Housebroken

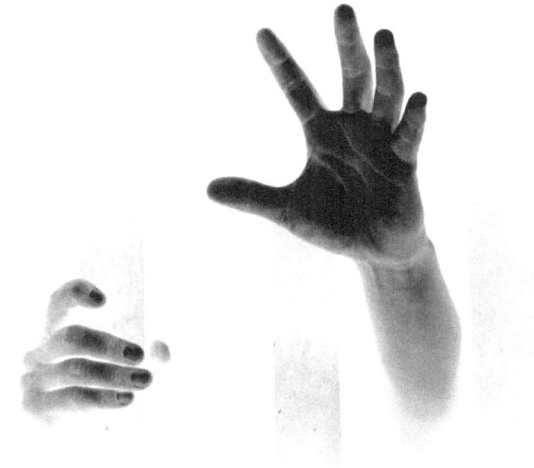

Also by The Behrg

Stillborn – A Short Horror Story

<u>The Creation Series (coming 2015)</u>
In The Beginning
Axis Mundi
Let There Be Death

Housebroken

A Novel

by The Behrg

Cover Design by Elder Lemon Design

ISBN-13: 978-0692413616
ISBN-10: 0692413618

Dedication

To the Bake and his lovely wife. Thank you for asking if after years of writing screenplays, I had ever considered writing a novel. Hopefully, at some point, you'll ask if I've ever considered becoming a millionaire.

Much love.

Prologue

Day Six

Shallow breaths. The tiny whine of a fly's wings.

Alighting on a thin black metal bar, the fly zipped up and out only to return, this time settling on an elbow pressed flush against the gridded wire squares. If Blake could have moved his arm even the smallest of degrees to keep those eyelash legs from tickling against his skin, he would have—even a touch as small as a fly's was a reminder of all he had lost.

His throat was dry, like swallowing chalk. At least he had accomplished what he had set out to, his screaming not meant for the ears of some random rescuer but an act of self-flagellation, the barbs of his own tongue sharper than any sword or whip.

Visions of what could be and what may have already been swirled through his head, though they were far from the only nightmares keeping Blake from sleep. His body was doubled over, head tucked between knees that had been raised to his chest, his back torqued in a sickly unnatural curve. His shoulders were stretched so far forward as to cause tiny tears in the sockets, his bare feet pressed flat against the tiny black bars. Purple spiderwebs of pain radiated up toward calf muscles so taut they fired in constant spasms. Swollen gridded squares of flesh were embedded across his almost-naked body. He wondered when the latticed skin might simply drop off, like

Play-Doh being shoved through a child's strainer.

There was little of Blake Crochet that wasn't pressed against some part of the cage that held him bound in his own kitchen, the cage that just a week ago had been used to crate train their dog, Conrad.

A week ago, Conrad had still been alive.

The worst part of his confinement wasn't the contusions forming on almost every muscle or the complete and utter lack of sleep. It wasn't the claustrophobia that hit after the first hour or the maddening numbness that followed. It wasn't even the painful few minutes of entering the cage one limb at a time, that feeling of trying to hammer a square peg through a round hole, knowing you wouldn't fit and that whatever didn't would soon no longer be a part of you. No, the worst part—the absolute worst—was not knowing what was taking place beyond those small and impenetrable bars.

Hot tears dropped from Blake's eyes, tears he couldn't wipe away had he wanted to.

His wife and son were gone.

Lost . . . *Taken.*

And for the first time in Blake's forty-two years of finding solutions where none were present, he couldn't think of a single way out.

It was like watching traffic, waiting at an intersection for that break you could pull out into, and when no break came, you just waited for a gap, half a car length of leeway or a driver testing his abilities to tweet or Facebook while behind the wheel. Only there were no gaps. The traffic running bumper-to-bumper never broke, and without the hint of a solution, the spark of an idea, Blake was no different than the fly tooling through the air, moving without purpose, moving only because it could.

At the moment, Blake couldn't even do that.

His only choice was to see the experiment through. The *pwoject.* To the very end.

If there was a chance, a single wild card in that deck of possibilities that could allow them to walk away unscathed, maybe not ahead—definitely not ahead—but at least alive and intact, *as a family* . . . well, it was worth betting all he had. The irony was watching the chips teeter from black to red, red to black, completely dependent on whether the House played by the rules. And from what

Blake knew about the fiery man running the show, he didn't like his odds.

He had helped fund an app once for both the Apple and Android markets that had made millions before it was shut down based on that simple concept. Spin the wheel, and place your bet. Better than anyone, he knew the awful reality: the House always wins.

If Blake could have bowed his head to weep further, he would have.

Chapter 1

"Pwe-Pwoject"

1

Blake Crochet finished the e-mail on his Cyborg XT phone while descending the cathedral-like ebony stairs. One of the benefits of communication in the digital age was that the recipient would never see the fury with which he pushed the tiny send button or notice the sweat stains beneath his armpits or have a clue how many times he had revised the phrasings of his e-mail, a sentence at a time, prior to sending it off into the cloud—a cloud that was forecasting thunder and precipitous storms.

Even more fortuitous, considering the recipient was his wife.

A dizzying display of refracted light danced across the adjacent wall, the glittery effect as mesmerizing as the house they had so recently moved into. Glancing at the overbearing chandelier along his descent, Blake was reminded of a bulbous rose bush that had grown too fast and thick, beauty transforming into monstrosity.

He had used similar analogies with some of the businesses he consulted with. The very act of pruning a rose bush, cutting, trimming, and destroying what otherwise looked healthy, was the only way to keep the plant from self-destruction. Most chieftains of commerce understood, much more succinctly than Blake's wife, that growth is often achieved through a perceived step backward. As to his and Jenna's relationship, mere steps in reverse had led to a full retreat in a direction from which no return was in sight.

Entering the foyer, he put off thoughts of Jenna, navigating through the web of e-mails and video messages that required his attention. Immediacy was a currency his network of C-level executives had come to depend upon. Exclusivity, on the other hand, was not.

His newest employer, a tech firm involved with predictive artificial intelligence interfacing, had commissioned the move from West Virginia to the sun-ensconced coast of California. And while from a business standpoint the timing had been perfect, no software had been needed to predict the challenges the move had created with the family.

Blake spoke into the blinking plastic tumor that had grown over his left ear and was only removed for showers and sex. He even kept the Bluetooth earpiece in place while sleeping. The DreameX app, which he had cofinanced, monitored both heart rate and REM, creating a constantly shifting cadence of sound and waves that enabled a truer, deeper slumber. The app required the earpiece, and Blake required the app in order to drift off. It was better than any sleeping pill.

"I want a full report on ScanneX. Move whatever mountains you need to in the next forty-eight so we can finalize A/B testing. Press release goes out Friday. Remember, cite *undisclosed* backers. I'll have JT in our corner by next week."

Blake counted the full three seconds it would take to translate his words, recording his message from English to Mandarin and sending out the appropriate text.

He suddenly stopped midstride. His left bare foot sunk into something that did not feel like Indonesian Makassar wood. He looked down.

Dog crap.

He could still see the moist bubbles waiting to break on the surface, pushing up between his toes. Definitely fresh.

"Damnit, Conrad!" A soft blip announced translation had begun on this new message. "No! Ah, shit."

He flipped the kill switch on the phone, shutting down all applications at once. China could wait.

Stepping with the heel of his left foot, Blake crossed through the family room over to the kitchen island, an expansive marble-topped counter brought in from Italy. The kitchen could have been transported straight from the pages of a magazine—fridge, ovens, and dishwasher camouflaged behind dark Persian cupboards, chrome pots, pans, and gadgets on the counters, shinier than if they'd just come out of a box.

Blake jumped onto the counter and bathed his foot in scalding water and liquid soap, hopping back down with a grunt. "Conrad!"

The jangling of her collar sounded as she darted from the room. *Stupid dog.*

He marched over to the back kitchen door. There she was, cowering in her crate.

A sleek black Labrador, Conrad had been a part of the family for three years. She was the quintessential dog—gentle and loving, playful but not needy, and so protective of Adam, who had decided when she was a puppy that he wanted her to be a boy. Blake had suggested Connie, but Adam had been insistent. The cross-gendered name stuck and was always a point of conversation on trips to the vet.

It hadn't been a question whether Conrad would accompany the family to their new home; what Blake hadn't counted on was the dog reverting back to her puppy stage. After two days of wet spots on the brand new carpet and strategically placed turds on the hardwood, Blake had once again purchased a doggy cage. Crate training all over again.

Blake yanked on Conrad's collar, pulling her from the crate and dragging her back into the foyer. He forced her face into what was left on the floor, tapping her on the nose gently.

"Help me out here, Connie. Potty outside."

Jing Jong.

The doorbell echoed, reverberating in the air like the ringing of a church bell. Jenna must have forgotten her keys on her morning run.

"Hold on," he shouted. Blake wasn't in the right frame of mind to handle the confrontation his wife would carry in with her, but he had little choice. He tapped Conrad's behind as she skittered off into the family room. Brown semiliquid tracks trailed behind every rise of her back paws where she had stepped in her own feces.

It was settled—he'd let Jenna clean it up.

That did cause him to laugh out loud.

Jing Jong.

"Coming!"

Blake slid the deadbolt back and turned the knob. As he opened the door, he took a quick step back, startled by the young man standing so close he was almost inside their house. Mid to late twenties with pumpkin-orange hair and a smile too big for his face, he seemed completely unaware of the shock he had caused.

"Good mauwning, sih."

Before Blake could react, Conrad darted through the gap, squeezing between him and the door. She leapt onto the kid outside, who toppled over, landing on his bulky backpack.

Blake shot forward, ripping the dog back by the collar. "Inside, Conrad!" She whined, pawing at the air.

The orange-haired kid smiled, kneeling up from the ground. "It's okay, sih. I weawy wike dawgs."

He reached into his bag, pulling out a doggy treat, and came forward on his knees, offering Conrad the reward.

"Yo a good dawgy, yes, you awe."

The young man got down in Conrad's face, grabbing at her front paws and darting in, as if about to attack. He bared his teeth, his low guttural growl met by Conrad's throaty whine, then pulled Conrad on top of him, ripping her from Blake's grasp. They rolled together on the porch, wrestling in one moment, the kid rubbing her belly the next. Conrad played along as if they had known each other for years, her flying slobber proof she had made a new friend.

A strange uneasiness settled over Blake as he observed the young man on the ground. Fiery curly hair clipped short and gelled back, shoes shined but edges peeling, a collared business shirt that was starting to fray . . . and what kind of person kept dog treats in their bag? What, for emergencies? As if the lisp weren't bad enough, he seemed to have a tic, blinking his left eye and opening his mouth as if yawning.

Blake stepped onto the porch, grabbing Conrad's collar, and ushered her into the house. He moved back inside, keeping the door open just a crack.

"Stay, Conrad. Stay!" He turned to the young man. "Sorry about that."

Conrad placed her nose against that sliver of an opening, sniffing for her new playmate. The orange-haired kid stood, brushing his clothes off. He cleared his throat, eyes down, then looked up with a smile that seemed to swallow the rest of his face.

Like a jack-o'-lantern, Blake thought, the kid's orange hair almost causing him to laugh.

"Hewe's yo newspeipo."

Blake couldn't shake the feeling that something was off. Terribly off. He opened the door just wide enough to grab the paper, every instinct screaming at him to slam the door, throw the lock, and walk away.

He kept it open, barely. Didn't want to seem quite that rude. "You the paper boy?"

"What? No, no, I don' wuhk fo' da newspeipo, sih." He laughed. "My name is Joje."

He held out his hand, that haunting smile back on display. After some hesitation, Blake opened the door wider, shaking the kid's hand. He kept his leg in place, blocking Conrad's attempted escape.

A confident shake. At least the kid had that.

"I noticed you wecentwee moved in. How do you wike da neighbohood?" George smiled.

Or should I call him Joje?

"You live here? Nearby?" Might explain something.

"Oh, no, I wish. I weawy wish."

The kid's left eye started blinking again, his mouth opening. He cocked his head and looked down. Cleared his throat. Then he was back as if nothing had happened. He continued with his lisp.

"I'm here for a school pwoject, to interview someone about their career." He gave a rehearsed shrug. "I like to think, why not start at the top. You know, go fo' fowce and ask the guys that are successful so maybe one day I can, you know, have the same success."

It took Blake a few seconds, but finally he got it. Go *full force*. He almost missed Joje's question.

"So what do you do for a living?"

"You realize this is a private community?"

"Oh, sure, but I'm not sowiciting. What is it you do?"

The tic was back. Some tiny inkling of decency made it hard not to feel bad for the kid. Some people were dealt a rotten hand, not his fault if he was trying to make the best of it. Still, Blake couldn't shake the creep factor emanating from this broken kid on his porch.

"I really don't have the time," Blake said as he closed the door. Or tried to.

The kid's foot was extended into the doorjamb, keeping it from shutting.

"You mind?" Blake asked, all pretenses of good-natured neighboring quickly fading.

Joje met him with the blankest of stares.

He really is a jack-o'-lantern, Blake thought. *There's nothing behind those eyes.* Then that winning smile not even a mother could have loved reappeared.

"Hi, deo!" Joje waved with his fingers past Blake.

Blake looked back. His son, Adam, was staring past him at the stranger on the doorstep.

Adam was tall for his age. At fourteen, he towered over his mother and would soon threaten his father for height dominance. With long, shaggy hair that though slept on, was about as styled as it would ever be, he immediately dismissed the young man on the porch.

"Thought maybe a kid wanted to play," Adam said through a yawn. "Should have remembered, you moved us somewhere there are no kids my age."

"Here, take the dog. I'll make breakfast," Blake said. "And put her in the crate." He turned back to Joje, ready to end their conversation.

"Tell your son I wanna pway," Joje said.

"Excuse me?"

"More questions. The, uh, missus? What does she do?"

The smile was back, but this time Blake wasn't having it. He opened the door and stepped out, closing it behind him. He was fit for his age, nothing like his wife, who seemed to work out twenty hours a day, but the bulk from his weight lifting days had never completely left, nor had it all turned to fat like so many of his college friends. More importantly, Blake knew how to be intimidating when he needed to be, and there was no question it had become one of those times.

"Why are you here?" he asked.

"For my pwoject."

"Cut the crap. Tell me what you're doing on my porch or I call the cops right now." Blake held up his phone, and true to his threat, the numbers nine-one-one appeared on the display as if he had keyed them in.

The AI he was beta-testing made Apple's Siri look like an Atari from the eighties. He still had so many questions about the technology—how, for instance, it had recognized the need to display the numbers but not actually place the call. The phone was a constant reminder that the move had been the right choice.

Joje looked down, blinking and opening his mouth. "I guess you don't become successful without weawning to wead a person, huh?"

"I can't even understand you."

The smile fell from Joje's face. "Wead," he pantomimed with his hands, "wike a book."

"I'd like you to leave. Now."

Joje slung his bag off one shoulder, unzipping it and pulling out a laminated card. Blake found himself translating the young man's crude speech impediment as if his Cyborg's language app had been hardwired to his mind. "I'm selling magazine subscriptions to pay for my schooling. Twenty dollars for the first, only ten for each additional subscription. I can even renew, uh, subscriptions you already have—"

"Get off my property, George."

"If every household bought one subscription, I could pay for my entire tuition in just a few weeks . . ."

Screw it. "Joje! Get off my property. Now."

"Are you making fun of me? My wisp?"

Blake couldn't help but chuckle. It really was too much. The blink was back, followed quickly by the yawning. This poor kid had no hope.

"You want some advice from our little interview? Pick a career other than sales. You see, in sales, people aren't buying a product, they're buying you, and even if by some miracle you suckered some poor old woman to open her purse because she felt sorry for you, as soon as you were gone, she'd realize her mistake and want her money back. It'd be the worst case of buyer's remorse in the history of sales. Just the memory of wasting three minutes of her time, as you've stolen from me today, would be too great a loss. So here's my advice.

Make a career change. Fast-food restaurants are always hiring. Or maybe aspire to be a greeter at Walmart."

He certainly had the smile for it.

"I'm counting to three," Blake continued. "One."

Joje looked down, clearing his throat, then looked back up. Blake couldn't pretend he hadn't noticed the moisture behind those eyes. He simply didn't care.

"I'd like to ask you to reconsider—" *Weconsido.*

"Two."

Backpedaling down the stone entryway, Joje stopped in front of the rock waterfall. Palm fronds tickled the top of his head.

"One subscwiption wiw weawy make a diffwence—" Joje looked off toward the driveway, his eyes moving down, then up, then back again.

Jenna suddenly walked past, sparing him barely a glance. She wore a purple designer sports bra some might consider too small for all it held and tiny black shorts, sweat glistening off her bronzed body. Blake found it difficult not to stare at his own wife, ten years his junior. He forced himself to look away, picking at an imaginary cobweb on the rock wall.

Jenna moved past him, touching him lightly on the shoulder. The muddled rattle from her earbuds sounded like planes crashing.

Joje stood gaping, his mouth literally hanging open.

"That's it! I'm calling the cops right now." Blake heard the first ring in his ear as the phone autodialed, picking up the need from their conversation. He tapped at his screen, ending the call before it was picked up. "It's ringing."

Joje looked at Blake as if waking from a dream. "Thank you, sih, fo' da oppotunity. Have a gweat day."

He set the laminated card down on a stone bench before disappearing around the corner.

2

When Blake reentered the family room, he found his son eating a bowl of ice cream on the couch, watching TV. An old rerun of *Family Feud*. Could he try any harder to be bored?

Conrad lay next to him, head resting in his lap, following Blake's movements with lazy eyes.

"I thought I told you to put her in the crate? And since when is she allowed on the couch?"

No response, from Adam or the dog. Blake sighed. "Really? Ice cream for breakfast?"

Adam shrugged.

"You know what? I want you to unpack your room today. Your mom and I both want you to." Blake paused, glancing at Jenna pulling out a bottle of Vitamin Water from the fridge. "Adam? You hear me?"

Without looking away from the TV, his son replied, "I hear you."

Blake followed his wife over to the kitchen, standing at the back sink. She moved rhythmically, earbuds still in, staring out through the open shutters at the sea.

The view from the house was spectacular, one of the things that had sold them on the place. The swimming pool jutted almost directly up against the receding cliffs with more than a thirty-foot drop down to the jagged and uninviting shore below, but from here it looked like the pool flowed straight into the ocean. The rocky beach wasn't the type to attract visitors, though the occasional surfer could be spotted bobbing out in the water.

They had one of only fourteen homes in this almost-hidden gated community in Malibu. Eight of those homes actually resided against the cliffs and shoreline, as theirs did. The others were set across the street yet raised up to still have at least a glimpse of the view.

It was the setting of paradise, though the past few days since the move had been anything but.

Jenna turned around, catching Blake staring at her. He hated himself for feeling guilty—she was his wife, this should be the most natural thing in the world. Still, he looked away.

Jenna grabbed the roll of paper towels from the counter and pushed it against his chest.

"Go clean up your shit," she said, louder than she probably realized. "I almost stepped in it."

Blake pulled the speaker buds from her ears. "I'm not the one who let Conrad out."

"So what, it's my fault she's having anxiety issues about the move? The cage isn't working."

"It's not a cage, it's a crate. And no, crate training doesn't work unless you reinforce the environment with good behavior, not bad."

Jenna set her Vitamin Water down, drops of liquid spurting out onto the counter. "Fine. I'll call a maid service on my way to Deb's. Have them come over to wipe up one little mess."

She swept past him.

"Deb? The interior designer who can't match her own outfit? What's wrong with the furniture we have, Jenn? I mean, why bring it if we were just going to replace it?"

She continued out of the room as if her earbuds were still in. "I'm jumping in the shower," she called back from the foyer.

It wasn't an invitation.

Blake grabbed her Vitamin Water, polishing it off with a grimace. Nasty stuff. He tossed it into the trash and grabbed the paper towels and a bottle of window cleaner from beneath the sink.

As Blake walked past, Adam stared at him with the hint of a smile that for some reason, reminded him of the lisper outside. Blake held up the paper towels and window cleaner. "Care to join me?"

The TV once again became the focal point of Adam's attention.

Blake continued from the room, thunderous applause following his retreat. What he really needed was an app on his phone that would help him understand his son. A teenage translator.

He smiled. Now that would be worth millions.

3

The furniture truck arrived just before two in the afternoon, more strangers walking through their house, carrying what Blake guessed passed for modern decor. A table that looked like a torture rack, vinyl couches so red and shiny they'd reflect the glint off a zipper, wall hangings and paintings he would just have to ignore.

The white grand piano was an especially nice touch, considering none of them played.

Deb was a complete delight, fussing over every detail as if the feng shui of the universe depended on it. She must have been the first woman Blake had met with a British accent who became less endearing when she spoke.

He locked himself in his study for the better part of the day, though he really had little work to do. And lucky Conrad was treated to three walks, each longer than the normal quick stroll through the neighborhood. It was on the third of these walks that Blake met one of his neighbors for the first and last time.

Conrad sniffed at the same bush she had explored earlier that afternoon while Blake poured over his portfolio on the small display of his Cyborg. The numbers hadn't changed since that morning but had occupied his mind all day.

His trade partner, Barry Hadley, had suggested some aggressive movements, and though Blake tried to read the market and pretended to follow the trends, he'd probably just tell Barry to go ahead. He had done well for him in the past.

He toggled back through the screens, initiating his auto-e-mail generator. A-mail, they were calling it, the name not nearly as mind-blowing as what it could do.

"Accept proposal," he said into his Bluetooth earpiece.

After the obligatory three-second delay, three windows popped up, each containing an e-mail reply varying in length. All three replies were written in the style of conversation Blake might have engaged in with Barry, yet each offered subtle changes, one even incorporating a hint of sarcasm, an ability that had been considered impossible when working within the confines of a programmed intelligence system.

It read, "Go ahead with the moves you mentioned. Keep up with this Milwaukee fever though, and I may find reason to start doubting your 'better judgment.'"

Betti, the name they were using for their AI interface, as in *better* than Siri, had gone to the length of following up on a conversation he and Barry had had a week ago about the Bruins. Barry was probably their only fan, Blake had joked, though Barry had been insistent this was their year. Well, Betti must have cross researched the results of their last two games (the Bruins, of course, had been slaughtered) and incorporated that within the autogenerated reply. Blake doubted he could have done better himself.

He hit send.

The key to Betti's success was the complete integration of all behavioral interactions captured on the Cyborg, literally *the* phone that would bridge the gap between home and mobile computers. Betti monitored every phone conversation, e-mail, or social media trend, every Google search and web interaction, even "listening" to the surroundings and conversation when the phone wasn't in use. And the more you incorporated real-life habits into the phone—whether purchasing, banking, or mindlessly seeking entertainment—Betti would more actively be able to interpret future actions and desires.

A-mail and the Cyborg phone itself would instantly create a billion-dollar platform, but the yet-to-be-established interactive and predictive marketing industry was bound to break into the trillions, a market Blake and his new company, Symbio, would be on the forefront of creating.

It was the reason he had brought his family out to the West Coast, had halted all but a few of his consulting gigs, keeping only those firms he had worked with for years. He was betting the farm with this one, placing it all on red, and he didn't see a single way he could lose.

Conrad suddenly lifted her head and barked once—yapped really, she had such a wussy bark—then bolted into the street.

Blake glanced up in time to see the black town car slam on its brakes. He pushed the button, locking the leash from extending farther, and yanked, ripping Conrad off her feet.

She hit the pavement on her side, inches from where the car came to a sudden stop.

"Sorry," Blake mouthed, with a wave of the hand to the idling car. He stepped off the curb and knelt down next to Conrad. She was already up, licking his outstretched hand.

Blake patted her down, brushing her silky coat, feeling each of her legs, making sure she was all right.

That had been close.

The car rolled forward another few inches, then stopped, the rear mirrored window lowering. A flush bearded face, silver whiskers betraying the black mop atop the massive head, glanced from canine to human, assigning equal value to the two of them.

"You should watch your dog." He had a deep voice as smooth as any radio jockey's Blake had heard.

"Your driver should watch the road. I said I was sorry."

The car started forward, then screeched to a halt at the

command of the bearded passenger, a mere lifting of the hand.

"You're the one purchased Welchsetzer's place. Tom Jones, Esquire, the third. Neighbor." He pointed to the massive home next door to the yard Conrad had been roaming in. At least Blake imagined the home was massive—a long driveway curved up behind a gated portico, disappearing behind the tall block wall that surrounded the place like a prison. The stones in the wall were black and rough, made of lava rock. Palm trees and landscaping peeked over the top of the walls.

"I'm Blake Crochet." He extended his hand into the window.

Tom put a sausage index finger into Blake's hand, as much acknowledgement as he was willing to offer. "Don't read much?"

"I'm sorry?"

"Public information. These cliffs recede almost eight inches a year. Half a decade, they'll be in the center of your home."

"Eight inches? Sounds like a small man's exaggeration to me," Blake said. He had dealt with plenty of men like Tom before. The only way to earn their respect was to throw it back in their face.

"As you can see, I'm no small man," Tom said.

"Well, it's a good thing my backyard is as big as it is."

"Halfway to your pool then. I've seen your yard. Never thought someone would buy that place, what with its history. Must have gotten it for a steal. What'd you pay? Two, two-five? Or'd they get you for three mil?"

Six point four actually, and this was the first Blake had heard of any questionable history. "Something like that," Blake said.

The gates to Tom Jones's driveway retracted. Blake took some pleasure in that his house was set against the ocean while Tom's backyard was lost into the forested mountains on the opposite side of the street.

"Can you even see the ocean with those walls around your place?" Blake asked.

"Not about seeing out but keeping people from getting in," Tom said. He flicked a business card into his pudgy hand like a cheap magician's trick. "You go nuts and murder your family, give me a call first. Get you off with a lot less than ol' Welchsetzer." He laughed, a rumble like an avalanche.

A single laugh escaped Blake like a bark. "I'll keep that in mind."

The card was glossy black with silver letters and a logo of two diamonds crushing each other inlaid with a picture of a much lighter, much younger Mr. Jones, Esquire. His cold stare in the photo was so intense he had either just witnessed a murder or committed one himself.

The caption beneath the picture made Blake want to gag: "Because the only crime is letting them put you away." He'd have to put it on the fridge. Jenna would get a kick out of it.

Conrad pulled against the leash, her collar catching and holding her back. Her tail began to wag.

Out of the corner of his eye, Blake caught movement—someone walking up the long, curved driveway to Tom Jones's home. The individual had bright-orange hair with a heavy backpack slung across one shoulder.

A smile broke over Blake's face. It was his buddy, Joje. He had to give the kid credit: he really put in the hours.

"Looks like you have company, Tom. I'd hate to keep you waiting."

Tom followed Blake's gaze. Without a word, the window began its ascent as the town car pulled forward, turning into the entrance and climbing up the driveway.

"Apparently, Southern hospitality doesn't extend to So Cal, huh, Connie?" He ruffled the fur on her head like a toddler's hair.

4

Jenna dipped her finger into her glass of wine, then brought it to her mouth. Leaning against the marbled island in the kitchen, she stared out at the room, her eyes wandering to each corner. Blake noticed she wasn't wearing a bra beneath her tank top. Hard not to notice. They'd need to talk about it—Adam was approaching that age where it could become a problem.

He decided the argument could wait for another day.

"Just pretend you like it," Jenna said.

Sitting on the red vinyl couch, anticipating the moment it would bounce him off like an ejector seat, Blake navigated through his presentation on his phone. Tomorrow would be his first official day at Symbio, and he needed to make an impression.

"I just wish we could have talked about it, that's all."

The house was quiet, Deb and her team of decor zombies gone for the day. The ticking of a square clock—*square clock?*—hanging above the TV was the only sound beyond the quiet hum of the refrigerator hidden behind faux cabinets.

"Nothing's permanent. We can exchange anything we aren't in love with."

"Sounds like our marriage." The words were out before Blake could recall them. So much for avoiding a fight.

Jenna drained her glass, filling it again from the bottle of Pinot. "I don't have the energy to go another round with you. Not tonight."

"I'm sorry. That was stupid. I know we're . . . trying."

"Is that what your e-mail was?" Jenna's accusatory glance was lost in the shake of her head as she circled round the kitchen island with her wine glass. Just another dangling conversation.

Instead of exiting the room as he had supposed she would, she opened the back kitchen door, where Conrad slid out into the night. Blake hadn't even registered the dog's whines.

He peeled his arms off the sticky vinyl couch. "I want you to start taking Conrad on your runs."

"Where'd that come from?"

"I met one of the neighbors. Let's just say I was less than impressed."

"So what, a creepy neighbor's going to kidnap me? Hope he can keep up." Jenna came back into the kitchen, pouring the last of the bottle into her empty glass.

"Women are ninety percent less likely to be abducted when accompanied by a large dog." Blake held up his phone. "Read it yourself."

Jenna's hands came up, just like he knew they would. He had made the statistic up, his display revealed nothing more than the agenda for his meeting tomorrow, though Betti would no doubt be searching for an article related to their conversation.

"I'd just feel better knowing she's with you, that's all," he continued. "This isn't West Virginia. There are weirdoes out here."

"Then we'll fit in great, won't we?"

"I'm serious, Jenn."

Jenna's chin crinkled into her pouty face. "I'll think about it."

"Be good for Conrad. Maybe help with the potty training."

"I said I'd think about it."

Which meant no.

There had been a time when he and his wife could hold conversations without someone having to win. He no longer kept score; they were both losing.

"If something bad happened with the previous owners here at the house, they'd have to disclose that with the sale, right?" he asked.

"Why? Neighbor say something?" In a previous life, Jenna had been a real estate agent. Before they had met. "If it devalues the property, then yeah, legally they'd have no choice. I don't think Rob and Ann were pulling a fast one on us."

"No, me neither."

"You Google it?"

She of course knew that he had. "Didn't find much. He had the previous owner right, though, a Jerry Welchsetzer. I don't know. Hard to believe anything the neighbor said. He was an ass."

Jenna chuckled, and Blake caught the it-takes-one-to-know-one implication. "What's he do? Business consulting?"

"Lawyer."

"Ouch."

"Criminal defense."

"Double ouch." She laughed. Blake did too.

He stood, setting his empty Heineken on the counter and pulling out the business card Tom Jones had given him. "He wanted me to give this to you. Don't expect a plate of cookies with it."

"Wow, maybe I'll let him abduct me."

"Just multiply the size of that face by two or three."

Jenna giggled.

"Wait till you hear him. Barry White would be jealous of that voice."

Jenna moaned as if impressed.

"I can arrange a meeting?"

"Stop," she said, resting her hand on his chest. "You're probably more his type than I am."

She smiled, and Blake joined her. It felt real, for a moment— their banter, their joking. He realized how much he missed her even though they saw each other every day.

The moment passed quicker than he would have liked. Jenna pulled her hand back, and Blake returned to his phone. "I'll check on

Adam," he said.

"He's fourteen. He doesn't need Mom or Dad turning on the night-light anymore."

"I'm glad you're happy. With the house."

She replied with a fake toast, holding her wine glass to the air before turning away and setting it on the counter. Whatever her silent toast had been, she didn't drink to it.

5

Blake had done more than a Google search on Jerry Welchsetzer, and his neighbor had been right—the man was in jail, but not for murder. He had been picked up two years ago for tax fraud and evasion, not the most harrowing of crimes, though he had been sentenced to eleven years.

Jerry had been a movie producer, bankrolling a hoard of B movies, mostly tit and torture flicks, not a single title Blake had recognized. Up to November 2010, Jerry's company had been involved in half a dozen releases a year—apparently the budgets on these movies created an opportunity for frequent productions; more productions meant more revenue.

As a movie producer, however, Jerry had overlooked one key demographic's interest in his filmography: Uncle Sam's.

Blake had read every article about the titan's demise, the closure of his production company, liquidation of assets. The fact that the house they were now living in had come up on the market as silently as it had was another testament to Jerry's fall. A few articles he found prior to the arrest harbored conspiracies about some of the titan's films being less theatrics and more reality, snuff films sold under the umbrella of entertainment. Blake had earmarked the articles on his phone, deciding they warranted a further look.

What he hadn't found was any mention of his family's death or murder—probably just another gross exaggeration from Tom Jones and his eight inches. Or at least Blake hoped so. Either way, he would have to look into it further. Not that he fancied himself an investigator, but if there had been a cover-up, he'd certainly demand a renegotiation on the home price.

Upstairs, Blake passed by twin antique bookshelves against the side of the hall, sort of a pre-Victorian feel. He had to admit he liked them, though the empty shelves carried with them a feeling of nonpermanence, as if this house were determined to not become a home.

He snapped a picture with his phone, Betti instantly bringing back the make and price. Shipped from a manufacturer in Germany, the bookcases were listed at $8,900 apiece. Reclaimed antique elm wood, whatever that meant. With phone apps and e-readers, Blake wondered if bookcases served a purpose anymore. Beyond collecting dust.

He opened the door to Adam's room. Unopened boxes, bed posts, and a mattress leaned against the wall, dressers and furniture stacked in a corner. Adam lay on an old sleeping bag in the closet, playing a portable video game, the new 3-D one he had gotten for his birthday.

Blake ducked into the closet, lying next to his son. He watched Adam tilt the screen and fire as his jet or spaceship followed his moves like a slightly lagging marionette.

Actually, not a bad idea. A marionette app could pick up a lot of traction. Completely useless, but useless often sold. Blake made a quick note on his phone. Not something for Symbio, certainly, but he could throw it to one of his boneyard hyenas, the little two-man operations hiding behind some three-lettered S-corps that could spin out an idea in a few weeks.

"Sleeping here tonight?" he asked.

The spacecraft flew through a heavily guarded tunnel, artillery tanks firing faster than Adam could respond. After a few dramatized hits, a wing flew off and the jet crashed, scattering pieces that looked as if they'd actually strike you.

"Yeah." Adam powered the game off. "Unless you wanna sleep here. I can take the couch."

For fourteen, he was frustratingly observant.

"Just wanted to say goodnight," Blake said, brushing dust from the sleeping bag. "You'll make new friends. Once school starts."

"I don't want new friends, Dad."

"This is," Blake paused, looking into his son's eyes, those eyes that wanted to cry but couldn't, not in front of Dad. Blake wondered if his son recognized the same look in his own eyes. Holding it together for his son's sake. "It's a big change for us all. Change is hard, but it forces us to grow. Helps us to become better than—I don't know—if we just . . ." He stopped. He wasn't even convincing himself.

"We're in this together, that's all. As a family." Blake patted his son on the back in a distant hug, the gesture left unreciprocated. "We'll celebrate tomorrow. Go out to dinner. Together."

Adam nodded, then fell back against the sleeping bag, his emotionless face lighting up in an eerie multihued glow as his game powered back on.

Blake closed his son's door, pausing just outside in the hall. The light to the master bedroom was aglow; Jenna must have already come up. That light shone like a beacon—calling, beckoning—but Blake's feet had planted roots. Some things, you couldn't forget. Or forgive.

Even with the passage of time, Blake was certain thick layers of dust and cobwebs wouldn't be enough to cover the gaping hole in their lives to forget the lilting echo of laughter that would never bounce through the halls of their new home.

Maybe there was hope for their little family, but in Blake's world, maybes evolved into inevitable regrets and unavoidable failures.

He returned to the staircase and began his descent.

The idea of hope would have to be enough. Like a drowning man offered a branch, he was willing to cling to it, knowing at any moment it could snap, leaving him to be swept away—but for now, it was enough.

He stepped into the foyer of the house he was but a stranger in. It would be another long night.

Chapter 2

Day One

1

Blake was running late.

In a dark Italian suit almost as shiny as the neighbor's business card, he grabbed his leather briefcase, tossing his tablet in as it powered down. His Bluetooth headset flashed every thirty seconds, its bluish-white light something he no longer even noticed.

He came out from his office, almost bumping into his wife. Coffee spilled down the rim of the mug she held out. He grabbed it, licking the bottom edge before it dripped.

Jenna moved in, surprising him by pressing her toned body up against his. "Good luck today."

She was already dressed for her run, her bleached hair pulled back in a ponytail.. He realized she was leaving later than normal, more than likely just to see him off.

"Thank you." He meant it. Bent down and kissed the top of her forehead.

Their embrace became the awkward exchange of a couple on a first date, neither knowing what to say next.

"Don't let me keep you," Jenna said, to which Blake nodded, remembering a time she would have.

He passed through the living room with the piano that would

never be played, the sheet folded on the couch where he had slept. At least it was more comfortable than the pontoon in the family room.

A dark spot on the carpet gave him pause.

"I swear I'm going to kill that dog. I don't have time—"

"I'll get it," Jenna said, following him into the kitchen, where he grabbed his keys. "I was thinking, maybe tonight, you could sleep upstairs. With me."

Blake looked up. She hadn't looked that fragile since, well, since the night they had agreed never to talk about. "I'd like that."

"I mean, we'll take it slow. But it'd be good for Adam to see us . . . trying." She picked up her Garmin watch next to the coffee machine and strapped it on. "Wasn't that the word you used?"

"Take Connie on your run?"

Jenna glanced back at him, rolling her eyes.

The hum of the engine of his convertible BMW M6 barely registered as Blake backed down the driveway. He was flipping through his phone's data-conferencing display when the phone vibrated in his hands—a profile of a faceless gray avatar displayed above the name JT. In some countries, that name was synonymous with asshole.

Despite his boss's lack of personal skills, or perhaps because of them, Blake pressed the button on his earpiece, answering the call.

"Hey, on my way," he said.

"Yeah, well I could have used you here an hour ago. Your presentation has got to be perfect, and I mean robotic, you've-practiced-this-speech-till-your-dick-dropped-off perfect."

"Don't worry. Our little Betti's going to do more than let down her skirt," Blake replied. "Trust me, the board will—"

The car shuddered, an audible crunch forcing Blake's foot to the brakes before he had time to even look up.

Shit!

He glanced in the rearview mirror—nothing behind him. No car at least.

He could still hear the whining voice of JT piping through the Bluetooth speaker, which had fallen from his ear onto his lap. Blake picked it up, pressing it to his face.

"Call you right back."

He pressed the button, effectively hanging up on his boss. He'd understand. Probably not, but Blake would cross that road when he needed to.

Blake dropped his cell and earpiece in the cup holder and left the engine running as he came around to the back of the car.

A mangled bike, wheel spoke and handlebars turning inward at sharp angles, lay like a wounded deer on the sidewalk and in the early morning shadows of his vehicle, a body lay crumpled on the ground. A line of blood trailed in a semicircle, coalescing beneath the form on the driveway.

"Gaw, damnit!"

Blake looked around. No neighbors out. No cars on the street. His trunk now sported a slight dent where they had collided, a few nicks and gouges on the bumper.

A moan brought him back to the body of an orange-haired young man.

"Ah, you've got to be kidding me."

Blake swatted the bike off of the kid, gently turning him over. Or at least more gently than he had handled the bike.

Joje stared blankly upward, blood smeared on his forehead.

Blake looked around again, street still empty. All he needed right now was Tom Jones rolling through in his town car. The bastard wasn't a personal injury attorney, but in this case, he'd probably make an exception.

"Hey, you okay?" he asked.

Moaning. The only answer he'd receive.

Blake felt for his phone. Realizing he had left it in the car, he glanced at his Rolex. Six twenty-six. Already the freeway would be backing up. He'd have to cut over the mountain and take side streets into the Valley.

"Look, uh, George, I'm going to carry you inside. We'll get you fixed up. First let me get rid of your bike, okay?"

Blake picked up the hunk of twisted aluminum and rubber. Piece of crap. There was no way the kid was riding home on that thing. How fast had he been going? He was just lucky it hadn't been a small kid or something behind him.

He tossed the bike into the center of the garage, not caring about the noise or additional damage it caused.

Pulling the keys from the car, he hurried toward the back. He'd have to move fast, clean the kid up, pay him off, and ship him out. It didn't have to take long.

"What happened?" Joje asked.

Blake moved to put his arm around him. "Come inside, you . . . had an accident."

Joje took one step and collapsed, slipping from Blake's arms. He hit the pavement with a resounding thud.

Blake looked skyward, ready to scream—he did *not* have time for this. After one final glance down the street, he bent over and lifted Joje as if carrying an injured dog. He was heavier, thicker than Blake would have guessed. His back began to groan in harmony with Joje's whimpers.

Into the garage and to the door leading into the house, Blake hit the curved button that started the garage's descent. It silently climbed down its tracks, not a peep or warning about the person who was being allowed entrance into their home.

2

"Jenna!"

Blake laid the bloodied Joje on the red couch. *At least you won't see the blood stains*, he thought.

Conrad bolted in from the foyer at full speed, preparing a leap that would land her right on top of the wounded Joje. Blake barely tackled her in time. Conrad whimpered as he dragged her back to the cage in the kitchen, sliding the bolt to lock her inside.

"Sorry, sweetie. Not now." He raised his voice. "Jenna!"

Opening cupboards and drawers, he searched for something to bring to Joje's aid: Band-Aids, gauze, Bubble Wrap. Blake couldn't make heads or tails out of the kitchen and whoever had unpacked their things. Even the paper towels were missing from the counter.

He ripped a hand towel from a decorative metal ring near the sink, wet it, and hurried back to the family room. On his way, he wiped absently at the stains on his slacks; the suit would be ruined.

"Jenna!"

"Jeez, you trying to wake the neighborhood? What? What'd you forget?" She walked in, carrying her running shoes and a wad of rolled-up paper towels that probably smelled of dog piss. "Oh, my god!"

"He rode right behind me as I was backing out. There was nothing I could do!"

"I'll call nine-one-one."

"Hold on. Let's see if he's okay first." Blake pressed the hand towel to Joje's head. *Should probably stop with the whole Joje thing.*

"He could have a concussion! We've got to get him to a hospital," Jenna said.

"Just wait a minute!"

Jenna picked up the house phone. "The line's dead."

"That's impossible. It's run through our Internet."

"Maybe the Internet's down?"

From the couch, "It is down."

Joje was sitting, the smeared blood on his forehead looking like a finger painting project gone wrong. Though, as Blake stared at the swirls of dark patterns, he couldn't find a source—not a single gash on that boldly protruding forehead.

"What are you doing, George?"

"You know him?" Jenna asked.

"Why wouldn't you buy fwom me?" Joje stared at Blake, his left eye blinking rapidly, mouth twitching open.

"What's he talking about, Blake?"

Blake hesitated. Something in him, some base human genome passed down through generations that in part took credit for mankind's propensity toward survival, was giving off clear warning bells. *Tread with caution.* Though that same part of him also admitted, much to his own dismay, that it might already be too late.

"You know, it was a mistake. You caught me at a bad time. How 'bout we sign up, and in fact, why don't I just, uh, give you everything I've got." Blake pulled out his wallet. "About five hundred bucks. That's a hell of a lot of magazine subscriptions."

Joje looked at the folded bills in Blake's hand. He cleared his throat, then looked up, that awful smile sweeping across his face. "I don't want yo money."

"What's wrong with him?" Jenna asked.

Blake wasn't sure if she was referencing his lisp or the nervous tic that was back. Or maybe it was that same intuition that had told Blake to slam the front door and flip the lock when they had first met.

"Look, I'm in a real hurry. What's this gonna cost me?"

"Always in a huwwy, huh, Bwake?"

"It seems to me you set this up," Blake said, "but name your price, asshole, while I'm still in a giving mood."

"No pwice. I just want help. With my pwoject."

"You're trespassing, and I'm calling the cops," Blake said, at once remembering his cell was dutifully waiting back in his car. Joje saw the hesitation.

"Oops. Leave your phone somewhere?" Joje said, with his deranged impediment. His eyes drifted to Jenna, who still held the house phone in her palm, not even a beep rising from the dead line.

Blake was through with threats. He moved toward Joje, intending to drag him off the couch, and was suddenly staring down the barrel of a black pistol pointed directly at his head.

Jenna screamed.

Joje brought the gun forward, its cool metal tip kissing Blake's forehead. Blake found himself raising his hands, staring into those dark, cold eyes.

Like a shark, he thought.

They had visited Sea World back when they were considering the move to California. The shark exhibit had been Adam's favorite, stepping into that curved glass tunnel, water surrounding them on all sides. The sharks had just been fed and darted back and forth in a frenzy, and while Adam had stood enthralled, Blake had been gripped with a sort of panic. It hadn't been the pressure of thousands of pounds of water bearing down on them nor the fact that mere inches of glass was all that separated them from those hungry monsters. It had simply been the look in their alien eyes. Not a dangerous look, like encountering a wild canine. The only word that came to mind was . . . apathetic. If the glass hadn't been there, they would have continued feasting, a second course consisting of Crochets coming right up. But the fact that the glass was there, it hadn't angered them. They simply didn't care. Eventually they would feed. Eventually they'd have their way.

That same soulless glare came hurtling toward him from those black eyes in Joje's skull. Make a move, and I pull the trigger, they said.

Only it would have been *twiggo*.

Blake realized he should have grabbed the gun, knocked it aside, and turned it on the kid threatening him and his family. Should have called his bluff—there was no way that thing was loaded—and slugged him in the jaw, permanently displacing that smile. Should have yelled for his wife to hide while he ducked into the other room, coming back with his own handgun, a .38 Special that was locked in a small beige safe on top of the highest shelf in his office, combination sixteen–forty-two–eleven.

"Stay calm." He wasn't sure if he was speaking for Jenna's sake, or his own. "I'll give you everything I've got, George, no lies. There's a safe." Blake swallowed. "Three grand in it. I won't even call the cops."

The tic was back, left eye twitching, mouth opening in that odd stretch. Joje looked down, clearing his throat.

I should move now. Attack. Take his gun.

Joje looked up in that instant.

Blake hit the handwoven Persian rug before he realized he had been struck. The floor felt like it was falling out from beneath him. Blood seeped into his eye. Real blood, not that fake crap Joje had used. Every heartbeat resounded through his head as if the task of pumping blood to his body had been handed over to his cerebrum.

"What—what do you want from us?" Jenna's voice. So distant.

Blake rose to his knees, pushing past the vertigo that threatened to send him back to the floor.

Joje wasn't smiling anymore.

"I'm sorry, Bwakey. I saw what you were thinking and, I don't like violence." He stood, seeming to bask in the scene of Blake kneeling before him. He continued, with his lisp, "No one's ever treated me like you, Bwake. With honesty. Not feeding me a bunch of lies. You made me realize how wrong my approach has been. What I really need is a mentor, someone who can help me navigate my way. The more I thought about it, I realized family plays just as big a role in success. Don't you think?"

He stood, his eyes hovering toward Jenna as he crept toward her, a predator stalking its prey.

"Don't you touch me," she spat.

"You misunderstand my intentions," Joje said.

"Oh, I read them. Loud and clear."

He suddenly reached out, grabbing Jenna and spinning her around. He pressed his body close to hers as he snapped back the top of the gun in one quick motion.

Blake closed his eyes as he heard the bullet enter the chamber, barrel now pointed at the back of his wife's head.

"Time for a family council. You, me, your son . . . and my little brother." *Wittle bwahtho*. Joje grinned. "We have an awful lot to talk about."

Joje's laughter scraped against the chalkboard in Blake's mind.

3

Seated on the couch he had called a bed last night, his wife and son next to him, Blake stared down at his Cesare Paciotti shoes. His reflection in them looked so small. The Band-Aid he was unable to find for Joje now plastered to his own forehead did little to help make his image on that shined canvas look anything but weak. At least the African drums in his head weren't beating quite as loudly.

Joje paced in front of them, his "brother" sitting on the piano bench or, rather, enveloping it like a gelatinous blob—not a single piece of the bench could be seen beneath his massive weight.

Introductions had already been made.

Joje called the newcomer Dwew, and despite his protestations, it was very apparent they were not related. Long dirty-blond hair that fell to his shoulders, pasty white skin, and a gut so heavy and full his shirt never had a chance of being tucked in. The kid was a brute, and while he looked like nothing but Jell-O, Blake sensed there was muscle beneath the mass.

Watching Drew fiddle with his phone, Blake couldn't keep the scowl from his face. Seeing those fat fingers rape Blake's Cyborg pissed him off more than the fact that they were being kidnapped in their own house.

Drew had been outside on the porch waiting for Joje to let him in, all part of their apparent plan. Had Jenna and Blake not shared a moment last night—a glimpse that repairing their marriage was at least a possibility—Jenna would have left earlier for her run instead of waiting to see Blake off and would have discovered the giant albino just outside. They would have been alerted to the fact that something was very, very wrong.

To think an act of kindness, an outreach toward patching things up, however small, had inadvertently prevented them from uncovering the situation they were now in was one of the most depressing thoughts floating through Blake's mind. He hoped Jenna wasn't thinking the same thing. The way she avoided his eyes let him know she had at least considered it.

The "pwoject" was insane. It could never work, and some part of Blake understood that's what made it so exciting to Joje. It was a kidnapping, but in all the wrong ways. No ransom, no demands; there was nothing they wanted—other than to *observe*.

Blake had never considered how invasive that word could sound.

Joje and Drew were moving in; they would follow his family's daily activities, watch their every move for seven days, an entire week. Joje would shadow Blake to work, to lunch, back home, to the bathroom, to the bedroom. He had made it clear there wouldn't be a moment he wasn't present. Somehow Drew would manage both Jenna and Adam, though how he'd keep up with Jenna's schedule alone Blake couldn't imagine.

"In order for the experiment to work," Joje had said, "we want you to pretend we're not even here. Like flies on the wall."

Would you like *fwies* with that?

"We are here strictly to observe."

Blake's pounding head contested otherwise.

Conrad suddenly yelped from her cage. She had been whining for some time. Now that she had found her voice, she wouldn't stop until she was let out.

"She needs to go potty," Jenna said.

"She can wait," Joje answered.

Blake sensed his wife fuming. It wouldn't take long before she'd go off, and it would be with a bang.

He put his hand on her knee, squeezing it gently. Not now, honey. The time may come soon, but not now.

"Let's go over the house rules," Joje said. "Three simple rules that keep everyone safe."

"What's a *woo*?" Adam asked. It was the first time he had spoken since he had been made aware of their predicament.

"Rule, Adam, house rules," Blake said. "Just listen, don't talk."

"But I can't understand a word this guy is—"

Blake grabbed his son's face, squeezing his mouth. He had never done anything like that before, and the shock was evident in Adam's eyes.

"Don't talk." Blake dropped his hand. *Please, Son, I'm doing this for you.*

Joje smiled. "A father's love. I just got goose pimples! See, we're learning already!"

Drew was oblivious to the conversation, lost in whatever was holding his attention on Blake's phone. It was more than disconcerting, considering the amount of information he would have access to. The phone should be able to read if someone other than the owner gained access to it, the AI interface supposedly able to recognize the change in behavior. Of course, the purpose of beta-testing was to uncover exactly those types of errors, and Drew didn't look capable of entertaining himself with a locked screen.

Conrad's yelping became incessant, a faucet whose leak had turned into a flow. Joje told Drew to go check on her. Blake imagined the legs of the piano bench snapping beneath Drew before he had time to rise. He was left disappointed.

"The house rules," Joje said. "One. Tell no one about our pwoject, who we are, or why we're here. No crazy stories about kidnappings. You don't mention us to the police, your friends at work, not even the gardener. No one."

Blake and Jenna nodded silently.

"Two. To help with rule one, no phones."

Joje stopped in front of the piano. Jenna's and Adam's cell phones as well as Blake's Bluetooth earpiece rested upon the tray for sheet music. The earpiece flashed with a reddish hue—he had messages.

"No cell phones, no home phones, no work phones. No pay phones. No borrowing someone's phone. And no e-mail or Internet."

Adam raised his hand. Blake shot him a glance that was ignored.

"You don't need to raise your hand, Adam. I'm not a teacher."

"What about video games?" Adam asked, his hand lowering halfway.

"Yeah, that's fine."

"But you can talk with people online through the games."

Joje smiled. "See, that's the level of trust I'm hoping we gain. The games are fine, Adam. I trust you. It's your parents I don't want getting ideas."

Blake shook his head. "If you want to see my job, I'll have nothing to show you. Ninety percent of what I do is conducted over web conferencing, computers, or my cell."

If Blake could get his hands on his phone, he'd have them out of this dilemma within minutes.

"I wowee you're not taking this serious, Bwake."

"No, I am, I just—I'll lose my job if I can't use a computer or phone."

Joje paused as if perplexed. "I can't jeopardize your job . . . We'll just run the calls through me. I'll be like your secretary. But with balls." He laughed, not realizing or perhaps caring that no one joined in. "Third and most important rule. Nothing changes from your routine. Nothing! Even if—especially if—it's something you wouldn't want others to know about. I can't emphasize this enough. Any questions?"

Adam spoke hesitantly. "What do we tell people, I mean, who do we say you are?"

Drew walked back into the room, Conrad's yelping growing more desperate.

"Tell them we're family," Joje said.

"She wants out," Drew said.

"No shit." Joje looked at Adam. "Can you take her out?"

Adam rose from the couch, Drew following him back to the kitchen. As soon as they were gone, Joje leaned in close to Blake and Jenna. His grip on the gun tightened, as if he felt a reminder was necessary.

"I'm a nice guy. And to prove it, I have rules too. But understand this, if you break one of your rules, I break one of mine. First rule? No one gets hurt. Second, your son"—Blake felt himself tensing—"stays with you."

Joje paused, letting that one sink in.

"Third rule. After the week's up, we leave. The pwoject's over, you never see us again. Though you might grow to miss us."

He smiled. Blake did everything within his power to not knock those teeth from his head.

The smile fell. "Don't make me break one of my rules. Adam seems like a nice kid. And I weawy hate viowence."

4

A tour of the house was the first order of business, all five of them awkwardly trolling from room to room. They started upstairs—Adam's room and the guest bath.

Adam's room, of course, hadn't changed; his bed still in pieces, dressers and unopened boxes in disarray. The guest bath was a Jack and Jill, attached to both Adam's bedroom and the guest bedroom. Toothpaste was crusted on both the mirror and the counter, wadded up tissues discarded near the sink. Blake was just glad Jenna didn't open the door to the toilet.

They entered the guest room through the bathroom. This was the first Blake had seen of the Deb-inspired decor.

Japanese-style hangings with brushed lettering climbed down the walls, a five-partition changing screen blocking a corner of the room. The bed and dressers were made of elegantly carved bamboo and reed wood.

A six-foot mortar statue of a giant Buddha and a samurai sword in its scabbard on the wall only hinted at what was really wrong with the room—it was like a Hollywood set where broad strokes were meant to hide the utter disregard for detail.

"You don't like it," Jenna said.

She was close. He hated it.

"What? You've complained about every other room," she said. "Might as well tell me what we did wrong here."

"What didn't you do wrong? You've got the statue of Buddha facing the bed. Do you have any idea how sacrilegious that is? It's like flaunting your sins before a god. He should be facing the door so those entering can give their respects."

"To that thing?" Adam asked.

"Yes, Adam, to that thing. You've got to understand other cultures don't operate on ignorance like Americans do. One wrong word or gesture and you've offended someone so deeply they won't hear another word you say. Like this sword?"

Blake moved to the wall where the sword was hung.

"It should be mounted with the handle on the left. A representation of peace. The way it's mounted now? It means aggression and danger to those who enter. It's the same direction it'd be drawn from in battle. Look, I'm sorry, but it's like we're living in some twisted bed-and-breakfast with themed rooms only someone as demented as Deb could come up with."

Jenna was silent. Blake knew he had hurt her. He also knew the frustrations rising to the surface went much deeper than ill-placed furniture.

"It was my idea," Jenna said, "not Deb's. It was going to be a surprise. We were going to hang the kamora or whatever you call it, the warrior garb you have in storage, against that wall there."

The kimono. Blake felt like an ass. He traveled to Asia several times a year on business, and Jenna knew how important it was to him—not just the deals or the money—the culture, the people.

"Guess we spoiled the surprise," Joje said.

"I'm sorry," Blake said, knowing the apology was as out of place as the East Asian decor. He found he couldn't take his eyes from the sword on the wall. When he considered their kidnapping, maybe it had been mounted the right direction.

"This will be your room," Jenna said. "Bed should be big enough, and we've got blow-up mattresses in the garage if you need them. You are guests after all. Make yourselves at home."

Drew dropped a faded duffel onto the bed, one end held together by strips of warped duct tape. It was all they had brought with them for an entire week.

"That won't be necessary," Joje said, picking the bag back up and handing it to Drew. "Unless, of course, you're in this room, I doubt we'll be visiting it much. Can't observe if we're not with you. At all times."

"Of course," Jenna said, her tone gone cold. "Should we continue?"

They did.

The theater room, upstairs loft with Jenna's vast array of workout equipment that would rival most gyms, the master bed and bath—almost as unfamiliar to Blake as it was to their "guests."

The procession continued as Blake slid more and more into himself. Maybe it was the realization of just how much access their kidnappers intended to intrude upon or that feeling of being judged, for how much excess they felt entitled to and how frivolously they spent their money. Perhaps it was the even harsher realization that in some regard, those judgments might be justified.

Back downstairs, Jenna led them to Blake's study. Double doors opened into a room lined with custom bookshelves that had been soundproofed to ensure Blake's ability to work from home without distraction. Blake had tested it himself, having Adam scream as loud as he could just outside his office and then sealing the doors. Not a whisper passed through.

A gilded oak desk sat in the center of the room like a throne, walls and shelves lined with accolades—awards and gifts and pictures of Blake with businessmen, politicians, men and women of power, and in each framed photo, Blake smiled, an arm around someone's shoulder or waist, wine glass, cigar, or beer bottle held in the air.

While Joje glanced at the pictures and awards, Drew picked up a gold-embossed model airplane from one of the shelves. It had been a gift from one of Blake's Chinese friends at BSC International. Blake had helped them win a contract with Boeing that took their company from twenty million in sales to over two hundred million. The golden plane was in reference to a Chinese proverb of the bird that wanted to fly to the sun; once he reached it, he was turned to gold, never to fly again.

The plane slipped from Drew's hands, falling to the floor. It hit with a loud thunk, a propeller and piece of wing breaking off.

Drew moved on to the next memento, not even bothering to retrieve the downed plane.

Never to fly again, Blake thought with a certain sadness.

Joje moved around the desk, sitting at Blake's chair. He waved his hand through a holographic clock, shook the wireless mouse, Blake's thirty-two-inch monitor awakening to a black screen. His laptop was still in his briefcase.

"So is this your office, or do you go in to an office?" Joje asked.

"Both. Most days I work from home so . . . this will be it."

"And today, when you hit me with your car?"

Blake was pretty sure Joje had been the one to do the hitting. "I was going in to work."

"Where's work?" *Wuhk.*

"Westlake. It's our corporate office."

"Uh-huh," Joje said. "So we should be there right now, not here. Are we late? Do we need to leave?"

Blake looked at Jenna, unsure how to answer.

"Do you think they postponed your meeting?" she asked.

Blake should be so lucky. "I doubt it."

"JT will understand," Jenna said, her voice unable to disguise her doubt.

Prior to being offered a position with Symbio, Blake had worked with them on a few projects, consulting with JT and, on occasion, his board. Jenna knew of their volatile relationship and the stress it had induced. Blake not showing for a meeting as important as today's would go beyond a screaming match. JT wouldn't fire him; he'd have Blake murdered.

"I screwed up your day, didn't I," Joje said, as if he hadn't considered the inconvenience kidnapping Blake and his family had caused. "Do you want me to call and explain things?"

"No!" Blake shouted. Too quickly, he realized, as Joje snapped his fingers, holding his hand out. Drew slid the Cyborg from his pocket, handing it over.

"Thirteen missed calls," Joje said. "JT's your boss?"

Murder would be too kind, Blake realized. JT would want him tortured.

"It's ringing," Joje said.

Blake's face fell. This was all wrong. He had to come up with a plan first, some reason for his absence that JT would at least consider.

"Remember our rules." Joje placed the phone to his ear.

"You're white," Adam said quietly, staring at Blake. "Your face."

"Tell him—tell him I've been in an accident . . . I won't be in until tomorrow, but I wanted him to know. And I'm okay!"

"You want me to lie to your boss?" Joje asked. "In front of your son?"

"No! I was in an accident, and I am okay—"

Blake fell silent as a blaring stream of unrecognizable screaming poured from the phone held to Joje's ear. Joje pulled the phone back.

"Hey!" Joje shouted, gripping the phone like a walkie-talkie. "No, wis—hey, no, you wissen! No . . . this . . ." He looked at Blake incredulously, as in *this* is what you deal with every day?

He hit the end key, disconnecting the call.

"Daaghhh!" Blake yelled. "I said don't call him!"

The screen lit up, phone vibrating in Joje's hand.

"Don't!" Blake said as Joje answered the call and brought the phone back to his ear.

"Wissen, oh I'm hanging up! Undohstand? I'm cauwing on behalf of Bwake . . ." A brief pause. "No, that's—that's not it. I'm—" Joje held his other hand up in the air in frustration.

Blake leaned in, yelling into the phone. "I'll explain tomorrow JT! I can't talk now. Tomorrow!"

Joje looked at Blake sharply, ending the call once again. "I said no phones."

"I, I wasn't—I just, it's my job."

"*No phones!*" Joje screamed into Blake's face.

Blake made the conscious decision to keep his feet planted, surprised by the amount of effort it took. He would not let this kid intimidate him. Not in front of his family. "If you're going to be my voice on the phone, I need you to listen to what I say with exactness," Blake said. "That's the only way this'll work."

Joje's dark eyes seemed to shrink beneath his protruding forehead. His face relaxed, features calming. "No more warnings," he said, his tic sweeping over his face. "You break a rule, however slightly, you force me to break one of mine."

Blake nodded, he understood.

His eyes swiveled to the closet behind his desk. His .38 Special, an antique handed down from his grandfather who had fought in the first World War, seemed to be screaming louder than JT had over the phone. He needed time—time, the cold steel of a pistol in his sweaty palm, and a beer or two in him to settle his nerves.

The targets he already had.

5

The day passed slowly, but unlike an idle day spent at the lake, this day dragged. It was as if every second were waiting until the absolute last chance to dart the short distance across the face of the clock. A day determined to extract a price for every minute's passage.

As Joje relentlessly inquired what the family would be doing, Blake began to wonder himself. What did they do to fill their day? He couldn't remember when they had spent this much time together, and the awkwardness was beginning to show.

Jenna ran her seven miles on the treadmill; there was no way

Drew could keep up with her on a real run. Blake joined her upstairs, lifting with free weights.

It was difficult staying focused with Drew's reflection in the background, a silent stalker on the fringe of a photo. His eyes never left Jenna's body, and Blake was frightened at the unspoken implications.

Joje had joined Blake, lifting as well and even spotting him on a few occasions while Adam had silently played his portable video games.

After the workout, Joje asked what they did next. Shower? Together?

The simple question caught them so off guard neither Blake nor Jenna had been able to reply. Adam, fortunately, had come to the rescue.

"They don't do anything together."

They fumbled over excuses until settling on their after-workout routine of going for a swim, and so, for the first time as a family since their move, they ventured out to their backyard.

The swimming pool was bookended by two hot tubs, one hidden behind a curtain of water from above, the other raised several feet above the pool around a curved stone tower. In the middle of the pool was a small island with a fire pit. At night, you could swim beneath the stars, waves crashing below with only the faint glow of the outdoor lanterns and flicker of flames rising from the pool's center to light your evening.

Both Jenna and Blake remained in their workout clothes to one extent or another, ducking into the raised spa. Joje opted to stay out, quietly observing from a patio chair below the straw umbrella hut. His gun never left his hands.

Drew and Adam had jumped in, playing volleyball with the net that spanned the pool until they grew tired with the amount of work required. Neither of them was very good.

When they decided to get out, Blake realized he and Jenna had sat across from each other the entire time like strangers in a hotel Jacuzzi, not a single word exchanged.

They went as a family to take the dog for a walk, dialogue so stilted and tired they stopped trying.

The TV was turned up louder than normal. Shows Blake had never seen proffered chuckles beneath breaths that were as forced as the conversation.

Blake tinkered in his office on his laptop for a bit, Joje breathing over his shoulder the entire time. Without Internet, he felt crippled.

Projects and deadlines floated through his thoughts like clouds he couldn't grasp. He went through the deck of slides he had failed to present, talking through some of the points with Joje, but found his attention hovering toward the Wi-Fi bar with a slash through it. No connections available. Seemed to sum up his life—with his computer, his son, and his wife.

After dinner, Conrad dropped her knotted rope throw toy at Joje's chair at the kitchen table, tail wagging furiously behind her. She never grew tired of the game, and Joje was inclined to indulge her.

He lobbed the gnarled rope back across the room. Conrad's feet slipped and slid as she picked up traction on the wooden floor.

"She likes you," Jenna said, grabbing the plate in front of Joje and adding it to her stack before returning to the sink.

Dinner had been anything but normal. The fact that they were eating together as a family was a novelty, but a home-cooked meal, despite being a once-a-year occurrence, had also been befuddled by an almost bare pantry. Mother Hubbard's cupboards hadn't gone dry; they had never been filled.

"Can I be excused?" Adam asked. His plate of scrambled eggs and toast had barely been touched.

"Sure," Blake said at the same time Joje said, "Yes."

Blake looked up sharply, but Joje seemed oblivious to it. Drew scraped Adam's eggs onto his own plate as Adam walked past, heading back into the family room.

"Dogs are so stupid. "Joje yanked the throw toy from Conrad's gritted teeth, then hurled the rope back into the family room. His trajectory was timed, the thick twisted rope swinging high and striking Adam in the back of the head.

"Ow!" Adam cried.

Blake's chair screeched as he stood. "Hey, do we have a problem?"

"We do. You're putting me in a position I don't want to be in. Already breaking the rules"

"We haven't even seen anyone," Jenna began. "How could we—"

"It's what my Sunday school teacher might have called a sin of omission," Joje said. "Do you think I'm stupid? That today was just an ordinary day? What was our third rule?"

Blake looked at Jenna, who shook her head ever so slightly.

"Nothing changes from our routine," Adam said from the family room.

"Someone paid attention," Joje said. "How much of today would you consider normal routine, Adam? That wasn't changed on account of us being here?"

Adam hesitated before answering. "Almost none of it."

"If you don't normally cook dinner? Then don't cook for us. If you don't know how to operate the dishwasher, don't pretend you do dishes every night. If you don't spend time together as a family, don't start now. If you don't like each other, don't act like you do. If your marriage is a sham? I want to see it. If you fight every night? I want to see it. If you're sleeping around? I want to see it! I want to see every sick and disgusting thing you wish you didn't even know about yourself! Are we clear?"

Yeah, we're queer, Blake thought.

The tension in the air felt like a living, breathing entity, choking all hope of normalcy in their supposed arrangement.

"Since you've all broken a rule, you force me to break one of mine," Joje said.

"George, we're trying—we're learning. Work with us here," Blake said.

"You're weak Bwake. It's why your dog shits on your floor, your wife resents you, and your son has no respect for you. The consequences were clearly laid out. If I don't follow them, you make me a liar. And I do not lie."

The gun, which had been in and out of Joje's hands all day, silently appeared, though this time with purpose. The thrumming in Blake's chest rose to his head; he instinctively moved out from the table, stepping between his son and Joje.

"Don't do anything you'll regret," Blake said.

"Precisely the lesson you need to learn," Joje said.

They stood facing each other like gunslingers in the Old West. Only Blake had no gun and was, in effect, begging for his life.

Joje's mouth twitched, his right eye blinking furiously. He finally broke the silence, tilting his head down and shrugging, gun in hand. "Tell you what. You broke your third rule, I'll break my third rule."

"Seven days," Jenna said. "You're not leaving after seven days?"

"Correct," Joje said. "We'll scratch this day off the calendar and start our week tomorrow. Unless you want me to break one of my other rules?"

"No, no, that's . . . more than fair," Blake said.

"Generous," Jenna said from the kitchen.

"Let's not have this talk again," Joje said.

"What about next time?" Drew asked.

Blake hadn't realized Drew had been paying attention to the conversation, though in hindsight, how could he not.

"Next time they break a rule?" Drew continued.

His quiet demeanor was a farce, Blake realized. If Joje hated violence, as he had stated—not that Blake believed that for an instant—Drew clearly hungered for it.

"Next time, we'll be forced to break one of our other rules, won't we?"

6

Night crept into the home like a silent stalker, slowly making its presence known. Shadows lurking in corners and darting between rooms spun Blake's thoughts into a torrent of despair. The seesaw rise and fall, a constant shifting of what he should do, how he should be reacting, was set upon a fulcrum where no balance could be reached.

Did he protect his family by fighting Joje and Drew, trying to eliminate the threat, or by falling in line with his "experiment" and avoiding any fallout?

What would be the consequence should he try and fail?

And what would they be if he didn't try?

The mental exertion of weighing options where no answer was in sight was exhausting. Blake's indecision was in itself a decision; he would have to give it more time, hope their kidnappers would grow comfortable and let their guards down should an opportune moment arise. He just hoped he would recognize that moment when it came.

That evening, they discussed the plans for the following day. It felt good to get out in the open their normal activities, especially after the draining day they had endured. Jenna and Adam had even laughed, reflecting on how torturous seven days like today would have been. Blake wasn't sure if laughter was the right response but had played along, smiling when needing to.

Tomorrow would be their first day apart, officially kicking off their grand adventure.

Joje would accompany Blake to the office in an attempt to save his job. He hadn't decided on a play that would get JT back on his side but hoped something would come to mind.

It had to.

Drew would be following Jenna through her day, bringing Adam along for the ride. It was agreed she would continue running at the home gym, but Joje wanted her to attend her Pilates class, go shopping—a trip to the grocery store was discussed, though that was typically not Jenna's forte—among the many other errands she had planned.

With the family being separated, and perhaps in response to Jenna's illusive errands, Joje presented a system to keep everyone in check, a safety net for him and Drew. Every fifteen minutes, one of them would text the other a coded message to ensure their party was behaving. A response was required with whatever "code" they had come up with. If at any interval one party failed to respond within twenty minutes, allowing for a five-minute leeway, the other party was to assume the worst.

The repercussions hadn't been discussed, but there was no question what they might be.

Blake expressed concerns of areas with no cell service or spotty reception or just one of them forgetting to check in. The plan was so full of holes it was almost guaranteed to go wrong. Joje had simply stated Blake and his family were as responsible as he and Drew. It was a matter of "teamwuhk," and no amount of arguing would get him to sway.

At 10:47, they decided to turn in, earlier than normal but close enough not to warrant an argument, not that Blake was expecting to sleep anytime soon. Take away the stress and strain of the day and the spinning mill in his mind searching for solutions, and he still would be missing his Bluetooth earpiece and his phone's sleep-inducing app.

It was going to be a rough night.

Jenna drained her glass of wine at the kitchen island and set it in the sink. It was her fourth glass, and she was clearly on a buzz. Adam powered down his gaming console and collected the other controller from Drew.

"Come on, Conrad, let's go potty," he said.

The dog leapt to her feet, collar jangling as she followed Adam to the back door. It was such an insignificant thing, Adam being responsible, but to Blake, it meant the world. Especially after a day like today.

The back door shushed closed, and Adam ushered the dog into her cage, the rattle of the metal door engaging. "Good girl," he said, probably slipping a treat in between the gridded bars of the crate.

Blake eyed the alarm system, which was set in the hall leading to the garage. One of the many things on the to-do list Jenna had given him.

He hit the lights, following Drew and Jenna down the hall to the foyer. An alarm wouldn't have protected them anyway, not from the dangers already inside their home.

It wasn't until Blake reached the stairs that the problem began.

"You're going upstairs?" Adam asked.

"It's time for bed," Blake said, not realizing what his son was asking.

"Oh, okay."

"What's the problem?" Joje asked, picking up on the exchange. Adam looked, for lack of a better word, guilty. "What is it, Adam? You can be honest. You need to be honest."

"I just, I don't want to get anyone in trouble."

And suddenly, Blake knew what was bothering his son—his son who picked up on details most kids his age would have missed.

"You sure about that?" Joje asked.

"It's been a long day. We can discuss this in the morning," Blake offered. He continued toward the stairs.

Joje raised his palm toward Blake.

Stop.

Surprisingly, Blake found himself doing just that.

"No one gets in trouble if you tell the truth." Joje hadn't broken eye contact with Adam, even with his display of power over Blake.

"My dad sleeps on the couch. At night." Adam looked down as if ashamed. "We just, we're supposed to keep our routine."

Joje looked at Blake. The sense of excitement, of violence bubbling at the surface, seemed difficult to assuage.

Blake kept his voice steady. "Your mom, earlier today, asked me to sleep with her tonight. We're turning over a new leaf."

He looked up at Jenna, who stood halfway up the stairs, massaging her head from the headache apparently encroaching. "That's right," she said.

"I think you should sleep down here, Bwake," Joje said, his eye blinking, mouth twitching. "As much as I'd enjoy watching you sleep together, I can't accept a lie."

"I'm not lying."

"Right now, I trust your son a lot more than I trust you. If he says you sleep on the couch, that's where you sleep. I'll stay here with you. Dwew will watch over Jenna."

"I am not sleeping in the same room as him!" Jenna spit the last word out like it carried poison.

Joje was smiling now. "Of course you are. And I know we didn't discuss this earlier, but we will be restraining you at night. For security reasons. I'm sure you understand."

Jenna looked at Blake, eyes pleading. "Don't let them do this."

"I'm drawing the line here," Blake said. "We stay together at night. Adam too."

"Your call, but if you break a rule, I break a rule," Joje said.

Drew continued up the stairs toward Jenna, who fell back, bumping into the railing. She began crawling up the stairs backward. "Stay away from me! You stay away!"

"You can't do this!" Blake said, moving toward the stairs.

"Drew?" Joje said.

Drew turned back around on the stairs, a sentinel standing guard. He was as big as any bouncer Blake had seen.

Blake paused on the bottom step. "If you touch her—"

"No one will touch anyone. You have it all wrong," Joje said.

"Just here to observe," Drew said, a complete lack of emotion on his face.

"He'll be in the same room as her, that's all. Watching," Joje said. "Adam, you'll be restrained but on your own tonight. Most nights, I imagine."

Adam nodded as if this made perfect sense.

"Why don't you bring your dad's toiletries down so we can avoid another outburst," Joje said.

Adam scampered up the stairs, giving Drew a wide berth.

Jenna's eyes burned down at Blake, and it wasn't from the alcohol.

Joje smiled. "Have a good night."

7

Adam lay atop his mattress set against the bed railings that had yet to be put together. His jaw ached from the grin on his face. His arm was bent backward, handcuffed to a bedpost, a bedpost as portable as a hockey stick.

What an idiot, Adam thought.

When Drew had pulled the handcuffs from their duffle bag, Adam hadn't complained or put up a fight. Instead he posed a question.

Where do you want me.

With no bed put together and his room looking like the aftermath of a garage sale, Drew had put the question back on Adam.

Just like Adam knew he would.

After cuffing him, Drew asked why his room was the only one not set up. Adam's reply had been planned, as had the response it garnered from the giant albino.

To piss off my dad.

Drew's smirk revealed everything Adam had hoped for. Make him think they were coconspirators, on the same side. Hell, maybe they were.

It had been a relief to discover Drew would be the one watching his mom and him. Joje scared him. Not because of the kidnapping; Adam was actually looking forward to the "pwoject"—it would at least make for an interesting end to his summer. Adam simply couldn't read Joje, not like he could other people, and that was more frightening than any amount of threats or hints of violence.

Adam had a gift, a way to know what someone would do before they did it, to predict their reactions, foresee their behavior, and he used it to get the results he desired. With teachers, friends, lately with girls, and especially with his parents. It was why he had been so upset about the move; his parents would never understand. He had followers back home.

Followers.

Like a *prophet*. And they obeyed Adam's command.

It was intoxicating, this power, and while he knew he could regroup and start over, "make new friends" as his father put it, he missed that feeling now. Of watching someone come to a decision they thought was their own, never realizing Adam had fit his arm up their ass, their head nodding when he moved up and down, mouth opening at the split of his thumb and forefinger, words repeating what he whispered in their ear.

He hadn't been born with his gift; it had been hard earned, though he didn't like thinking about that.

He knew he was gifted, because he had never been caught. No one realized how he turned the conversation or how they forgot what they had initially come to him about. His response or lack of response always elicited the results he wanted.

People were so stupid.

But Joje, he was something else. It was like he could see through Adam, see what he was really after. Like when Adam set up his dad to take the fall, pretending to just want to follow the rules—Joje knew what he had been doing.

Pulling the I-don't-want-anyone-to-get-hurt card, Joje had called his bluff. Straight out.

"You sure?" he had asked.

It had taken Adam so off guard he hadn't known how to respond. Luckily his father hadn't caught on.

But while Joje was something of a mystery, Drew could have been hypnotized by a kindergartener. Before Drew had left his room, Adam had shared with him a little secret—since after all, they were coconspirators.

"She sleeps naked. Don't tell her I told you."

If a fire had burned behind Drew's eyes, it would have been stoked to blazing.

And with that, Adam had him. It was a lie, of course, but one he'd never be caught for. He only wished he could be in the room when Drew demanded she sleep in the nude.

Jenna always walked around her room naked; Adam had plenty of recordings, though he kept them well hidden. This would be something completely different, however, and her looks, instead of helping to talk her way out of a situation, would only make things worse. If only he could have caught it on film.

Jenna relied far too much on the looks she got from other men, at the gym, at Starbucks, anywhere her fake boobs and tanned pelican legs would take her. Adam still remembered the teacher-parent conference four years ago with Mr. Morrison.

No wife of mine will ever get away with that kind of behavior, he thought.

He smiled, chained up in his room, yet, for the first time since they had arrived in this awful new house, feeling so free.

This would be a fun seven days.

Chapter 3

Day Two

1

Blake walked up to the mirrored glass doors of his office building, hoping the reflection of his shaking hands was just a warp in the glass. "Fake it till you make it" wasn't supposed to apply to someone his age or at his level. His plan, however, was as thin as the line he was walking with Joje. One misstep and there would be no going back.

On the drive up, Blake couldn't count the number of times he had contemplated finding a nice piece of wall to ram his M6 into. Maybe the center divider at an angle that would propel Joje up and over, straight into oncoming traffic, or a quick plunge off the rise of a cliff into unforgiving waves.

Unfortunately, he knew where that would lead his family, a death not nearly as quick as a watery grave.

One long breath to clear his mind and turn that interior switch to the on position. He'd only have one chance. It was all he would need.

Blake entered the building.

He did not hold the door for Joje.

The front receptionist, Cyndi, with the *Y* and *I* reversed in a failed attempt at chic originality, greeted them coolly. Thin to the point of anorexic, her beady eyes bored into Blake as if she held some personal grudge against him.

She gave a light toss of her head, her too-blond hair barely acknowledging the movement. Blake had met her once before and hadn't cared for her then either.

"Could you let Jim know I need to see him?" Blake asked as he continued past.

"Actually, Mr. Crochet"—she leaned over her massive glass desk to call after him—"Mr. Crochet?"

Blake stopped. Joje stood behind him, looking completely out of place. This wasn't going to work.

"Who is this?" Cyndi asked.

"*He*, not *this*. And in the future, take care how you refer to a potential partner," Blake said.

Joje smiled, once again not helping the situation.

"Mr. Tanner actually suggested, should I see you come in today," she paused, denoting the apparent question that had been, "that I have you wait in the lobby for him."

Blake stared down at Cyndi. This twenty-something secretary who thought being a bitch was part of the job requirement, stringy bleached hair cut to look like a mannequin, stunning dress revealing all leg but covering everything up top—not that there was much to showcase. He was certain she had to show her tiny tits three times a day to some minor executive just to stay employed.

"Cyndi. Let Jim know my guest and I are on our way to his office."

"Well, your guest will need to sign in." She brought out a thin tablet they used as a digital clipboard. All about presentation.

Blake's eyes never left hers. He supposed some men got off on reigning in that kind of attitude. "Don't ever talk down to me again."

He ushered Joje past the hall to the glass staircase leading up to JT's office. As they began their ascent, he noticed Cyndi on the phone, watching them go.

"Do you always lie at your job," Joje asked.

"You haven't left me much of a choice. Unless you want me to tell them the truth?"

Joje's left eyed twitched, blinking rapidly. His face drew down in an awkward yawn. "I want this to be as close to real life as possible."

Blake suddenly shoved Joje up against the side of the staircase.

They were in that perfect position where no one could see them, from above or below. Blake held him close, the back of his arm pressed against Joje's throat, faces almost touching. He could feel the tremble in Joje's frame.

"What the hell do you think this is? Real life . . . ? I'm doing what you asked, playing by your rules, but here, you play by mine. I've got one chance here. One!"

Joje's lips curled up in a tight smile as if he were enjoying this display. Blake pressed harder against his throat. It took every ounce of constraint to allow Joje to keep breathing; he wanted to close his hands around that neck and never let go.

His phone suddenly buzzed. In Joje's pocket.

"You want me to respond," Joje said.

Blake released his grip, disgusted with his companion, more disgusted with himself for playing along in this mad charade.

He continued up the stairs. Joje followed, typing a response one finger at a time into the phone. The smile that crept over his face was more frightening than the realization that Blake could have ended Joje's life—had, in fact, wanted to. And strangely, he didn't think Joje would have stopped him.

It made Blake shudder. What outcome was Joje hoping for in all this?

One chance. That's all he needed. It just had to be the right one.

2

A light breeze carried the smell of the ocean mixed with the gargled taint of car exhaust. Still, Jenna sensed drifting on that breeze a freedom she could almost reach out and grab.

Across from the small sloped parking lot, past the Pacific Coast Highway with its occasional passing car, she stared out at the end of the world. At least that's how she pictured it.

The ocean shook, roared, consumed.

She breathed deep, inspired—feeling braver, stronger.

The Escalade chirped, alarm setting. Turning back to the one-roomed wooden building that was Sunrise Yoga, faded blue paint now an almost colorless gray, Jenna felt the breeze die, air turn stale.

First, her morning runs. Now these bastards would take this from her. One less hour in the day to lose herself; how desperately she needed to remain lost.

Drew stood on the cracked sidewalk, watching her, his eyes never leaving her chest. She shuddered, a cold sweat trickling down her back as she thought about last night. Drew might not have touched her, but she couldn't escape the feeling of having been raped.

Where has that breeze gone?

"So are we doing this today?" Adam stood next to Drew by the side of the building, sulking even more than usual. Not that she could blame him. Reluctantly, she joined them.

"There's a skate park in Santa Monica I wanna check out when you're done," Adam continued.

"I've got a hair appointment after this," Jenna said. Adam rolled his eyes in response. "This is a women-only facility. You'll have to wait outside. It's one room. There's nowhere I can go."

"I'm supposed to stay with you," Drew said.

"And I'm telling you if you want me to maintain my routine, we'll need to compromise. Your . . . brother was adamant we keep our schedule."

Drew ran his hands through his greasy hair. "I should call George."

Adam's face suddenly lit up, his eyes brightening. "I thought he put you in charge of us? You call the shots. You don't need his permission."

Careful, Adam.

Jenna reached out to put her hand on his shoulder, but he ducked her, drawing closer to Drew.

"It's not like you can be with both of us at all times anyway," Adam continued. "Think about it—Jenna runs around to a million places, I've got my things that I do. You're going to have to trust one of us to be on our own. Unless you keep us both locked up at the house."

Damnit!

Jenna almost slapped Adam; the kid had no finesse. As soon as she got inside, she'd be able to get help. Sure, it'd be embarrassing, but there were far worse things to worry about. Their bedtime routine, for one.

"I'm going to be late."

"Wait," Drew said.

Jenna continued toward the front corner of the studio. From there, she could sprint to the building, get inside before he even realized what was happening.

"Ow!" Adam cried out.

"I said wait!"

Drew had Adam's arm twisted behind his back, causing Jenna to halt. The boy was up on his tiptoes, trying to release the pressure, a grimace on his face. The parking spaces in front of the bike and surf shops were empty, not a single passerby or witness around.

"You want to see your son, get back in the car."

Jenna hesitated. And Adam saw it.

"She doesn't care," he said. "She's not my real mom."

His words couldn't have been more damning. She left the side of the building, rushing to Adam and cradling him in her arms. He pulled away from Drew, returning the embrace.

"I am your mother. And I won't let anything happen to you."

Adam responded with a choked gasp, his head resting against her bosom. Despite having made the right decision Jenna couldn't help but feel like an invisible glass had just been lowered over her, walling her in on every side.

A gear ticked another notch closer to a darkness as consuming as the ocean, an ink stain sickness that knew only how to feed and multiply.

"Get in the car," Drew said. "I'll drive." He took the keys from her, opening the passenger door. A true gentleman.

She slid in, the closing of that door sending the gear tumbling yet another notch.

"Love you, Jenna," Adam said from the backseat.

"You too, kiddo. You too."

3

The clear glass walls of JT's office transformed to an opaque beige, something accomplished with the push of a button. He closed the double doors behind him, rubbing his hand against the gray-tinged goatee on his pocked face, the only hair on his head that still grew. He was young to be the CEO of a global company, the framed *Forbes* issue with the cover story "Thirty CEOs to Watch in Their Thirties" hanging in the hallway a sign he was not only aware of it, but defined by it.

Blake noticed he was wearing his suit jacket. Not a good sign.

"JT, let me introduce you to a . . . friend. A potential partner." He motioned to Joje who looked as confused as Blake's boss.

JT shook his hand and nodded, turning his attention back to Blake. "A word?" He nodded to his office.

Blake pressed forward. "George, this is Jim Tanner, or JT. He's the vision behind the numbers and science. One of the youngest CEOs to build a Fortune-Five from the ground up. If things progress like I believe they will, he would be the one to carry this deal through."

He turned to JT. "This is George. I've . . ." He paused. "It's a little complicated. I promised not to reveal his last name or the . . . company he's associated with but—"

"I didn't know we were looking for partners," JT said.

"A partnership is where both parties mutually benefit," Blake quipped. "Sometimes they're not sought after. They just appear, knocking at your front door. But only a fool turns away what he hasn't considered."

JT looked Joje over once more, no doubt noticing the same discrepancies Blake had upon their first meeting. Blake could only hope he ascribed them to eccentricities.

He took JT aside, speaking softly, but still in range of Joje being able to overhear. "Look, you hired me not only because of what I can do, but who I know. This is big. It could change everything."

"One of my many concerns," JT whispered back, the menace in his words not lost in the lowered volume. He smiled briefly at Joje, then continued. "I run this business. I make these decisions. Maybe that wasn't clear when you interviewed." He spit out this last word as if it were the most horrendous curse in a sailor's dictionary.

Joje's left eye started blinking rapidly, his mouth opening in a constant yawn—the hushed tones were becoming a problem.

"I don't want a fricking excuse for yesterday, and I don't want to be accosted by some freak show clown you owe a favor to. All I want is for you to invent a damn time machine so you can bring my presentation to the meeting that happened twenty-four hours ago! And maybe, just maybe, you'll even travel back to a time when you were still employed here!" JT's voice had risen so loud his entire frame was shaking. "I want your phone before you leave. I'll send a driver to pick up the rest."

Blake forced himself to remain calm. A shouting match would only seal his fate. He pointed instead toward the *Forbes* article, hoping to God his hand would stop shaking.

"You're on that wall because when the stakes get too high and others fold, you go all in. You know when to stay in the game. And this—right now—is a moment you will always regret. If you back out." Blake lowered his tone to a whispered hush. "Without even knowing what's to gain."

Joje cleared his throat, glancing down, then spoke. "Wiw find someone else." He gave a dismissive glance toward JT and started down the stairs.

Blake realized he was holding his breath. He let it out, counting the seconds. He only got to four, but it felt like hours.

"Your argument better improve from here," JT said. Then he was pounding down the stairs in pursuit of Joje.

Forty minutes later, they left JT's office. An assistant in tight snow-leopard pants and a loose blouse cut so low it left little to the imagination led the way, showing them to Blake's office.

It had worked. JT had bought the pitch, the potential for an earth-shattering transformation enough to keep his interest piqued. He hadn't been thrilled with being kept in the dark, had demanded information, but Blake had finally convinced him he had no option. It was play by their rules or they would move on to one of his competitors. Lying to his boss on the first day was not the way he wanted to start with this organization, but he had to remember all he was really doing was buying time.

Joje had performed unbelievably well, his nuances accentuating the fact that this "partnership" was real. And somewhat frighteningly enough, it actually felt like a partnership—the give and take, the playing off each other; Blake had to admit he was impressed. He never would have guessed Joje had that kind of potential. To sell someone at JT's level on any amount of bullshit was difficult at best. To get him to purchase the whole dung pile? Next to impossible. Joje had truly done well.

As they marched down the hall, Blake couldn't help but feel the elation that always came after closing a deal—a high that would carry him for days. Usually, this would mark a night when he would take his wife to bed, one conquest followed quickly by another. That feeling of near invincibility always translated well in the bedroom.

But not tonight. Whether Joje and friends were staying or not.

Joje's hand almost hit Blake in the head—not in an attack, but in what was meant to be a high five. So much for the class he had shown earlier.

"That was amazing," Joje said as they followed the brunette, his smile pure jubilation. "This is so right, I can tell already, I'm gonna learn a lot from you."

"We'll be learning from each other. Especially if the trial period's a success and both parties decide to make the partnership official." Blake nodded toward the assistant, hoping Joje would understand. He hoped she had been hired for her looks, not her cognizant abilities.

"You want us sticking around longer than seven days?"

Blake's reaction must have been horrific, because Joje laughed, punching him in the shoulder. "Just messin' with you. Even if you asked, I couldn't possibly fit it in my schedule."

He laughed again, then skipped down the hall. Actually skipped. They were attracting more than passing glances from the offices and associates they passed.

Joje cleared his throat, staring at the assistant leading them, her tight rear end swishing back and forth like a metronome. He reached out, pretending to grab her ass, but instead tapped her on the shoulder. To her credit, she didn't jump.

"Uh, miss? I'm sorry, what was your name?"

The assistant lowered the digital clipboard she was holding in front of her chest and smiled. "Lucy."

"I wove Wucy," Joje said, trying out each word as if sipping at champagne.

"Like the TV show." She was good. Blake barely noticed the scowl on her face as she turned around and continued forward. They arrived at the door to Blake's office.

"JT asked me to apologize. Your actual office, Mr. Crochet, is in renovations. He hoped this would suffice until your—little partnership—is cleared up."

Apparently she had been paying attention.

"I'm sure this will be fine. Thank you," Blake said.

"JT also asked for an update each day, keeping him abreast of the situation."

"A breast?" Joje asked, his impediment making the inference even more idiotic.

"Two, actually," Lucy said, anger like a passing cloud flashing across her face as she stared at Joje, whose eyes still had not risen from her cleavage.

"You're stunning," he said with his lisp. "Forgive me for taking notice."

Lucy paused as if unsure whether to thank him or slap him. Probably the latter.

"I would love to get coffee with you sometime."

"I don't drink coffee. As of right now. Have a good day." She left them there, walking briskly back down the long hallway.

"You can't tell me you wouldn't sleep with her, given the chance?" Joje asked. "She's gorgeous!"

"I'm married."

"And how's that working out?"

Blake refused to rise to the bait.

"Seriously, if she threw herself at you, what would you do? These are the kind of things I need to know! Have you ever cheated on your wife? Would you?"

"We need to work on some tact when it comes to business," Blake said. "What's appropriate, and what's not."

He opened the door to his office, met by a windowless room. Storage racks with cardboard boxes of toiletries and cleaning supplies greeted him. A weathered desk that looked like it had just been brought in from the street was propped against the wall, one leg shorter than the others. Two paint-stained metal fold-out chairs were propped against some open pipes.

No wonder JT had kept them so long. They had needed time to "prep" his office.

His boss hadn't bought a word. If this partnership wasn't something Blake could prove useful, this would be his last stop on his way out. Losing a relationship with Symbio would go much further than just costing him his job; it would be the first topple of a domino that could bring Blake's whole world down.

How could he have thought they had won this battle? There was no partner, no big plan; it was all words, colorful words with empty promises.

He looked at the only "partner" in his office who had already taken one of the fold-out chairs and was sitting on it. Backward.

He was screwed.

4

They arrived home shortly after seven following a gruelingly unproductive day. Blake couldn't remember the last time he had accomplished so little while putting in that kind of hours. At least he still had a job.

For now.

Conrad came running and leapt up onto Blake's suit pants. Ordinarily, he'd have ordered the dog down. He just didn't have it in him today.

He dropped his briefcase gently to the floor and bent down, petting her neck and rubbing behind her ears. "Connie, Connie, Connie. Did you miss me?"

The dog squirmed from beneath him, abandoning Blake for Joje as he came through the garage door.

Maybe Joje was right—dogs were stupid.

Jenna appeared in the hall, looking just as anxious to greet him. She rushed forward, embracing him.

"You okay?" he asked.

"Fine, just, happy you're home safe." She laughed, such a forced bit of mirth. Blake wasn't sure what their day had entailed, but he had a feeling it was as bad as, or worse than, his own.

"You're sure you're okay?"

"Yeah, sure. Day just . . . didn't go as planned," she said.

If Blake had once been able to read Jenna's thoughts, as all married couples occasionally do, those days had long passed. Something had happened, but he wasn't going to get it out of her. Not here anyway. Maybe not ever.

Adam sat on the couch with Drew, video game controllers in hand. Some soldier shoot-'em-up game, the kind that always made

Blake nauseous just looking at it.

He finally has a friend.

The thought was beyond disturbing.

"How was your day?" Jenna asked, reaching out and touching his chest as if making sure he wasn't a phantom.

"Productive," Blake lied. "I think Joje—"

Damnit! He had to stop thinking of him like that.

"Uh, George is going to be a fast learner."

If Joje was bothered by the play on his lisp or name, he didn't react.

"Think you can find him a position? Somewhere to start or maybe an interview with one of your dealers?"

Blake realized how little his wife understood of what he really did. "I hadn't thought of that. It's something we can explore."

Joje's smile appeared, like a stamp on his face. "We'll see."

"I'm starving," Adam said from the couch without looking up.

"I wasn't sure what to do for dinner," Jenna said. "We didn't have a chance to go by the store."

Blake wanted to ask what they had done all day but knew it wasn't the time.

"We never did celebrate," Adam interjected.

Blake's heart leapt just a little. On the drive home in bumper-to-bumper traffic, an idea had begun to crown—the birth of an idea was always messy. Blood, sinews, false starts between painful contractions. Unknowingly, Adam had just grabbed the forceps and was helping to now pull that baby out.

"I told Adam we'd go to dinner to celebrate the move. I completely forgot. Are we okay to do something like that?"

"You don't need my permission. We're here just to observe," Joje said.

Now Blake just had to make sure that slime-covered newborn didn't fall through his hands when it shot out.

They exited at Westlake Boulevard off the Ventura Freeway heading to The Promenade in Thousand Oaks. There were closer restaurants in Santa Monica, but Blake was looking for a real mall, somewhere with security cameras, crowds, and a lot of traffic. No one had objected to the drive.

He felt more aware behind the wheel than he had in a long time. It reminded him of when Adam had been born; the drive home from the hospital had been the first time in his life he had held his hands at ten and two. That feeling of carrying precious cargo, and knowing that somewhere, some force was determined to take it all away.

Jenna and Adam sat in the back with Drew between them. He stared at Blake in the rearview mirror, and Blake quickly looked away. Joje sat shotgun in the front.

One big, happy family.

They were enjoying one of the luxuries of living in California—a perpetual state of traffic no matter the hour. Blake wasn't sure he'd ever get used to it. With cars in front, in back, and on both sides of the Escalade, he felt suddenly claustrophobic.

He glanced out his window at the coupe to his side. A young family. Two car seats in back. The woman in front laughed silently.

Their lane started to move, a service van for an HVAC company replacing the coupe. A beefy Mexican, shirt sleeves rolled up, tattoo dripping down his forearm, drank a bottle of Coke Zero with the window rolled down. Enjoying the evening breeze.

It made Blake wonder how many times he had driven past someone trapped in the car next to him? A woman or man caught by an angry ex-lover? A child picked up by a stranger who had no intention of returning their stolen wares? A family that from all appearances, looked happy but that was really being dragged through hell by a psychotic kidnapper with a lisp?

It probably wasn't a high number, but the law of averages meant it had occurred at least once, maybe more. Someone staring forlornly out their window, praying the car next to them would glance their way and realize their predicament.

He'd never look at driving the same way again.

"Are you always this melancholy on your way to dinner?" Joje asked. "Come on. What do you normally talk about?"

"No one talks in this family," Adam said, one earbud hanging out.

The light turned yellow and Blake hit the brakes. The car ahead of him committed to a race with the camera flash that would be an indisputable ticket.

The idea that followed required action without contemplation, decisions made in the fraction of a second.

Just as the light turned red, Blake slammed his foot on the gas, gunning the engine. The Escalade jerked, catching itself then revving from first to third. A bright flash poured down from the lamp overhead. Blake's action caused not one but three cars to honk from opposing lanes. In an instant of instinct winning over reason, Blake even pointed at Joje with his left hand for the picture, following through to scratch his stubbled cheek. They made it through the intersection without harm.

"Sorry," Blake said as they cruised toward another line of cars waiting at the next intersection. "This traffic drives me insane."

"That was smart," Joje said, a hint of a smile betraying his curiosity. "Unfortunately, we'll be long gone by the time that—memento—arrives in the mail."

He held Blake's phone up, the camera on back turned toward them. "If you wanted a picture to remember me by, you only had to ask. Smile!"

Joje's left hand shot out, catching Blake on the side of the jaw and completely unprepared as the flash went off. The car swerved. Jenna screamed. Blake quickly corrected, pulling back into his lane as a truck's horn swept past.

"I'm driving!" Blake shouted. His face was red. And throbbing. But not nearly as fast as his heart.

Joje was the picture of calm. "What better time to be reminded your actions have consequences."

"I didn't break any rules."

"Let's not squabble over definitions."

They arrived at The Promenade a quarter past eight. The endless rows of parked vehicles never ceased to amaze Blake. The real drug of America—retail shopping.

He parked in the back next to a lamppost. If there were cameras, they'd be mounted near the lights.

Sounds of everyday life swarmed over Blake and his family . . . cars driving, parking, honking; the distant babble of conversation; a child screaming, parent scolding; a car radio blasting bass and little else—it all sounded so foreign, so out of place. Blake felt accosted by the normalcy of it all.

Life continues on in spite of our best efforts, Blake thought. Walking next to Jenna, he felt the need to grab her hand, if only to remind himself that this was real, that he wasn't dreaming. But even in his dreams, his guilt kept him from reaching out.

"Best behavior, everyone," Joje said.

If this was going to work, it would be crucial to keep Joje's guard down. "I'm sorry about earlier," Blake said. "I shouldn't have done that in the car. It wasn't worth the risk."

"Apology accepted." Joje smiled. "Let's go have some sushi!"

5

They were brought back to a corner booth at the far end of the restaurant. Joje insisted the family slide in to the middle with him and Drew on either end. Menus were placed on the table before the hostess quickly disappeared.

"I need to use the ladies' room," Jenna said.

"Drew?" Joje said, proffering one hand out in open invitation. Drew stood, allowing Jenna to climb out. "Don't let her out of your sight."

"Order some edamame," Adam said, oblivious to the conversation. "And pot stickers." His face was hidden behind the menu, and not for the first time, Blake was grateful for his son's innocence.

"Sure," Blake said. Then, as if it had just occurred to him, he let out a long sigh. "I don't have my phone."

Adam lowered the menu, his face sinking.

"What's wrong?" Joje asked.

"It's nothing," Blake said.

"Dad does this thing on his phone where he can translate our order to Chinese or Japanese. It's fun. The waiters get a kick."

"Well, let's do it." Joje brought out Blake's phone. The soft glow of the blinking light confirming messages and e-mails were going unchecked. "What do I need to do?"

"It's . . ." Blake paused. His head throbbed with every pulse of light blaring from his phone. "It's kind of tricky. Not just a push of a button."

Joje flipped the phone around in his hand end over end.

"We'll just order regular," Blake said. "It's fine."

"Then we won't be following what we really do, how we really act," Adam said.

Blake could have kissed him.

Adam continued, "Just set it to airplane mode so he can't make a call."

And the kiss was being retracted.

The information gathered by the Cyborg included much more than what was done on the phone; every conversation that took place around it was sent out to some off-site server of Symbio's for analysis, part of their predictive algorithms. However, Blake was fairly certain little human interaction took place within that analysis. He had been hoping for the chance to blind copy that data to one of his contacts—any of his contacts—to send out, in effect, a message in a digital bottle. Airplane mode would effectively set his plan to a crash course, preventing any data from moving to or from the phone.

"How do I do that?" Joje asked.

Adam reached across the table, grabbing the phone from Joje. Surprisingly, Joje let him have it. He toggled through a few screens, finding the mode setting and shutting down all communication with outside towers.

There had to be another way.

"See? The little slash through the phone at the top?" Adam said.

Joje took the phone, handing it to Blake. "I'm trusting you."

"I understand," Blake said, wondering just what Joje's "twust" entailed.

Jenna and Drew returned, Jenna moving back in next to Blake without a word.

"Any problems?" Joje asked.

"She wouldn't let me wipe," Drew said.

"There's always next time," Joje replied.

Blake seethed inside. He had to do something. As he keyed in their orders for appetizers and drinks, he realized Adam may have come to the rescue without even knowing it.

When the server finally arrived, Blake had everything ready. He asked if he spoke Japanese. The server said he did. Setting the language to Japanese, he hit the translate button. After the three-second delay, their order was spoken in perfect Japanese by a surprisingly warm and interactive voice. The server grinned and made the appropriate notes on his pad, asking if there was anything else.

No, but there would be.

Joje was ecstatic. "You have to show me how that works! This could revolutionize the world . . . no one will need to study a foreign language ever again!"

Blake nodded along. It wouldn't *"wevowooshinize"* the world but, as Adam had said, it was fun. As orders were finalized, Blake keyed them once again into his system. The message before the order was the only one he was really concerned with getting right.

With the arrival of the appetizers, the server stood at the ready for their order. "Wait, wait," he said. "My boss coming."

Perfect, Blake thought.

"I wanna do it," Joje said. "Let me do it, Bwake. I don't want you doing it."

Blake pressed a button, quickly hiding the message that would be translated. He handed the phone back, his fingers lingering on it a second too long.

"Where's the order?" Joje asked.

"Just hit the button on the upper right that says translate."

The server's manager arrived, a stout middle-aged woman with a large mole on one of her double chins. The server told her she had to listen to this. He then looked at Blake expectantly. "Can you do Cantonese?"

"Sure," Blake said, reaching for the phone.

Joje held it back. "Show me. How do I switch the language?"

"I need to see it. I don't have it memorized."

Joje held the screen out for him to see, though he clearly intended to maintain control. The manager looked at her employee with a hurried glance that said he was wasting her time. She put a smile back on as she faced the table.

"Tap the circle in the upper left. There's a drop-down menu," Blake said.

Joje flipped the phone back around. "Then I hit language? Ok, Cantonese . . . and then what?"

"Translate."

Joje held the phone out in the middle of the table for all to hear. His smile couldn't have been any larger. After the initial three-second pause, the warm voice returned, this time speaking in perfect English:

"Please nod along and laugh as if nothing is wrong. The two men sitting with my family have kidnapped us. I need you to call the police and have them wait outside. This is not a joke, this is real. My family's life is in your hands. Please help us."

Their order then began to play.

Blake swallowed. He didn't dare look up.

"I hit the wrong button," Joje said. "Let's try it in Cantonese." He pushed a few buttons on the phone and the message repeated in the hard syllabic Cantonese dialect.

Jenna's hand on Blake's knee should have been reassuring. It felt more like a farewell.

The manager's plump cheeks rose into her eyes in a forced smile. She glanced between Joje and their server, who looked equally confused.

"Do the one that says it's a stickup, that we're holding up the restaurant!" Joje said, holding the phone out to Blake. At Blake's lack of response, he continued, "There are some really funny ones on here. One that says, 'Where's your bathroom? I shit myself!'" He laughed, the only one at the table to do so.

Drew glanced nervously around the restaurant though no one had taken notice of the awkward exchange.

"It's a joke?" the manager asked.

"Yeah, it's a joke. We'll find some better ones. Come back later," Joje said, waving her away as he continued fiddling with the phone.

She emitted a tinselly laugh, raising her eyebrows at the server as she left. The server looked back at Joje and asked if he could repeat the order.

In fact, he could.

They ate in silence. Sushi had never tasted so bland. Drew ended up ordering a plate of teriyaki chicken after almost gagging on his first roll; his late order, and an additional round of nigiri for Joje, had given Joje plenty of time to try out other phrasings on the phone, effectively diluting the message Blake had attempted.

As they waited for the bill, Joje asked for the keys, handing them to Drew and telling him to take Adam and bring the car up. Blake should have tried to stop him, but they left for the entrance before he could say a word. Just one failure after another.

Jenna's accusatory look did not help.

Blake picked up the tab, though Joje insisted on getting the tip. He snatched the small leather-bound book, making sure Blake couldn't write some desperate message.

"Pick a number between one and ten, Bwake. Bwake?"

"Eight." He was growing tired of the games.

"What about you, Gem?" Joje asked.

"Excuse me?" Jenna said.

"Do you prefer Jenna or Jenn? Or Jennifo?"

"I prefer Mrs. Crochet from you."

Joje laughed. "Pick a number between one and ten."

"One."

"You know, you can tell a lot about a person through that simple exercise. Sixty percent of people choose four through seven. They're your typical, average Americans. Playing it safe. Those choosing two or three generally lack self-confidence. They see themselves as below average, little aspirations in life. Eights and nines are more like your husband. Successful. Arrogant. Think they're better than everyone. Some may be right, don't get me wrong," he said, looking directly at Blake. "But most aren't. Now ones and tens, they're the most exciting. They share a certain psychosis, shaping the world around them. They're like a spark—unpredictable but commanding attention."

Blake sighed loudly. He couldn't take much more of this crap.

"You know the most compatible of matches?" Joje continued. "A one and a ten. They're the perfect match."

"And let me guess," Jenna said. "You're a ten."

Joje just smiled, scribbling something on the receipt. His phone buzzed—Blake's phone—and Joje typed out a reply. Once he had finished, he looked up. "Time to go."

Jenna linked her arm with Blake's as they rose from the table. "What are we gonna do?" she whispered.

"I don't know," Blake said.

Most of the tables were now empty, just a few remaining stragglers enjoying conversation as much as the food. *Sort of a lost art form*, Blake thought.

"It's okay," he whispered. "We'll be okay."

The hostess bade them farewell from behind her podium.

Yes, everything was great.

Delicious.

Joje had her laughing within seconds.

The fogged windows made it impossible to see anything outside. Blake couldn't help but wonder if something might have gotten through to the manager; she had avoided their corner of the room for the rest of the evening. Was it because she found them annoying, or had she called the police in case it was more than a joke? Maybe they had picked up Drew as soon as he walked outside. Maybe that text—if it had been a text—had been sent to disarm Joje into believing everything was okay.

They stepped outside.

The night was a little darker, air a little colder. No one pointed guns or announced over a megaphone the jig was up.

Even though Blake had been expecting it, the disappointment took a moment to settle in. Maybe it sensed how long of a stay it was looking at.

And then Jenna was running.

It happened so fast nothing registered until she was ten feet away.

"Don't move," Joje said. His gun was pressed into the back of Blake's head. Then into his phone, he said, "The bitch is on the move. Yeah, take the boy."

Jenna called for help.

Three women and a young girl backpedaled away from her toward the nearest shop. Other clusters gathered but at a distance, staring, watching, whispering, and pointing, but no one reached out. No one took her in. No one offered help. With raised hands, they retreated as if she were the one with the gun, she the one threatening instead of being threatened.

Blake heard her screaming at two teenagers, her voice going raw. "Give me your phone! Give it to me!"

The young girl in a black jacket that had to be her boyfriend's deferred to the taller boy, his long face accentuated by the bowler cap on his head. He pulled a cell from his pocket and leaned out to hand it to her.

Drew suddenly appeared from behind, encasing Jenna in his arms and lifting her from the ground. The phone fell. Jenna screamed, kicking her feet as Drew carried her to the Escalade at the curb.

Blake started moving.

A gunshot brought him to a stop.

He looked down to see if he had been shot, adrenaline clouding his mind. He didn't see any blood.

"That's your only warning," Joje said from behind him.

Phones were being held up, thrust out, pointing in his direction and at the now-fleeing Escalade. Drew must have gotten her inside.

Blake turned around to face his assailant, anger and rage no longer in check.

"It's over," Blake said. "Look around! There are too many witnesses!" To his surprise, Joje smiled. "We won't press charges. Just leave my family alone."

"This isn't close to being over, Bwakey."

"It's over! We're finished playing your sick game!"

Joje looked at him. Was that disappointment in his eyes? "Stay here then. I don't care. This pwoject is not working out like I had hoped."

He stepped off the curb just as the Escalade braked to a harsh stop in front of him, passenger door already swinging open. He was inside and the vehicle was moving before Blake realized he was being left behind.

Without his family.

6

Blake ran, momentum carrying him so fast he tripped over his feet, almost face-planting on the asphalt. He hit a passing car on the hood with both hands, trying to get them to stop, the frightened faces inside probably mirroring his own.

He shouted to the gathering crowd. "Call nine-one-one! They've got my family!"

He cut across an island of plants and bushes toward the mall's exit. He had to beat them there.

As he cleared the planter, landing back on the road, a silver Tacoma screeched before him. Blake rushed the driver's door, throwing it open. "I need your car!"

A young man who probably couldn't even grow a beard stared back at him. Then the vehicle started rolling. Blake reached out, grabbing the kid by his shirt and dragging him out. Luckily, he hadn't been wearing a seatbelt. The kid hit the ground hard, and the truck stalled.

Blake jumped inside, letting the speed of the vehicle close the door for him as he turned the key and hit the gas. Slamming on the brakes, he yanked the wheel to the left. The truck fishtailed over the center divider, almost overturning.

There! The Escalade was just beginning to turn onto the main road.

Blake sped past the line of cars, barely maneuvering the truck between them and the divider. He ignored the honking around him.

Then he heard the baby cry.

Behind the passenger seat on the back bench was a rear-facing car seat.

Shit!

He couldn't see into it, but the wail emanating behind him was fierce. He didn't slow down, couldn't slow down.

Something suddenly shot over his head, yanking his neck back against the headrest—a leather strap pressed into his bulging neck. Blake lost his grip on the wheel, his hands clamoring at the tightening noose. It was no longer just the baby screaming; the mother behind him added her voice, a high-pitched screech joining the hysterical wails.

Blake's vision blurred as he realized they were pulling out into the intersection.

Into oncoming traffic.

Pulling out, but not turning.

The impact on the driver's side spun the truck a harsh ninety degrees—the airbag sprang, catching the side of Blake's face as the strap around his neck broke the skin, ripping so tight he heard a distinct snap. Glass splintered and flew, the angry noise like a steam train breaking down the door. Blake hadn't had time to tense, the only thing that kept him from blacking out when the strap tightened around his neck. The pressure released, though Blake's lungs refused to fill—it was like being held underwater, the sight of air just above the sullen waves, and for all his thrashing and kicking and struggling, the surface remained out of reach. He lifted the purse strap from around his neck, flinging it down, air escaping his flirtations. The mother's cries, the baby's short and constant wails, it was as if all sound had harmonized into one gigantic, thrumming note, vibrating now through his head. He was losing consciousness. His lungs remained empty, throat on fire.

In a moment of searing pain, air rushed down his damaged larynx, filling his lungs. He held it in, the pain so intense he wasn't sure he could exhale. And then the truck was hit again.

A vehicle barreled into them from behind, from the lane they had been pushed into. The truck jolted up onto the median. Blake flew into the dash, his head connecting with the windshield, sending a spider web of cracks across the glass. He landed in the passenger's seat, his shoulder jammed against the door.

The truck finally came to a stop.

Blake looked back at the young mother hugging her child to her. At least they had both been belted in.

"You okay?" Blake asked though no sound came out. His throat throbbed. He was barely aware of the blood rolling down his face.

He threw his bruised shoulder against the passenger door. It opened, and he fell backward to the ground. People rushed toward him. Faces. Asking questions. Was he okay. Was anyone hurt. What happened. Phones pressed to ears. People calling nine-one-one.

Finally.

In his peripheral vision, he noticed a white Escalade pulled against the side of the road thirty yards ahead, thin wisps trailing from its exhaust.

"No Idling Allowed."

A memory floated before Blake's vision of him standing on the dock at the Port of Nagoya in Japan, workers scuttling about like beetles in the rain. A yellowed sign had been stuck to one of the wooden posts on the dock, layers upon layers of tape peeling from its edges: "No Idling Allowed."

It had been the only sign in English.

Blake stumbled forward on the open road, desperate to maintain consciousness. After a few steps, he picked up speed, ignoring the yells behind him. His steps turned into a shuffle, turned into a jog, turned into a sprint as he let the air disappear from his lungs with only one concern on his mind.

His family.

He approached the driver's side, the window already rolled down. "Get in," Drew said, with barely a glance.

Blake opened the back passenger door, unaware of the pounding footsteps approaching as he climbed into the vehicle. All he saw was his wife and son . . . and Joje. For once he wasn't smiling.

"I woweed you wouldn't make it."

Jenna leaned against him, embracing him as best she could, her hands lashed crudely together in front of her with tape.

Drew accelerated, leaving the scene behind. Distantly, Blake heard the locks engage, the child-lock feature meant for safety taking on a quiet reversal of roles.

Jenna's head fell against the cradle of his neck—despite the pain, Blake refused to flinch or have her move. "I'm sorry," she whispered.

Tears came, unbidden, unwelcome, Blake too exhausted to wipe them away. He watched as flashing blue and red lights passed on the opposite side of the road. Two, three cop cars. And an ambulance. He continued seeing a ghost image of those lights long after they disappeared.

He awoke with a start as Drew rolled down the window in front of the gate to their community. Drew tapped at the box, the gates retracting. As they rolled forward, Blake realized they hadn't asked for the code.

His head felt like a driving range, the plocking of random heartbeats slamming so hard against the back of his skull he wasn't sure how long he'd remain coherent. His shoulder jolted in short, successive spasms. Jenna had gone blank, lost in her mind's projection of their inevitable "talk" with Joje.

An eye for an eye, rule for a rule. The laws of an unforgiving god.

Adam met Blake's gaze with a single nod.

The homes they passed were dark; few had more than automated exterior lights brightening the occasional palm tree or bush. He wondered how many of the homes they passed were even occupied.

Most of these mansions, their Realtors had told them, weren't primary residences but vacation homes with only the occasional visitor. At the time, that had seemed a plus. Now Blake wasn't so sure.

Everything else was black—sky, road, even the space between homes. Beyond their street, nothing was visible but an empty nothingness that was supposed to be an ocean.

We should never have moved here, Blake thought. Why hadn't they recognized the darkness that was here?

They pulled into the garage and Drew turned the engine off, closing the garage door with the press of a button. No one exited the vehicle. They sat in silence until the overhead lights flickered back off.

"We're home," Joje said.

7

As soon as they entered the house, Conrad began her yapping. Blake sat at the kitchen counter, a wave of dizziness sweeping over him. Jenna was pulling his shirt off.

"We need to get you to a hospital," she said. "Adam, honey, can you get the dog?"

"No hospitals," Joje said.

Blake winced as Jenna lifted his arm. Nausea suddenly hit, and warm vomit splattered onto the counter. The sushi looked even more decorative coming back out. What little Blake swallowed burned on its way back down. His body started shivering.

"He's going into shock!" It was Jenna. Jenna's voice. Moving away from him.

Conrad clawed her paws up onto Blake's legs, licking the spittle from his face. In the next moment, Blake was on the floor, his face pressed against the cool wood. He couldn't remember sliding from the stool, but the reverberations from hitting the ground continued to resonate. Conrad whined, nestling her face into Blake's.

He heard his wife yelling. Struggling. Something crashed to the floor, metal ringing out. If Blake could have spoken, he would have told them all to be quiet. The noise wasn't helping his head.

Conrad was up, moving away from him, growling then barking, though not in her usual tone—her bark was low, menacing. A promise of violence.

"Get it—"

"Drop da knife!"

"Adam, run!"

"This ends wight now!"

Conrad snarled, bodies shuffling, colliding. Grunts, then a man's yell followed by a thud that shortened Blake's breath.

Whimpering. Conrad's or Jenna's? Or his own?

"Ah, gawd, my hand!"

More snarling. "Get her in the cage!"

The rattle of the latch snapping into place.

"Get some ice." Joje.

"He bit through my hand!" Drew.

"I said get some ice!"

It's a she, Blake thought. The dog is a she.

Conrad's barking became desperate. She finally found her voice. From the angle Blake had landed, he couldn't see past the counter wall. Blinking required effort.

And then the yelling began.

"You think this is a game?"

Thud.

"That I'm joking?"

Another thud. Blake heard Jenna gasping for air.

"That I won't follow through on my promise?"

It came again, that muffled thump. And again.

Moisture pooled beneath Blake's cheek on the kitchen floor, and he realized he was crying.

"Don't you *ever* break a rule again!" Joje's lisp was brought even more to the forefront than normal.

Thud.

"You break a rule? I break a rule!"

Thump. Jenna, choking on her gasps.

Blake tried to get up. His muscles rebelled. Like trying to command the body of a corpse.

"That's enough!" Adam's voice, shrill and higher than normal. "That's enough."

Silence. Even Conrad's barking stopped. Blake had never heard his son talk like that before, with such authority.

A final thud. Blake shuddered.

"Now it's enough," Joje said. "Wrap your hand and get her upstairs. Cuff her to the bed. And you." There was a pause. "That was brave. I'm proud of you, protecting your family. Now help me carry your old man."

Blake passed back out before they had a chance to lift him.

Chapter 4

Day Three

1

"California Dreamin'" pulled Blake from a dreamless sleep—the alarm playing from his phone. He had always loved that song, though now that he was here, he wished he were anywhere else. Who knew, maybe that was the point of the song? The dream infinitely better than reality. He reached out to silence it but found he couldn't move—or rather, he could move only so far.

His arm was restrained, handcuffed to the headboard behind him. Every muscle in his body groaned with the slightest of movements. *His face colliding into the rushing airbag, a noose wrapping around his neck, his head smashing against the windshield, shoulder slamming into the car door.* Memories resurfaced, reminding him how their California dream had become a prison. Two days they had survived, though by Joje's count, they still had six to go.

Lying beside him, Jenna stared into his face with one eye. Her other was swollen shut, her face a blotched mask of purple and black. She blinked, the deranged wink of some villainous monster.

"It was nice . . ." Blake paused, trying to clear his throat, realizing there was nothing to clear. He swallowed glass. "Nice sleeping with you again."

Jenna smiled, as much as her lips would rise. She wore an old nightgown. Blake wondered how she had changed into it or if she had been the one to make the change. Her cuffs were tighter than his, her wrists chaffed and reddened. The angle of the bonds kept her from lying flat against the bed, her spine arced. It had to have been a sleepless night.

"How do you feel? Sorry," she said, turning her face from his. "Morning breath."

"No, you smell good. And I feel great." Two lies to start the day.

"You look like shit." Jenna giggled.

"Probably make a good pair then, don't we?"

"Always have," she said.

"Not always," he said.

Her eyes flitted around his face, exploring him as if it were their first night together, though maybe it was the bruises, cuts, and scrapes that held her attention.

"I'm sorry—" they both began at the same time, then laughed. Or at least Jenna did; Blake only croaked.

An energetic "Good mauwning!" sent the smiles into hiding. Joje crossed from the foot of the bed to Blake's nightstand, pulling his phone from the charger. "Now just pretend I'm not here while you two do your thing. Morning routine, right?"

He buried a key into the cuff around Blake's chained hand, then went around to the other side of the bed, releasing Jenna. "You should really consider makeup before seducing your husband. Just a little constructive feedback."

Her clasps came undone, and Jenna collapsed against the headboard with a sigh of relief.

"And . . . action!" Joje stared at them as if watching magicians about to perform their final act.

Jenna began to laugh. Blake couldn't help but join her, the ridiculousness of their situation moving past fear into a plane of utter insanity.

"Do not laugh at me!"

They only laughed harder, Joje's lisp adding to the absurdity. It was like watching a child in the throes of their first tantrum.

"This was part of our deal—I will observe your sex life!"

"I can barely speak," Blake said. "Or move."

"Right back atcha." Jenna buried her head in the pillow. "Ooh, though I could still sleep for days."

"Guess I'll have to demonstrate how it's done myself," Joje said.

Their laughter died. The veins in Joje's neck were throbbing, his face flushed with anger.

"I've seen what happens when we break your rules," Blake said, "and I'm not willing to break another. In this case, that means *not* having sex with my wife. We haven't been . . . intimate in a long time."

Joje was quiet. The lack of a smile was almost as disconcerting as the hideous jackal's grin that normally adorned his face.

"We'll follow your rules, but don't expect to watch a live porno in here. This is real life. It's not always as grand as it appears from the outside," Jenna said.

"I want you to follow your routine, but that routine had better include patching up your relationship because this . . . excuse? It won't work a second time."

Not out of the woods yet, Blake thought to himself. Not even close.

Blake showered. He wasn't timid by nature or afraid of locker-room culture, but standing naked in their open rock shower while Joje watched a mere three feet away was one of the most awkward moments of his adult life. Still, the almost-scalding water was a welcome sensation and gave the false impression of washing away the aches and pains of the previous day.

Nothing seemed broken, at least noticeably. The left side of his face was a seared red from the airbag, and his neck looked like he had tried to hang himself and failed. Countless gashes and bruises, but above all, his body just ached, a deep, underlying pain he welcomed with every movement of joint and muscle.

It meant he was still alive.

He dressed, a light-gray Armani with a blue Italian shirt. Joje watched him in his walk-in closet—Jenna's was twice the size of his—racks of suits, tuxedos, and dress shirts. Blake snapped his cufflinks on, slipped into a pair of leather shoes. Joje wore the same tan kakis as the past two days, though he had found a new wrinkled polo with brown and white stripes.

In the hall, Blake stopped in front of his son's door, pushing it open. Adam was crashed out on the floor, his feet climbing vertically up the bed that had yet to be put together. One of the taped-up boxes had been split open, Lord of the Rings figurines with tiny plastic axes, swords, and shields spilling out onto the floor. The aftermath of a battle gone wrong.

Blake backed out of the room, bumping into Joje behind him. Shadow, indeed.

"You know, I never had a father?" Joje said.

"How tragic," Blake said. "I'm sure no one can relate. It must be the cause of every misdeed you've ever committed in your life."

Joje laughed. Blake wasn't sure what reaction he had been hoping for, but that certainly hadn't been it. They started down the stairs.

"We got an e-mail from JT this morning. He wants an update," Joje said.

"And what would you tell him?"

"I wowee about your commitment to this pwoject."

No longer talking about work, are we, Blake thought.

As they passed his office, Blake couldn't stop from seeing the image of his beige safe hidden at the top of his closet. Thirty seconds alone, and Joje would quickly learn how serious Blake was taking his "pwoject."

The unmistakable aroma of cooking bacon hit them as they walked into the family room. Drew stood shirtless in front of the stove wearing an apron with orange and purple flowers on it. The apron had been a gift, a joke since Jenna refused to cook. She had found it so amusing she had brought it with them; as unsentimental as she was, she occasionally clung to the most random things, things that had made her smile. Blake wondered if he hadn't already been lumped into that category, Jenna keeping him around to remind her of better and happier times.

"How do you like your omelet?" Drew asked, attempting to flip runny eggs over in the pan. He was soaked in sweat as if he had just stepped from a steam room, his shoulder-length hair tangled and moist, droplets rolling from his face and thick arms and falling into the pan with an added sizzle.

"None for me," Blake said. "Just coffee." Preferably without Drew sweat. "How's the hand?"

Drew brought his left hand close to his chest, thick gauze and tape making it three times the size of his other hand.

Good girl, Blake thought. He'd give Conrad as many treats as she wanted.

Drew stared back at him with his deadpan eyes. "You know, I don't even feel sorry for you. Or your family."

Joje crossed in front of Drew, grabbing a plate with a greasy omelet on it. Smoke rose from the one in the pan.

"Where's Jenna?" Blake asked, realizing she wasn't in the room. He moved to the back of the kitchen, the dog crate was also empty.

"Went for a run," Drew said.

Blake glanced at Joje who seemed unconcerned as he took a monster bite out of his omelet. Cheese hung from his lip, connected to his fork.

"With the dog?" Blake asked. "By herself?"

Drew just stared back at Blake across the kitchen island. Joje shoveled another steaming bite into his mouth.

"Where is she?" Blake said, his throat burning from the increased force of his words.

"He told you," Joje said. "She went for a run."

"Might be her last," Drew said.

"I swear if you've—"

"Consequences, Bwakey," Joje said, mouth full, steam pouring from that gaping hole as if he were a devil. "Your wife is learning a valuable lesson."

Blake strode to the counter, prepared to teach Joje a *"valuable wesson,"* but all the knives in the block had been removed. His thoughts were moving so slow he had no idea what to do next. "Please," he found himself saying.

Drew sniffed loudly. "She's out back. Better hurry."

Blake pulled the slits open at the shuttered doors leading to the covered patio in the backyard. It took several seconds for his mind to make sense of what he was seeing. When he realized he was looking at his wife, no damage to his throat or vocal cords could have kept him from screaming.

2

Adam heard yelling. His room was almost directly above the kitchen, and in spite of the immensity of the house, he could hear almost everything.

He had been awake, thinking about last night, Jenna getting the crap kicked out of her. He had almost joined in; it was so hard just to watch, and then he had cried out for it to stop. He still wasn't sure why. Had he actually wanted it to stop, or had he been testing his ability to influence Joje? He wasn't sure. People were complicated, he knew, their decisions rarely set against a backdrop of one color or tone.

But his father's cry broke his concentration. He heard the back door of the kitchen slam, and the walls of his room shuddered with the vibrations from below. He scrambled to his feet, picking up the headboard he had been cuffed to last night.

In his closet, he zipped open a camping backpack, grabbing the handheld camcorder he kept hidden beneath the other junk. Boy Scouts served some purpose. He regretted not having the time to fast-forward past where the video was paused—Jenna, in one of her better performances, trying on shirt after shirt. There was something about the act of a woman removing her shirt that appealed to Adam so much more than just seeing her topless.

He flipped the camera on, changing the mode to record. The headboard dragged across the carpet, hitting into boxes behind him. He had to catch whatever was happening outside on film.

At the window, he angled the camera and zoomed in. His breath caught. Was he really seeing what he thought he was?

An uncontrolled shiver ran through his body like a premature orgasm. He no longer regretted losing the other footage—this would be something he'd be able to watch over and over and over and over.

3

Blake threw the patio door open in a full sprint toward the pool. The peaceful oasis of their backyard had become a horror so unspeakable it couldn't be real.

Jenna hung over the pool, strung up and tethered to the volleyball net, her body directly over the fire pit. A fire pit whose flames were dancing. Her arms were separated, tied or cuffed to the top of the net, her legs kicking wildly, swinging over the open flames as if she were running in midair.

She went for a run. Might be her last.

Blake was going to kill Drew.

He leapt into the pool, not giving his suit pants and silk shirt a second thought, and swam the few feet to the island. The key for the gas to the pit had been removed.

Without thinking, Blake climbed from the pool, standing on the ring around the pit. The heat of the flames pressed against him like a physical presence. That's when he noticed Conrad. Or what was left of her.

The beautiful Lab he had so recently scolded was literally burning alive, staked to the fire pit. The flames licking Jenna's legs sprang off of Conrad's back. Her hair was gone, her face melting like a snowman, eyes oozing, snout running, and yet Blake could still see the fast thump of her struggling heart.

A thousand competing thoughts screamed through Blake's brain, not one carrying a solution. His hands rose to his mouth of their own accord. He could hear Conrad whining, the slow leak of a tire, barely more than a whisper.

"I'm so sorry," Jenna said, tears rolling down her face. Blisters floated up her feet and calves. The intensity of the heat was already beginning to dry Blake's sopping suit. He couldn't think, he just had to act.

He leapt over the dying dog, on top of Jenna, gripping the top of the net and bearing his whole weight down on it, on her. The net shifted, bending forward and backward at once. Blake lost his balance, almost went head over and back into the pool, but Jenna brought up her legs, wrapping them around him and pulling him close. He could feel the heat emanating from them, singeing his back. She cried out but held firm. The combined weight had the effect Blake had hoped for, the net tearing at one end and then plunging them into the water.

Blake was tangled, caught in the netting and limbs of his wife—she kicked out and connected with his groin. Air left in a flurry of bubbles, and for the second time in less than twenty-four hours, he was drowning, only this time he was actually beneath water. Jenna's face was suddenly next to his, pulling him up by his shirt. Blake kicked, and the surface moved toward him.

"Hunnnhhh!" Blake gasped for air, the net still wrapped around his legs and torso. He glanced about frantically for his wife.

Her head surfaced and then sank back beneath the water. Blake pulled her up, then swam to the edge of the pool, holding her tight.

"Shhh, I've got you," he said.

He thrust her toward the side, and she grabbed on, the net still attached to her reddened wrists. She was bleeding out, the gashes in her wrists wrapped tightly to the net with fishing line. The blood spread, pool water carrying it outward.

He untangled the net from his body and lifted Jenna from the pool, sliding her onto her side. Her eyes were starting to cloud.

"Stay with me!" he yelled, cradling her in his arms. Her exposed legs and bare feet were a charcoaled red, skin peeling back like bark from a dead tree. Blood continued seeping from the gashes in her wrists, the skin folds like the Cheshire cat's smile.

Blake heard clapping.

Joje stood just outside the patio door. "Bravo! What a performance!"

"I am going to kill you!" Blake shouted, voice cracking.

"You're under a little duress, so I'll let that slide," Joje said. He turned, looking up toward the house. "Good mauwning, Adam!"

Blake glanced up in time to see Adam's shutters slide closed. Joje threw something toward him. A towel opened up, falling short on the stamped colored concrete.

Blake set Jenna gently on the ground, running to snatch it, then hurried back to her. He wrapped both her hands in the towel, applying pressure to her wrists. He went to lift her, but she refused.

"I'm okay. I need to watch."

She lay in his arms as they silently observed the flames consume the rest of their dog. In the end, she never howled, never barked, and eventually, her extinguishing whine was no more. The fire crackled, both over the pool and inside Blake, a white-hot fury the likes of which he had never before known.

4

Blake laid Jenna on the couch, her body so limp and lifeless he couldn't tear his eyes from the rise and fall of her chest, the only proof she was still alive. Joje too stared at her chest, though for other obvious reasons—the wet nightgown clung to her body, as see-through as plastic wrap.

"Get a blanket. Linen closet's upstairs next to the bathroom." To Blake's surprise, Joje immediately left.

"You're gonna be okay," he said, combing back Jenna's hair from her face. "We're gonna be okay."

Oh, God, let her be okay . . .

Blake went to the kitchen, tearing through the bottom cupboard where Jenna had found the Band-Aids the other day. That seemed a lifetime ago. He grabbed a roll of gauze, what was left of it, searching through bottles of tanning lotion.

No burn cream. *Damnit!*

He grabbed a large bottle of aloe vera, realizing at the same time he should just leave it there. "For temporary relief of minor sunburns and pains," it read. Jenna would need something a little stronger. Like morphine.

"Your omelet's cold."

Blake stopped halfway to the family room. Drew stood on the other side of the island, a smug smile on his face. It was the most absurd thing someone could have said in the moment, and Blake's fractured mind struggled to make sense of it. That ridiculous apron, that pale white skin still wet and shiny—not from sweat, Blake realized. From water.

Pool water.

Blake leapt against the island in a surge of adrenaline, reaching across and grabbing a surprised Drew by the apron and pulling him forward. The metal rack holding fruit on the island went reeling, mangoes and oranges tumbling and spinning to the floor. Blake tried to slam Drew's head against the counter, but his reach was too far extended, and the momentum didn't carry. Drew twisted back, wriggling from his grasp.

"Boys!" Joje said, having reentered the room.

That sliding noise of a gun cocking was enough to bring Blake back to his senses and reprioritize his agenda. It was a skill he had mastered, as had every successful individual he'd ever known—attack the most important task first without losing sight of what's next in line.

As Blake moved back to his wife, retrieving the blanket from the ground, he went through the list in his head.

One, get Jenna help.

Two, kill Drew.

Three, kill Joje.

Four, save his family.

The order of those last few might need to be rearranged, but he couldn't think right now. Anger clouded judgment.

Joje kept his distance, gun still pointed toward him. Blake laid the blanket lightly over Jenna, praying her skin wouldn't stick to it when he would need to pull it back. He knelt beside her, sliding the fishing line down and wrapping her wrists with gauze. The trickle of blood had all but ceased. He paused as he worked, really seeing her for the first time in a long time. She was so beautiful. Without makeup, her face swollen and bruised, eye crusted shut, she was still perfect. He tucked her hair behind her ear, and she opened her one eye, looking into his.

"Conrad," she said.

Before Blake could shake his head, she had fallen back under. Her legs were shaking, spasming beneath the blanket. He pulled it up to take a closer look.

Blisters and boils dotted her legs and feet like raindrops stuck to a pane of glass. Several of the toes on her right foot had fused together, skin melting into one connected piece. The bottle of aloe vera slipped from his hands to the floor.

"I can't do this," he said. "I can't play this game anymore."

"Think of all we've accomplished in just two days," Joje said. "Convincing your boss to keep your job. The lengths you went to to save your family? Your wife's still alive. You still have your son. That's a lot worth continuing for."

"I'm taking her to the hospital," Blake said.

"We never intended for anyone to get hurt," Joje continued. "It doesn't have to be like this, but that's up to you. Not me, not Dwew. You determine how we behave."

Blake stood, moving back into the kitchen to the rack of keys.

"I wowee you're not listening," Joje said.

They were gone. The car keys, gone.

"Where are they? The keys!" Blake yelled.

"Dwew, will you kindly fetch Adam?"

Drew removed the apron and headed out the kitchen through the living room, shirtless.

Blake opened a cupboard, then another. He wasn't looking for medicine, he was looking for something—anything—that would give him a chance to take on Joje.

"She really is exquisite." Joje stood over Jenna. "Was your first wife this beautiful? Or did you upgrade after your success?"

Blake slammed the cupboards closed, grabbing the only thing that came to mind—the frying pan from the stove. Still warm. He rushed into the family room with it.

"This won't end well," Joje said. "Put it down."

Blake swung at Joje who sidestepped the pass with the practiced efficiency of a martial artist. Blake realized how little he really knew about his captor.

Adam peeked his head from the corner of the entryway, Drew undoubtedly behind him. Blake yelled, charging forward and swinging the pan left, right, and down, whooshing through air with each attempted strike and never seeing the opening when Joje moved in, his fist catching Blake in the throat. His bruised, swollen throat.

Blake's vision went black; when it returned, he was on his knees, leaning against the couch next to Jenna. To not return to that void beckoning to him as he inhaled and exhaled required all his concentration. He felt Joje's breath on the back of his neck.

"You still don't understand how this works. You can't fight it. When you try, you only hurt the ones you love. And next time?"

Joje grabbed Blake by the hair, tilting his neck back to stare at Adam, who stood wide-eyed in the hallway. "It will be your son."

5

Blake drove to the pharmacy with Joje in the same vehicle that had started it all. Joje's refusal to allow Blake to take his wife to a hospital forced him to take the only alternative he could get. Joje made calls on Blake's behalf, playing secretary in an effort to track down a physician of a friend of a friend; they hadn't had the time or the need to locate a doctor since the move. The spotty reception along the coast kept Joje occupied.

Eventually, they got a contact for a physician who dealt with patients only through e-mail. For what he charged, those e-mails should have performed surgery. The sense of urgency must have come through, as half a dozen prescriptions for pain meds, antibiotics, and some enzyme cream called Santyl were waiting at the pharmacy for them.

The pharmacist, a tall man with thick white hair and a thicker mustache, couldn't take his eyes from Blake as he scanned the drugs. His bifocals slid down the bridge of his nose as he asked, "How's the other guy?"

It took Blake a moment to remember how bruised and cut up his face was. "Pretty sure he came out ahead."

Joje made conversation as Blake confirmed he understood the risks of the prescriptions on the digital keypad and swiped his card. Joje then asked the pharmacist how to treat a burn wound on a canine.

"How bad are the burns?"

"I'd say pretty bad, wouldn't you, Bwake?"

"Card Declined" flashed on the screen, giving Blake pause. He swiped it again.

"You talking blisters? Pus?" the pharmacist asked.

"Blistered," Blake said. "Skin's . . . cracked. Like dry leather."

The small display repeated its ominous message: "Card Declined."

Blake took a step back. His Cyborg—the phone— was connected to every one of his accounts. Savings, checking, even his slush account Jenna didn't know about. Had he really handed Joje a skeleton key to every locked vault in his name?

He brought out another card, a black American Express he rarely used, slid it through the reader, awaiting the confirmation of his fears.

The pharmacist continued his conversation with Joje, politely pretending not to notice Blake's predicament. "Second, maybe third-degree burns. Take her to a vet. She's going to need fluid, IVs. Burns that severe require serious treatment."

Joje held up one of the pill bottles. "Why we have these."

"For a dog?" the pharmacist asked. "You trying to kill her?"

The display above the reader spit out the same message. Blake held his wallet in his hand, realizing how utterly worthless the plastic he carried had become.

"I got it, Bwakey," Joje said, throwing two hundred-dollar bills onto the counter. "You can pay me back later."

Blake's demeanor must have revealed the absolute horror he was feeling. The pharmacist snatched the bills, taking a step back from the register.

"If we don't take her to a vet, will she live?" Blake asked.

"Without treatment? You won't be able to stave off infection. That cream will do as much good as handing two aspirin to someone who's broken an arm."

"Dogs don't have arms," Joje said.

"What kind of dog is it?" the pharmacist asked.

"Just a bitch," Joje said.

The pharmacist placed the change from the register on the counter, backing away.

"Take her to a vet. Or a hospital. If you'll excuse me." He stepped behind the partition into the adjoining room of licensed drugs and plastic containers. It was the only time Blake had seen someone use prescription drugs as an escape without actually swallowing a pill.

The BMW's tires spun beneath the loose gravel on the road as Blake took a turn too fast on the drive back up the coast. His thoughts were spinning even faster, but on a hamster's wheel, never making progress. The ping from his phone announcing an incoming message or e-mail was gasoline to the fire.

The conversation with the pharmacist had left him rattled. He had to get Jenna to a hospital, he just wasn't sure how. Add to that complication the fact that his captors were secretly robbing him blind.

"How much have you taken?" he asked.

"Taken?"

"My money!"

"We're not robbing you, Bwakey. I'm no thief. It's all there. You just won't have access to it. Not during the next phase of our pwoject."

"The next phase?"

"I'll be honest. I got a little upset when I saw how many zeroes were attached to the numbers in your bank, and yet you wouldn't buy a ten-dollar subscription?"

"That has nothing to do with why you're here," Blake said.

"It has everything to do with it. Can't you see? Who would you be without your money, your success? That's all I'm interested in finding out."

Another ping. This time Joje answered the text, silently typing a short reply, probably to Drew.

"You can have it all—take it! Just leave me and my family alone. Take Drew, take this car, I don't care, but leave! Get out of our lives, just—just leave."

"You know I can't do that," Joje said.

"Then let me take my wife to the hospital. We can leave her there. Continue at home with your project. No one will know!"

"You have nothing to bargain with."

"Oh, no?" Blake skidded around another corner, pushing his rage into the machine that was his car. The speedometer climbed, fifty . . . sixty . . . seventy. He took the next curve without hitting the brakes, tires chirping as they grabbed and slid, grabbed and slid, the BMW fishtailing before catching. And still Blake refused to let off the gas. Seventy . . . seventy-five . . . eighty.

"Do I look afraid, Bwake? Or concerned?" Joje's voice was calm, relaxed, even as Blake's knuckles turned white from gripping the wheel.

Flashing lights and a burping whirl suddenly sprang from behind them, an unexpected answer to prayer. *There's my bargaining chip, you bastard*, Blake thought.

"Don't pull over," Joje said as Blake braked. "No, pull over."

Blake slowed but continued driving, a floodgate of ideas breaking through the dam of depression. One way or another, he had stumbled onto their way out.

"Pull over!" Joje said, glancing behind them. Blake continued driving, passing a gravel turnout with more than enough room to have stopped. Joje laughed. "Bwake, I'm trying to help you."

"No, but this cop might. Should I lead him to the house?"

"Lead him wherever you want," Joje said. "Just whatever you do, don't let him open your trunk."

"What are you talking about?"

"I left a little insurance in there," Joje said. "In the off chance we might need it."

Another wide turnout was ahead. Blake brought the car over,

gravel grinding beneath the wheels. He put the car in park, a cloud of dirt sweeping past them.

"What the hell is in my trunk?"

"You can't believe I wouldn't have a plan for something like this?" Joje asked. "Get the cop to leave, or you will never see your family again. In more ways than one."

"What's in there?" Blake repeated.

"Not what. Who."

"What—?"

"Your fingerprints on the body, murder weapon in your house," Joje said.

"Bullshit."

"Think. Do I need to bluff?" Joje held up Blake's phone. "One button and your family disappears forever, long before any cops can arrive. No, the insurance is for something more, for when you're no longer afraid to lose your family."

Blake looked in the rearview mirror. It was a motorcycle cop. He couldn't see the face beneath the helmet from this distance. "Whose body is it?" he asked.

"Does it matter?"

"Whose body!"

"Your neighbor. The one you were arguing with on the street." Joje's lips pulled to the side, his tic taking over. "Your little dispute was convincing on camera—his, not mine. Probably provide a nice motive. He had a lot of surveillance, that one."

Tom Jones. He'd never be placing his sausage finger into someone's handshake again. Blake wanted to believe it was all a fabrication, an elaborate lie to keep Blake from talking. The emblem of Tom's business card spun in Blake's mind—a diamond being crushed by another diamond, just as Joje was crushing him now.

Because the only crime is letting them put you away.

Blake wondered if Tom would think so now. "How do I know you're not lying?" he asked.

"Because. I don't lie."

"Fine. I won't say a word, but in exchange, I'm taking Jenna to the hospital."

"No," Joje said.

"She'll die if I don't!"

"She won't die."

"I promise—I'll play by your rules. I won't say anything!" Blake said. "Just let me get her help."

A knock at the window. Blake jumped. The uniformed cop was at Joje's door.

"Promise me I can take her," Blake said.

"I can't make that promise."

"Promise me, Joje—she's my wife!"

Another knock. Joje glanced outside, held his finger up. One minute. It should have been a hilarious gesture, given to a police officer. Blake only wished he had held up two fingers; he needed more time.

"You will never step foot in a hospital while we're here," Joje said. "Play by the rules, and no one else gets hurt. Or call my bluff. But you should have said your good-byes before we left."

Without looking away from Blake, Joje pressed the tiny lever, lowering his window. A light shone directly into Blake's face, causing him to squint. As he shielded his eyes, he watched Joje's smile creep onto his face like a spider scurrying from beneath shadows. Phone in hand, thumb rested lightly against the button that would decide the fate of Blake's family, Joje broke eye contact.

"Good mauwning, offisoh."

6

Adam sat on one of the swing-out chairs attached to the kitchen island, having finished the bacon and eggs Drew had made for him. Greasy dishes and pans were piled in the sink like the blocks of a Jenga game after one wrong move.

There have been a lot of wrong moves lately, Adam thought.

"*Modern Warfare?*" Drew asked.

"Yeah, sure.".

Jenna lay on the couch in front of the TV, still covered in blankets. She wasn't shivering anymore, and the even rise and fall of her chest suggested she was asleep. Drew and Adam both hovered over her, their shadows enwrapping her in yet another layer.

"Why'd you do it?" Adam asked. Drew stood there a long time without answering, so long Adam began to wonder if he had vocalized his question.

"She has to learn," Drew replied, as if it was answer enough. In a way, Adam supposed it was. "Sorry about your dog."

"Sorry about your hand."

Drew nodded.

In some ways, they were so similar. Sacrifices had to be made in order to demonstrate how far one was willing to go. If anyone understood, it would be Adam. Still, he was fairly certain Jenna was a far way off from "learning her lesson." Her injuries wouldn't turn her into the submissive housewife Drew and Joje were hoping for. You don't tame a lioness by breaking its legs; you just piss it off.

Beneath her closed lids, Jenna's eyes hadn't moved since Adam and Drew had stood over her. She was playing dead. Adam wanted to smile.

"You wanna play upstairs? In the theater room?" he asked.

A pause. "We need to stay down here, to watch her."

"She's not going anywhere. I've never played on the projection screen. It'd be awesome. Life-size soldiers, bombs exploding, bullets whizzing by in surround sound."

"Why haven't you played there?" Drew asked.

"My dad won't let me. But he's not here."

"We can't be there when George gets back," Drew said.

Bingo. Adam went to the TV, unplugging the game console from beneath the mounted racks. "Grab some Pepsis?"

Drew moved to the kitchen without a word, so used to following orders. Holding the console and controllers against his chest, Adam went back over to Jenna. With his other hand, he reached out, gently squeezing her hand. He had expected her to return the squeeze, let him know she understood the time he was buying her. Instead, her hand lay limp against his, cold to the touch. Maybe she wasn't faking.

Adam felt Drew's presence before he heard him. For such a big guy, Adam was surprised by his stealth.

"You trying to wake her?" Drew asked.

"Just wanted to be sure," Adam said. "I don't want us to get in trouble." Let him think they were in this together. Who knew, maybe they were?

Drew reached down, his hand sliding beneath the blanket as he groped Jenna's chest. She gave no reaction. For the first time, Adam felt a twinge of fear from the pale face next to him. Eyes that seemed to look but not see. Like a stuffed animal.

Maybe they weren't that similar.

Adam led the way through the foyer and up the stairs to the theater room. By the time Jenna's eyes popped open, they were both immersed in their game.

7

"I interrupting?"

The cop did not sound happy, a short, pudgy Asian with a clean-shaven face that made him look much younger than he probably was. He had a dark, fat mole where his left nostril met his cheek that looked like an obscene and bloody pimple. His suit was pressed, badge shined, hair trimmed so short it wasn't possible to have it out of place.

"Sorry, officer," Joje said. "Been a long day. Our dog just died."

"Eat your homework too?" He ignored Joje's laugh, eyes training on Blake. "You been drinking?"

"I don't drink, sir," Joje said.

"Not you."

Blake opened his mouth, a plea for help preparing to leap from his tongue. The words collided head-on in a pileup that went on for unspoken paragraphs.

"You look a little banged up. Something I need to know about?"

A lot he needed to know about. Joje's finger circling around the send button on the phone had a way of rejuvenating Blake's vocal chords. "Uh, no, sir. Just an accident."

"Uh-huh. Where you headed?"

"Home," Joje said. Blake couldn't stop the shiver that raced through his body. Joje may not have noticed, but the police officer certainly did.

"Where's home?"

"Couple miles up ahead. What's the address, Bwakey?"

"Sixteen Vanilla Banks," Blake said.

"Have it for the weekend?"

"Seven days," Blake replied. He looked up. "I mean, we bought it. We've only been there, well, about seven days."

"So the Welchsetzer home sold." The officer's lips curled up on the left side of his face, making the mole widen as his nostrils flared.

"Moving trucks should have given it away," Joje said.

It had to Joje, apparently, though Blake was having a hard time believing their encounter was nothing more than chance. Someone must have sent them. And if they were sent, it meant they were after something, something more than Blake's money.

The officer stuck his hand through the window, and Joje took it.

"Officer Randall," he said, reaching across Joje and offering his hand to Blake. "Welcome to the neighborhood. Me and Deputy McClellan run tight end D on the PCH. Anyone not local, we make sure they're running from point A to point B. No pit stops in between. I'm sure you've heard, crime rate in Malibu is the lowest in all of LA County." He paused as if in a high school play, waiting for the line the other actor was struggling to remember.

Blake nodded after a moment. "Thank you."

"Hey, it's what we do. I don't want you to think the locals get a free pass or anything, but," he shrugged, "we look the other way, you know, when we need to. Malibu is sort of a throwback to the Old West. A town where . . . money still talks." He laughed, then looked out over the car toward the ocean. "We make it a point to know the residents on a personal basis. We'd love to come by. You married? Family?"

"Yes," Blake said, almost too eagerly. Joje's face was crinkled as if he were squinting, though the sun was overhead.

"I don't want to invite ourselves . . . ," Randall said, implying quite the opposite.

"Now's a bad time," Blake said. "We might be going to the hospital, right George?"

"Someone sick?" Randall asked.

"My wife," Blake said.

"You don't want to go to the hospital, trust me—you're new here, there's a lot to learn. Here, the hospital comes to you. I mean, you're living in Mount Olympus. Even the cops are like your own personal escorts." The left side of his mouth curled up again in that half-spawned smile. "Here," Randall pulled out a business card and jotted a number down on the back, handing it to Joje. "Dr. Cheverou. From Russia or something. Makes house calls. I hear he's phenomenal. And discreet."

"Thank you," Joje said.

"My number's on the front. Give me a buzz once you're settled. McClellan and I can swing in one evening at shift's end. For drinks or something." He glanced between the two of them one final time. "You sure everything's all right?"

Joje conceded to Blake, it was the moment to either fold or go all in. Joje's finger continued its swirling pattern on the phone's keypad in his lap. How long would it take Drew to respond to that text? Minutes? Seconds?

"Just, the dog dying has really shaken us up," Blake said.

"Oh, shit—I thought that was a joke! Oh, man, I'm sorry. Happens a lot you know, after a move. Dog tries to get back to where home was, not realizing where home is. They have sort of a sixth sense thing about that. You, uh, get him cleaned up off the road or need me to get animal services?"

"No, we're good," Blake said.

Randall tapped the top of the car. "We'll be seeing you then." He winked before leaving. Apparently, that was acceptable in the throwback town of Malibu.

8

Jenna sat on the couch, staring at the legs that had to be someone else's appendages. The sight made her stomach churn. Blotched patterns, misshapen bubbles, and deformations had replaced her normally sleek and tanned calves. Her feet were even worse, like they were simply rotting away. If they healed—a big if—she'd have nothing more than nubs at the end of her legs. Stumps, like a tree that had outgrown its usefulness.

I'll never be able to run again.

The thought was paralyzing, and for a moment, Jenna couldn't breathe. She wasn't sure she wanted to. That this was the first moment she had been left alone since Joje and Drew's arrival, she knew she had to use it for what it was. An opportunity. One that might be her last.

She forced herself to regulate her breathing as she did before any race, deep, even breaths in with a slow exhalation. The same pattern she had used in childbirth.

Her breathing stopped. Jenna thought her heart might have also. Bricks crumbled from the wall she had constructed, toppling down in an avalanche of memories.

These memories were more painful than the screaming of her legs or the thought of never being able to run again.

These memories were death. These memories, suicide.

Her feet, bare, stepped onto the dried weeds and craggily grass of the path that wasn't a path, just a slightly trampled trail leading through the trees to the spot where kids went to smoke cigarettes or pronounce their love by branding a tree with a blade. Discarded condoms hanging from bushes proved there were other ways love had been pronounced. With each step, she felt a poking or prodding, something sharp trying to break beneath her skin—a rock, a twig, a jagged piece of aluminum from a pellet-riddled Coke can.

Poisonous clouds dropped so low they grazed the tops of the trees. They seemed to move from the sky into her head where they were waiting to burst. Wind shook the dead leaves from skeletal trees whose limbs were turned down like claws reaching for her. Dead leaves, dying trees, dark clouds. A day with a complete absence of color.

Her legs carried her forward as if she were on a moving platform, an escalator that never ascended but pushed her toward what she didn't want to see. What she could not believe. The permanently dried pond, two boulders stacked on top of each other where countless teenagers had sat. Her feet gave way to her knees and later to her whole body lying prostrate against the carpet of prickly leaves and grass.

A child's body lay at the bottom of the rocks, long, strangled hair swept over the face turned at an angle that could only be achieved on a doll.

That's what she was: a doll. Cold. Lifeless.

Unmoving.

Adam screaming. "Maaaaaaaaum! Maaaaaaaauuum!" Shadows leapt around her, birds flitting from tree to tree, cawing their mourner's cry.

Her little girl. Her baby.

She gasped, air returning as she wept, unearthed grief so new and fresh it felt like it had just happened yesterday. She wept for a life that had ceased to exist that day. Their daughter's, yes, but also her own. Nothing had ever been the same.

She could hear Evaline, her soft honeyed voice, her words an unsung song. "Lub you. Lub you, Momma."

"Maaaaaaaaaum!"

Jenna closed her eyes, reveling in the pain that was her escape. It was why she ran, why she worked herself past the point of exhaustion. It may have even been the reason she stayed with Blake. Pain—blinding, intoxicating, consuming, addictive pain—it made her forget.

Luckily, pain was in ample supply.

She brought her arms to her left leg, one under the knee, the other slid beneath her calf. Grimacing, she lifted the leg and set it over the couch, ignoring the tears leaking from her eyes and her shortened breaths. Her right leg followed. She spun her torso with its movement, now facing forward toward the TV.

A furnace's flame scaled her legs, so intense it felt almost mind-numbingly cold. Still, the memories were there, Evaline's face, her laugh, her crystal-blue eyes.

She put the slightest amount of weight onto her feet resting against the hardwood floor, an incendiary pulse racing through her entire body. Droplets of sweat slid from her forehead down her temples. Her fists were clenched, stomach muscles tightened.

Breathe.

She would use the pain to forget; use this chance to live. The den might as well have been across the Sahara, but the kitchen, well, it was the impossibility that had always brought her to the starting line. They had taken the knives, but she could find something—a screwdriver, can opener, it didn't matter. Something for when their guards were down, and right now, in her condition, the amount of resistance they'd expect was virtually nonexistent.

Jenna scooted herself toward the edge of the couch, picking up her legs to inch them forward. She could do this.

Fists against the cushion, she pushed off, raising herself up. Her left leg screamed at her but eventually slid back the two inches she'd need to steady herself. She hovered, her arms bearing most of her weight, still resting on the cushions. She started rocking forward, letting the momentum build.

She could do this. She could do this. She could do this!

She launched herself upward, pushing off with her arms. Both knees buckled like links in a chain, her weight throwing her right knee sideways while she toppled. The resulting pop burst through her ears, rattling through her head. She collapsed, her arms shielding her head from the floor but not from lying across her right knee, twisted at an awful angle. Her breath came in short, jagged bursts, barely muffling the agonizing screech dying to leap out.

She forced herself into a push-up position with her arms, twisting her body around so that her back was to the floor. Her legs jolted with the turn, moving of their own accord like the lifeless limbs of a rag doll.

And just like that, the memory was back.

Evaline. Her doll.

This time, she was unable to silence her screaming.

9

Blake pulled into the driveway, putting the BMW in park. He wasn't ready to go inside, not without getting what he had really gone out for.

"What will it take to get help for my wife?" he asked.

"We just did get help," Joje said, shaking the pharmacy bag of boxes and pills.

"Real help. You heard the pharmacist, she's—those aren't minor burns."

"I said no, Bwake. I meant it. No hospitals."

"The card, the doctor the cop referred. He said he's discreet."

"No," Joje said.

"You're the one who wanted to observe what I do—if my wife was seriously injured? Nothing would stop me from getting her the help she needs. Nothing."

Joje cleared his throat, the tic disappearing from his face. "All right, Bwake. If she's not doing better tomorrow, maybe we call the good doctor."

"Maybe?" Blake asked.

Joje smiled. "You are such a good mentor."

The garage door climbed upward at the press of a button. The door leading into the house opened. Adam's face was more grim than his usual teenager self.

"Mom needs help!"

Blake was inside the house, following his son into the family room before Joje had exited the car. He realized too late how easily he could have locked the garage door, keeping Joje out. If he only had to deal with one of them, he was confident he could win. Or at least have a fighting chance. He had to be more aware of the opportunities parading as normal occurrences if he was going to save his family. Escape wouldn't necessarily require a big event.

Jenna was on the floor, her body flailing in spasms—legs flittering, head shaking, one open eye rolled far above her eyelid.

He was going to lose her.

"Joje, the pills!" Blake ran to his wife's side, kneeling and cradling her head in his lap. "How long ago did it start?"

"We heard a scream. She was like this when we came down," Adam said.

Joje entered from the hall. "What do you mean when you came down?"

Adam looked at Drew, then dropped his gaze.

"Pills!" Blake screamed. Joje threw him the bag. "Adam, get me water—now!"

Adam went to the kitchen, looking relieved to slink from Joje's attention.

"You left her alone?" Joje asked.

Blake was too concerned with his wife to give more than a passing thought to the argument beginning to build. He had the first of the small medicine jars unscrewed, pills spilling onto the ground around him as he jerked a few into his palm.

"She could've gotten away," Joje continued.

Drew took a step back. "It was only for a minute."

"What if she had gotten away!"

"Look at her—she can't even cross the room!" Drew said.

Adam handed Blake a bottle of the flavored water, liquid sloshing over the lip and onto the floor. *Please let this work.* Doubt filled Blake's mind—how was pain medication going to stop convulsions?—until he saw Jenna's eye.

She was alert, in control, as she always was. Blake looked at her thrashing body then back at her face. The hint of a smile crept onto her lips and a single tear snuck from the corner of her eye, gliding down her face.

"You could have ruined everything!" Joje screamed.

He came rushing at them. Blake hovered over Jenna to protect her, but Joje wasn't coming for them. His fists swung furiously toward Drew—left, right, right, left, face, stomach, neck, face—until the colossal giant came crashing down into the eighty-inch flat screen. It broke his fall only slightly, forcing him to the floor with a shattering of glass.

Joje brushed a fallen piece off his arm, standing over his "brother" like a victor in a ring. His foot came down on Drew's bandaged hand. Drew screamed out in pain. "There are consequences for us too. Everyone plays by the rules."

He kicked Drew in the face with such force Drew's entire body flipped over, tumbling another few rolls. *An eye for an eye, "woo" for a "woo."* Drew lay there, unmoving—either unconscious or wishing that he were. Blake had to look away—as much hatred as he harnessed toward the large oaf, he couldn't watch this outrageous display.

But Joje wasn't finished yet. He continued his attack. The sound of Drew's beating was so similar to that of Jenna's from the previous night. Blake held his wife, preparing to retaliate if the attacks turned in their direction.

Finally, Joje stopped, his breathing slowing. "I'm sorry you had to see that. I really hate violence." He paused. "The pills helped?"

Blake looked down at Jenna, her body's thralls silenced. Whether involuntary or forced, they seemed to have stopped with the shock of what they had just witnessed.

"For now," Blake said.

"Good."

"Help me move her to the couch?" Blake asked.

They lifted her with care, Adam joining to help, and still a deafening yelp leapt from her tiny frame. Blake noticed how swollen her right knee was, the ball twisted sideways with her leg straight below it. Had Drew hurt her while they had been gone? Or had Blake landed on her wrong when they fell into the pool? He couldn't remember but would have sworn that injury was new.

He knelt beside her, the resolve to protect her and Adam stronger than it had ever been. He grasped her hands, pulling them together. What he felt made him swallow back the tears, his thoughts replaced with fear.

Gripped in his wife's fist was something foreign, something hard. Her fist relaxed in his grip and his fingers wrapped around hers, exploring the object beneath.

A corkscrew, its wound, curved metal ending in a sharpened spike. The injury was new, and Jenna had done more than just fall from the couch.

Though the waves outside crashing against the cliffs could barely be heard, Blake felt their sheer force hurtling through his mind. So many variables, so many risks. Had she hoped Drew or Joje would be the one to lean down and take hold of her? That metal coil waiting to pierce flesh?

And what if she had tried and failed? What then.

He pried the corkscrew from her fingers, her tensing grip proof she was more aware than she was letting on. But he couldn't let her make a mistake. Not again.

He shoved the corkscrew into his pocket, making sure Joje hadn't seen the exchange. If there was a mistake to be made, this time he would be the one to make it.

Chapter 5

Day Four

1

They buried Conrad beneath the stone walk leading from the pool to the sand volleyball court, her remains placed in a small moving box. The recycling logo and "Handle with Care" imprinted on the side were hard to ignore, considering the circumstance.

The gray waves of the ocean disappeared beneath the edge of their backyard. Despite being unable to see the impact, their soft roar was as guaranteed as the rise of tomorrow's sun. They were about the only two things Blake could guarantee at the moment, the routineness of his life slipping away like the eroding cliff's edge.

For an instant, he thought of throwing himself over, just leaping from the cliff into the shattering waves. He had to get a grip, but he wasn't sure what he was grasping at.

"Dad, can you say something?"

Blake's hands went into his pockets. He rubbed the metal corkscrew between his thumb and forefinger like a good-luck charm. The words didn't come easy; hard to know what to say at a funeral when the murderers were standing beside you, pretending to mourn.

"Conrad was a part of this family. She was a protector, a friend, a beloved pet, a family member. Her life was taken unjustly."

He paused at the crashing of another wave.

"But her memory lives on. Let us remember her love, her friendship. Let us learn from her example in these times of trial, and—"

He paused, his mind wandering over rocky terrain.

"And never give up."

A chorus of amens surrounded him. Blake grabbed his son, pulling him close. For a nonreligious guy, it was the best he could do. "I'm sorry, buddy," he whispered.

"It's okay, Dad. It wasn't your fault."

But wasn't it? For not acting sooner? Not finding a way out of this entrapment they had been forced into? Or could he have prevented this from happening, his wife being hurt, by convincing his family to just live within the confines of their "woos." Rules made to be broken.

If there was a God, Blake wondered if he hadn't done the same—created rules that were impossible not to break. Maybe he liked seeing his children suffer while claiming, as Joje did, that he "hated violence." Or maybe that torture really was a refiner's fire. Either way, Blake knew he was on his own. No "god in the machine" happy ending for his family.

He squeezed his son hard, bringing his mouth close to Adam's ear. "Take the first chance you get and run. Don't worry about your mom or me. Just go as fast and as far as you can. Understand?"

It was hard to know if Adam's upturned face and complacent nod meant he would listen. Blake could only hope. And maybe pray.

Back inside, Jenna lay motionless on the couch. She had slept there all night, flitting through restless bouts of sleep and pain. Blake had lain beside her on the rug, barely convincing Joje to let him stay there. Administering pills, converting a bowl into a bedpan, and coating Jenna's legs repeatedly with enzyme cream had made for a restless night.

"We need to call that doctor," Blake said.

Drew came out from the bathroom, the flush of the toilet like thunder following lightning. The sink, however, had never been turned on. His right eyebrow had been split open and stapled shut with a staple gun from the garage. Blake still shuddered thinking about it. His bottom lip was swollen, giving him the look of a pouting child. "What doctor?" he asked.

"What we need to do is some work," Joje replied. "You've been getting some angry e-mails lately, a lot of very upset customers. Time you teach me how to work your magic."

"George, you said—"

"It's Joje!" His eyes met Blake's, and in them, Blake saw only murder.

"We saw what happens when Drew breaks a rule, but what happens when you do?" Blake asked.

"I do not break my own rules."

"You're breaking one now by refusing to let me keep my routine! My wife is dying on the couch! She's dying, Joje. Look at her." He couldn't keep his voice from cracking. A light blanket had been draped around her body, but Jenna's face had gone gaunt, her color almost mirroring Drew's skin. "This is my family," Blake continued. "Not a game."

"How'd you find a doctor without Internet?" Adam asked. He was sitting on the counter, his legs kicking beneath him.

"A policeman, yesterday," Blake said. "He gave us the number."

"And you didn't say anything to him? About us? Or them?" Adam asked.

Blake's left eye twitched, his head throbbing. Soon he'd look like Joje, with some hideous tic. "I'm doing what I have to, Adam, to keep our family safe."

Adam didn't say a word, but the look he bore made Blake begin to question even himself.

Joje sighed, removing a thin wallet from his back pocket. He took out the card from inside and threw it into the room. It spiraled down like a fallen leaf. "Call the doc. Just remember, once you make your own bed, you lie in it."

Blake grabbed the card, turning it over in his hand. On one side, Officer Randall's information—station address, office number, *cell*. On the other, a scribbled name and phone number. It was a double-sided coin; either way, he couldn't lose.

"What are we doing about the TV?" Drew asked.

"If you let me online, I'll order a new one," Adam said.

"That's fine. What's the number, Bwake?" Joje asked.

Blake read the digits, and Joje punched them in on the Cyborg.

"If it's not too much to ask, Joje, I'd love to look for another dog?" Adam asked.

"That's a great idea," Joje said, glancing up from the phone. "Let's do it."

Blake felt like he had been sucker-punched, his son asking their kidnapper instead of him. And yet, he hadn't even considered how Adam must be grieving. He should never have told Adam to run; his son needed someone to hold him right now, not push that kind of burden onto his shoulders.

Joje tossed Blake the phone just as he was about to go to his son. Joje went to Adam instead. The victory Blake had just achieved was swallowed up as Adam wrapped his arms around Joje's back in a tight embrace.

"Thank you," Adam said, "for understanding."

The ringing of the phone was like a whirlpool sucking Blake down. When the doctor finally answered, it took Blake a long moment to remember why he had called.

2

Blake and Joje locked themselves in his office, diving into the semantics of the various projects he was embedded in. Like spinning plates. But with the impossibility of communication, these plates were dropping from their poles and shattering on the ground.

Two of the major corporations Blake had consulted with for years had sent notice they would no longer be employing his services due, in one form or another, to his lack of communication. One he had expected: the ScanneX project, an app that would convert a phone into a millimeter-wave scanner, was one he had dropped the ball on. Using technology similar to airport scanners, the thought was to allow a phone to take, in effect, medical X rays of the body without the radiation. The other company had been a shock, and yet Blake's business model, promising immediacy and an unparalleled level of service, was a noose he had knotted with his own hands.

With Symbio on the rocks and his relationship with JT hanging by threads, Blake could soon find himself in a position he would have considered impossible a week ago. Penniless. He didn't want to think about what would happen when the many C-corps he employed deposited checks attached to accounts now emptied.

Blake's phone lit up, vibrating across his desk like some tantalizing stripper—look all you want, but don't touch. Not without consequences. He glanced at the hologram clock on his desk. Eleven forty-six. The doctor he had called should be here any minute.

Joje moved between the shelves on the wall of Blake's library, studying the plaques, degrees, and pictures. He seemed not to notice the phone. He pulled a book down from one of the top shelves, turning it around and reading the back.

As Blake surveyed the room, he realized not one photo contained a picture of his wife or son. There were no photos of family trips to the Grand Canyon or Hawaii, not a single shot of him with Adam earning an award at Boy Scouts or at a school project. Impossible to have pictures of events that never took place or, worse, took place without him. His success had come at a cost he may not have realized. No, that wasn't true; he had always been aware of the sacrifice, it had just seemed necessary at the time.

The phone started its phantom spasms again, screen leaping back to life as it continued its death march across his desk. Blake leaned forward, looking at the caller ID on the screen.

"It's JT. I wouldn't miss his call. Especially twice," he said.

"I've never seen anyone in such a huff to impress their boss," Joje said, setting the book down on a ledge and bringing the phone to his ear. "Hehwo?"

"Who the hell is this?" JT's voice blared from the phone. Joje must have accidentally pushed speaker. Or maybe it hadn't been an accident.

"It's your—what'd you call it, Bwake—potential partner?" Joje said.

"JT, I'm here—you're on speaker," Blake said.

"Caught the cozy couple together," JT said. "A driver's en route to pick up your equipment. Laptop, phone, any other material you've taken from the office. I expect cooperation."

"What? What happened to our arrangement?" Blake said.

"Nothing happened, that's the problem. Not a single update? For a guy as wired in as you, Blake, that reeks of bullshit. Cooperate when the driver arrives, or I'll be sending another out to deliver a subpoena."

"We're making progress! I'll send you a report right now!" Blake sputtered.

"You haven't gone outside five miles of your home in the past two days! What progress could you possibly be making?"

"How does he know that?" Joje asked.

"What, are you stupid? Your phone!" JT shouted. "We've tracked your every movement since our little meeting. And don't think we won't be analyzing every conversation that's taken place with Betti in earshot. You forget, Blake? That bitch is always listening. If you've so much as given anyone the lint collected on that phone, we'll know, and you won't be facing a law suit, my friend. It'll be a jumpsuit. A nice bright-orange one with a big sign on the back that says 'Enter Here.'"

Blake stared into the phone. If JT's threats weren't idle, and Blake didn't believe they were, then the monkeys in IT would be combing through every bit of data collected from Betti. They'd be able to recapture the progress of their kidnapping one conversation thread at a time.

So why wasn't Blake rejoicing? Why the feeling of mounting dread?

An image flashed before Blake, of digging a grave, only this one was much larger than Conrad's, and in it he laid his son and his wife, the recycling logo on the boxes replaced with skull and crossbones.

"I'm on my way to you," Blake said. "Call back the driver. I'll— I'll come in, bring it to you myself."

"No need—"

"No, there is a need," Blake said, cutting JT off. "Look, I'm sorry things have gone the way they have, this—it was out of my control. Least I can do is come in and shake your hand on my way out."

Silence from the phone. Then JT finally spoke. "I have a meeting in an hour. Be here before then." He hung up without waiting for a reply.

Joje tossed the phone back onto Blake's desk. It clanged against the back of his monitor. "That was the best you could come up with? We'll come to you?"

"What are you talking about?"

"And you knew this whole time and failed to mention your phone has some kind of spy surveillance crap on it?"

"Artificial intelligence, and yes, it listens to every conversation," Blake said. "It's recorded every word you've uttered since arriving here, and you better believe JT will be contacting the police."

Joje shook his head. "I chose my mentor so poorly."

"Excuse me?"

"You don't fight for anything, do you? Not your family—that's already been established—but I thought then maybe you'd fight for your job? You didn't even try to dissuade him! 'Let's shake hands on my way out!' I don't think there's anything to learn from you. You stumbled into success—you never earned it! You don't deserve . . ." Joje looked around the room, then threw his hands up. "Any of this! Your wife, your son, your job, your success? It was never yours! You were just keeping the seat warm for someone who deserves to sit there."

He's going to kill me, Blake realized. This was never a game, it was an usurpation, a coup, and Blake was the one being replaced.

Joje grabbed a crystal globe the size of a softball from the corner of Blake's desk, then brought it down, crushing the phone beneath—electronics, glass, and plastic splintered off like broken limbs. "Problem solved. Good luck getting recordings from that!"

Blake stared at the shattered phone that had consumed so much of his life just a few days ago. He thought its loss would have been catastrophic, and yet instead he felt as if a weight had lifted. Its destruction could become his family's salvation.

"At least one of us knows how to fix things," Joje said.

Betti's data wasn't stored on the actual phone; that was a sheer impossibility. But if Blake led Joje to believe he had solved their problem, he wouldn't know JT still had access to all that had transpired the past few days. JT might resent having to act on it, but Blake knew the bastard wouldn't have a choice—he would call the cops.

The real question was whether that would save his family or result in their deaths.

Jing Jong.

The doorbell caused Blake to jump in his seat, the soft chimes seeping into the room through the open door. The last time he had heard that sound was when Joje had entered his life.

"Looks like the good doctor's arrived," Joje said. "Remember the rules?"

Blake nodded.

"Do you? Really, Bwake? Or do you just remember the ones you think I made?" Joje gave a bitter laugh. "I never said you have to let us do whatever we want. Never said you couldn't fight back. But that's your routine, isn't it. Letting your son, your wife, your boss walk all over you."

Jing Jong. Jing Jong. Jing Jong.

"You're pathetic," Joje said.

Blake stood, picking up the crystal globe. No amount of CPR would save Betti. "Let me do the talking," he said. "If you want there to be no questions, just let me handle it."

They suddenly heard screaming.

"Help! Help us! Please, God, help us!" Jenna's cries echoed down the hall.

"Where the hell is Dwew?" Joje said, moving toward the door.

Falling in step behind him, Blake raised the globe above his head. He brought it down, throwing his entire weight into that blow on the back of Joje's head. The globe shattered, pieces breaking off like continents separating from a prehistoric Pangaea.

Joje slumped forward. Blake followed him down, thrown off balance from the torque of his attack.

Joje hit the side of a chair, rebounding and collapsing to the floor.

Blake caught himself on the cushioned seat, dropping to one knee. In his other hand, he still held the jagged remains of the globe, blood dripping down the side of the broken world and from the bottom of his hand.

His blood or Joje's? It didn't matter.

Joje pushed himself up, then collapsed back to the ground, dazed. Blake had to get his gun. He pounced on top of him, driving his knee into Joje's back and pinning him down. He wrapped Joje's arms behind his back as if he were a cop on a crime drama, though with nothing to bind him.

A string of relentless *Jings* and *Jongs* rattled through the house, but Blake was so swept up in the moment he could only focus on his downed opponent and keeping him restrained. So much so that he failed to hear or see Drew step into the office.

The blow to Blake's head was much more severe than a shattered globe. He never saw what Drew used, but as he flew off

Joje toward the desk, he welcomed the darkness so quick to embrace him.

3

Adam's fingers glided over the keyboard of his father's laptop like a concert pianist preparing to play his first note. The TV was the first purchase he'd be making, followed by ordering dinner, then a wheelchair for Jenna, Joje's orders. He'd see what else he had time for before they decided the computer should be put away.

Alone in the kitchen, he scrolled the cursor through the icons at the bottom of his father's laptop. He hovered over the symbol that read "a-mail." He knew what it was: Blake's secret e-mail software that was supposed to read your mind or something. His heart beat a little faster as he considered opening it and sending out a one word e-mail to Blake's list of contacts.

Help.

At the very least, it would make things interesting.

He moved past it, instead launching Chrome. It was too late for help.

His father was gone, probably had brain damage from that blow to the head. Drew had held nothing back when he swung that golf club. They had dragged Blake into the garage. Who the hell knew what they were doing in there?

Adam clicked order on an eighty-five-inch 8k ultra HD TV without looking at the price. It was a model not being released yet to the general public, eight times the definition of 1080p with 3-D technology that didn't even require glasses.

He entered his father's credit card info from memory, a card Blake didn't even know he had. They had gone to a Nailers game a few years ago though neither of them followed hockey. It had been right after his sister was born, and Adam suspected Blake just wanted out of the house. One of the booths out front had been giving away jerseys if you signed up for a credit card. Blake had been on a conference call or something but told Adam to fill out wrong info for him to sign just so Adam could get the jersey. But the jersey wasn't what Adam had been interested in.

Since then he had mastered his father's signature and now had a dozen or so credit cards in order to bounce balances back and forth. Intercepting the mail had never been a problem, and each new card came with a limit Adam would never reach. He clicked on the twenty-four hour delivery and watched as a spinning wheel began processing his order.

His eyes flitted from the bright screen to Jenna on the couch. She lay staring blankly at the ceiling, her swollen eye barely cracked open. IVs ran from hanging bags of clear liquid the doctor had brought, connecting to her neck and arms. It may keep her alive, but it wouldn't help the real problem.

She was addicted to antidepressants, and Adam conveniently "forgot" to add those pills to the pain meds he was in charge of bringing her. Considering the stress of their current situation coupled with her injuries, he gave her another day at most before she turned into a total vegetable. She'd be so unresponsive Joje and Drew would be able to do anything to her.

An ache grew in the back of his eyes like a physical weight. There was a good chance Blake wouldn't be coming back around. Jenna was a mess, and Adam couldn't imagine living with her alone. For the first time in a long time, he thought about his sister.

Blake had been right. He should run away.

He opened a new window and began searching for wheelchairs. The door to the garage opened, and Joje entered from the connecting hall. Blake and Drew weren't with him.

"How's my dad?"

"Bweathing," Joje said, which didn't say much. "And how's awe good docto feewing?"

The doctor was tied to a chair in front of the broken TV, duct tape covering his mouth. A true kidnapping. His white eyes bulged from his wrinkled and saggy cheeks, his bald and spotted head shiny from all the sweat. He stared at Adam, begging, pleading.

Adam wondered if the doctor had known when he woke that morning that today would be the last day of his life. He couldn't even pronounce the guy's name.

The doctor squirmed in his chair, beating against the back of it, as Joje approached.

"Can I go for a swim?" Adam asked. The question clearly caught Joje off guard. Adam kept himself from smiling.

"Sawee, I need Dwew wight now."

It always took Adam a minute to understand Joje. "I'm bored. I already ordered the TV and wheelchair. They'll be here tomorrow. I just need to get out of the house for a bit."

Adam could almost see the turning gears behind Joje's eyes as he considered the possible outcomes. "That's fine."

Joje came forward, putting his hand on Adam's shoulder. "Thank you again, fo' expwaining about the phone. I'm pwoud of you."

Adam shrugged, letting Joje's hand slip off his shoulder.

"I want my son to be just wike you." As he returned to the family room, Joje pointed at Jenna on the couch. "Stay," he said, laughing as he continued back to the garage.

"Bye, Jenna," Adam said in a whisper. He went to the back door, passing Conrad's empty cage, and stepped outside. Joje's misplaced trust was something he had worked hard to earn, but Adam was beginning to realize how much he had underestimated their kidnappers.

With Joje, he felt like he had fallen into a wormhole, popping out and meeting his future self. It had been intoxicating at first—frightening, sure—but no different than smoking his first joint or bedding his first girl. A fear more thrilling than it was scary. But soon he'd be alone with that future iteration, his parents out of the equation, and he was no longer sure that mirrored projection was who he wanted to be.

First his sister, now his parents.

And it was all his fault.

He ripped off his shirt and dove into the pool. The collision with the water cleared his mind, ideas floating to the surface like rising bubbles of air.

Blake's words, "Take the first chance you get and run."

Joje telling him, "I'm pwoud of you."

And Adam left with nothing to say for himself.

He broke the surface, swimming to the far side of the pool. Maybe there was nothing left to say. Had he known when he woke that morning that today would be the last day of his life?

Joje's pwoject would soon be coming to an end.

At least for him.

4

Blake awoke with a gasp. From the base of his skull running to the middle of his forehead, it felt like someone had pried their fingers deep into the spongy tissue of his head, and was about to peel it back like the skin of an orange. It was a new and much more intimate acquaintance with the term "splitting headache."

Water poured over his face, which had most likely ripped him from unconsciousness. He tried to shake it off, but its source was bent on drowning him. He coughed, his lungs suddenly burning. With dread, he realized it wasn't water.

It was gasoline.

Fumes climbed down his throat and nose, causing Blake to choke and snort. At last the flow of liquid stopped, his clothing drenched and sticking to him as he lay in a gathering puddle of fuel. It took a moment for his eyes to focus, even longer to connect image to thought. Speckled pavement, artificial light, shelving filled with boxes . . . and a twisted and bent bicycle lying on the floor.

His garage.

He rolled to a crouching position, rising to his hands and knees. His head hung, eyes closing to stop the dizzying effect of the room spiraling beneath him. It didn't help.

"I'm only going to ask this once, Bwake, so pay attention," Joje said.

Blake hacked through another bout of coughing, his lungs trying to eject the fumes inhaled with every breath. When he was through, Drew bent down, forcing Blake's head up.

"Where are the files stored?" Joje asked.

His sight was so blurry Blake barely recognized Joje, though it could have been because he wasn't smiling. He blinked through the pain, the burning sensation in his eyes making him wonder if they hadn't already lit a match.

"From your phone," Joje continued. "Where are they stored?"

"Go to hell—"

Drew's fist cuffed Blake across the chin, and his head lolled backward. He could have sworn he heard marbles clicking around somewhere inside his skull. More gasoline poured over his face, the toxic air doubling him over, a wretched and wet cough forcing its way out.

"Let's try again. Where do they keep the record of the files from your phone?"

"I don't know. I didn't—"

Air shut off like a valve closing as Drew's hand clamped over Blake's mouth. His neck was forced back, eyes squinting at the blinding lights overhead. Just as Blake felt unconsciousness circling above him, Drew removed his hand.

Blake gasped for air. What he found instead was gasoline.

Liquid flame fought its way down his throat, into his lungs, gasoline dribbling through the passageway of his nose. He felt it floating in his head, his throat burning from the inside out; if there had been a flame, he could have spewed fire. Chortled gags and the painful wrenching of stomach muscles no longer in his control brought up meals in puddles of blood-ridden fuel.

"Please," Blake said, a line of spittle hanging from his open mouth. "I don't know where—"

A match burst alive in Joje's outstretched thumb and forefinger. Blake could smell the burning sulfur, see the flame's sway in both of Joje's eyes.

"Do it," Drew said, backing away from Blake. "We can take care of the others, be gone before anyone finds out."

"We still have unfinished business." The flame climbed down toward the bottom of the match, lighting upon Joje's fingers. He didn't so much as flinch.

Blake sputtered, trying to catch his breath. "There are . . . warehouses—it could be anywhere or backed up at every one. I have no idea. I'm not involved in any of that."

Joje dropped the match.

Blake's heart fluttered, a miniscule comet breaking Earth's atmosphere, carrying with it only death. The last of its flame snuffed out a second before striking the ground, its smoking top put out by the puddle of gasoline.

"You're going to fix this, Bwake. And I'll show you why. Bring him."

Drew lifted Blake from his armpits, dragging him toward the front of the garage. They crossed from where the Escalade was parked over to the back of Blake's midnight blue M6.

"Pop the trunk," Joje said.

Drew dropped Blake to the floor, moving to the driver's door and reaching in.

"I believe you know a bit about poker, Bwake? Have even played in a tournament or two? You probably know the old saying, never show your cards unless you have to. If everyone folds and you take the hand, you drop the cards facedown. But I believe there's power in showing your hand. In letting your opponent know you're not bluffing."

Blake felt Drew's hands pick him back up, dragging him toward Joje. Toward the trunk.

Drew lifted him to his feet. Blake had to catch himself from falling, placing his hands against the rail of the open trunk. The smell hit him before he could register what he was seeing.

Legs. Arms. Detached from a thick torso that was cut into fourths like a sandwich. And tucked beneath the crook of an elbow, the back of a head, a mass of matted black hair like lichen crawling upward.

Blake bent forward, vomiting onto the side of his car, then backed away, the garage door clanging as he smacked into it.

"You said you were tired of games, right? So no more games. Find a way to fix this, or you've just seen what becomes of your lovely wife and son."

Wuv-wee indeed.

Inside the house the first thing Blake noticed was the rolling metal arms with hanging bags of clear fluid, wires and tubes snaking over to Jenna's arms, one biting into her neck. He approached her hesitantly, every step wobbly, aware of the fumes and stink of gasoline surrounding him like a cloud. Her eyes were closed, and as much as he wanted to put his hand on her head and run his fingers through her hair, he stayed himself.

Drew was unwinding a rope Blake had used to tie down a Christmas tree to the top of their Jeep one year back in West Virginia. The tree had only made it halfway to their house, sliding from the roof of the car and bouncing along the barren curved road of slush behind them. They had gone fake every year since.

Beneath the rope was a frail, wizened old man. Drew ripped the tape from his mouth with a stinging pull that stole the color from the man's cheeks. He raised his hands tentatively, the wrinkles in his forehead spreading like ripples in a pond as he arched his eyebrows.

"Please? I can leave?"

Dr. Cheverou was a relic from another age caught in a world moving too fast. And this time it was bound to get him hurt.

"No leave," Joje said. He pointed to Blake. "Make sure he's . . . okay in the head."

Dr. Cheverou smiled as if he were used to people speaking to him like a three-year-old.

"Make it quick," Drew said.

"Sit please?" The doctor's thick accent rolled his sentences into one continuous word.

Blake lowered himself onto the loveseat perpendicular to Jenna. He wasn't sure he'd be able to get back up. "Where's Adam?" he asked, suddenly realizing his son was missing.

"In the pool," Drew said. He must have seen the fear sweep over Blake's face because he added, "He's just swimming."

"I need my tools?" the doctor asked.

"No tools," Joje said.

Dr. Cheverou turned back to Blake with a scowl that had been perfected over a lifetime.

"Thank you for helping my wife," Blake said. "She looks better, her face . . . it has color."

Dr. Cheverou only grunted.

"Where are you from?" Blake asked.

"Look up," the doctor intoned. He moved his face forward, mere inches from Blake's. Blake could smell the musk of the doctor's cologne over the reek of gasoline, an odd cocktail of engine oil and old man smell mixed with sweat. And fear.

Dr. Cheverou's fingers prodded around Blake's eyes. "I am from Ukraine. Lugansk. Is like little Los Angeles." He turned Blake's head to the side, massaging around the back of his skull. Blake winced, a piercing spike spreading forward all the way to his eyes. "Fingers."

Blake held out his hands, not understanding it was a question until the blurring of his vision settled to a more muted amplification.

"Oh, uh, three. Two. Six . . . or seven."

Dr. Cheverou's face back in Blake's. Their eyes met, and in the doctor's Blake saw pity. Then the doctor slapped him across the face, hard—jolting.

"You bring me here? To these monsters?"

Another slap, Blake too slow to stop it or move out of its way.

Maybe it hadn't been pity.

"Whoa, whoa, Doc!" Joje was suddenly there, grabbing the doctor's upraised hand and saving Blake from . . . what? Shame?

Dr. Cheverou spat in Blake's face, then glared at Joje. "Let me go. No one will know about this. I know to keep secrets."

Blake watched as the doctor's face turned from a grimace of hate to pain. He bent downward, Joje no longer holding his hand, but squeezing it—crushing it.

"I don't want to hear you asking to leave again, Doc. Understand?" Joje said.

Dr. Cheverou nodded through welling eyes.

Joje stood over the now-kneeling doctor, not an edge of menace in his voice despite his vice-like grip on Dr. Cheverou's hand. "You're a guest and this . . . is like a vacation. Well, more like a staycation. I'm going to need the password to your phone as well as your e-mail so we can make sure your staff knows you left town."

Dr. Cheverou nodded.

"Now how's our boy doing? Is he okay?"

"Is poor light . . . difficult without tools," the doctor said.

"You're not getting your tools," Joje said.

Dr. Cheverou snorted. "He has concussion."

"Will he be okay?" Joje asked.

"Please. I've done nothing wrong."

Joje twisted the doctor's hand so abruptly the string of bones snapping sounded more like a line of firecrackers, one going off after another. He released the hand, and the doctor crumbled to the floor, weeping.

"Thank you, Doc," Joje said. "And remember our rules."

"You are a small man with small dreams," the doctor said, spit flying with his words.

Joje's tic was back, his right eye blinking, mouth twitching in spasms. "This, Bwake, is the kind of fight I had hoped you would have." He spun on the doctor with such speed, foot rising to Dr. Cheverou's chest, it lifted the doctor almost completely from the floor as he barreled into the wall, wheezing.

The doctor reached for his fallen glasses with his good hand, bringing them slowly to his face, hand trembling. He had barely caught his breath when he looked back up at Joje. "I was wrong, not small man. Puny."

Joje just smiled. "Tie him back up, Dwew. And mind the doc's hand. Bwake and I need to do some planning."

<h1 style="text-align:center">5</h1>

There were two main warehouses where Symbio housed servers in California, one in Lancaster, the other in Indio, and while they were only separated by about 150 miles, the amount of time to cross that distance in traffic would be more akin to six hours. Give or take an hour. Add the fact that if the files had been requested, they'd already be in someone's hard drive in the Westlake office, and they needed to be in three places at once. Salvaging what remained of Joje's "pwoject" would be more difficult than resuscitating Betti on Blake's shattered Cyborg phone.

He shared with Joje his honest opinion: they were too late. There was no way to know where the information was being housed, at whose terminal, on which server or location. They were looking for a needle in the sewage tunnels of Los Angeles, and in the sewers of LA, there was an abundance of discarded needles.

"If you can't find a way, we're going to need a larger trunk," Joje said, arms folded as he sat across from Blake at his office desk. "Are we clear?"

Yeah, we're queer, Blake thought.

He had a way, it just wasn't one he was comfortable employing. But it wouldn't be the first time he had been left with no options. "I've got a guy," he said.

"How long will it take?"

"Depends. On what he wants."

Joje's mouth began to twitch, his lip riding down the side of his face. "Whatever you need can be arranged. Your money's safe."

It was Blake's turn to smile. "It won't be that easy."

Rory Shepherd was the Neo of hackers. In the early 2000s, he had hacked his way into the top ten companies of the Fortune 100, sending the CEO of each company an interoffice e-mail from the former CEO demanding their immediate resignation. A third of those e-mails had been sent from the grave.

In '06 he breached the security of the top twenty universities, lowering tuitions by sliding a decimal point one step to the left. In the twenty-four to forty-eight hours it took for the universities to become aware, there was a combined total of over fourteen million in lost revenues, though most universities had gone back and successfully litigated the difference from those enrolling.

In 2009 Rory stormed the gates of Google, sending, albeit for a brief minute and six seconds, users of the one box search engine giant to an "under construction" page. Rumors abounded that Mark Zuckerberg had sent the request to Rory as a dare, one to which Rory responded by simultaneously sending Facebook users to the almost-abandoned wastelands of Myspace. To Zuckerberg's credit, the lapse in time of that leap was a fraction of Google's, lasting just under twenty-four seconds.

That Rory and Blake were on a first-name basis was something Blake both was proud of and despised. It also meant Blake's chances of getting his help would be next to impossible.

A paranoid recluse, Rory had a system that prevented him from being discovered by authorities and those who would have loved to extradite him, among other things. He only worked with a client once. No exceptions.

And somehow Blake needed to change his mind.

"I'm going to need to break some of your rules for this to work," Blake said.

Joje looked at Blake with skepticism. "Go on."

"There's only one person I know who could get what we want out of Symbio. The problem is, I don't think he'll do it."

"Unless?"

"I tell him what's really happening," Blake said. "I don't think he'll do anything about it, like calling the cops. I'd stake my life on it. This guy—he's . . . disconnected from the world in a way that's hard to explain. It's like everything to him is a big video game. People's lives—they're just actors, mannequins. He doesn't care about anyone or anything."

"So why would he care about you?" Joje asked.

"He won't. But maybe he'll be fascinated enough to want to watch, to be a part of it, and that's what we need. He doesn't do jobs for money. What he requests, it's . . . well, it's always something you'll regret giving. He wants people to pay for his service. And the people that know him or how to reach him? Let's just say money would be too easy."

"I like this guy already," Joje said. "What do we need to do?"

"Send a fax."

Joje picked up a small shard of the crystal globe, barely recognizable. He turned it over in his hand. "I'd have no idea who you're sending it to."

"Neither would I," Blake said. "That's just the way it works."

Blake could see Joje's mind tearing the idea apart. "Joje, I will do anything to keep my family alive, and this is the only way I can think to keep those files from JT's hands."

"There are other ways to destroy files than over the Internet," Joje said.

"Not at three locations. Say you blow up one. The cops will be all over Symbio so fast we'd never reach the parking lot of the others. This is the best I've got. It's all I've got."

The fax had just gone through when Drew broke into the room, double doors splitting apart and banging against either wall.

"Adam's gone."

The front yard was empty, the only motion on the street from a few errant seagulls circling overhead. In the rear of the house, a discarded shirt, still inside out, lay on the patio, the only sign Adam had been there.

He did it.

A quiet calm filled Blake as he watched the waves tumble in below the edge of their backyard. That feeling, that things could only get worse, was a sailboat set to sea, so small he could barely make it out. Adam was safe. The rest, well, it no longer mattered.

Joje ordered Blake back inside. He carried a chair from the kitchen, placing it next to the bound doctor, telling Blake to sit. Dr. Cheverou's hand had turned a blistering purple, beads of sweat dripping from his forehead onto the fresh duct tape covering his mouth.

"Where is he?" Joje asked.

"How the hell should I know? I was unconscious," Blake said.

"You're the one who said he could go without me," Drew quipped, wanting to avoid whatever outburst was about to happen.

"So where would he go?" Joje asked.

"The police?" Blake said.

"No. He's having too much fun for that." The certainty in Joje's words was frightening. He pushed aside one of the metal racks and pressed his hand to Jenna's face. Then slapped her.

Jenna opened her eyes wide, the memory of her whereabouts seeming to slowly sink back in. Blake felt his heart racing. He also found himself unable to lift a finger to stop him.

"Adam's gone," Joje said. "Did he tell you where he was going? Did he say anything?"

Jenna arched her back, repositioning her body on the couch without moving her legs. After a long moment she responded. "He said good-bye."

She looked at Blake with a heaviness he hadn't seen in years. Suddenly he wasn't so certain about Adam's escape.

"I haven't given him enough attention. I've been so preoccupied," Joje said. The sincerity and hurt on his face was at odds with everything Blake thought he had known about Joje. "Will you help me look for him?" he asked.

"He's my son," Blake said.

"Dwew, I, uh . . . I'm gonna have to leave you, but I'll need the gun. Don't yet trust Bwakey. Will you be okay?"

Drew glanced between his two hostages, an old man with a shattered hand, gagged and tied to a chair, and a crippled woman without the ability to even stand on her own. "Wait here," he said, disappearing down the hall.

Joje began to pace. "Does he surf?"

Blake shook his head. Not a lot of surfing instructors in West Virginia.

"He asked if he could go for a swim," Joje continued, his mind keeping pace with his feet. "Bwake, you were out. He wouldn't have known if you were coming back . . . Jenna immobile . . . it's the first time he's been separated from Dwew . . ."

A loud scraping sound echoed from the hall, preceding Drew's arrival, the sound of a metal cabinet being dragged across the floor. Blake flinched, the grinding noise reminding him of a dentist's drill. Drew finally appeared, the noise coming to a screeching halt. He lifted the object triumphantly in the air.

It wasn't nearly as heavy as it had sounded, the metal grinding against wood surprisingly deceptive. In his hands Drew held the katana that had been mounted in the guest room. The Japanese sword. The scabbard's end was tipped in metal, decorative red and gold lines running down its length. Like the gouged line now running down the grain of the floor to his hall, Blake imagined.

Awkwardly hefting the sheath in the crook of his arm, Drew slid the sword out with his unbandaged right hand. The blade was two and a half feet long and shone like liquid, a long groove running along the upper end of both sides, what Blake had heard referred to as a "blood groove." Their decorator may have gotten most things wrong, but this blade was without doubt authentic.

The sword swooshed through the air, the sharp whine like three whistles simultaneously blowing. "Who needs a gun?" Drew asked.

Joje only smiled.

6

Blake drove slowly, riding his brakes as they followed the curve of Vanilla Banks Road toward its eventual dead end. He had only driven past their house the first time they had come to the Cliffs, when it was still one of thirty or so houses they had been looking at. How any house goes from one of thirty to "the one" was still a mystery to him.

The road sank into shadows, the sky at its tipping point, night winning the siege against day. The last of the sun's rays swabbed at the clouds, pinks and oranges fading into coarser replications only hinting of their former beauty.

"We may need to go door-to-door," Joje said between yelling Adam's name. With his lisp it almost sounded like he wanted Blake to dance do-si-do.

The top of the convertible was down. Blake wondered if there was anyone on the street to even hear them.

They passed a modern behemoth of a house, its tetragonal center feeding off into castled pillars, at least three stories high. Like lighthouses. The roundabout driveway behind its elaborate gate was empty, not a single light on in the house.

Adam wouldn't hole up in an abandoned house as empty as his own. With no sirens in the distance or helicopters swirling overhead, Blake was resigned to agree with Joje that his son hadn't gone to the cops. So where the hell would he have gone?

The paved street dead-ended into a spectacular rock formation, a natural jutting of black stone sticking from the ground as if the gods had hurled down spears that had petrified over the ages. Wisps of sand blew and circled across their tops. Beyond, a gloomy blanket of ocean stretched endlessly, the rotation of waves crashing forward, then drawing back.

Forward and back. Forward and back. An eternity of marching in the same place with only the guise of progress to keep you from stopping.

Blake put the car in park and turned the engine off.

Adam said he was *going for a swim.*

As the colors in the sky bled out their final dribbles, Blake realized how close he was to losing his son for good.

Forward and back. Forward and back.

He hoped he was wrong, but in the mental state his son had left in, he couldn't imagine any other outcome. Not for a forlorn teenager whose family had just been ripped away in a sweeping moment.

At the cliff's edge they peered down at the waves crashing against the base. The noise of their breaking was formidable, white froth flying into the air, mist on their faces despite the distance. There would have been a beach there just two hours ago—a small one, granted, but wide enough to trod across for a boy with nowhere to go. Boys with nowhere to go rarely required wide paths.

The cliff curved around a bend moving inland. The dirt at Blake's feet suddenly crumbled beneath him, a stone dislodging and tumbling down. He took a step back, his foot catching on a rock and sending him reeling forward—his arms flailed. He was going to fall . . .

Joje reached out, grabbing ahold of him by the shoulder. That was all it took. Blake's sense of vertigo passed, and he stepped safely back.

"This way," he said.

They followed the curve of the cliff side, leaving the illustrious lights of civilization behind. Not a building or home could have been built along these rocky steps, the ground jutting at odd angles and broken boulders. Periodically they would glance down over the edge. Adam wasn't below.

The cliffs became overgrown with trees and vegetation, beginning their ascent much higher than the twenty or thirty feet above the water they now stood at. In the distance they appeared to rise sixty, seventy feet into the air. The roads beyond those mountains would begin to curve upward into the hills, carrying their passengers over into the Valley.

The sky had grown increasingly dark, the sun immersed in a baptism that set the water at the horizon on fire. Without thinking, Blake began to unbutton his shirt.

"What are you doing?" Joje asked.

"He's down there."

"Where? I can't see him."

"Neither can I, but I know he's there. He needs my help."

Blake peeled back his shirt, a sudden gust of wind surprisingly cold. It was easy to forget just how cool the temperatures could drop along the coast, even in the middle of summer.

"I can't let you do this," Joje said.

Blake handed Joje his shirt, kicking off his shoes and removing his socks.

"If I fall . . ." he broke off, unable to finish his thoughts. Joje wouldn't get help. He couldn't. Not without getting himself caught. "I won't fall."

Joje looked out over the edge, squinting into the distance.

Blake forced from his mind the image of tackling Joje, both of them plummeting to the rock strewn beach below. "You said you never had a father? Well, this is what a father does. Descends into the darkness to save his son even when he can't see him. Because he knows he's there."

And Blake did know. He could feel it. And time was running out.

"That's ridiculous," Joje said. "He has no reason to go down there. How would he get back up?"

"I don't think he was planning on coming back up."

Understanding stole over Joje's face. "Has he tried something like this before?"

"Once," Blake said. "It's been a few years."

"I'll follow, from above."

Blake knew he wouldn't be able to. Joje may think he could, and would for a time, but Blake's guess was that Adam had passed far beyond where the cliff walls rose. He wished he had grabbed the flashlight from the trunk of his car, but Tom Jones's bulbous corpse stood watch, guarding the flashlight and jumper cables from beyond the grave.

Blake crouched, studying the cliff he intended to scale. This spot was as good as any. The outcroppings and jutting rocks made for plenty of handholds. As long as they didn't give out or crumble beneath his weight.

He gripped one of the sharp rocks at the cliff's edge and swung his body out and over, finding, with a few misplaced steps of dirt tumbling loose beneath him, footholds where he could rest his weight. Or at least part of it. He began his descent.

7

The rippled strokes of paint on the ceiling stirred like clouds in the air, disconnected lines forming scenes, people and creatures constantly shifting, deconstructing. A woman hanging from a noose, blood seeping from her eyes and forming a pool, a sea where a child was drowning, then sinking, then decomposing, specs of flesh floating back to the surface on bubbles that became smoke leaping from a burning house, tiny devils watching it burn, circling, chanting, transforming into a whirlpool that became a dragon spewing flames that became a baby placing a shotgun to its mouth . . . The images revolved like the outer doors of a hotel, its lobby inventing new horrors with every turn.

The noise of running water in the downstairs bathroom suddenly shut off. Jenna felt her body tense. It wasn't the sink that had been running, it was the tub, a nightmare that had leapt from the ceiling, becoming reality.

Blake had abandoned her. Had left without a second glance. And the spider that had been biding its time was now preparing its lair for matters far worse than death.

She caught the eyes of the doctor seated on the hard wooden chair across from her. She had never seen a less sympathetic stare. A few final drips plunked from the bathroom then Drew entered, the long sword in his hands unsheathed.

"Help!" she screamed. "Help us! Help me!"

He approached, his thick lips curling upward, then he slapped her so hard her head rolled completely to the other side, staring into the cushions. He held his bandaged hand close to him, and she hoped it had hurt him more than it had her.

She felt the needles in her arm and neck pull at her skin, a burning sensation, then a tearing as they ripped free, dangling from the metal racks. Drew rolled the racks back toward the broken television, Jenna watching the blood coalesce in the crook of her arm.

"Nothing to worry about," Drew said. "Just giving you a bath."

His bulge was back. And throbbing. He placed the sword against the love seat, then lifted Jenna, throwing her over his shoulder like a child's toy. Lightning pounded through her legs carrying all the way to her lungs where that energy was released in an electric cry.

It was several minutes before her breathing returned to normal. Drew set her on the closed toilet seat. Jenna arched her back to take as much pressure from her legs as possible. The bathroom mirror was still fogged from the recent steam.

"Do you need help undressing?" Drew asked.

"You can't do this—"

"I'm helping you," Drew said. "So you don't break a rule."

"You can't—I don't think you can put burns like this in water!"

"You can. The soaking will help."

"You don't know that!" Jenna cried. "What if, what if it . . ." Staring down at the grotesquery that had become her legs she felt a tightening in her chest. This wasn't happening. "We need to wait!"

Drew eyed her hungrily. "We're not waiting."

"The doctor—ask him, he'll know! I'll do what you say, I promise, just—make sure it's not going to kill me?"

He stepped in front of the bath, staring down at the water, both glass partitions slid to one side. Deb had been right, that beveled glass looked ridiculous, though the thought was equally flippant.

"At least bring my pills?" She hated the defeat in her voice. "To help with the pain?"

Drew's face was unresponsive. Jenna wasn't sure if he had heard her. She was just about to speak again when he moved toward the bathroom door, his foot bumping into her outstretched legs. She swallowed the scream breaking at the surface, her entire body convulsing.

"Your shirt better be off by the time I'm back." Drew's version of an apology.

Leaning her head against the wall, she did her best to focus on her breathing. Maybe Drew would bring the whole bottle and she could end this before he had time to realize what she had done. The black currents of those pills beckoned.

She sat upright, staring at the open door within her grasp. Before she could change her mind, she flung it shut. The door slid into the doorjamb and back out a quarter of an inch, not completely closed.

Gripping the towel rack against the wall, one hand propped on the toilet seat, she shoved her body forward. Her knees buckled, bombs exploding, as she collapsed into the door, rolling to the ground with limbs beneath her that no longer worked.

The door clicked closed.

She heard Drew in the family room running toward her. Squinting through the tears, her fingers searched for the button that would lock the door. She found it, pushing it in just as Drew's weight slammed against the other side.

The handle shook, the door rattling in its frame as he shouldered his weight against it. "Open the door, you cunt!"

Jenna let her head fall back against the wall, reveling in the peace and quiet, Drew's threats and curses shouted at someone else, someone far away.

His foot crashed against the other side of the door, the lower half moving an inch outward then falling back in place. It wouldn't hold forever.

If only she were in her bathroom upstairs or even the guest, cabinets filled with junk—dryers, curlers, *scissors*—anything she could get her hands on as some kind of weapon. This bathroom had only a sink that rose from the ground like a thin vase, flowering at the top. No cupboards, no accessories, just a hollow aluminum rack holding toilet paper and a liquid soap dispenser at the sink.

As she lay on the floor looking at the other objects in the room—carpeted mats, towels hanging from the walls—she realized there might be something she could use. The painting on the wall was a Kazimir Malevich. She had always loved abstract art; something about it appealed to her sense of finding order in chaos or chaos in order, she was never sure which. She didn't know the name of this particular piece but remembered buying it at auction for over a hundred thousand.

And here I have it hanging on my bathroom wall, she thought.

Something heavy struck the door handle on the other side, a

loud clang emanating through the wall. "When I get in there . . ."—clang—"you're going to wish . . ."—clang—"you had died in that fire!" Another loud clash.

She knew what she had to do. She lifted her arms above her, fingers barely reaching the edge of the framed painting. She pushed. The frame barely budged. Of course Debbie's team would have hung it with more than a loose nail. The door shuddered next to her. She was running out of time.

And then she saw it. So simple.

She wriggled her body over to reach the aluminum rack holding the toilet paper, emptying the rolls onto the floor. She looked up at the painting. Definitely chaos in order.

The aluminum rack crashed against the frame, glass shattering despite its rounded tip. Shards rained down around her, gathering in her hair, on her clothes. She grabbed a long, jagged piece the size of her fist and held it in her hand, turning her body to rest her head against the tub. Now all she had to do was wait.

8

Blake lowered his foot, blindly searching for an alcove or ledge, a rock jutting from the cliff face. He found it, something upon which his toes landed, the ball of his foot stretching over the cold, sharp stone. He allowed his weight to shift, testing the foothold. So far, so good.

Hanging on to the coral rock at the cliff's edge with his left hand, he brought his right down, grabbing a shallow crevice that made for an excellent handhold. He'd be able to follow it down a ways. He pulled against it, making sure it was as solid as it looked. With a deep breath he let go of the rock at the top, allowing his body to drop over the ledge.

The breeze transformed into violent gales around him, thrashing, pushing, and pulling in a malevolent desire to tear him from the cliff's face. The moment passed, the winds drawing back, content to observe his inevitable fall with or without their assistance.

What little light remained in the skies was slipping behind the inkblot that was night. Blake continued his way down, one harried step at a time. Twice his footholds gave out, his body flinging from the cliff, kept from falling only by his tightening grip on whatever rock or crevice his hand was wrapped around. When he finally leapt the last few feet down, his feet and pants were submerged in water, then the tide rolled back in.

A wave crashed against him, barreling into his back and sending him staggering toward the canyon wall. Before he had a chance to regain his balance, another wave toppled into him. He lost his footing, going down. He snagged onto a rock formation in time to barely avoid that pull from sucking him back out.

"Bwakey! Bwakey!"

He heard Joje's frantic yells over the assault of another wave. The sprawling climb looked more daunting than he would have thought possible. Whatever else Joje was trying to communicate was lost as another wave dashed itself against the rocks. He started making his way along the canyon wall.

As his toes and bare feet slammed into fallen rocks and boulders, Blake asked himself why they hadn't picked a house in Malibu where there were actually beaches. With sand and a shoreline and life guards sitting in towers spotting missing children who happened to wander by. Privacy came at such a high cost.

Despite his pounding heart and a level of activity Blake hadn't sustained in years, he was shivering. The water felt fifty degrees or colder; add the chill of the wind, and he'd only have so much time before his body went rigid and numb. He continued on, walking through water when he could, swimming when he couldn't.

"Adam! Adam!"

He yelled though he knew his words would be lost against the backdrop of tossing water. He had to be getting close. He had to be.

And then he saw him.

His son.

Or rather his body.

Slipping beneath the undertow of a forming wave, Adam floated facedown in the water. Blake lost sight of him, the torrid water thrashing and falling. Adam's body bobbed back up only to submerge once more.

"No!" Blake screamed, flinging himself from the wall and diving into an oncoming wave. It hammered into him, forcing him to the ground and sending his feet flailing over his head. He launched back up, gasping and lunging toward where he had seen Adam last. Another wave fell, propelling him back toward the canyon wall.

"Adam!"

His son wasn't there.

Another wave hit. Blake wiped the stinging water from his eyes. Where was he?

Floating on top of a cresting wave was the driftwood Blake had mistaken for his son. A waterlogged branch as thick as Blake's thigh tumbled beneath a wave, flecks of wood churning and gathering back on the surface.

His tears mixed with the salty water on his face. Up above he caught no sign of Joje. More than likely he was tripping over roots and vines as the landscape changed from sand-covered rock to tree-spotted forest. If Blake was in any real luck, Joje would lose his balance and tumble right over.

A wave caught him by surprise, immersing him completely. As he drew back up out of the water, he heard the squawk of seagulls. He jumped into another wave, letting the water carry him up and back into the jutting canyon wall.

"Dad! Dad!"

It was Adam.

Blake heard his son's cry, and exhaustion left as quickly as the tide pulling away. It would be back, Blake had no doubt, but he could handle another wave.

"Adam!" He searched, squinting in the waning light and following the coast that continued like a drunkard's walk.

"Dad! . . . Help!"

Rushing water forced Blake back against the wall. He let it carry him, turning to grasp the edge of an alcove and lift himself up. He needed to be higher; he needed to be able to see.

"Bwake!" The voice came from above. Blake glanced up at Joje, who must have been kneeling at the edge of the cliff, his body hanging halfway over the lip. Joje pointed out toward the water, not the coastline. "There! Out there!"

Blake's eyes probed against the dark skyline and murky waters. And then he saw it—a rock outcropping that barely rose above the surface of the water as if standing on its tippy toes, gasping for air. The silhouette of a body clung to it. The shape of a boy.

His boy.

Without hesitation, Blake dove into the oncoming wave. It swept him right back to the base of the cliff. He kicked off, swimming lower when another wave burrowed down, flipping him over with its crushing force and flattening him against the floor of the sea. He reached the top of the surface in time to catch half a breath before the next wave struck. His limbs wrenched around in a half circle as he was brought back to the alcove he had seconds ago left. Blake reached up, hanging on as he allowed himself a moment to catch his breath.

"Bwake!" Joje was yelling at him from above, but Blake gave him no heed. He had to get his son.

He waited for the water to start drawing back before he dove in, swimming with all his might. The wave that met him was like a garbage truck sweeping aside a fly. Blake broke back into the water, thrashing against its pull, thrashing, but not gaining. He topped one wave's crest only to be met by a secondary rise that carried him right back to the canyon wall. The alcove was now to his left, his panicked attempts at swimming moving him farther down the coastline—farther away from his son.

Blake's chest was heaving. He was no longer cold, he was sweating, and his body ached with a deepness he recognized as something much more dangerous than exhaustion. He was closing on the brink of utter fatigue.

A rope suddenly caught around his neck, and he was transported back into that truck, the purse strap cinching off his airway, throat bulging, burning. He grappled with it, coming away with a tangle of seaweed that had wrapped itself around him. He threw it, or did his best to, the long strand barely moving a few feet, already gliding back toward him.

He thought he heard his son calling his name.

"I'm coming!" he cried, then plummeted back into the water. This would be his last attempt—not a matter of choice, just an undeniable fact.

He broke over the first wave, his arms carrying his body past just as the rise began to fall. Gulping a half breath of air, he lowered himself, gliding beneath the next rush while still being swept back. He swam, the air in his lungs burning, legs kicking, arms cutting. At last he resurfaced, stopping a moment to get his bearings. A wave began forming just past him, crest rising quickly before burying itself into the mountain's edge.

He had made it.

The island of rock was barely visible above the water. Slowly he swam toward it. He thought he heard hooting and applause coming from above. Angels rejoicing or an orange-haired devil responding to its lengthened stay.

Blake swam on.

The rock was smaller than he had thought and slippery, his hands sliding off until a better purchase was had. Adam held on to the other side, knuckles and hands white against the dark rock. Blake took hold of his son, clinging to him, hugging him, kissing the top of his wet, greasy hair. Adam, for once, didn't seem to mind.

"You came!" he said.

"I did," Blake said between heavy breaths. "I always will."

The water tugged, a taut force ripping at Blake, trying to separate him from his son. Despite the pull, he refused to let go.

"I'm sorry, Dad. I thought—I thought I could swim around to get away."

"Shhh, it's okay," Blake said, ignoring the lie.

"Did you kill him? Joje?"

"No. No, he's . . . here. Up above." Blake pointed to the cliffs behind them. They looked so high from down here. Insurmountable. Adam's body was shivering, teeth chattering. They needed to get out of this water and soon.

"I thought you were dead," Adam said.

"It doesn't matter. You're safe. That's all I care about."

And with the words, Blake felt the crushing blow of Adam's choice. His son could have gone to the cops, could have run away. Instead he came out here seeking a more permanent escape.

"Can you swim?" he asked.

"Yeah," Adam said.

"Okay. Follow me to the cliffs. From there we'll circle around, find a way up."

Adam's face was pallid.

"You can do this! I know you can. The water will carry you. I'll be right behind. I won't let you out of my sight."

Adam nodded. As if on command, a gust of wind blew into them. Blake couldn't feel his fingers or toes. He glanced up at the top of the cliff, trying to spot an eager Joje. Whether he was there or not,

Blake couldn't tell.

They pushed off. The pull of the water carried them farther from the alcove Blake had hoped to swim to, but both he and Adam made it to the cliffs without incident. Just meant more ground they would need to retrace. The waves now crashing against the walls were violent, blinding in their ferocity. Blake had Adam lead as they began the slow path around the curve of the cliffs, buffeted by the assaulting waves. They were both shivering now.

Adam continued to glance back, making sure his father was behind him. The travel was slow, clinging to rocks and earth as the waves struck, racing the few steps they could manage when the ocean inhaled. At one point dirt and loose rocks fell from above, Blake reminded of Joje's looming presence. Weariness circled him like a whirlpool almost pulling him into its dark abyss.

They made it back to where Blake had descended; at least he thought it was the spot. From their vantage point he had no idea how he had made it down in one piece. Joje knelt above, calling down to them, though his words were lost with the noise of the ocean in their ears.

"This is where I came down," Blake said, studying the cliff side.

"And you made it without falling?"

Blake laughed, an expression that felt oddly foreign.

"Keep going," Adam said. "There's an easier path where the canyons meet. Someone set up a rope."

Of course. Blake looked up at Joje and pointed his arm in the direction they were traveling. Hopefully, he'd understand they had to continue. They passed beneath the moonlit shadows of massive mansions hidden behind a wall of earth until arriving at the area Adam had described. It did look like two canyons meeting, one cliff falling away into its jutting brother, creating a tiny slot canyon too narrow for a person to crawl through. But it did allow for an easy path down and back up, especially with the gnarled rope hanging over the lip of the first drop less than ten feet above.

"It's where the surfers come down," Adam said.

Blake nodded. He should have known there would have been an easier way. Adam reached up, grabbed the end of the rope, and used it to scramble up the side of the cliff, walking almost perpendicular to the mountain. He pushed himself over the edge, then swung the rope back out.

It took Blake much longer to climb the same distance, his exhaustion no longer at arm's length. Adam took his hand, helping him with the final push up and over the edge. Blake collapsed into his son, his breathing as ragged as when he had been sucking in gasoline. At least that smell had been washed away.

"Where's Joje?" Adam asked.

"Shhh," Blake said, closing his eyes and resting his head against his son.

"We should go, now, before he gets here!"

"Okay." Blake's eyes wouldn't open, his breathing slowing. He thought Adam was speaking again, but before syllables could register as words, he was out, the systematic crashing of waves in his ear the sleeping pill he had been missing for the past several days.

9

The glass shard in Jenna's hand rattled against her wedding ring, making a clink, clink, clink sound as if someone were preparing to give a toast. Or a eulogy. Wood fractured around the handle of the door with another thud.

Please, God, Jenna thought, let it be quick.

With a harrowing thump the door burst in, a long side board from Adam's bed continuing through like a battering ram. It hit into the sink, turning up into the mirror, which cracked, splintering into smaller, distorted views. She lifted her arms to keep the board from landing on her legs, and then Drew was there, grabbing her hands and yanking her forward. The glass shard dropped to the floor.

He dragged her from the tiny bathroom into the family room, her legs like logs trolling behind her. The pain was beyond anything she could have imagined.

Drew rolled part of the rug back so that her back was pressed to the hard floor. Jenna's shrill cries bounced off the walls unheeded. Forcing her hands down and pinning them to the floor, Drew jumped atop her, his weight crushing into her.

"This is the place, the exact spot. The husband was there," he pointed with his head, "watching the entire time while we raped his daughter and wife over and over. Joje told them we'd stop if they could be quiet." Drew's fat lips spread in a grin, his breath reeking. "Eventually they got real quiet."

Jenna's eyes brimmed with tears, her vision blurring.

"Blake's not here, but maybe the doctor could watch? What do you say, Doc?" He looked up at the old man tied to the chair. "Did you piss yourself? Joje isn't gonna like that."

"You've done this before?" Jenna asked, more a statement than a question.

"Yeah, we've done this before. Now I sorta have a thing, see. I don't like the smell of a woman's goody bag. You all reek. It's in you and on you, but you take the bath, I make this as painless as possible. Maybe even forget you locked me out."

"I knew," Jenna said. "From the first day you arrived, I knew why you were here. What you were after."

"You don't have a clue what we're after."

"I hope Adam didn't go to the cops," she said.

"Why's that."

"Because I want the pleasure of killing you myself."

"The hard way it is," Drew said.

He hopped back up, grabbing her by the feet. Jenna floated in and out of consciousness as he hauled her back to the bathroom. She vaguely remembered clawing at the end table, lamp tipping, magazines spilling to the floor.

Drew ripped at her shirt, pulling it over her head. It got caught in her hair; he just yanked harder. His finger ran down her face, trailing the lines of her neck, cupping her breasts beneath the sports bra. She felt ill, the pain so intense she might throw up.

"My pills . . . ," she managed to get out.

"Here." He unscrewed the cap, tipping the bottle. The white tablets poured not into her hands but into the toilet. He opened a second jar, shaking them out at a trickle at first, then dumping them with the first. Two more bottles followed, hundreds of pills floating in the round bowl before her like drowning maggots.

"Care to bob for apples?" Drew asked.

Sadly, had Jenna been able to move closer to the toilet, she might have done just that. With an exaggerated motion he flushed them down, the noise of that water spinning like a jackhammer in her skull.

"You're going to feel everything from here on out," he said.

"Starting with your bath. And instead of just a soak, I think your legs need a good scrub."

Jenna's hands searched the floor around her, finding only slivers of glass.

A shudder suddenly broke through the house, vibrating against the wall of the bathroom. It was the garage door rising. They were home!

Drew slipped from the bathroom without a word. When he came back in, he was holding the sword. He brought its tip an inch from her face. "One word about any of this, and I cut out your eye. Do you believe me?"

She did.

"Goes for you too, Doc," he yelled out the bathroom door. His bandaged hand reached down, lifting her face toward his. "To be continued.".

Jenna had faced her share of monsters in her life, her father, bad boyfriends, and the oily darkness that swam around her, circling even when things were going right. Yet none had prepared her for this. Regardless of who came through that garage door, she knew if she was ever alone with Drew again, she would be finished.

Chapter 6

Day Five

1

Blake lay in his bed, alone. It was an odd sensation, the unruffled bedspread and sheets beside him a stark reminder of pre-California days when he had retired to bed without knowing if or when Jenna would come in. Blake had no context to determine whether Joje's absence was a good or bad thing.

He decided on bad.

The pulsing in his head made thoughts difficult to piece together, every muscle twanging with the slightest movement. His body was telling him what he already knew.

Enough.

We give.

Uncle.

At least Adam was safe; but no, Blake knew even that wasn't true. When playing Russian roulette, you don't relax when the gun clicks instead of fires. Especially when you're the only one playing.

Guilt threatened to tip him over an edge and into an abyss with no end, an edge he couldn't afford to look over. Not now.

Jenna's already there, he thought, or thought he thought. It was so difficult to tell which were his own. He should join her. He knew who was there with her, the reason Jenna had descended to such depths and stayed for so long.

Their daughter was down there.

Evaline.

That he had awoken to a day that would be filled with new horrors he had no doubt, but the memories of his daughter, her tiny fingers gripped around his one, were more than he could bear. He started down the path toward her, tree branches slapping against his arms and shoulders, raking across his face. He tripped over a root or rock, one knee scraping against the ground, leaving a smeared stain of rotting leaves and soil. The soft burble of a brook drew near, though no water had passed here for months. It wasn't trickling water; it was the sound of racking sobs.

A blade of sunlight brought him back to their bedroom. It slid through slanted shutters, past shaded screens and wood partitions to break into the room. He realized that he wasn't shackled. Joje had either forgotten or no longer considered Blake a threat.

He sat up, glancing around the room. Throw pillows had been discarded in a tangle at the foot of the half wall separating the upper landing with their bed from the rest of the room, but beyond that the bedroom was immaculate. Immaculate and sad. The glossy-eyed baby alligator head on the nightstand was the only item in the room he and Jenna had purchased together. The COO at a midsize oil company in Mississippi had insisted on taking him and Jenna on a safari cruise much different from the one they had experienced at Disneyland. They had purchased the head as a souvenir, laughing the entire time.

God, he missed her laugh, missed that feeling of being in love.

Her excitement the day she had told him she was pregnant. Pulling that urine-stained stick that looked like a purple and blue thermometer from her purse at the Lemaire in Richmond, fumbling it in her excitement, the waiter bending down to retrieve it and holding it out, proudly displaying it for Blake to see. "Congratulations," he had said. "Now if you'll excuse me, I need to wash my hands."

Blake washed his own, after relieving himself in the bathroom. He could barely look at his reflection in the mirror, and in those brief glances, all he saw was contempt.

Suds of soap overflowed from the small basin at the sink, but his hands were still dirty, covered in filth and dirt and broken leaves.

And hair.

Matted in blood.

It clung to his fingers and the backs of his hands like sap. He was crying again, not sure he wanted it removed. The last of his baby girl; they had already taken the body away.

Her face was covered by tangles of hair, as it often was, her thin brown curls as obedient as the child they belonged to, but it was the angle of her head that was wrong, an equation that simply didn't work. One arm lost beneath her, the other outstretched, tiny fingers splayed as if reaching for something just out of grasp. Maybe life.

A bird chirped, its woodland song belonging in that moment no more than any of them, and then Blake was rushing past his fallen wife and forgotten son, picking her up, bringing her to his chest, cradling her cold skin against his own, her cheek touching his cheek, his hand running through her crusted hair, patting her back, twisting her neck back into place only to watch it flump back again, his tears bathing her face, soaking her locks and the collar of her sundress, its bright orange and yellow flowers turning a muddied amber and molten brown. He called her name. Sang it. Screamed it. Waiting for her to place her hands against his face, squeeze his cheeks and bury her nose into his as she did every morning, or at least the mornings he was home. Her name became a prayer, became a word so holy he could no longer say it, his speech dissolving into the anguished cries of a father who has lost everything, sending squirrels and birds fleeing. And all the while Adam's illicit voice, like a merry-go-round's jilted tune, "It's my fault, it's my fault, it's my fault."

Had he ever told his son that it wasn't?

Blake shut the water off, drying his hands. A storm was growing behind his eyelids; this time it just might sink him.

He dressed, blue jeans and a faded black Rolling Stones T-shirt. There were no pretenses to keep up any longer. He went down the hall and descended the stairs, feeling like he was riding an escalator, that dreamlike sensation of moving without moving, a hamster on a wheel.

The deep groove in the hallway floor led him to the family room. What he witnessed came as a complete surprise.

Jenna was at the fridge, the open door blocking her face, the top of a wheelchair poking above the back of the island counter. Joje and Adam laughed at the far end of the island, seated on the swing-out chairs. Drew was seated on the couch where Jenna had been lying, the first to spot Blake, a smug look on his face. Even the doctor was no longer tied up; his arm was in a sling, and he walked from the pantry back into the kitchen.

They all seemed so . . . *normal*.

They could have been a regular family on an ordinary weekend, catching up, enjoying their time together. At least if you removed the shattered TV and the Japanese sword leaning against the couch, and both Drew's and Jenna's multiple bruises.

"Dad!" Adam called.

"Welcome to the land of the living," Joje said with a laugh.

The *waahnd* of the *wiving*. Blake wasn't sure it was a place he wanted to be a part of.

The fridge door closed, and Jenna held Blake's gaze. "You're okay." Not a question, though she certainly looked to have her doubts. The square clock above her showed quarter of twelve.

"Sorry," Blake said, not knowing if it was because he had slept in or if he was merely apologizing for a lifetime of mistakes.

"Did you know your son knows how to twirl a gun? Like in the Old West," Joje said, jumping up from his seat. "Show him!"

Adam only kicked his chair out from the island, letting it reel him back in. "Nah, that's okay."

"Come on, show him," Joje pressed. Adam stood reluctantly. "Now turn this way, Bwake. That's it, like you're about to duel."

Adam stood facing Blake, half a room apart.

"Now!" Joje shouted.

Adam swiped at his side, twirling a pistol from his belt forward and pointing it directly at Blake.

"Bang," Joje said.

Adam spun the gun in his hand before rotating it back, slipping it into his belt.

It took a conscious effort to breathe. Blake glanced at Jenna who just turned her head, looking away. "We don't play with guns," he said lamely.

"Just stuff we learned in Scouts," Adam said.

"I don't want my son playing with guns," Blake repeated.

"The party pooper's arrived," Joje said.

"May I use your restroom?" Dr. Cheverou asked, bowing slightly to Joje. His hostility to his captor seemed to have fled.

"Go," Joje said, shooing the doctor away. "We got a response, Bwake. From the fax you sent. Your mystery man is on the case!"

Blake felt his stomach tighten. He had almost hoped Rory would refuse, had expected he might. If he had accepted, that meant he had also completed his part, deleting the files and any evidence of Joje and Drew's stay. Deleting the only means of someone coming to their aid.

"I need to . . . need to sit," Blake said. He moved to the love seat, falling into it. Drew didn't bother to even lift his outstretched feet.

If the fax had come in, not only would Rory have completed his part, he'd have listed his demands. Payment for services rendered.

Doing business with Rory was unlike any Blake had conducted—the price was never discussed beforehand, arriving only after Rory had accomplished what others might deem impossible. There were no negotiations, no backing out. And Rory always collected, one way or another.

Blake had heard rumors of those who refused to pay, who thought the price he demanded too extreme. Every one of them ended not in financial ruin, but in public extirpation. It wasn't enough to steal your identity, wipe your bank accounts, erase your history; those were events someone could climb back from. No, these rumors ended with life sentences for inside trading or embezzlement, children and spouses taken and sold into sex trafficking rings, one-way admissions into experimental hospitals where pleas of sanity fell on deaf walls. These were the consequences for those who didn't pay, disasters you couldn't come back from. The senator that had first introduced Blake to Rory had warned him he'd be better off selling his soul to the devil. At least that way Blake would know what he was giving up.

Joje pulled a folded sheet of paper from his pocket, looking it over. "He deleted the files. Even wiped them from a C-T-O-S computer."

"That's a—it's not a specific computer. It means the chief technology officer's computer," Blake said. "JT wasn't taking his threat lightly."

"What threat . . . what's going on?" Jenna asked.

"Your husband is just fixing one of his many mistakes," Joje said.

"My phone, it recorded everything that's happened over the past few days," Blake said.

"And you're helping them destroy those files?" Jenna asked, a thickness to her voice that wasn't from the Vitamin Water she was drinking. "You and Adam both. You're going to get us killed."

She wheeled her chair away from him, bumping into the kitchen table with a jolt.

"Did I miss something?" Blake asked.

"That crazy decorator chick came over earlier when Jenna was asleep," Adam said. "She got mad I sent her away."

Probably saved her life, Blake thought, though he wasn't willing to voice it right now. Jenna's words hung on him like weights. Everything he was doing was to protect her and Adam, couldn't she see that? The rolling of her wheels on wood softened to carpet, the vaulted living room only amplifying her sobs.

Without a word Drew stood, grabbing his sword and silently following Blake's wife.

Joje returned to the fax. "There's more. Says here he couldn't get into one of the outside storage centers because it's offline. Is that a problem?"

Blake paused. "Yeah."

"And then there's something about a zip drive, but he thinks it's JT's? I don't know." Joje came over, handing the paper to Blake. "I thought you said he was expensive?"

Blake snatched the page, reading through the bullets of info that always accompanied Rory's acceptance and list of demands. Joje was right, two loose ends—a storage facility in Lancaster and, far worse, the zip drive, most likely JT's based on the IP address of the computer. It made Rory's services nearly useless, far too many copies available to staunch the flow. Yet it hadn't stopped from him listing his demands. What Joje hadn't been right about was Rory being inexpensive.

For payment he asked just two things: a nickel and a strand of hair.

The nickel was a 1913 Liberty nickel. Blake had come across an article about JT a few years back when he had just begun his relationship with Symbio that centered around the CEO's purchase of a five-cent piece for over five million dollars. The article went into some detail about the coin, apparently one of the most sought-after collector's items in the history of the US. All Blake had thought about when reading the article was how many nickels it would take to make five million dollars. He had done the math: one hundred million. At twenty-two pounds of weight per hundred dollars, it came to a grand total of a million and one hundred thousand pounds of nickels. Blake had one of his programmers in China to thank for those details.

The article had been more an insight into the mind of JT; a man willing to spend that kind of cash on something that couldn't purchase a lollypop in today's economy was a man you could influence through ego. Ego and perception. With Rory asking for the one item that defined JT along with a strand of his hair, he might as well have been asking Blake to murder his old boss.

"It's impossible," Blake said. "What he's asking us to do? What he wants?"

"You told me you could fix this," Joje said. His tic began pressing on his face like an invisible string pulling at his bottom lip and the skin around his eye.

"You're talking breaking and entering. And even if we got into this storage facility, I wouldn't begin to know how to wipe just the data we need. If JT has a backup, it's pointless anyway. It's going to get out."

"Not if we stop JT," Joje said.

"And how do you propose we do that?"

"Second page," Joje said.

A cancerous pit grew in Blake's stomach as he continued reading. The specs of the warehouse were included as well as a guarantee that security cameras and alarms would be disabled after eleven. Tonight only. As to JT, Rory had left a back door open into his laptop that would immediately notify him the next time the machine booted up and connected to the Internet. He would scramble any attempt at accessing the flash drive for the next two days. Payment was expected on the third.

Blake closed his eyes, massaging the pressure points beneath his eyebrows.

"Can it be done?" Joje asked.

Can it be done. A question Blake had never answered no to. Because if you wanted something badly enough, there was always a way.

"Bwake, can it be done?"

"Maybe," he said, answering a question much more important

than whether they could get the phone's data. Because maybe, just maybe, he'd be able to get his family out of this alive.

"Can I help?" Adam asked.

"No!" Blake said, but Joje's "sure" seemed to trump his reply.

Joje continued, "We'll need a third man. Dwew can't help. He'll be watching these two." He paused, then moved toward the bathroom. "Everything coming out okay, Doc? Been in there awhile."

The bathroom door looked split, doorknob hanging loose and knocking against the wood as Joje gave it a light shove. He stopped just inside the doorway. Adam pushed off from the chair on the counter and crossed through the family room, following him.

"Adam, wait," Blake said, but his son continued without a pause.

When his son turned to look back at him, his face was long and unflinching. Joje joined him, completely unfazed. "Staycation's over," Joje said. "Doc decided to check out early."

2

Blood. At the sink, dripping down the basin, globs on the marble floor, coagulating along the grains of grout, pooling near the base of the toilet, smeared against its side, its cover, the walls, the towels, the glass partitions to the tub. Some of the stains showed where the doctor's trembling fingers had swiped in the final throes of death. As quietly as he had gone out, he had made sure to leave his mark.

They moved his body outside, wrapping him in the Persian rug that had occupied most of their family room. One arm swung out, dangling down from the folded carpet, Dr. Cheverou's wrist split wide like a fish opening its mouth. Joje set Drew on digging duty. Blake was on cleanup.

Red-drenched towels gave way to copper-stained rags piled against the bathroom wall like the sopped aftermath of a carwash fundraiser. Adam moved the towels into a black trash bag, the pattering drips against the tile floor louder than they had any right to be.

Blake was on his hands and knees with a safety pin, running the grout of the tile, scratching out the grime and dried blood, when Joje entered.

"Who knew it took so long to clean up after a dead body? All those CSI shows seem to skip that part," he said. Blake caught his smile in the reflection of the cracked mirror. "What are we doing for dinner?"

The lingering stink of blood and death masked beneath ammonia caused Blake to gag. At least he didn't vomit; not that he hadn't earlier. "Just . . . order something," he finally said.

"Easy, Bwake. It's not like I offed the good doc."

Yeah, but he knew it was coming, Blake thought. Am I the only blind one who can't see it?

"I need some air," he said, standing and walking out of the small bathroom. Those walls had shrunk over the past several hours.

He went to the back door, throwing it open and stepping out. Sunlight glinted off of the ocean just beyond their backyard, wavering like a mirage. He breathed deep, holding it in, the crisp sea air igniting something in him, reminding him what he was fighting for. A light breeze tossed his hair, caressed his whiskered face.

"Bwake?"

Joje passed the pool and continued to the cliff's edge, the large palm trees to the right offering intertwining columns of shade from the sun now on its decline. Blake didn't remember walking to the edge. Maybe that was something you never remembered.

They stood there in silence, watching the moving sea with a quiet reverence.

"I want to bring Jenna out here," Blake said. "Can I bring her out?"

Five minutes later, Blake was sitting beside his wife on the white piano bench. He had set it near the edge of the cliff but not close enough for her to fall or purposely leap from. As distant as they had become, he still knew her well. Joje had brought out a small stool they kept in the pantry for her legs to rest on. She was as comfortable as she could be under the circumstances. Joje remained unseen behind them, for the first time in a long time, silently observing.

Jenna looked on the verge of crying, tears held in by sheer force of will. "It's beautiful," she said.

Blake only nodded. He wanted so badly to wrap his arms around her but wasn't sure the gesture would be reciprocated. Glassy reflections of light danced across the water.

"Do you think, the doctor . . . maybe that's our only way out?"

"No," Blake said, too quickly.

A moment passed before she spoke again. "Nothing will ever be the same."

"Nothing ever has," Blake said, knowing he was speaking of this week as well as the past two years.

She leaned her head on his shoulder, speaking even softer, her voice barely audible above the breaking waves. "They killed the family that lived here before us. Drew told me. The neighbor was right. They were *here* before we were. Both of them."

She paused, giving him time to lean his head onto the top of hers. "What does it mean?"

Blake hated his response but had no idea what else to tell her. "They've had this planned a long time."

Jenna sniffed, a tear skirting down her cheek.

Blake wrapped his arm around her, not caring whether she wanted him to or not. Right now it was what he wanted to do. Some apologies weren't meant to be voiced, would in fact lessen their value by being put into words. So he held her instead, telling her how sorry he was for so much gone wrong without ever opening his mouth.

From a distance, their heads leaning in and bodies close, they looked like a couple without a care in the world who longed to do nothing more than be together. A couple in love.

"Someone's at the door," Adam called from the back door. The mirage shattered.

"Pizza man," Joje announced loudly. "Go ahead and sign it."

The spell was broken, a subtle reminder that they weren't just a couple sitting out in their yard, watching the sunset.

"You smell awful," Jenna said, a laugh escaping.

Blake couldn't help but join her. "I think I'll burn these clothes with the towels."

"No more talk of burning," she said, her smile disappearing.

Without letting her see, he stole a glance at her mutilated legs, stoking the flames within him. They looked as coarse as a leather glove left out in the sun for months.

God, how did this happen to us? he thought.

God didn't answer, but Adam did, his words equally as revelatory. "It's not the pizza man," he called. "It's the police."

3

Adam's words were like pulling a fire alarm at a school assembly. Chaos erupted. Jenna bent forward to get to her feet, momentarily forgetting her plight and crying out in a short jagged burst. Drew knocked Adam through the doorway, putting him in a headlock with his massive arm, the sword held tightly against his side. Jenna fell from the bench, pebbles kicking up, Blake scrambling beneath to support her, lift her, keep her from falling, all the while tracking the movements of his captors, their distance, the seconds he had to act, think.

Joje hadn't even risen from his stool. "Stay calm."

His words had a way of slowing time down.

"Bwake, take off your shirt, in the pool then out, rinse that smell off you. Jenna, you're staying here. One word and I let Dwew finish what he started, and Dwew? Anyone comes out those doors before me, you put that little knife to good use."

"What about me?" Adam asked.

"Help keep your mom quiet."

There was a moment of stillness, even the swell of waves seemed to pause and reflect, and then Blake was removing his shirt. He set Jenna back against the bench, stepping over brush and flowers to get to the pool. His jeans, he realized, looked like tomatoes had been thrown at him, their dried drippings extending to the end of the leg.

"Yeah, pants too," Joje said.

Blake unfastened the buttons, pulling the jeans off. Drew moved past him with Adam.

"Blake, help us," Jenna said, her words both imploring and questioning at the same time.

"I am," he said, then dove into the pool in his silk boxers, swimming across to the other side. Joje met him there with a towel, which he wrapped around his waist.

"I don't have to warn you, do I?" Joje asked.

Blake looked across at Adam, who sat beside Jenna on the bench. Drew stood behind them, the katana slipping free of its sheath. "No, you don't."

They moved from the kitchen through the living room, stepping up from the white carpet to the hardwood tile of the foyer. The front door was open; Adam must have hoped they would hear something, put them on alert. Officer Randall stood squinting, one hand raised to shield his eyes, the setting sun glaring through the top window in the back of the entryway. His partner wisely wore shades, though the shiny reflective lenses were a model at least a decade out of style. He stood a good foot and a half taller than Randall, one stud earring in his left ear with a thin goatee just beginning to show gray.

"Sorry," Blake said, "we were in the pool."

"Hell, it's where I'd be if roles were reversed," Randall said with a grin. "It was Blake, right? This is Deputy McClellan I was telling you about. We were hoping to take you up on that offer."

McClellan didn't offer a hand or greeting, just continued chewing a wad of gum. In comparison to Randall, McClellan looked like a slob, his shirt too large for his lanky frame, bulging in awkward places and clearly unpressed. He was just along for the ride.

"Now's a, uh, bad time," Blake said, Joje leaning against the door beside him.

"I never caught your name last we met," Randall said, eyebrows raising.

"Biw," Joje said, following McClellan's lead by keeping his hands at his side. "Bwake's wife's bwahtho."

"We won't stay long," Randall said.

"Another night might be better," Blake said. "Next week maybe."

Randall glanced at his partner. "Well, it's not purely a social call."

"What do you mean?" Blake asked.

"Have a few questions for you, that's all, won't take but a minute."

"Okay if we talk outside? Wife has a migraine," Blake said.

They stepped aside to give Blake space. Joje stayed in the open doorway, arms folded, looking as uncasual as possible. Blake wobbled forward, all too aware of how weak he felt.

"Whoa, you all right?" Randall asked.

"Yeah, fine," Blake said.

"You were in an accident, right? The bruising on your face? Was that a car accident?" Randall asked.

Blake nodded, unsure if this was small talk or if the questioning had begun.

"When did you say that occurred, and do you recall the

location?"

Definitely being questioned.

"I'm sorry, you said you were here on business?" Blake asked.

"That's right," Randall said. "Where was that accident at?"

"Am I in trouble here?"

"Not at all," Randall said, his words as unconvincing as his stance. He was apparently still waiting for Blake to answer.

"Uh, it was just a stupid accident—no one else was involved, I . . ." Blake laughed awkwardly. "I sort of ran off the road late at night. Hit into a tree."

"You file a police report?"

"No, no, the car wasn't worth much. I was picking it up for my son, to start practicing."

"How old's your son?" Randall asked.

"Fourteen," Blake said.

"Is it in a shop? The car?" McClellan asked. His words were clipped, enunciated to a T. Blake wasn't sure if that was how he always spoke or if it was in response to his own babbling and Joje's speech impediment. Blake nodded. "We'd like to see the paperwork on it, if you don't mind."

"I can, yeah, I can certainly get that to you," Blake said.

"You wouldn't mind if Deputy McClellan snapped a few pictures of your bruising now, would you?" Randall asked.

Blake blinked, realizing for the first time the gangly cop held a small digital camera by the drawstrings at his side. "Is that normal protocol for an accident where no one's hurt? I'm not sure I understand what this is all about."

"Call your lawyer," Joje said. "Don't put up with this bullshit."

I can't afford my lawyer, Blake thought. Not anymore.

"No, no, he's not under arrest. We're just ruling out possibilities," Randall said.

"For what?" Blake asked.

"You've seen the squad cars across the street all day?" Randall asked.

"I've been inside mostly." Blake couldn't see any police cars.

"Just a few doors down and across the street," Randall said, pointing. And suddenly Blake knew—Tom Jones. His face, he realized too late, had probably given away much more than he should have. A change occurred in both officers' stance, though they hadn't moved. It was more an awareness, their muscles and bodies tensing, preparing for the unexpected. Blake wondered if he led them to the trunk in his garage how prepared they'd really be.

"When's the last time you saw your neighbor?" McClellan asked. So he would play the role of bad cop.

"We don't see anyone here. Neighborhood's like a ghost town," Blake said.

"Thomas Jones," McClellan continued as if Blake hadn't spoken. "Twenty-three Vanilla Banks. You two haven't met?"

Blake felt his face flush. Water dripped from his hair into his eyes. Or was that sweat? "No, I don't—I don't think so."

"You don't think so?" McClellan asked.

Blake glanced back inside his house, Joje standing silently in the doorway. "No, I haven't met any of the neighbors."

"Call your lawyer, Bwake, trust me on this one." Joje shifted his weight to the other side of the doorway.

McClellan turned to look at his partner. "Well, I'm a little confused."

Randall came to his partner's rescue. "We have a video of you and Mr. Jones having an . . . altercation . . . just outside his property. I believe you gave him the bird after he drove off?"

Of course they had that on video. Joje had said the attorney's surveillance was par none. Convenient editing on Joje's part.

"Oh, was that his name?" Blake asked. "And he lives on this street? I just, I thought he was visiting someone here, but yeah, we did meet, though I certainly wouldn't call the conversation heated."

"That's not how the driver remembered it," McClellan said.

"Is it against the law to flip someone off in Malibu?" Blake said, plastering a smile onto his face.

"No, of course not," Randall said. "Thomas Jones has gone missing."

This was the moment they had been waiting for, the crescendo of a rising classical piece of music, all of the dancing back and forth leading to one second, to get Blake's reaction.

While he knew they were watching him, looking for a tell that would give him away, Blake had absolutely no idea what reaction they'd perceive as being guilty. Shock? Indifference? Even without a reaction, Blake realized how guilty their entire conversation had made him appear.

A blue Ford Focus pulled to the curb of the house, a sign like a taxi driver's stuck to the top with "Delivery" on it in yellow.

Be grateful for small miracles, Blake thought. The screaming and double bass thump of death metal tumbling from the car distracted even the two officers.

"About time," Joje said loudly as the driver approached. He was husky, tattoos of topless girls lying with dragons on both of his sleeveless arms. His walk slowed significantly when he noticed the cops.

"Sixty-seven nineteen," he said. Joje took the two flat boxes from him. Dark patches of grease had soaked through the bottom box.

Joje scribbled on the receipt copy, and the kid quickly turned to leave. Halfway down the path he glanced back. "Nice tip. Thanks, man."

The interruption had clearly destroyed the momentum of the officers' rehearsed interrogation. Blake picked up where they had left off, hoping to bring it to a quick end. "Look, I don't know where my neighbor is. I don't know where he works, where he goes in his free time, or who he spends it with. Like I said, we barely spoke. He almost hit my dog, was a complete asshole, I flipped him off, will even plead guilty to doing so, but I haven't seen him since."

They waited on the porch as if trying to recall what their next lines were supposed to be. "Couldn't he have just gone on vacation?" Joje asked.

"Most people don't bleed out four to five liters of blood before going on vacation," McClellan said.

"Sorry to disturb you. Clearly you've got dinner waiting. Here's my card," Randall said, "in case you lost the first. You remember anything from the past few days, give us a buzz."

He started down the stone path with his partner. Almost as an afterthought he turned back, but Blake knew it was no afterthought. "How was that, uh, doctor I referred to you?"

"We never called him," Blake said.

Randall nodded slowly. "Strange, he had you on his books yesterday. His office assistant's a good friend. Guess I'll have drinks and a conversation with her a little later."

Blake nodded; not much else he could do. If Malibu was like the Old West as Randall had intoned on their first meeting, then Blake and his family were the unwelcome newcomers about to be driven out by the local sheriff and deputy. The more frightening realization was that should his family survive the week, by the time the police were ready to issue a warrant, Joje and his accomplice would be gone.

4

The pizza was cold and dripping with grease. There was only one parlor in the Palisades that would deliver this far out. For the price it should have tasted much better than it did.

The house had a peculiar stink to it now, an odor that sat heavy like a cloud about to burst that went much further than the gore the Ukrainian doctor had left behind. Plates of discarded food and open containers fell from the full sink onto the counters. Drew was surprisingly an okay cook; a housecleaner he was not, and whatever he opened or pulled from the fridge stayed there, growing interesting shades of mold. Even the fruit on the metal rack on the kitchen island was beginning to go bad. Add to that the smell of Jenna's legs, which equally stunk of rot, and the stench of Drew and Joje, which could have rivaled the most ostentatious homeless couple. Blake wasn't aware of either of them showering since their arrival, the pimples bubbling beneath Drew's oily face a sickly sight.

"Can I be excused?" Adam asked.

"Sure," Joje said before Blake could reply.

Adam skirted away from the table, his chair scraping against the floor. His plate with the five uneaten pizza crusts remained on the table. "I'm going upstairs," he called back.

"Take Dwew," Joje said. Drew grabbed the remaining slice in the box and left through the living room. "We wouldn't want another mess to clean up like the good doctor." He smiled conspiratorially.

Blake did not smile back.

"I'm joking, Bwake. If Adam really wanted to off himself, trust me, he'd be dead. He's a lot smarter than you give him credit for. Now while you were on your cleaning spree, I made a few calls in preparation for tonight."

"You're going through with this?" Jenna asked. She looked like a child sitting at the grown-ups' table, her wheelchair so much lower than the other chairs.

"I don't have a choice," Blake said.

"Just like you had no choice but to let the police leave while our kidnappers have free rein of the house?"

"You know what would have happened, Jenn, if I had tipped them off."

"But you don't know what's going to happen from you keeping your mouth shut," she said. Angry tears were forming at the corners of her eyes. "Sometimes I wonder whose side you're really on."

"Come on, that's ridiculous!" Blake couldn't keep his voice from rising. "I'm doing everything I can to keep you and Adam from getting hurt. Worse than you already are. It's not worth the risk."

"I guess I'm old-fashioned. I had always hoped our family was worth the risk. Any risk." Jenna pushed away from the table, her hands guiding the chair back.

"Jenna . . . ," Blake said, but she continued wheeling herself into the family room. He stood, chair knocking backward and ringing off the hardwood floor. He wasn't going to lose this fight, not this time, not by letting her walk away.

"What do you want me to do?" he yelled. "Not help get these files? Until Drew starts using that sword of his, hacking off fingers and limbs from you, me, *our son*? You and I both know that eventually I'd end up helping anyway. I'd have no choice. And say I had told the police, what do you think would've happened then? A gunfight in our living room? And let's just say one of those cops were sharper than they looked and shot Joje before he could respond, they come storming outside, and guess what. That blade, that decorative sword you and Deb hung on our wall, would be slipping against yours and Adam's throat before they'd have a chance to get off another shot. So tell me, Jenna, what am I doing wrong here? How am I not protecting my family by doing things I don't want to do? Tell me!"

He could hear her sobs, her chair facing away from him, toward their garage.

"What do you want me to do?" he asked, trying to soften his voice and failing.

"I want you to leave," she said. "Do whatever they want, just . . . if we get through this, the next few days, and they go like they said? *If* that happens, I want you to leave."

Blake had always wondered when their arguments would culminate in a request for divorce. He found the fight had gone out of him, words unable to repair the damage done. He stood behind her for some time, wanting to reach out, hold her, tell her he was trying—God, how he was trying. Instead he left her there in the family room. In that small way he could give her what she wanted.

Joje's smile was more pronounced than ever, a black spec between his front teeth from the pizza. "Thank you for opening yourselves up like that. That was fun to watch."

Blake pulled a beer from the pantry, knocking its top free on the rough-edged kitchen counter. He had always liked his beer warm. "You were saying? About tonight?"

"Right, we're gonna need some supwise."

"Surprise?"

"No, supwise . . . spehshowized equipment."

Supplies. Great.

"I know a guy," Joje continued, "but he only takes cash, so we need your money."

Blake waited for the punch line to the joke. "You have all my money."

"Cash, Bwake. The three grand you had stashed away? I don't know if it's enough, but it's worth a shot."

Blake couldn't remember telling Joje about any cash.

"You tried to buy me off, Bwake, remember? After you hit me with your car?"

"You hit me," Blake said.

Joje just smiled. "Let's go see that safe you told me about."

5

Blake rolled his desk chair toward the closet, climbing atop and balancing as the seat spun beneath him. Reaching up to the dial, he felt like he was having an out-of-body experience, that he was looking down on himself, ashamed at his own actions. This safe, it was the last part of his life Joje had yet to stick his filthy hands into. And now Blake was granting him access. Maybe Jenna wasn't so far off from the truth.

He turned the dials slowly. Sixteen–forty-two–eleven. The safe door popped open. Inside were stacks of bills wrapped in rubber bands—much more than three thousand—two manila envelopes bowed with the amount of contents they contained, a flash drive in a Ziploc bag, and two cartons of bullets next to his .38 Special. The Smith & Wesson's wooden handle was turned toward him, six-inch barrel pointed toward the back of the safe. He always kept it loaded.

I had always hoped our family was worth the risk.

Drew was upstairs with Adam. Would he hear the gunshot? Undoubtedly. And what would his reaction be with Blake's son at his side? And if something went wrong? If the gun misfired or, worse, he missed?

Blake felt that sharp ache behind his eyes again. He reached in, his palm knocking against the six-shooter, and grabbed a stack of bills. "Here," he said, tossing it down to Joje, who was sitting on the desk.

"Empty it," Joje said.

Twelve stacks, crisp hundred-dollar bills bending around the bands at their center as he handed them down. Each small stack contained one hundred bills, a hundred twenty grand in total. He had always kept cash on hand in case of an emergency, though real emergencies, he had come to learn, couldn't be solved with any amount of money.

"I never realized how much three thousand looks like," Joje said.

Blake grabbed the final two bundles. "A hundred and twenty thousand," he said.

Joje had the cash stacked neatly on Blake's desk, next to his wireless keyboard. "Don't you get tired of all the lies, Bwake? Three thousand . . . What else have you got in there?"

Breathing harder, the pain behind his eye like a needle plunging its way through his oracular orb, he wrapped his sweaty palm around the wood stock of the gun. It felt so solid in his hand, its weight balanced. He hadn't brought the gun out since he had put it in the safe, shortly before Adam was born. His first wife had hated guns, made him promise never to even show it to their then unborn son. It was a promise he had kept even after her death.

One of the few, he thought.

The gun hadn't been shot for over fifteen years, its last cleaning long before that. So many things could go wrong, would go wrong if he made a mistake.

"Bwake?"

He loosened his grip on the revolver and grabbed the two manila envelopes, dragging them along the bottom of the safe. "Here," he said.

Any risk.

Joje opened the first envelope, spilling its contents onto the desk and shuffling through them. It contained every legal document for Blake's holdings—rental properties in Park City, Utah, and Jackson Hole, Wyoming; a list of the corporations he had an interest in; stock certificates and trade ventures—it was all there, the final pieces of Blake's wealth.

"You'll sign these over to me," Joje said, "just as a precaution. After our week is through, it'll all be returned of course."

"Of course," Blake said.

Joje ripped into the second envelope, much thinner than the first. Out fell passports, social security cards, birth certificates, marriage and death certificates; the latter, documents Blake had never read. Joje took much longer with these, studying them, reading each one through. He rearranged them, setting a few side by side.

"Rachel Lynette Green. Your first wife? Pretty name."

Not when it was pronounced *Wachel Gween*. Blake felt the loss as if it had happened yesterday. Odd, he rarely thought of her these days, and yet having Joje go through these private moments, he felt more dismayed than the thought of signing over any of his holdings or stock.

These were locked here for a reason—memories and regrets no one had a right to peruse.

"Married January first, nineteen ninety-six. New Year's Day. Was that right after college?"

"During," Blake said, still standing on the roll-out chair. "My senior year."

"College sweethearts. Quite the commitment that young. So, married in ninety-six, four years later Adam Green Crochet is born, February nineteenth, the year double zero. Five pounds, three ounces. Small." Joje looked up as if it were a question.

"There were complications. He came early."

"More complications two and a half years later it seems. US standard certificate of death," Joje read. "Lot of boxes to be filled out. And there's your signature . . . did you pronounce or certify her death?"

Blake felt his jaw clenching.

"Cause of death: caowdiopulmanao-wee awest, ductal . . . How the hell do you pronounce that? Adeno . . .?"

"Pancreatic cancer," Blake said.

"They could have just written that. So let's see, your wife, to whom you were so in love you couldn't wait to finish college before marrying, dies . . . and six months later you remarry. Jenna Shurtleff. No middle name. I like that."

Joje turned another paper over, laying it beside the others. "No kids, no kids, and then after nine years, boom—a daughter. Evaline Stacy Crochet. Evaleen or Evalin?"

"Evalin," Blake said.

Joje held up two pieces of paper, shuffling them back and forth. "Birth and death certificates only two years apart. Life can be tragic."

The lump in Blake's throat was hard.

"You know I haven't seen a single picture of her in the whole house. Was there a fire? In your previous home? Were all your photos destroyed?"

Blake felt his hand tightening on the grip of the gun.

"Must be tough losing your wife and daughter, though you don't seem one to grieve long. Upgraded your wife after six months, how many days before you took down the photos of your little girl? What, did the dog take her place?"

I had always hoped our family was worth the risk.

"I guess in the end our lives are nothing more than dates and numbers on a sheet of paper," Joje said. "All that blank space on the page? The details of our lives between the numbers? No one remembers that. They're just locked up in some forgotten vault."

Any risk.

Blake closed his eyes, steeling himself for the moment to come. Just as he began pulling his hand from the safe, the hilt of the revolver pressed firmly in his grasp, he felt the cold steel of Joje's own gun against the nape of his neck.

Joje had been waiting for him.

"I had such high hopes for you, Bwake. Did you really think staying on that chair looked natural? Like you had nothing to hide? Open the cartridge and empty the chamber."

His hands trembling, Blake did as he was told, letting the six-shooter slide open, the bullets dropping and bouncing off the chair.

"I'm gonna need that gun." Joje extended one hand around the chair in front of Blake. It was gloved in the plastic bag the flash drive had been in.

Blake lowered the empty revolver, chamber still hanging to the side like a lifeless limb. At the last second, he whirled against the chair, the tall back whipping Joje in the side and slapping his hand away. Joje's gun went off right next to Blake's ear, the blast deafening. He fell from the chair, hitting into the closet on his way to the floor. The chair suddenly came reeling toward him, Blake barely able to bring his hands up in time to keep it from his head.

Joje stood where it had been, his face twitching. He set Blake's .38 on the desk with a loud clunk. "You, Bwake, are testing my patience."

He ran one arm against the desk, sweeping off its contents—the stacks of money, legal documents, clock, keyboard, and mouse all flying from the desk, crashing into the chairs and bookshelves carved into the wall. The rubber band on one of the wads of cash must have broken, hundred-dollar bills streaming outward and floating down like leaves in autumn.

"You're sitting on the bullets. Pick one up. Come on, Bwake, do it!" Joje ripped one of the drawers from his desk off its hinges, dumping the contents to the ground. Mini drives and DVDs spilled to the floor, scattering along with the assortment of pens, staplers, letter openers, and all the little knickknacks that collect at the bottom of desk drawers.

"Pick up a bullet!" The next drawer came out, this one full of files. Business plans and financials, the confidential information of industry leaders converged into a heap of stapled papers and opened folders.

Blake shifted slightly, picking up one of the copper-cased bullets that had rolled beneath his foot. He held it, his hand shaking so violently he could have had Parkinson's.

Joje tore out the contents of the small bureau in the corner, wires and cables, electronic gadgets and components, most of it junk that Blake had kept in case he needed it one day. The monitor on Blake's desk followed them to the floor.

"Go ahead, Bwake, load your gun!"

"No," Blake said.

Joje crossed to the other side of the desk, grabbing the gold-trimmed lamp and ripping it from the wall. He used it like a baseball bat, swatting at the bookcase, framed pictures, trophies, and artifacts tumbling from the shelves. One shelf broke, collapsing into the one below it, hardbound books, some rare editions, others signed with dedications to Blake, spilled from the shelf, a waterfall of turning pages.

"Put the bullet in the gun, Bwake!"

"No!" Blake shouted.

The US Civil Affairs challenge coin Blake had received from Major Blackledge with its display case flew across the room, shattering on the wall. The ceramic rooster Michiyoshi at Fujitsu had given him in Japan wobbled, now splintered and headless. Countless treasures, testaments of his accomplishments and triumphs, were discarded and destroyed, trampled on by Joje who callously walked back to Blake's desk, book bindings ripping and glass popping beneath his feet.

"Why? Why won't you load the gun, point it at my head, and pull the trigger? Why?"

"You'll kill me," Blake said. "And my family."

"I would," Joje said, looking at Blake like a wounded dog. "I will. If you don't get your act together."

Blake glanced behind Joje, wondering why Adam and Drew hadn't come in yet? The gunshot alone should have triggered a reaction, not to mention Joje's rampage of destruction.

But his office doors were closed. He remembered screaming at the top of his lungs as Adam stood just outside his doors only a few days ago. A few days that felt like a few years.

Joje snapped his fingers in front of Blake's face, dragging him from his reverie. "Are you going to be a problem tonight, Bwake?"

"No." No *pwobwum*.

"Are you going to try to escape? Or get help?"

"No," Blake said again. There was no *hewp*.

"Are you going to follow my orders with exactness?"

Blake's head hung. "Yes."

"Because if you don't?"

"You'll kill me and my family."

"Say it one more time," Joje said. "Like you mean it. What will happen if you disobey?"

Blake closed his eyes, wanting to believe that whimper was coming from someone else. "You'll kill me. And my family," he said.

"Such a fast learner," Joje said. "I'm glad we had this talk."

Chapter 7

Day Five Continued

1

A single police cruiser was parked halfway up Tom Jones's driveway, its rotating lights bathing the shadows in unwanted color. Where the gate normally stretched across that driveway, a line of police tape ran connecting black stone wall to black stone wall.

Blake wondered if the cops had finished inside and were there only to keep an eye on him and his family. Would they be following them tonight? Only a part of him hoped they might.

Joje drove Jenna's Escalade, and Adam sat in the back dressed in all black—pants, long-sleeve shirt, he even had a black beanie he was turning in his hands. Blake and Joje were both dressed similarly. Blake wore black gym pants and a dark zip-up sweatshirt with a hood. Joje had needed to borrow a set of clothes, though they hung much looser on him.

Dark streets and darker alleys shot past as Joje drove them to a part of LA Blake was unfamiliar with. The small houses they passed were painted in what once were bright colors, now dulled with time. Reds faded to swollen pinks, yellows rotting, violets tinged with black streaks as if it had recently rained tar. Bars lined the exterior of every window, rusted gates encircling yards, big signs warning of dogs or guns or gangs depending on the amount of graffiti.

East LA? Compton?

Blake supposed it could be a lot of neighborhoods in Los Angeles. The street signs floating past were as blurred as his thoughts. He was just grateful they weren't in his convertible.

He wondered if Joje had grown up in a similar neighborhood, the product a cesspool like this spits out. But Joje had risen above. He had taken the streets to those who thought they were immune, those unprepared to fight back—dirt for dirt, blood for blood, rule for rule.

A phone buzzed, vibrating in the cup holder. For a second Blake thought it was his shattered Cyborg, then recognized Jenna's jewel-encrusted case. Joje glanced at the screen, smiling. "They're ready for us."

"How are you keeping in touch with Drew if you have Jenna's phone?" Blake asked. "Your twenty-minute rule?"

"Some rules change."

After a few turns that put them into a section of town without streetlamps, they pulled into an abandoned gas station. Two rows of pumps were set like headstones in a cemetery, hoses and nozzles long removed. The small booth in the center of the station that should have conveniently stored candy, beef jerky sticks, beer, and soda was now inhabited with spiders, cockroaches, and rats. Its windows were covered in boards decorated with the sprayed ink of whatever gang had claimed the deserted relic, like dogs pissing on a tree, marking their territory.

In the back near a dumpster, a large white box truck with dark windows idled. Shadows clung to it, and Blake felt his mouth go dry.

"Stay cool," Joje said. Blake hadn't realized Joje was nervous as well. Maybe this was even outside his element.

They drove slowly ahead, stopping a few feet short of the truck that looked like a U-Haul that had been painted over. No front license plate, two indistinct men in the cab.

Blake felt himself tensing. "You know these guys?"

"These aren't the type of guys you know. They're the type you know of," Joje said.

He shut off the engine and climbed out, the ding of the open door bleating in Blake's ear. Which meant the keys were still in the ignition.

Blake didn't think, he leapt across the gap between the front seats, clawing at the driver's door. He slammed it shut, engaging the locks and turning the key. The engine purred quietly to life. Blake cranked the gear into reverse, tearing out from the gas station, leaving a bewildered Joje behind.

But no, he was still sitting in his seat, that every-other-second ding pounding through his head. Because it would go wrong.

He'd crash into the abandoned convenience store. The men in the truck would open fire, spreading his brains against the headrest. Joje would call Drew, and Jenna would be waiting for them back at home on their couch, headless.

Adam stood outside the car, looking through the driver's window. He held the black duffle bag Drew and Joje had brought with them, now stuffed with Blake's cash from the safe.

One of the men opened the passenger door of the cab and stood, looking out over the frame with what looked like an automatic rifle slung over one shoulder.

Blake stepped out. Though he closed the SUV's door, he still heard the ding.

Gloved hands assaulted him from behind, shoving him against the white truck. His son grunted as the man moved down the line, checking every pocket and crevice. The man wore a faded ball cap on his head, a thick brown beard tinged with random strokes of red draped over his shirt like a bib. Curls spilled from the sides of his hat, as greasy and dirty as the charcoal jumpsuit he had on.

"There's a gun in my back pocket," Joje said.

The man lifted the gun out and threw it onto the asphalt. "Take off your shoes."

Blake bent down.

"Stand up! Just kick 'em off."

Blake stood, his heart thrumming in his chest. He kicked his shoes free, squeezing his feet out. He thought he heard the truck's engine rev, though it could have been his imagination. The other gunman still stood above the open door, rifle trained down on them.

"Follow me," the man said.

They walked toward the back of the truck, loose rocks and torn asphalt pressing into the bottom of Blake's feet. The bearded man watched them with beady eyes buried beneath all that fur on his face. At the rear of the truck, he unhitched the lever, rear door climbing upward with a rattling roar. No light came on from within.

"Climb up, don't cross the yellow line."

Blake hoisted himself up then bent down, offering Adam a hand. Adam ignored it, scrambling up on his own, Joje following. They stood at the edge of the trailer's entrance, a barely visible line of paint running across the flooring in front of them. Beyond that line the floor went black, lost in shadows as dark as any cave. Blake thought he heard the slightest of sounds, a quiet shuffle, but that could have been anything in a truck whose engine still sputtered.

"Make up yo mind alweady!" Joje suddenly said.

A blue light pierced the darkness from the top of the back of the truck, blinding in its intensity. In that brief glimpse of light, Blake thought he saw a giant insect with huge, bulbous eyes toting what had to be an automatic rifle pointed at them. It was gone before he had time to process it.

An overhead dome light swelled. Blake felt his son grab onto his arm, then quickly let go.

In the center of the vehicle stood a man who looked like the actor from *The Fly* halfway through his metamorphosis. He wore a black mask that covered his face, with dark elongated eyes extending out, a green grated panel for a nose. Bands stuck out at odd angles with a shroud that draped over his shoulders and neck. He was dressed in black fatigues that made their own getups look like ninja-themed pajamas, the kind that go on clearance before Halloween.

The walls of the trailer were lined with high-caliber artillery, wide racks sporting guns so large they were probably meant to be mounted on vehicles. Bins were filled with actual rockets and grenades, other gadgets and weapons Blake could only guess at.

"Be glad it was the blue light," Joje said softly.

"Security stays," the bearded man said, hefting himself up. "No questions about the merch. If you don't know what it can do, you don't need it. If you don't know what you need, you've come to the wrong store."

"Fair enough," Joje said.

Bug Man quietly released the clasps from boots strapped into the floor of the trailer and withdrew to the corner. His gun never wavered from staying on them.

Joje went up and down the racks, pointing at certain bins, tubs, and weapons. The bearded man followed, nodding like a waiter mentally taking notes. It was over quickly. Blake didn't hear the negotiations, but Joje only took out two stacks of bills. Instead of handing the bearded man the two stacks, he handed him the bag.

"You clear our arrangement?" Joje asked.

The bearded man glanced at Blake then Adam, possibly looking for an interpretation. If Blake hadn't been spending so much time around Joje, even he might not have understood that last sentence. "We're good." The bearded man closed the roll-up door. "Be a few minutes."

They waited while Bug Man assembled their equipment. The night was oddly humid, Blake's shirt soaked through in sweat, clinging to the small of his back and chest. He tried to convince himself it was just the humidity.

"Think Mom's okay?" Adam asked.

"Let's hope so."

A loud clang sounded against the rolling door. Their escort undid the hatch, the door rising a mere foot and a half, their gear passing through. A hundred thousand dollars had just purchased a few clunky items zipped inside Joje's duffle bag, three milk jugs full of a clearish substance, and a red canister that looked like an undersized propane tank. Expensive store.

Joje grabbed the jugs. "Let's go." Adam grabbed the duffel, groaning at its weight.

"Let me help," Blake said, taking the bag by the other side while hefting the tank. As they turned to leave Blake caught a glimpse of Bug Man lying on the floor, goggle mask still in place, one bulging eye staring back at him.

The other was lost behind the rifle aimed at his head.

The rolling door crashed closed, Blake breathing a sigh of relief. These guys certainly didn't take chances.

Blake and Adam moved to the back of the SUV with the red canister and duffel bag. The back was popped open, milk jugs inside.

The soft crunch of gravel announced they weren't alone.

A thin older man with gray hair bunched into a ponytail stepped from behind the car next to Joje. His face was hard, wrinkles and lines earned from more than just the passage of time. He wore a tight leather jacket, his hands gloved as well, tapping a gun with a long, thick nozzle on it against his leg.

A silencer.

Blake swallowed hard. "Is there a problem?"

"You forgot yer shoes," the man said.

The bearded man appeared behind them, blocking their passage the way they had come. A shortened double-barrel shotgun extended out from his hip. He carried it low, like a head-banger guitarist plucking chords at his knees.

This was going to go badly.

"Look, we're not with him," Blake said.

The older man with the ponytail cocked his head. "We know." He stepped forward, gun barrel centered on Blake's head. "Don't do anything stupid. Your son's coming with us."

Blake barely felt his muscles tense before the shotgun slammed into the back of his knees from behind. He crumbled, hands scraping against the graveled pavement. He cried out, answered only by Adam. Shouting.

"No!" Blake yelled.

Ponytail pressed a syringe into Adam's neck, Blake's son going limp in the man's arms.

The bearded man locked the shotgun over Blake's head, pulling against his neck with enough force going after Adam was the furthest thing from his mind. Black spots swam across his vision, then he was shoved forward, forehead cracking against the bumper, before he fell back to the loosely paved floor.

Ponytail was already gone, Adam's shouting silenced.

Blake spun, his arm flying out to disarm the bearded man, but he wasn't there. Joje watched as Blake rushed to the other side of the SUV, no sign of his son. He ran, covering the distance of the Escalade in seconds, his socks sliding as he fought for purchase on the gravel beneath him.

He heard the driver's door to the truck rattle closed just as he came around the SUV. At the rear of the truck, Bug Man stood, bulb eyes staring at Blake. Adam was now flung over Bug Man's shoulder. His son wasn't moving, a child who had fallen asleep in his father's arms.

Bug Man gave the slightest of nods, then disappeared around the back. Before Blake had begun to move, the truck lurched forward, Blake's feeble screams doing nothing to halt its progress. The cab of the truck was already past when Blake began to run, forcing his legs to move despite the flare of pain. His arms pumped in a full sprint, each second bringing him farther along the truck's side. He was gaining—and then he felt his foot slide out from beneath him, the gristle and gravel carrying his shoeless feet forward but not up.

He went down hard, skipping across the pavement. In the seconds it took for him to recover and regain his feet, the truck was already jostling between the deserted gas pumps, approaching the street. The rolling door in back was closed.

Blake had a clear mental image of Bug Man hanging upside down from the truck in a cocoon-like web while Adam bounced back and forth into sharp racks and cages in the dark.

At the gas station's entrance, the truck didn't slow as Blake had expected but pulled straight out, making a sharp turn, its rear wheels falling over the high curb and sending the trailer into one last bounce before accelerating down the dark road.

Blake stopped at the curb, bending over to catch his breath. Every heartbeat was a kick to the groin, every inhalation a dagger in both ears. A headache so powerful came on he thought he might vomit.

He did. Retching so hard he felt he had coughed out the inner lining of his throat.

A pair of headlights approached from down the street. Maybe Blake could wave them over. Given his condition he wasn't sure who would stop for him, but he never got that far. The Escalade pulled up beside him, window rolling down.

"Get in," Joje said.

Blake stared at the vomit on the ground as if the chunks and spoiled texture could divine him his future. If it could, it certainly wasn't bright.

He opened the passenger door and climbed into the SUV.

2

Sweat dripped down Jenna's face, her exertion rivaling any of her normal workouts. She tensed her abdomen, lifting herself backward up another stair. The movement was slow, strained.

How many seconds did she have?

Blake had left without a word before she had a chance to apologize. Before she could beg him not to go. Before she could tell him to take her with him, take her anywhere but here. Alone. With Drew.

Her palms flattened against the back of the next step as she slid her body upward, the distance of one stair as far as a marathon. Her legs clacked below her, and she prayed she wouldn't pass out.

Drew's words came back to her: "Time for a little game of hide-and-seek."

And she was the one hiding.

Her wheelchair lay on its side beneath the chandelier, front door thrown open. If she could convince him she had fled outside, it might buy her a few more seconds.

Seconds were all she had.

She rose another step, legs sliding like deadweight beneath her. *If Blake had only left me with that corkscrew*, she thought bitterly.

A part of her knew it would have gotten her killed, the other part argued that dying was a better alternative.

Drew's voice boomed from the kitchen. "Ready or not, here I come!"

Jenna flipped over, her knees and the front of her legs scraping against the offset wooden stairs as she clawed her way up at a faster pace. It felt like being skinned alive. She reached the top, pulling herself forward until she lay prostrate against the hard floor.

No time to rest, no time!

Her body trembled as she inched forward, head sliding against the floor. He was coming. Her seconds were up.

3

Blake felt hollow, a Russian nesting doll that was nothing more than the outer shell. Pop that sucker open and gone were the wife and child, dog and baby that should have been layered within. He stared out the passenger window unaware of the passing landscape. All he saw was his gaunt and haunted face, empty eyes searching for a will to go on.

The clock on the dash read 12:23. He thought of congratulating himself on making it another day but knew there was nothing to celebrate. Despite having slept late, Blake felt destroyed, the weariness crawling through every cell of his body.

"Your shoes are in the back," Joje said.

It was the first thing either of them had said since Blake had gotten in the car, at least a half hour. Blake couldn't form a reply; he had nothing left to say. Not to Joje.

"You gave me no choice, you know. All this time together and I still don't know if I can trust you."

Blake continued staring out at the dark night.

"Adam will be fine, you don't need to worry. He's just a little insurance to make sure you do your part tonight."

Constricted city blocks and houses with no yards gave way to older homes with open fields of grass and weeds. Foreclosure signs replaced the "Beware of Dog" placards, street lights growing farther and farther apart. Blake had never been to Lancaster before. Now he knew why. The city reminded him of a child trying so hard to get his parents attention that once earned, the child realized he had nothing to show or say.

The soft cackle from the radio was turned so low no song could be distinguished.

"Bwake, you with me, buddy?" Joje asked after another prolonged silence.

"I'm not your buddy," Blake said.

"There you are," Joje said with a smile.

"You took my son," Blake said, each word coming with a forceful current of air. "Why would I ever help you now?"

"Temporarily, Bwake, just temporarily. Focus on what we're here to accomplish, and you'll see him in the morning. Have I ever lied to you?"

They continued in silence, Blake's guilt offering an abundance of inner dialogue. Houses were replaced by an industrial track with winding roads, large buildings appearing at every turn. At the bottom of a hill, they came to a large warehouse, a bland brick-and-mortar building indistinguishable from the others in the area except for the company's logo splashed across the top.

Symbio.

The name had been a play on the symbiotic relationship between artificial intelligence and the consumers who would end up using it, an almost malicious joke. The data contained in this warehouse was more valuable than any of Blake's possessions. In some ways he had always known this would be the real target in Joje's project. It had never been about his family—Joje wanted what was in these walls.

They drove over the curb and grass to avoid the large yellow bars that gated the driveway's entrance. Not much of a security deterrent. Joje circled around the back to a loading dock where three large roll-up doors were secured. Not a single car in the lot, not at this hour.

"What are we really here for?" Blake asked. "What are you after? What is it you want?"

Joje appeared baffled. "I'm here for you. To help you save your family. Now let's make this quick. Your boy cut surveillance at midnight?"

"Eleven, I think."

Joje pulled a black ski mask over his face, stretching it out. Only his eyes and mouth appeared beneath the lined wool. He didn't offer one to Blake. They met at the rear of the SUV.

Joje dug through the opened duffel bag while Blake slid his shoes on. From the bag Joje removed a short metal contraption half the size of a baseball bat with metal prongs springing from one end like a claw.

"Remember, your son's depending on you right now. For once, be the hero. Keep the rules and save your son."

Blake nodded absently.

Joje shoved the duffel bag into Blake's chest. As they climbed the stairs to the loading dock, he pointed to the camera above the door. "Better hope your boy isn't setting you up."

Blake stared at the security camera, wishing there were a person on the other side, watching them. The camera failed to track their movement as they passed beneath.

Joje approached the door with a confidence Blake didn't understand. Roles certainly had reversed from the last time they had entered a building owned by Symbio. The metal wand Joje carried fit snuggly around the handle of the door, those claws cinching closed around it. There was a mechanic whir, followed by a clicking sound.

Joje manipulated the wand, the metal rungs turning while the rod remained still. More clicks, like metal gears notching into place. After a minute or two, there was a loud pop followed by the wand disengaging from the handle of the door.

The doorknob fell to the ground, clattering at Joje's feet. He tapped against the remaining bracket where the handle had been with an outstretched finger—it plopped out, falling on the inside of the building.

"Voilà," Joje said, though with his lisp it came out "*Wa-la.*" He reached his hand into the hole and pulled the door open. He slid the wand against the door to hold it in place.

Blake grabbed Joje by the shoulder. "Where did they take him? Adam?"

Joje shrugged his hand off. "Even if I knew do you think I would tell you? You're only chance of seeing him again is to destroy these files. I'm doing this for you!"

"That's not good enough!" Blake yelled back. "I need to know he's safe!"

Before Joje could respond, a piercing wail erupted from just inside the building. Joje cringed, and Blake's own hands instinctively rose to his ears.

"Take this," Joje said, leaning into Blake's ear and pushing something into his hand.

A gun—Blake's gun.

Before Joje could enter the building, Blake discharged the gun, emptying the clip into his kidnapper's back. The staccato firing of round after round synced with Blake's pounding heart, rational thought swept beneath the siren's cacophonous noise.

Joje fell to the cement floor, but his body disappeared. Only his clothing remained in the wrinkled outline of a body.

He really is a phantom, Blake thought. A ghost. A demon.

"Bwakey? You with me?"

Joje stood at the door, looking back at him with concern. Blake wiped at his eyes with the back of a hand. Wavering in his outstretched hand was a flashlight pointed at Joje's back.

"I'm good," he said.

"Bring the bag."

Blake followed Joje into the warehouse.

4

The loading dock was a small area closed in by double doors still swinging from Joje's passage. Blake continued past into a small hallway. A blinking red dot swept outward from the end of the hall in time with the deafening alarm.

Blake's thoughts turned to Adam. He wondered where his son was right now. Were they still driving? Had they arrived to whatever hell they would lock him in? He pictured Adam chained in a dark room, frightened, possibly even hurt. No food, no water, his captors waiting for a call that would only come if he did what Joje required.

It's all a game, Blake thought, to see how far I'm willing to go.

Pressing his back into the door at the end of the hall, he stepped into what could have passed as the interior of a spaceship. The room was colossal—ceilings extending forty feet or higher, the length of the warehouse going back the distance of a football field. Rows of black towers with tiny LED lights aglow were stationed throughout the room like the monuments of some superior and future race. Sharp blues, reds, and oranges, winking at him, sharing their secrets. It was incredible the amount of equipment that went into making an end user's experience on the cloud seem a thing of ease.

Joje was halfway down one of the aisles, motioning for him to hurry. For once Blake had no problem following orders. As he rounded the corner of a server tower, he found Joje standing before a column extending to the ceiling. Blake scanned the room, noting a total of six similar pillars. They coalesced toward the center of the roof, arching outward with giant support beams. Joje wasn't planning on destroying the servers, Blake realized; he was going to bring down the entire building.

Joje grabbed the bag, rummaging through it and pulling out something wrapped in cellophane. He set it down, removing a spool of wire and handing it to Blake. "Run this to the car, then bring the red tank back with you. Try not to get any kinks in it?"

Blake uncoiled the spool as he went, his mind slowly unraveling with it. If they made it out of this alive, he didn't know what to expect. There was no way they'd avoid prosecution; at least Blake wouldn't. The bodies of his neighbor and Dr. Cheverou he might be able to lay at Joje's feet, but being under coercion wouldn't excuse his actions right now in any court of law.

The alarm was beginning to sound like the maniacal laugh in that Pink Floyd song; he couldn't remember the name, but he knew it was on *The Dark Side of the Moon*. He made it past the double doors and into the loading area when the wire ran out. He was still twenty, maybe thirty feet from the SUV.

Blake moved back through the hall and into the warehouse, spotting Joje at another column.

"Where's the tank?" Joje asked.

"Wire's too short—it won't reach."

"Shit!" Joje looked around as if a solution might be hanging from one of the server towers. "Did you bring the tank?"

It was Blake's turn to look around blankly.

"We're running out of time! Do you want to get caught? Go get it!"

This time Blake ran. Outside he opened the back of the SUV, hefting the tank out and closing the rear door. Black block letters ran across the side of the small red tank. Though Blake had no idea what it meant, he knew what it spelled. Disaster.

The faint yet unmistakable sound of sirens pushed through in the distance. Their window of opportunity was about to come to a suffocating close.

Blake carried the tank up the outer steps and into the loading area. Out of the corner of his eye, he almost thought he saw the mounted camera swivel toward him. Through the double doors and down the dark hall, he pushed through the door into the warehouse.

Joje stood directly in front of him. "Someone's here."

"I heard sirens—"

"No, inside the building. This gas should ignite at the slightest spark, will that be enough?" He pointed to the servers.

"The towers?"

"All those components, that electricity?"

"I . . . I have no idea," Blake said.

"Start at the far pillar, break the seal, crank that valve, then run that tank between the other two pillars on your way back. Then get your ass out to the car."

Blake's hesitation was more than visible.

"Just think of your son. I have faith in you."

"What about whoever's in here?"

"Run fast." Joje patted him on the shoulder, the door closing behind him.

A second alarm seemed to go off in Blake's head. Joje was going to leave him. Blake would walk out, the building crumbling behind him, to a squad of cop cars and guns pointed at his head. Just a disgruntled ex-employee exacting revenge on the company that had recently let him go. Guilty as charged.

He stared out at the dark warehouse floor, wishing he could simply wait and turn himself in, ending this nightmare in at least some fashion. Instead, with the tank clanking against his leg, he took the first step forward into a world where he would be the villain.

5

The truck finally shuddered to a stop, a giant beast resting its head on the ground after an arduous journey. Adam could almost feel the walls of the trailer breathing in and out, the final vibrations and groans of machinery settling. While everything around him was cooling down, his body's temperature spiked, the rhythmic pulsing of his heart going into overdrive.

The trip had been long—too long for him to follow the twists and turns of their course. It pissed him off that Joje was once again using him as the object lesson for Blake's mistakes. The vendetta Joje carried against his father had become personal. Adam wished he understood the motivation behind it; with that knowledge he might finally get a peek into the workings of Joje's mind. After all, understanding someone was the first step in learning to control them.

The darkness in the trailer was absolute. Adam released his grip from the metal rack attached to the wall and pondered how much longer he had to live. Just yesterday he had been ready to walk into that ocean without looking back; now he had returned to plotting, manipulating, *living*.

As he stepped away from the rack, one arm blindly reaching in front of him, his foot collided with the body on the ground.

There you are.

He bent down, hand out, a finger pressing into the fallen man's nostril and quickly pulling back. Still not moving. That was a good sign. He hoped.

The guy's helmet with night-vision goggles had fallen loose during their scuffle, the only reason Adam was standing while the other guy was on the ground. He had expected Adam to be frightened, docile, willing to please. But Adam wasn't any of those things.

His father would have let himself be tied up, counting on his cooperation to buy him rapport for good behavior. Joje, on the other hand, would have slipped the noose from around his own neck into doleful strings, his captors quickly becoming marionettes to dance at his beck and call.

Who would Adam emulate? Who was he most like?

The question hadn't been difficult, and the body—unconscious only because Adam hadn't dared fire a weapon with the amount of explosives in here—was the only proof he needed.

The truck doors slammed closed outside. His nerves were racing—these were the moments he really felt alive. Hundreds of scenarios played before him, projected onto a gridded chessboard. Thousands of possibilities. So many weapons at his disposal.

Hell of a place to keep a prisoner, he thought.

Light sprang into the back of the truck as the door rolled upward, causing Adam to squint. Two silhouetted men, black phantoms of shadow, loomed before him. And as was often the case, Adam found himself embracing the most unlikely of moves, pulling strings he hadn't known were there.

"Please, help me!" He curled up into the fetal position, dropping to the bed of the truck and holding his arms over his face.

"Milt? Milton!" one of the men outside called.

"What the hell happened?"

Sobs came, on cue.

"Neither of 'em were strapped in, coulda hit his head."

"Please don't kill me," Adam said. "I don't want to die!"

"You think he did something to him?"

"He's a kid."

Adam smiled, hidden behind his raised arms.

6

Slithering along the rug that stretched across the upstairs hall, Jenna paused as the front door slammed. It seemed to send vibrations down the length of her body. She wouldn't have time to make it to her bedroom. Up on her elbows she clawed her way to the guest bedroom, almost shutting the door and pressing the button inward on the flimsy lock.

Better to make him think I'm not here, she thought, leaving the door cracked. The stone Buddha in the corner may have been facing the bed, but it felt like the statue was making sidelong glances in her direction.

Halfway to the bed something roared from outside. It sounded like the ocean had broken through the walls of their home; a head-on collision with two cars made of glass. Thunder, tinkling crystal, and shattering glass echoed down the hall on a continuous loop, its noise refusing to end.

After what felt like minutes, the rattle of glass and crystal, chains and light bulbs, came to a settled silence. Their chandelier now lay in pieces on the wooden floor of their foyer.

Jenna ducked her head, barely squeezing beneath the rail of the bed, its uneven bamboo reeds scratching at her face and back like fingernails as she pulled herself beneath.

More noise broke from down the hall, filled with anger and immediacy. Furniture breaking, trinkets falling, objects being hurled at walls.

"You're not behind the bookcase," Drew announced from the hall.

She heard the glass from a picture frame shatter, something hard thudding against a wall.

"Not in your son's room," he shouted. Jenna heard the door to the Jack and Jill bathroom open from Adam's end, the clutter of colognes and lotions, candles and pebbles on display racks being swept to the tiled floor. "Not on the toilet or shower."

The door flung open to the guest room from the bathroom. Jenna kept her breathing slow, though she could do nothing about the pounding in her chest. She had positioned herself with her head at the end of the bed so she could watch him come for her, know when he was in the room.

Drew's boots stepped farther in, the rubber soles worn, frayed strings dangling from their sides. She saw the tip of the sword dip in and out of view, heard him swinging it like a cane or umbrella. She had nothing—nothing she could use to stop him from finding her or stop him when he did. He walked along the edge of the room, the sword rising above her view. He swatted at the wall hangings, the matted Japanese symbols hitting the ground, frames breaking, slashes making them more indecipherable than they already were. A wooden chest was thrown over, its hinges snapping, its top resting at an angle that would never close again. Wooden spools and balls of different sizes tumbled from its depths. Drew made sure to step on each one, the intricately carved and formed wood pieces cracking and popping beneath his heavy feet.

"Not hiding in the chest. On guard," he shouted, jumping forward and slashing at the screen partition next to the bed. Fabric pieces fell like confetti. Overturning it he moved on, dragging the blade against the wall, that grinding sound causing the fillings in Jenna's teeth to ache.

No more, she thought. He knows I'm here.

She opened her mouth to give herself up when she felt the mattress above her sink down as Drew jumped onto the bed. It bowed, boards creaking, the curved mattress almost touching her.

"This bed is crap," Drew said. "No wonder she wanted us sleeping here."

She heard the sword swish through the air, its whine stopped by a muffled catch at the end. Again and again, he swung, feathers falling over both sides of the bed. Pillows came next, thrown to the corners of the room in pieces, fluff flying out with them. The weight from the bed raised then plunged down, Drew jumping as if he were a child, and then with a large jump the blade sank through, nicking her right shoulder as it slid off. She didn't dare move; he would hear her if she did. It came again, this time far from where she lay. She felt his weight come down toward the top of the bed once, twice. And then the sword slid down from above, an inch from her face, every muscle in her control going taut. With a final bounce Drew jumped from the bed back to the floor.

"Not in the guest room," he shouted loudly, slapping the side of the blade against the stone Buddha's belly. "For good luck," he said before exiting back into the hall.

She heard the crashing of the projector and other equipment from the theater room across the hall. Still her body refused to relax, as if she were clinging to the side of a building twelve stories up instead of resting beneath a bed on the floor.

The bedroom door crashed back open with a bang. Jenna barely kept herself from screaming. Drew was breathing hard, the exertion of his activities apparent.

"You're not there, are you?"

He dropped to the floor a few feet from the bed, his head parallel to hers. "Hi."

Jenna closed her eyes, feeling the tears leak down the contours of her face.

"You're like a rat. Squeeze through anything," he said. "Let's see what can squeeze into you."

His hands came reaching for her, barely fitting beneath the bed siding. As he began pulling her out, her head knocking into the rail, she realized she didn't even have another scream to summon.

7

Blake darted between obelisks of electronics, thick weaves of braided cables waiting to ensnare him at every turn. He arrived at the far column of the building without seeing anyone, immediately finding Joje's handiwork. A pale, thick paste had been carelessly slopped onto the column, small tubes peeking through, cemented against the plaster. Two wires descended from the tubes, connecting on the floor into the cable Blake had unrolled earlier.

Blake had no idea how plastic explosives worked, but he had a pretty good idea he didn't want to be here when they went off. The column of the building stood about three feet away from the nearest server tower. How long would it take the gas to disseminate enough to catch the electricity from these machines?

If it caught at all.

A rattle of something bumping into a nearby tower brought him back to the moment at hand. They were closing in. Whoever *they* were.

He broke the seal around the canister's turn handle and with a last inhalation of unpolluted air twisted the dial until he heard the soft sssssisp of gas spitting from the nozzle. No turning back now.

He pointed the nozzle toward Joje's masterpiece, the weight of the tubes held in the pale plaster already starting to pull from the wall. Hopefully, they'd hold long enough. As the plaster started dripping from the spray of gas, he ran, dodging server towers through the diagonal path toward the second column. How long did he have? And would Joje let his family go if he didn't make it out alive?

The building column surprised Blake, arriving around a turn when he had thought he still had another few to go. The tubes on this column had already pulled free and were lying on the floor. Blake turned the nozzle on the tubes, dousing them in the spray of air. Tiny droplets of moisture percolated on the tubes. It would have to be enough.

Darting back in a nearly opposite diagonal angle toward the last column and his eventual exit, he rounded the corner of a blinking tower, colliding into one of his pursuers. The tank released from his grasp, clanging down the aisle as they both went down in a flurry of motion. Blake rolled to his side, bringing up the flashlight. He looked into the wide eyes of a gaunt-faced youth, the stubble on his face like the patchwork of wild weeds, without design. He wore a light ball cap pulled low onto his head with a matching jumpsuit—at least in the amount of stains they both had.

A janitor. The bucket of slop had spilled on the floor, a mop entangled between the kid's legs.

"Get out!" Blake yelled, rising to his feet and recovering the canister. "Go! Now!"

The kid stared at him blankly. Blake half expected a long line of drool to drip from his open mouth. "Go! Get out! The building is going to blow!"

His threat, or really his attempt to help, was lost behind a flash of light and heat that Blake had only ever experienced when sitting in the front row of a big-staged magic show. The room was no longer dark. From the rear of the warehouse, where Blake had come from, an intense light swarmed like a sun lifting above the horizon. The gas had ignited. It would follow the currents in the air much like a trail of gasoline on the ground until it reached its source: the canister in the aisle.

The wide-eyed youth hadn't moved. Blake looked into his uncomprehending eyes, turned, and ran.

The entire room was now aglow, the cry of the alarm lost behind the gaseous explosions behind him. It was like a pyrotechnics show gone horribly wrong, each blast of combustible air multiplying, setting off the charges next to it.

Blake could feel the oxygen being pulled from the room, his chest tightening, his clothing becoming damp against his body. He changed his trajectory to the outer door.

He slammed it, throwing the door wide. Flames leapt above his head into the open corridor in a scorching fireball, rushing and consuming the oxygen in the fresh room. Blake dropped to the floor, sure he would be aflame. To his surprise only his hand had caught fire—the hand that had held the nozzle of the tank. Unnatural blue flames flickered behind the orange glow covering his right hand like a glove.

Stumbling to his feet and keeping his head low, he ran toward the end of the corridor. He pulled his sweatshirt over his head, wrapping his hand in it and squelching the flames. He burst into the loading area at the rear of the building, no fireballs following him out. His run was now the staunch gait of an injured animal, kept in motion only by the instinct to survive.

As Blake poured out from the back door, he expected Joje to be gone, was almost certain he would be. This was a suicide mission, a sacrificial offering to an orange-haired devil in exchange for the life of Blake's son. Not a rule for a rule, but a soul for a soul.

To his surprise the Escalade was there, idling in the loading dock. A cry escaped from Blake that sounded almost like a laugh. He ran the final steps across the dock, ignoring the stairs, and hurtled onto the top of the Escalade's roof. He gripped the bike rail with his good hand as he tapped the top of the roof with a furious thump. The SUV leapt backward, and Blake barely managed to keep from toppling off.

They shot across the rear parking lot until the Escalade came to an abrupt stop. Blake rolled backward over the roof, his body spilling onto the pavement in a drop that left him mostly breathless. Police sirens were no longer in the distance, they were coming at Blake from every direction.

Surrounded.

"Bwake, you do it?" Joje asked, leaning out the driver's window.

Blake sat up, looking for the cruisers that should have been closing in. Through the far, shaded gate he could see siren lights whirling. He made out the shape of at least three cop cars.

They had gone to the wrong building?

Confused, Blake moved to the door behind Joje, opening it and climbing into the backseat. He lay across it, looking up at the ceiling.

He closed his eyes. He didn't want to see this next part.

"Did it work?" Joje asked.

Blake held up his quivering hand. The outer layer of skin had completely melted away, leaving a mucous-like membrane covering the pulsing pink-and-burned flesh beneath.

"You weren't supposed to light yourself," Joje said.

"There's a janitor . . . inside," Blake said. "Just a kid . . ."

The car was moving, the motion lolling Blake further into darkness.

"Dumbass just doing his job, huh?" Joje said.

Before Blake could answer, his thoughts were lost in the sheer force of the explosion behind them. It felt like the world was caving in, the car caught in a whirlwind like Dorothy's crippled house. Windows shattered, a violent gale rocking them back, tires screeching at the unexpected thrust. And suddenly the explosion doubled, tripled in size—a nuclear detonation, the fiery glow coursing into the vehicle a preview of hell.

Joje laughed, the cackle of a psychopath, as their vehicle increased its speed. Blake glimpsed out the shattered passenger window at the building hidden behind a rumbling thunderstorm of black clouds. The sight was more impressive than he could have imagined, in the most disturbing of ways. Within that churning smoke, another blast ignited, house-sized chunks of concrete and rubble spewing out as if a volcano had erupted.

And somewhere in that building was the body of a stubble-faced youth who had probably been working for eight bucks an hour. Blake could almost see the janitor's face, still unable to make a sound. The janitor and building weren't the only things burning back there—a part of Blake's humanity had been torched, a piece of his psyche that he would never get back.

Because this murder—this death—was on him.

He let his head fall back to the seat of the car. Joje would take him wherever he intended to, Blake only knew where that road wouldn't   lead: redemption.

Chapter 8

Day Six

1

Sunlight leaked through the edges of boarded-up windows, scuttling beneath the wide gap at the bottom of the door. A flurry of moths and mosquitos bounced in the air, the occasional wanderer causing Adam to slap at his own face or arms. Bites covered his exposed flesh, the only really bothersome one at the corner of his lower lip like a pimple, causing his lip to hang slightly down.

If he could figure out how to twitch his left eye, he might really look like Joje.

With the light creeping into the otherwise dark storage shed, Adam could finally make out some of the objects he had lain against. Sealed wooden crates were stacked to the ceiling along the walls of the shed, covered in dust as thick as sand. The wing of a small airplane skewered through the boxes, its end terminating in dangling cables and bent jagged metal like a limb that had been torn free. Discarded seats from a car and other pieces of machinery and rusty antiques that looked almost petrified in their disuse lay in heaps, a large metal chain coiled on top, flakes of red rust shedding like a second skin. Cobwebs, broken light bulbs, and an abandoned water heater so full of holes it had clearly served its life sentence as target practice.

There wasn't a lot he could use here, but he also had the feeling he wouldn't need to. Joje was showing off to his father, strutting his feathers in a display that had little to do with Adam.

And if I'm wrong?

Footsteps approached from outside, the soft crunch against trodden dirt. Adam remained quiet, listening to a padlock disengage. Blinding light rushed in as the metal door flung wide. Adam's eyes were accosted at the sudden change. When they had partially adjusted, he saw one of the men standing before him, the one with the thick beard.

"If you want breakfast, follow me."

Adam fell in step behind the man. It was impossible not to notice their surroundings, but he tried his best not to look like he was noticing. The property was huge—Adam couldn't see a fence or wall, and the abundance of trees and smell of juniper reminded him of their home in West Virginia. The ground was covered with dried leaves, needles, and bullet casings, as if they too fell from the surrounding trees.. The cabin they walked toward was certainly no luxury rent-by-the-week model and had the look of a house that held the stories of generations within its walls.

They passed a well covered with wooden planks and continued toward the cabin entrance, or exit, considering they were entering through the back. The smell of fried meat and potatoes brought moisture to Adam's mouth.

"This way," the guy with the beard said. He wore a beanie today with flaps that hung down around his ears, knotted cords dangling beneath. A flannel shirt and jeans that certainly could have stood on their own.

The kitchen was small and quaint, a gas stove, washtub sink, tiled dark blue counters with a swirly cream-colored pattern none of these men would have picked out. The grout between them was a dark encrusted black. Adam recognized the older lanky gentleman at the table as the one who had driven their arsenal on wheels, the one who had taken him at first. He was halfway through his plate, steam still rising from every forkful.

"That's Gary," the bearded man said pointing to the gray-haired man with the ponytail. "I'm Stu. The one you hit over the head is Milton."

Adam thought better than to apologize. Hopefully, they would take his actions as a normal response to being kidnapped and instead harass Milton for letting a kid get the better of him.

He loaded a red plastic plate up with the stringy meat-and-potato concoction out of the pot on the stove. "So what's the plan? How long will I be here?"

"I told you I like this kid," Stu said.

Gary grunted. "We ain't no babysitters, so stay outta the way."

Adam nodded, sliding onto the bench across from Gary. "How well do you know Joje? Or George, I guess."

Gary held his fork halfway to his mouth. "An' don' talk."

Adam continued, feeling emboldened. "He's putting you in a lot of jeopardy right now. It's obvious you're not kidnappers. So what, you sell illegal arms—not like people wouldn't get them somewhere else—but why do this? You owe him a favor? Is it the money?"

Stu pulled up a tall stump to the table that had been carved into a seat, a grin spreading across his face.

Gary shoved his plate back into the center of the table and stood. "Put him back in the shed when he's done. I don' need more bullshit." After walking from the room, he came back to retrieve his plate and fork, carrying the food out with him. "An' wipe that damn smirk off your face," he shouted back.

Stu burst into laughter.

2

Blake took the stairs with a cautious limp, clinging to the railing with his left hand. His other hand was brought in close to his center, as if he expected an attack at any second and needed to protect it. It shook like a metronome on its fastest setting, the flesh wet and red, raw hamburger or chewed meat. How Jenna had managed the pain for so long was beyond him, though he was certainly looking forward to uncapping one of her pill bottles and swallowing them dry.

Joje stood at the bottom of the steps, and the comical idea of him tapping his toes sprang to mind. The dead-eye look on his face kept Blake from laughing.

They had to clamber over the blockade in the foyer to get to the front door. Blake looked up at the remaining end of chain still dangling from the ceiling. Crystal and glass cracked beneath their every step. They opened the front door just as the chimes rung a second time.

Jing Jong.

The sound of death.

It wasn't the police as Blake had thought. Officer McClellan and his gangly partner were out doing what they did best—protecting the residents of Malibu from Looky Lous and purveyors of celebrity maps. Instead, it was a delivery guy. Two of them actually.

"Shouldn't you have been here yesterday?" Joje asked. "Twenty-four hour delivery?"

"You want it or not," one of the men said.

It took several minutes to clear a way through the front room, several more to come up with a story about the chandelier. Joje joked that they were doing a reproduction of *The Phantom of the Opera*.

They wheeled the ginormous screen encased in cardboard and plastic into the family room, the wheels catching on the groove from Drew's sword in the hall. They were professional and courteous, accepting waters when asked, mounting the screen where the previous one had been and even configuring Blake's electronics and remotes to the new TV. One of them had tattoos stretching down below his rolled-up sleeves all the way to his wrists. Had the sleeves not been rolled up, no one would ever know his body was covered in ink.

We all hide who we really are from each other, Blake thought.

As the one with tattoos showed Blake the functions on the new remote, his gum doing little to hide the bitter aroma of cigarettes from his breath, Blake noticed the scene being displayed. Channel Seven News on the bottom of the screen, an aerial shot taking up the wide expanse of eighty-five inches above it.

The picture was of the remnants of the warehouse they had destroyed last night.

Pieces of the building had spread in a quarter-mile radius; debris, concrete, and the charred remains of server-related equipment looked like the fallen corpses of a robot war. The scroll at the bottom of the screen read, "Two deaths reported in bombing of tech firm's storage facility. Police citing a 'deliberate act of terror.'"

The camera switched to a different location, outside the glass building of Symbio's headquarters in Westlake Village, their logo brightly lit. JT walked from the parking lot to the front of the building, a swarm of media around him. He spoke rapidly into a microphone, distracted and in a hurry.

"Turn up the volume," Blake said.

The delivery tech raised the remote, and JT's voice went from a whisper to a shout from the surround speakers in the family room. ". . . of the event is something we have no doubt. The launch of our OS is going to revolutionize the industry—obviously there are those who stand to lose from that. But if anything, this gives us the confidence we're so far ahead of our competition they have to resort to terrorist-like attacks to try and derail us. The tragic part isn't the loss of data and equipment, however, it's the loss of innocent lives."

The female reporter in the brown fashion-less suit jogging alongside JT pulled the microphone back. "Do you have anything to say to your attackers?"

JT stopped just before the door to the building, two security guards stepping from off camera to the door and holding it open for him. He pulled the small mirrored shades from his eyes, heavy bags displaying the long night he must have had. He looked right into the camera.

"We know who you are. And you'll wish you could invent a time machine to make sure your parents never met when we're through with you."

JT's face and the Symbio office disappeared, replaced with two news anchors behind a long desk. The anchors began explaining that Symbio's lawyers had clarified JT's statement, emphasizing it wasn't intended as a threat but rather a business reaction to the legal ramifications of such sabotage. Despite JT's statement, no suspects had yet to be arrested; the authorities were actively investigating several leads.

"Turn it off."

The screen went close on one of the anchors, a male with hair so stiff it could have been thrown like a Frisbee, the space next to him displaying information on Symbio as he began to highlight the company's profile. Then the television burst into a digital implosion ending with a blank black screen.

"Everything all right?" the tech asked.

Blake looked at the delivery guy as if seeing him for the first time.

"With the picture and color?" the tech added.

Blake signed paperwork awkwardly with his left hand and walked the two men back to the door. Jenna had oddly been absent from the couch, the revelation of the deaths Blake was responsible for yet to add to her already tainted view of him. She wasn't in the living room, nor had she been upstairs, but Blake knew better than to ask when in company.

He went to tip the two men on their way out, then remembered he didn't have a dollar to his name. He looked to Joje but found no help.

"I, uh, apologize," Blake said. "Don't have any cash on me." He felt like a complete asshole as he closed the door softly behind them. He sunk down to the floor, head resting against the door's frame.

Two deaths.

A deliberate act of terror.

The weight pressed down on him, a thumb squashing an ant, boot snapping a twig. When the cops finally caught up with him, there'd be no question where Blake would spend his retirement.

Checkmate.

He could almost hear the word spoken in Joje's lisping voice.

"Where's Jenna?" he asked.

"Who?"

"My wife," Blake said.

"I'm sorry, I'm not sure who you're talking about," Joje said.

"*Jenna!*" Blake called for her as he got to his feet. "Where is she?"

"You must have hit your head one too many times, Bwake. Jenna's my wife. You're in my home. And I'm growing rather tired of your 'visit.'"

"No. No, no, nooo! Tell me where she is!"

Joje stood at the lip of the step down into the living room, a white sea of carpet behind him. "I'm making sure she's safe, something you failed to do. I'm not even sure I should bring Adam home, with all your recent failings. But there's no need to concern yourself with my problems. Let's concentrate on yours. Like what you're going to do about the payment to your Internet whiz kid."

"I don't give a crap about him. I have done everything you've asked, given you everything you wanted. Now bring my family back!" Blake's finger stabbed at the air as if he could puncture Joje with it.

Joje just peered back at him with derision. "I need to be going."

"Are we getting Adam first or Jenna?" Blake asked.

"We? There is no more *we*. This whole pwoject? It's failed. It's over! What can I possibly learn from you? How to lose a job? Check. How to screw up a marriage? Check. How to be an absent father? Raise a kid who resents you? Check! I may be partly to blame—I did choose you as my mentor—but you have failed! You've dug your own grave with the golden spoon you were handed—thinking you earned this . . ." Joje shook his arms, indicating the house. "Deserved . . . any of this? In one week, Bwake—less than a week— you've been brought down to nothing! And I'd love to take credit for it, I really would, but I give credit where credit's due. So congratulations!" He clapped, hands turned sideways. "We've been witness to the fall you've been building toward your entire life."

White heat rumbled inside Blake; he was almost surprised it wasn't shining from his fingertips. Joje could see the change in his face; he drew up, planting his feet on the wooden floor in front of the step down. They both knew where this was going; it was where Joje had guided Blake from the beginning, a channel allowing the water to think it flowed where it wished.

Joje's tic pulled at the left side of his face. He didn't bother trying to make it go away, not this time. "There you are, Bwakey. Welcome back."

It felt good to be back.

Joje slipped the gun from behind his back but instead of pointing it at Blake he released the cartridge, stepping down onto the plush carpet. Walking backward, he set both pieces on the piano, in the run where sheet music would have been had anyone in the house known how to read sheet music. His eyes were wild.

"I won't stop," Blake said.

"I always hoped you wouldn't."

Blake screamed—a primitive cry so ancestral no words were needed for it to be understood. He lunged forward, a hurricane of fury. There was no premeditation, no plan, just an outpouring of indignation. Joje had been expecting Blake to take a swing, what he hadn't expected was all of him.

Blake barreled into Joje with such force it drove him back, lifting him from his feet, his back colliding with the spine of the grand piano. The propped up lid fell, crashing down with an awful clack, piano strings vibrating with a low twang as Blake drove Joje harder into the polished surface. A tall lamp tilted and fell, Joje sliding, Blake following him down until he landed on top of him against the padded carpet.

Joje slammed his open palms against Blake's ears. Specks of white light floated across Blake's vision.

Blake drove his knee upward into Joje's crotch, and a howl escaped from the diaphragm Blake rested atop.

Joje tried to flip himself beneath Blake, but the muscle memories of Blake's wrestling days were kicking in. He pinned Joje back to the floor, swiping at the hands flying toward his face.

Instinct drove him. Ignoring the flaring in his burned hand, he brought his head down, forehead barreling into the bridge of Joje's nose. Blood erupted, spouting up, almost drowning out the noise of crunching bones.

Joje cried out in pain. Blake scrambled off his opponent and crawled back on the floor. His hand reached up onto the piano bench, higher, striking a random key, a reverberating bong sounding in low E, searching, higher, fingers scraping against wood, searching, his side pressed into the bench, ribs aching, hand shaking, searching, searching . . .

And finding.

He scrambled to his feet, the click of the clip snapping into the butt of the gun, sounding as righteous as a church choir.

The freckled kid with orange hair was now glistening in blood. Streams streaked down the varied peaks and valleys of his face, speckling the carpet below. He was up on his elbows, blinking hard, his legs stretched out in front of him. A red-stained handprint was matted into the threaded carpet, yet still he smiled, his teeth covered in a slimy, bloody glaze.

"That was a good one, Bwake," Joje said. "You got me."

Both his hands came up, palms out, one a pink fleshy color, the other rippled in blood.

Blake walked forward, not nearly as confident with the gun in his left hand, yet at point-blank range he could have been holding it with his toes. He trained it on Joje's chest. He had been waiting for this moment so long he was worried it wouldn't live up to the anticipation.

A phone buzzed, vibrating in Joje's pocket.

"Give it to me. Slowly," Blake said.

With one hand Joje reached into the pocket of his jeans, drawing the cellphone out. Jenna's phone.

"Pwabowee Dwew, checking in." Blood sputtered from his mouth as he spoke.

He tossed it to Blake, who caught it with his burned hand, grimacing. He glanced at it for only half-second intervals. He couldn't afford to take his eyes off Joje.

"You said you were done with that. Checking in."

"I lied," Joje said.

"I thought you never lie."

"Guess I learned something from you after all."

"Here's what's going to happen. You're going to tell me where my son is and where Drew has taken my wife, then we are going to go get them. If anyone even tries to stop us I will put a bullet through your head—something I've learned from watching you."

Joje was shaking his head. He wiped at his face with the back of his hand, smearing it across the carpet. "You need me more than I need you."

"You're wrong."

"Then good luck finding your family."

The phone began vibrating again, this time in Blake's hand. He looked down at it, only for a second. A text message, same as before, but completely undecipherable: *D2*D3VIRA*.

"What does it mean?" Blake asked, holding the phone for Joje to see.

"They've arrived. If he doesn't get the right text back, you won't have to bother looking for your wife," Joje said.

"I will make you feel more pain than you have ever felt. What do I text him back? What do I say!"

"Doesn't work that way."

"Tell me, damnit!"

"You might as well shoot me," Joje said, resting his hands back on the carpet.

"You think I won't?"

"Come on, pull the trigger! Right here!" Joje tapped at his

forehead furiously.

Blake's hand ached from his tightening grip on the barrel. "Last chance! Please, Joje, tell me where they are."

"Come on, you can do this." Joje lifted his head, back straightening to look squarely into the barrel. In the reflection of his eyes, Blake caught a glimpse of himself—bruised, battered, bloodied, and as insane as the man he was staring at. The reflection of a complete stranger.

"One," Blake said.

With his busted nose and blood slithering down his face, Joje's smile was the creepiest it had ever been.

"Two," Blake shouted.

Joje closed his eyes, face held high.

"Three!"

Blake pulled the trigger.

3

"Steady your shoulders, now slide your head forward, that's it, nose touching the charging handle—it won't move on you. Now deep breath, exhale partially, hold . . . and squeeze that trigger like your lady's thighs."

The M4 burst in a staccato of automatic fire, Adam's arms through his torso vibrating all the way to his bones. He kept the nozzle from rising and watched as the aluminum hull of a rowboat disintegrated.

The clip ran dry. He let the gun drop in his hands, admiring his handiwork. Bullet holes began in a migratory path, then condensed in one area, punching a much wider gap through the metal. Brush and wild weeds could be seen on the other side.

"Pretty awesome, huh?" Stu said.

"Yeah. One more round?" Adam asked.

"Thirty more rounds—one more clip. But that's it."

Adam handed the automatic machine gun back to Stu, who discharged the spent clip.

"There's no cell reception up here?" Adam asked.

"Not out here in the boonies," Stu replied.

"So how will we know when I'm supposed to go back?"

Stu squinted, looking off into the distance and avoiding Adam's eyes. He wiped down the rifle with a black cloth, pressing it into the empty chamber where the clip had gone. "We wait till we get word. No more questions unless you want to go back in the shed."

"You've gotta have some way of communicating. Do you have, what do you call those radio things?"

"Walkie-talkie?"

"No, the one you need a license for?"

"Oh, a ham radio? No. Milt or Gary go down once a day to get messages. George ain't our only client, you know. But we prefer staying out of reach," Stu said, handing Adam the gun. "This time I want you to try making an *X*." He stood back, arms folded, allowing Adam to do it on his own.

Adam pushed the butt of the gun into the crook of his shoulder, lining the sight up and bringing his head forward. He was able to control his breathing, but his heart was racing, turning the last corner with the finish line in sight. Now or never, it screamed.

Would he be heralded as the boy who saved his family from these monsters or become a monster himself?

A light breeze jostled the scraggly weeds topped with little purple flowers, as if that little color could hide what they really were.

Now or never.

He spun his body toward Stu, gun positioned so tightly it didn't move, his heart thumping louder, ghetto-blasting his intentions as the bearded young man began to rise, eyes widening, realizing exactly what Adam was planning.

"The hell you two doin'?"

The voice shouted from the bottom of the hill. Adam broke his gaze to track the other gunman. *Gary*. He was unarmed, a hand held to his head to block the sun. Stu ripped the machine gun from Adam, a silver pistol appearing in his other hand, catching the sun's rays and sending them back out.

Adam forced himself to exhale.

"What do you need, Gare?" Stu shouted, his eyes never leaving Adam's face.

"You teachin' him to shoot or becoming the target?" Gary called back, a cold laugh following.

Stu nodded at Adam to walk back down in Gary's direction. In that look Adam knew no matter what he said or did he was no longer "just a kid."

"Milton wants the boy," Gary said as they got closer.

"He can have him," Stu said, shoving Adam in the back. The ground came out from beneath him. He fell, stickered weeds and hot dirt raking his hands and arms as he tumbled the remaining few feet down the hill.

4

The blindfold was lifted over Jenna's head. A dull light revealed walls that had aged from white to the color of bone—a shade not quite white, not quite gray, but equally disturbing. She moved to fix her hair, then thought better of it. She didn't care how she looked to these assholes.

Drew hadn't been gentle in getting her out of the house. Thankfully the bruises on her arms and aching in her legs were all she had suffered from his wrath.

At least so far.

She felt his breath against the back of her neck. His hands clamped down on the handles behind her shoulders as he turned her chair, the fold-out metal stops her legs rested upon scraping against the side of that pale wall.

The carpet was thin and ancient, a light purple with dried splotches of white paint near the baseboards. She didn't recognize where they were, passing a tiny bathroom on the left, its hard yellow-tiled walls and small taupe-colored toilet reminding her of her grandmother's house in Nebraska. Even at five years old she had known the reek in that house had been of old people, no cinnamon candle or potpourri sufficiently able to mask the stench.

She could almost smell that candle now, that sweet scent mixed with the delicious aroma of wood chips burning in the stove . . . and then the smell began to change. Cinnamon warping into the rot of burning meat, flesh going black, charcoaled and continuing to burn . . . Her legs blistered beneath her, the meat's juices dripping between the openings in the grill, flames leaping higher, smoke rising to her mouth and nose, slipping down her throat, tendrils grasping, clutching, puncturing, and no matter how she turned her head, she could still smell herself cooking, melting beneath the flames.

She wiped at the dampness on her forehead. There was nothing she could do about the moisture beneath her arms or between her legs. Did this house have no air conditioning?

The hall ended in a plain white wooden door, round brass handle no longer holding a speck of its coppery shine. Drew reached over her, his gut pressing into her face, to open it. He banged the wheelchair forward against the door. The room caused her breath to catch.

Pink wallpaper in bright spotted patterns sporting cherubs and clouds, flowers and hearts, swallowed the room, making it seem at once a vast hall and a shrinking cell. The ceiling had small circular mirrors spaced apart to give the appearance of stepping stones leading from one corner to the other. A large mural of an elegant woman with long, straight black hair running over her neck and covering one breast, her other exposed, was the only picture in the room. The woman's cheek was bruised, her eye just beginning to show its shine. The rest of the wall was covered with more glass— circular mirrors, rectangular mirrors, mirrors with paintings of flowers along the edges or dancing across the bottom, some hand mirrors awkwardly hung, some in frames, some without. Lights spun as if a disco ball had been hung with all the reflections of pinks and reds.

In the center, taking up almost the entire bedroom, was a large heart-shaped bed, its headboard made of foam or cloth and forming lips in an upturned smirk. Candles and dried rose petals adorned the few shelves in the room, though covered in dust. A small glass statue of a naked woman arching her back, disproportionate breasts thrust into the air, the lone decoration atop the dresser in the back.

This wasn't a room, it was a torture chamber.

"You know where we are? Whose house this is?" Drew asked.

Jenna shook her head, almost imperceptibly.

"The old owner of your house. Jerry Welchsetzer. Lucky for us this property was kept off the books. You know what line of business he was in?"

Jenna's head continued to shake.

"Porn. Movies mainly, but the special ones were all shot here. The productions with a very limited release. Often filmed for a party of one."

Jenna noticed the cameras for the first time, mounted in the corners of the room. How many were hidden in other objects—frames, mirrors, naked statues?

"No actors. Just a guy and a girl and only one leaves the room alive," Drew said.

"How do you know all this?"

"I worked for him. Mr. Welchsetzer." He said the name with contempt. "Always liked the movie industry, but Jerry, he made a mistake. Tried screwing over the wrong guy."

Drew grabbed her head, her body tensing as he dropped down, whispering into her ear. "This is what George has planned for you, once he's finished with Blake. He doesn't know I brought you here, but I needed you to understand. What your options are. Do you? Understand?"

Jenna whimpered beneath his grasp.

"I can help you. Protect you. If you help me," he said.

Her breaths came in gasps, her eyes no longer seeing.

"We can run away, you and I. From this. From George. But it's your choice."

Some choice, Jenna thought.

"And Joje is not as gentle as I am," Drew continued.

"He'll come after you. After us," she said. Let him think there was an *us*. If it kept her alive a little longer.

"Then I'll kill him," Drew's lips whispered in her ear, his tongue brushing against it. She shuddered, unable to stop her body from reacting. "Come with me. Or I'll kill you."

5

Click.

The empty chamber resonated through Blake's teeth, as quiet as a trickle of water, yet more forceful than a waterfall. He could have sworn he felt a recoil, though the gun had barely moved. Joje looked up at him with that smile, blood spouting from his nose.

"No," Blake screamed, firing again and again.

Click, click, click, click.

He held his hands out in front of him, turning the gun so it faced down. He tossed it onto the piano, metal striking wood, making gouges that no longer mattered.

He was done. He had failed. Perhaps for the last time.

They won't even know I tried.

It was perhaps the worst thought. Adam and Jenna. There would be torture, agony, and in the end they would die believing Blake had been incapable of helping them, unwilling to even try.

Joje rose to his feet, pulling a mix of hanging snot and blood and flinging it to the carpet.

"I'll get your son. And your wife, but you are staying here."

"Your gun was loaded . . . before," Blake said, mind still trying to make the leap that would catch up to the present. "In my office?"

"Blanks. Did you find a bullet hole in your wall?"

Blake felt the walls collapse in around him.

"Mine's never been loaded. I told you from the beginning, I don't like violence." Joje walked past the dining room table into the kitchen. "Come."

As Blake entered the kitchen, he found Joje standing next to the table, a large butcher knife in his hand.

"Don't make me use this," he said, then pointed to Conrad's crate next to the wall. "Get in."

Blake's bare feet felt cold against the wooden floor. "You can't be serious."

"Very," Joje answered, his busted nose making him sound more nasally. Combined with his lisp, he could have been voicing a cartoon character on some Nickelodeon show.

"I won't fit in there," Blake said.

Joje brandished the knife. "Then I'll make you fit. Fight me on this, and your wife and son will come home to your corpse."

Conrad's cage took on the role of a gaping mouth, its thin black bars sharpened teeth, preparing to swallow Blake whole. It was small, stretching about four feet in length, three feet wide, three—maybe three and a half—high. They had purchased it when Conrad had been a puppy. Blake really should have gotten a larger one when he had started using it here in their new home but had decided the cramped space would be part of the punishment.

"Go ahead. You can tie me up, gag me, throw me in a closet, a trunk. I don't care! Just . . . I'll be quiet." Blake tossed his hands in the air and sat on one of the kitchen chairs. "It doesn't matter anymore."

"What about your family?"

Blake shook his head, breathing heavily to keep from crying. "I sometimes meet with business owners looking to restructure, revive a business that's already gone too far. Buried in debt, fighting markets that have passed them by. There are times when your only option is to fold."

"What are you trying to tell me?"

"Just do it already!" Blake yelled. "End this. Kill me!"

A spike of pain flashed through Blake's hand resting on the table, causing him to jump up. Joje pulled the butcher knife out of Blake's hand with a quick tug.

"I don't have time for you to feel sorry for yourself," he said. "Now get in that cage, or I will cut you into a thousand little pieces and feed you to your son. As bad as things are, they can always get worse."

Blake looked from the gash in the back of his already-burned hand to Joje's face. "What did I ever do to you?"

Joje slammed the blade down again, and Blake pulled his hand back just in time to see the blade sink an inch into the table. "Two minutes," Joje said. "Whatever's not in that cage is coming off."

Blake knelt in front of the crate, heart pulsing. The opening was the size of his laptop screen, maybe a little taller, but no wider. Probably smaller than his waist. The cage became a complex Rubik's Cube puzzle, Blake envisioning one body part at a time moving into the tiny wired box, folding limbs back, rolling shoulders, stretching, cramming.

And failing to fit.

"A minute forty-two."

"I can't—" Blake said.

"Then prepare yourself for real pain."

"Promise you won't hurt my family," Blake said.

"I only make promises I know I can keep. And I can promise you'll see them again."

Blake could feel his exhaustion—a living, breathing entity that had entered his body, demanding him to stop.

Stop trying, stop caring, stop fighting.

Stop.

Adrenaline long gone, he let out a long breath, then brought one arm into the cage. It felt like shoveling the first scoop of dirt onto his own grave. He lowered his head, turning onto his back and sliding farther in. With some contortions, and a slice through his shirt, he was able to pop the top half of his body through. His head hit the back of the cage, waist and legs still hanging out.

"One minute," Joje said.

Blake tucked his head forward, scooting farther into the cage and raising his head up. It rattled against the top bars. He breathed out, already feeling a bout of claustrophobia gripping him. His waist was caught at the opening, the rounded edges of the thin bars surprisingly unsmooth, digging into his skin. He floundered to the side of the cage, seeing if it would open up more room to bring his knees up. It didn't. He was still only halfway into the cage with no idea how to get the rest of him inside.

"We can do without your legs. I'm sure Jenna can empathize."

"Wait, damnit!" Blake shouted.

He hunched up, ducking his head and bringing it forward to the center of the cage, his back arching. It enabled him to slide back another few inches, his waist falling through the opening, gashes scouring the small of his back and hips. Now his butt was against the floor of the cage, a hard plastic lining that ran from end to end. With the back of his neck craning against the top of the cage, Blake realized he had no leverage to move forward or backward. He tried to wriggle his body in farther, but there was nowhere to go.

"I'm stuck."

"Thirty seconds," Joje said.

"I'm serious, I can't move!" Blake tried inching his head forward, but it was levered up at an angle that blocked him from any movement. He strained his neck to the other side, his head notching forward an inch, or at least a single square grid in the cage. His back was shaking, but he forced it flush against the end of the cage. Still his legs dangled out, nowhere near close enough to bring up his knees." There's not enough room—this isn't going to work!"

"Make it work!"

The cage felt like it was shrinking, and though the gridded bars had no way of blocking the passage of air, Blake could feel the oxygen expiring. He had to get out.

With effort he managed to bring his body back into a lying

position, then wriggle slowly back out. He knelt on the wooden floor, sucking in air like he had just come up from beneath a wave. He felt lightheaded. Had he been holding his breath in there? Maybe it had just been the contortions of his body preventing him from drawing in a normal breath.

"I . . . I can't, I can't," Blake said. Blood trickled down from the palm of his right hand running the length of his arm.

"I ever tell you I've been here before?" Joje asked. "In this house? Your office was a wine room. That's why it has its own temperature control."

"Welchsetzer?" Blake asked.

Joje smiled. "How much do you know?"

"I don't. The neighbor—the lawyer you murdered—he told me."

"Told you what?"

"That Jerry went crazy. Murdered his family," Blake said. "Wife, kids."

"You believed him?"

"No. Yes, but no. I never found anything. But it was you, wasn't it? You killed them?"

"They had a large oak table here, you know, thick legs . . . like Dwew's?" He smiled before continuing. "China cabinet against the wall. Drapes—this awful pattern. And a signed Marilyn Monroe against that wall—the one where she's laying backward on the couch, topless, not the typical skirt-flying-up-trying-to-hold-it-down pose. Always felt bad for those kids, their girls."

He shook his head. "I took his wife right here, on the table, Jerry standing about where you are now, my head banging into the light fixture with every thrust, her ass slapping and sticking to the tabletop, and then when I had finished, I bent forward looking into her eyes—she had remarkable eyes. She was a dark woman, European I guess, but her eyes were this emerald green with specks of gray, just breathtaking. She was looking at me by then, and while we stared into each other's souls, I put a knife just like this through her side. Punctured her liver. Then I went farther, deeper, driving the blade up, my hand thrust inside her, our eyes never leaving each other. The light in those beautiful eyes dripping away till they were nothing more than cheap marbles."

Joje stepped back, taking a long breath. Blake leaned against the cage, crying, and yet, just like Jerry's wife, unable to take his eyes off Joje. "I guess I'm telling you this so that you understand. I keep my promises, Bwake, but I also keep my threats. Now get in the cage."

Blake bowed his head. He was ruined. Broken. Stripped of all he had been, all he had believed, his sense of the world, that if you did right and worked hard, good things would come and that when challenges appeared, there were always solutions. Always.

But not anymore.

As bad as things are, they can always get worse.

"Why this house?" he asked, swallowing hard. "What, what is it you want?"

Joje looked like a patient parent determining how to answer a child's silly question. "I don't care about your house. I have everything I could ever want. Except what you took."

The statement felt like hitting the ground after a fifty-foot fall. Blake's mind began spinning.

"Try going in backward. Feet first."

"What is it you think I took?" Blake asked, feeling an urgent need to understand why this was happening, that it wasn't meaningless.

Joje spun the knife in his hand and started forward.

"No, no! I'm going!" Blake said. He turned around, still on his knees, but now facing away from the cage. The tears that dripped from his eyes were hot. He backed his legs into the cage, bringing his knees in, toes striking the back before he could think of ducking his waist in.

"Lower your legs like you're kneeling but with your upper body slack against the floor."

Blake did as he was told, crouching while flattening his chest to the floor.

"Scoot to the side, closer to me. Now rotate your knees down, lying sideways."

The edges of the bars on the opening gouged into his side as he now lay vertically through the opening.

"Good," Joje said. He was really getting into it now. "Can you— bring an arm in?"

"Not yet," Blake said, keeping his tone blank of emotion.

"You're gonna have to stretch your legs out above you lengthwise, fold in half like a sandwich. Here, I'll help," Joje said.

Eventually, that's what worked, Joje pressing Blake's legs back through the bars once he had them extended as far as he could. Blake's glutes and hamstrings screamed at him as they moved an inch at a time until finally popping out above him, extending against the top of the cage. Blake's back was spasming, the angle of his body compressing bones and nerves in a way never intended. With more assistance from Joje, he was able to squeeze his arms and shoulders through, hunching his head into the small cavity created between the top and bottom halves of his body in an upside down sandwich.

He heard the rattle of the cage close, latch locking into place. Then Joje's breath on the back of his head as a lock was snapped shut. Then another one.

Not a lock, Blake realized. The handcuffs.

With the cage closed, Blake tried to let his body relax, filling out the additional space before realizing there wasn't any. His attempt at shuffling his shoulders, wiggling side to side, or stretching his feet that were pressed flat against the front of the cage were met with the same results. He didn't have an extra breath of room.

"Comfortable?"

Blake's breath disappeared, his diaphragm pushed so tight he couldn't form words if he tried. Blood rushed to his head so fast it seemed he would drown.

"You're turning a little white. Hold tight. I'm gonna flip you."

The world twirled, Blake's limbs and back squeezed against the gridded bars. Like a Tilt-A-Whirl, the cage flipped forward another ninety degrees. His body settled in, his legs pressed now against the bottom of the crossed bars. The hard plastic plate that had been on the floor was now above him and had dropped down, leaning against the top of his head and closing off what little space had existed there.

The air was suddenly gone, the space between the bars no longer allowing its passage. Blake screamed, the last of his air escaping, even though the scream had only been in his mind.

Joje's face appeared next to him, though Blake could only glimpse him out of the corner of his eye—turning his head was an impossibility. "This will work beautifully," he said.

Could he tell Blake was dying?

"Breathe, Bwakey, it's okay, you're okay, just normal claustrophobia setting in."

But Blake had forgotten how to breathe. What did you have to do to make your chest rise and fall? One arm was compressed against the side, the other he was practically sitting on; how could he bring them up to force his lungs to expand and compress?

"Breathe, focus on it—come on, Bwake!"

Blake closed his eyes, shutting everything out, the cage, the world, their predicament, Joje.

Forget everything. Just breathe.

In. Out. In.

"There you go!" Joje said. "See, you'll be fine. I'm a man of my word. I'll be back before tonight. With your family."

Out. In. Out.

Joje whistled as he moved back into the kitchen, keys tinkling together.

In. Out. In.

When the garage door closed, Blake missed a breath. The whoosh of that door sealing shut reminded him of the dirt falling from his shovel onto the bodies in the open graves he had dug in his own backyard.

But whose bodies?

Jenna's? Adam's?

Evaline's?

Or was he watching the reel upon the completion of his life, reliving the events that had led to his death?

In.

Out.

In.

Chapter 9

Day Six Continued

1

Adam drew in a sharp breath; he hadn't expected it to be this bad. Milton sat in a wooden chair so rickety it would've been better used as firewood. It was the only piece of furniture in the room beyond a filthy rug rolling up at the edges, discolored with age.

Stu and Gary may have known their weapons, but Milton was a soldier, and it only took one glance to recognize it. He was lean, cut, muscles moving beneath his clothing with every breath. And his face looked like a pumpkin that had been smashed in on Halloween.

An open gash at least an inch wide, wider in parts, ran from his hairline down the curve of his forehead and over his right brow. His eye was black—not the bruised purple and black from a blow near the socket, but the actual eye itself, black, only half of it floating where it should be, the rest covered in tissue and film that reminded Adam of a swamp. He could almost picture flies buzzing around it.

Adam had hit him with the end of a canister, knocking Milton out before he had a chance to realize Adam was a danger. And then Adam had brought the canister down again, and again. He had to be sure, and in the complete darkness of the trailer, he had no idea if the guy had just been thrown off balance or was down for the count.

Apparently   it   had   been   the   latter.

His goggles, the night-vision headset he wore, must have shattered inward with the blows. If the canister hadn't been torn from Adam's hands as he toppled over when the truck made a sharp turn, he didn't think Milton would have been here. At least not sitting in a chair.

Whatever ground Adam had hoped to gain, he knew was lost. Why had he hesitated outside? That may have been his only chance. But he was just a kid, just a young, stupid kid who had been taken from his parents, frightened out of his mind, reacting without thinking, not knowing how much damage he could have caused.

He couldn't convince them if he didn't believe it himself.

"Sit."

Adam looked around for another chair, though he knew there wasn't one. From behind, someone kicked in his left knee, forcing him to the ground. He stayed down, hoping it showed some sign of vulnerability. Pretending to be scared for the moment wasn't a challenge.

"Who are you?"

Milton's voice was like glass.

"I'm Adam—"

A hand raked across his cheek, Adam's vision blurring.

"Not you, your family. Who are we holding? A senator's son? Police chief's? A warden?" Milton leaned down, that cesspool of an eye unblinking. "Why do you matter?"

"I don't. We don't. My dad's in technology, does consulting. He just started working for a new company? I don't think his old business was going that well."

Adam stopped talking. Milton had only tilted his head, but the gesture had been enough. As scared as he was, he also felt a sense of awe—this guy could get people to do what he wanted without even opening his mouth.

"What company?"

"Uh, Symbio?"

Milton brought up his hands, rubbing them together. A mucous-like liquid was forming in the gash on his face like a bronzing glaze. He glanced over Adam, and suddenly arms were pulling him back, holding him so tightly he felt his ribs might break.

"Always easier to make nobody disappear," Milton said.

They dragged Adam across the floor, his knees scraping, the

cloth of his jeans catching.

"No, wait!" he called. "I lied!"

The two men stopped just in front of the door. They didn't release him, and Adam understood that if he was dragged from this room, it would be to die. His breath tumbled from him in whopping gasps. He looked at the one-eyed man in front of him, injured so badly he should have been in a hospital, and shuddered.

Such power. Such command.

"I know why he chose us, our family," Adam said. He waited like watching a lion deciding whether it was going to rip you apart or drag you back to its lair to dine on at its leisure. Milton's eyes once again flicked upward, and Adam felt the hands release him. He hit the floor, breathed in a sigh of relief.

Now he just had to come up with a believable lie.

2

Jenna was belted into the passenger seat, doors and windows set to child lock on the SUV. Not that she could have jumped out and started running had they been unlocked. Worse than the pain in her legs was the lack of pain she felt in her right foot and calf. They might as well have not been attached—she felt nothing there.

Drew stuffed a handful of french fries into his mouth, washing them down with a slurp of his extra-large Coke. He eased behind a BMW, getting back onto the Santa Monica 10 Freeway heading east. The smell of greasy fries and chicken made her stomach both turn sour and groan with the pangs of hunger.

As they merged onto the freeway, Drew told her to eat. She didn't argue. "Where are we meeting them?" she asked.

"Him," Drew corrected. "Just George."

"He's left them? Blake and Adam?"

Fries were traded for breaded chicken balls. Drew chomped loudly, mouth open.

"Are they alive? Why would he leave them?"

"Why do you ask so many questions," Drew said. "You made your choice, live with it."

She knew it was a choice she wouldn't live with long.

Traffic moved, and Jenna realized she had no idea what day it was. A weekday? Weekend? Drew took the 110 interchange, the overpass floating above the Staples Center off to the right. They converged with the mass of vehicles migrating north.

"Please, Drew, tell me. Are they okay?"

"None of you are, not with George."

"Are you going to kill him?"

Drew glanced at her sharply. "Don't breathe a word of that to anyone! You don't know him like I do. You think something, he'll find out."

"If you protect my family from him, if they're alive? I'll give you everything you want."

She was surprised to realize she meant it.

Past the conglomeration of intersecting off-ramps, the 110 opened up into a smaller interstate, one that reminded Jenna of being back home. West Virginia never felt so far away.

Drew followed the GPS on his phone, the freeway eventually dissolving into a street in Pasadena, Arroyo Parkway. Jenna followed every turn and street name, hoping somehow, someway, she might be able to retrace these steps.

They turned left on Colorado, right on Fair Oaks, sidewalks as busy as the streets of New York. Drew pulled into a Shell station at the corner of Walnut, weaving between the cars lined up for gas and passing the large yellow sign with red-lettered words: "Snack Shop." On the other side of the gas station, he parked in front of the air and water hoses.

Drew stepped out without a word, the beep of the alarm enough warning to not open a door or call for help. Jenna watched in the side mirror, turning it to follow him until he disappeared into the convenience store next to the open garage. Her entire body seemed to release a breath she had been holding for days.

A small pickup truck that had once been white but was now plastered in mud or maybe cement pulled in beside her. The driver, a dark Latino with bushy sideburns and eyebrows, opened the door too hard, its edge banging into Jenna's door. The alarm chirped.

Jenna met his eyes as he realized someone was in the car he had just marked, maybe dented. He looked like he might crawl back into his truck and drive off. Jenna held up her hands, cuffed at the wrists, for him to see.

"Help me," she said, hoping her bruised face would be clear through the tinted windows.

The man outside her door wet his lips with his tongue, then glanced down, averting his eyes.

Jenna put her palm to the window, still peering out at him.

"Please! Help me!"

A fist pounded against the glass on the other side of her palm—Jenna jumped back in her seat, a cry leaping from her mouth. Her heart rate had gone from still to sprint in half a second. The Latino man outside pressed flat against his truck as he let another body slip by.

Joje.

He looked in at her, smile splitting across his face. His nose was swollen, flesh a nasty purplish red. He pointed at the lock, motioning for her to open. The man at the truck was already gone, Joje's frame in the side mirror blocking Jenna from seeing him slink away.

She turned from the window, staring into a windshield that might as well have been blank. She was still lost in her thoughts when Drew climbed into the backseat and Joje pulled out onto the street, a street she no longer cared about. Another freeway, another off ramp, busy roads turned into lonely side streets turned into dirt paths no vehicle was meant to drive on.

Wherever they were leading her, it wouldn't matter if she knew her way back—it had always been a one-way ticket.

3

The clock ticked forward another notch, the rift between passing seconds wide enough to swallow Blake whole. He swam in a black pool of ethos, kicking, clawing, wrestling his way to the surface and yet still being pulled beneath. His movements were restrained—the flaring of a nostril, the tremor of a muscle, an itch tickling the hairs on his leg like a silky worm—as restrained as the tired hand moving mercilessly around the corners of the clock.

Round and round we go.

"Hello?" he called.

"Hello!" he answered. Round and round and round.

His body had long passed the point of discomfort, giving up its demands to move, stretch, *breathe*. He had entered a cocoon of paralysis, only his mind wandering from the small wire crate in the kitchen to roam the dark corners of his imagination; thoughts, memories, and regrets colliding into nightmares almost as frightening as the truth.

His wife was in one such corner, her body sinking into the hospital bed. Monitors blinked and beeped, drooping bags of poison running their tubes into her wrists like the stinging tail of a chimera.

This was a corner Blake had learned to avoid, one he hadn't visited in years.

He brushed at the cobwebs clinging to his face, his hair, and stepped a little closer, close enough to see her face.

Her cheeks were sunken, skin pulling inward as if she were wearing a mask that had been fitted to her face. Her normally vibrant eyes now clouded behind the drugs. She had lost so much weight she no longer resembled the woman he had married—in truth, she no longer looked human.

"I'm here," he said.

A tear ran from the corner of one closed eye, trailing down the side of her face and disappearing on the white sheets of the bed.

She's crying because you're not here, you're never here, and even when you are you don't want to be, you want to be anywhere but here, looking at anyone but her.

Her bony chest rose beneath the hospital bedding then fell, her body appearing to sink farther into the sheets.

"You should have told me you were coming."

Her voice was hoarse, the whisper of a breeze through dried leaves barely clinging to a tree in early November. It wasn't from the cancer; it was from disuse. The closer they got to the end, they had so little to talk about.

"Where's Mommy?"

Adam stood at the open curtain—Blake had told her to keep him out, he wasn't going to be long. Cobwebs hung from above, a transparent curtain the boy seemed not to notice.

Blake's wife covered her face, a movement that probably caused her immense pain. "I don't want him to see me like this! Take him out—take him away!"

Where's Mommy?

Adam had been looking right at her when he asked the question. An innocent inquiry for a child not quite three, a damning one for the mother on her deathbed.

"I don't want him to see me!" she screamed.

Jenna entered the room, her young face flushed red. She scooped Adam up and nestled her lips against his neck, blowing on him and making him laugh. Through his giggles he cried out, "Stop!" She looked at Blake, mouthed, "Sorry," and then left, taking Adam with her.

Blake watched her go, unable to peel his eyes off her. He was surprised to feel stirrings down low, especially in the presence of his dying wife. Not so surprising considering where he and Jenna had come from. Or where they were going after.

She was staring at him when he turned around, and through sheer force of will, he was able to meet her eyes. Wounded eyes. Rachel eyes. If she hadn't known before, she knew now.

She had known before.

"Tell him I love him," she said.

"You'll tell him when—"

"No." They both knew she wouldn't be getting better. "Tell him."

"I will," he said.

"Every day."

"I promise."

The words were as hollow as the empty room he spoke to. Finally Blake heard the soft tick of another second pass by.

4

Adam sat across the hall in a bedroom a quarter the size of his own on a low mattress as hard as the concrete ground he had slept on the night before. The blankets were tousled, with stains larger than any of Conrad's puddles. He had fed Milton his story and now, like an accused criminal, awaited his fate. As the voices across the hall grew louder, he suspected that fate would fall far from his favor.

"That's just what he wants you to think!" Gary's voice.

"This gets out, that we crossed one of our own? Who does

business with us will be the least of our concerns." That was Stu.

"There's always business," Gary countered.

"You want the people we sell to comin' for us?" Stu again.

"Nah, nothin' here is what it seems."

"I agree with Gary." Milton, a voice no one argued with.

Adam had made the mistake of thinking they feared Joje. He had been under the impression the whole song and pony dance when they had purchased the weapons was all for Blake's sake.

He had been wrong.

He bent forward, unlacing his shoes and pulling them from his feet. The bed groaned, old springs singing at the shift of weight. Within seconds Gary was at the open doorway, no doors to any of the bedrooms.

"The hell you doin'?"

"I barely slept last night. I was just gonna lay down?"

Gary looked at the bed then back at Adam. "Don't get comfortable." He snorted, then left, rejoining the others.

When Adam stood, the noise of the bed sounded the same as if he were lying across it. He stepped cautiously, testing each floorboard before letting his weight fall. His back against the wall, he listened to the men arguing a few feet away.

". . . Whole thing feels like a setup." Milton. Or maybe Gary.

"Good money for the amount of merch." Definitely Stu.

"Not for the kid." No, that was Milton.

"Ain't no amount enough for that." Gary.

Milton, Gary, and Stu, the three stooges, Adam thought. And they trusted Joje as much as his father did.

He peeked around the corner, pulling immediately back. The open doorway diagonal from his own was blocked with Stu's bulky frame. He stood, back to Adam, leaning against the frame with one arm. Another glance—Adam couldn't see past him, which meant Gary and Milton couldn't see him.

He stepped into the hall closing his eyes, something he had done as a child. The mere act of walking with his eyes shut always made him feel invisible. He crept to his right toward, presumably, the front of the cabin.

"Then we pick him up and end this quietly before it begins!" a voice shouted, causing Adam to freeze. He thought it was Gary but couldn't be sure. He didn't glance back. If they noticed him, Adam was certain he'd know.

The end of the short hall opened not into a front room as he had hoped, but into a bathroom, a showerhead that would run onto tiled floor, no tub or wall separating it from the single toilet and bucket of water next to it.

How could there not be a front entrance?

Looking back down the short hall, he noticed the door he had somehow missed—an actual door, fitted into one of the smaller doorways. A thin plate of glass ran through the upper half, a sort of window looking onto a staircase, winding down.

Of course the front entrance would have to be lower than the back. Just open the door enough to squeeze through, creep down the stairs, and he was home free, though he had no idea where he'd go from there.

He wasn't even sure where home was. Not for him.

Turning the handle, an old round knob that spun with ease, he pulled it slowly toward him.

Creeeeeeeaaaaaak.

The hinges couldn't have announced his exit any louder. He spun into the narrow stairway, slamming the door closed behind him and taking the stairs two at a time. Before he hit the final step the door flung open above.

The bottom landing opened into a room the size of a closet; cement floor, a door to the right, one to the left. Adam chose the one away from the house, leading outside. He flipped the deadbolt and rushed through.

Sunlight hit him, cement changing to dirt, rocks pressing through his socks and into his feet. He ran, bracing against the pain with each step, his socks flopping, beginning to slide off.

He leapt over a ridge of dirt and rock at a curve in the rough road that lead away from the cabin just as he heard the men spill from the front door. He ducked lower, flattening himself to the dirt.

Had they seen where he had gone? How many options were there, and how long before they narrowed them down?

Not long.

Ten feet away the first of a forest of trees staggered up from the ground. Tall thick trunks, dense enough that he might be able to lose them. Getting that far would be the trouble.

He inched along the raised ridge on his belly, following its gentle curve. Ahead, the trees drew closer to the road. It also put more distance between him and the cabin, him and his captors.

His new captors.

"Don't anyone touch him," Milton shouted. "I want the pleasure."

Adam couldn't wait any longer—he shot forward in a full sprint, loose rocks kicking out from beneath his feet.

"There!" someone shouted.

Adam looked back. Gary stood on a ridge, rifle at his shoulder. Adam leapt, still a few feet from the trees that might offer some protection. He hit the dirt, the whirl of a bullet whistling overhead. His legs found purchase, half crawling, half running toward the slope of trees.

He reached the first tree and wrapped himself around it just as another bullet plunked into the wood behind him.

"I said don't touch him!"

"You want him to get away?"

"He ain't goin' nowhere. Not out here."

Adam's breathing was labored, his feet burning, rocks and stickers driven into the soft flesh of his feet. No time to do anything about it.

He pushed off the trunk just as a body stepped into his path, blocking his way. A branch snapped beneath the man's weight.

Stu.

His automatic rifle, the one Adam had shot, was held down at his side.

"Please. Let me go?" Adam knew it was pathetic begging for his life, but the tears just under the surface weren't fake. Neither was his quivering lip. "Help me?"

Stu gave the slightest of nods and stepped to the side.

Breath returned, Adam's heart beat again. He stepped past the large, bearded man, a whirl of motion following him.

A weight slammed into the back of his head. The world tilted—leaves, branches, rocks, pulling toward him, drawing up from the ground.

When he hit, he slid, the sharp twangs of pain in his feet now plunging into his stomach, arms, palms, and face. He pushed himself up, legs still down behind him, and managed to crawl another inch or two before collapsing.

Somewhere between the haze of his throbbing head and the darkness swirling before his eyes, he heard the words "I am."

5

The bouncing of the SUV along the uneven dirt path had taken its toll on Jenna's body, her legs flaring beneath her seat. They had followed a trail that lead nowhere but up at an angle she hadn't known her Escalade could handle. Trees swarmed around them, pressing in. Soon the road would be too narrow to traverse.

"Our friends don't know we're coming," Joje said, "and they're not keen on visitors."

She heard Drew rustling in the back, something clanging against her folded-up wheelchair. It was the sword. Drew set it between his legs, a samurai meditating before battle. An extremely overweight albino samurai.

His eyes flickered toward her, then away. Was he thinking of doing it? Thrusting the sword through the seat into Joje's back? Was he capable of doing it?

"Not sure that'll help, Dwew, when the bullets begin to fly."

"It'll help," Drew answered.

"I thought you said they were friends of yours?" Jenna said.

"They were."

They continued in relative silence, the noise of tires churning over rocks and jostle of shocks and undercarriage replacing conversation. The dirt road banked up high on the right, and as they came around the corner, they felt rather than heard the first gunshot. A plink of metal followed. The vehicle shuddered.

Joje hit the gas. They topped the crest, view opening up to a cabin a hundred yards out. Jenna saw a man disappearing behind it.

She felt Drew's hand on her arm. "Get down," he said.

Light reflected off to the right in the trees, and then the windshield lit up with bullet holes, glass splintering outward, puffs of air streaming past Jenna's head. Drew had crouched low, as low as his large frame would allow, and Joje screamed—not in pain, in exultation.

He cranked the wheel hard to the left. The back of the Escalade turned and spun on the rough dirt, and then the vehicle jerked, its momentum carrying it in a direction its tires no longer allowed. They lifted into the air.

Jenna braced for impact.

It came quick, the back of the vehicle slamming down on its side first, then rolling, tumbling, sky above, below, rotated to the side, glass and the terrible sound of crunching metal. Airbags sprang, from the side, from the front, and when the vehicle finally came to rest, Jenna lay on her side, gravity pulling her toward her door.

She was breathing, uninjured as far as she could tell, except for the aggravated throbs pulsing from her legs. She turned her head and felt a stiffness there that would certainly grow.

Joje suddenly fell into her with abandon, an elbow colliding into her chest, his head knocking against hers. He pushed off with a grunt, stepping onto the armrest. "Keep down and stay quiet."

The windshield in front of them was shattered, glass clinging to the outer edges of the frame. Joje reached down, wiping something from Jenna's face.

Blood.

She hadn't even registered the pain. Still couldn't.

He winked at her, then began to moan. He kicked at the glass, making a wider hole, then crawled through. It was a weird sensation watching him stand just outside, a sense of vertigo gripping Jenna like she had never felt before.

Joje spit a glob of blood onto the ground, hands on his knees, wavering.

A man stepped from the trees into the clearing, a large gun strapped around him and held near his waist. He approached with caution. Jenna almost shouted a warning but thought better of it. She should be so lucky.

Joje fell to his knees, arms raised, hands coming together on the back of his head.

"How'd you find us?" the man asked. He was old, thin. "No one knows about this place."

"You can't think I'd do business with someone I don't know?" Joje said. "Gary Blanchard?"

The man, Gary, tightened his grip on the rifle.

"Ex-marine, served from sixty-eight to seventy-one in Southern Quảng Trị, Regimental Landing Team Twenty-Six. Court martialed

December eleventh of seventy-one and deserted shortly after. In seventy-five you came back to the States in part due to our dear President Ford's proclamation that changed your discharge from dishonorable to a mere clemency discharge. You were in Florida till nineteen eighty, mostly in construction, then moved to Montana with the gal pal you were shacking with at the time, Elizabeth Hulton. Fathered a daughter, and that's when the records get a little light. But I don't stop at light. You joined the Militia of Montana that holed up in the Gallatin Mountains outside of Bozeman, later deserting to the King's Mountain Militia somewhere in the early nineties. In the wake of the Oklahoma City bombing, you left the King's Men, spending a few years in Mexico where you also fathered a son, one you never knew about. He died before his tenth birthday, so no love lost there. Entered California in oh-six, whereupon you regrouped with Milton Steed, a former King's Man himself. And here you've built your enterprise selling to the same groups you once believed in, customers like John Trochmann, Mark Koernke, and Chris Kerodin and his Threepers."

Gary looked visibly shaken, like he should be the one on the ground, Joje standing over him with a gun.

"Did I miss anything?" Joje asked.

"Milton was right. You are dangerous."

"More than you could ever know."

Gary's gun drew up, but not before Drew appeared beside him, sword whirling in his hands—he thrust it through the man's chest, a single shot releasing from Gary's rifle before the blade was withdrawn. Gary toppled to the ground. Drew kicked the rifle away and then squatted in front of the man, blocking Jenna's view. The arc of his blade, however, was clear enough, as was the spray of blood that spread outward onto the parched dirt.

"Took your time, didn't you?" Joje said.

And then Jenna heard a cry. "Mom! Dad?"

It was Adam. Her *son.*

6

"Adam!"

Jenna's voice broke through the clearing, and Adam felt something swell in his chest, then a boot slammed into his backside and he stumbled forward another few feet, falling onto one knee. His parents' Escalade lay on its side, his mom calling from within.

"Drop it or the little guy eats dirt," Stu shouted behind Adam.

Drew stood over the body of Gary on the ground, one foot on the man's head as if he had stopped a soccer ball. The head, which was no longer connected to the rest of his body.

"Okay, okay." Joje flung a small pistol away.

"The, uh, sword? You can drop that too."

It took Drew longer, but he leaned down, sliding it their direction in the dirt.

Where was his dad? Hiding? Had they all really come to rescue him?

"Adam! Are you okay?" Jenna asked. Adam could see motion through the windshield, Jenna trying to move or get out.

"I'm good," Adam yelled, expecting a kick but receiving none.

Joje didn't seem that concerned with the automatic rifle Stu had pointed at them. He kept looking toward the cabin, moving gradually away from the car. One wheel still spun lazily in the air. "We're just here for the boy," Joje shouted. "No one else needs to get hurt!"

Adam caught movement out of the corner of his eye near the cabin.

Milton knelt in the rocks, raising a large cylindrical tube to his shoulders. *It's a rocket launcher*—Adam almost wanted to laugh. Milton's angle kept him out of view from both Joje and Drew, though he had a perfect shot at the vehicle.

Jenna. Trapped within.

"No!" Adam turned, jumping onto Stu, clawing at his face.

The rifle connected with Adam's jaw, sending him sprawling. He heard commotion behind him, someone running.

"Get my mom out!" he shouted.

Stu was on one knee, bringing the rifle up in a quick and trained motion. Adam leapt at him again, causing his first shot to go wild. Stu held Adam back with his left hand pressed into Adam's face.

"Stop it, kid—I'm on your side!" He shoved Adam back down, raising the rifle up and firing. No aim, no scope, and only one shot. Its noise rang out.

Adam followed the direction Stu had fired.

Toward the cabin.

Stu rose onto his toes to see if his shot had landed. Joje was still running, reached the corner of the cabin and turned back toward them, arms waving in the air.

Man down, or whatever the hell it meant.

Adam reached his arm up toward the bulky bearded man to have him help him to his feet. "You were with them the whole time?"

Stu took it, pulling Adam up, then shoved him forward with such thrust Adam flew back to the ground, barely keeping from hitting his head. He slid in the dirt, a prickly weed scratching at the side of his face.

"You could have gotten someone killed," Stu said, clearly pissed. As if that wasn't exactly what Stu had done? He left Adam there, walking toward Joje and the cabin.

Adam went to the Escalade.

He lay down in the dirt, hand reaching through the broken windshield to take hold of Jenna's. A lock of hair had fallen over the left side of her face, and Adam could see it had darkened near her forehead.

"I wanted to come to you," she said.

She was bleeding. How bad?

"Where's Dad?"

"Home. I think." Her tone lost any of its brightness. "They're going to kill us."

"They saved us!"

"No, Adam, they are going to kill us." Her grip tightened on his until it hurt.

"I won't let them," he said.

Her lips rose in a forced smile. She didn't think he could.

"I don't know why, but I mean something to them. I can protect you," Adam said.

"I'm glad I'm your mother," she replied.

And for the first time that Adam could remember, he didn't know what to say.

She pushed at the hair falling over her face, and it fell out in one large chunk. Adam gasped—it looked like someone had taken a cheese grater to the side of her head. The pink and gristly material that had formed like mold on her scalp pulsed with a heartbeat of its own. Her head fell forward, grip releasing from his hand.

"Help!" Adam screamed. "We need help!"

7

Milton felt the chains wrapped around his body, preventing him from rising. The bullet had severed the carotid artery in his neck, and he could feel himself slipping away. It was more dreamlike than he would have thought, the pain someone else's.

The clear blue sky shimmered like puddles on a paved road in the dead of summer.

Only a mirage.

Joje appeared over him. The gurgle of blood was the only curse Milton could utter.

"I wowee . . . you don't know who I am," Joje said.

And suddenly he did know. If Milton had had any color left in his cheeks, it'd be gone now.

How had he not seen it before?

How had he not been prepared?

But who could prepare for this—for *him*?

The corner of Joje's face drew down, his left eye drooping. "I wanted you to know. So you didn't think this was . . . random."

The boy began screaming in the background but noise was already fading . . . fading . . . playing in another room, over the radio in a busy diner where, no matter how hard you tried, you could never recognize the song, playing not to be heard but to fill the gaps between dishes clanging and forks scraping and uncomfortable lulls in conversation that always accompanied those who ate at diners.

The shakily drawn version of Joje lifted a gun, his form going jagged like scribbles where staying in the lines no longer mattered— had it ever mattered? He pointed it, shakily, gun splitting into two, three distorted versions of itself, in his direction, his colors darkening . . . darkening . . . and of all the regrets that could have flashed through Milton's mind, only one burrowed its way out.

He had known this day was coming. They all had known. He just never would've suspected it'd be Joje.

8

Jing Jong, Jing Jong, Jing Jong.

The doorbell resonated through Blake's mind, replacing thought with instinct, instinct with dread. He knew he was losing all rationality.

He also knew the doorbell wasn't ringing.

Jing Jong, sing along, in a cell forever long.

The forbidden corners of his mind had melded into a giant hole as large as the squares between the gridded bars around him. He could no longer lose himself in something as simple as memory.

He thought of his son. He thought of Jenna.

He thought of all the ways he could kill himself.

Suffocating wasn't possible, no matter his willpower, he was unable to keep his nose and mouth pressed into the crook of his arm past a certain point—lungs burning, eyes watering, head both sinking and floating away at the same time. There wasn't enough leverage or enough force for him to break his own neck. His back and spine may have felt like they were at the brittle point of bursting, but there wasn't room to push them any farther. Wiggling or flexing muscles proved almost impossible, drawing enough movement to break or even cut into his own skin, also out of the question. He had even tried to keep his eyes open when sneezing—an old child's maxim he had never believed but was at least willing to try. Conrad's hair and dandruff in the cage had gotten to him over time, his nose now a dribbling mess.

At some point he had let himself urinate, the urge far stronger than sensibility.

Humpty Dumpty sat on the wall, Humpty Dumpty had a great fall . . .

At times he was falling. Like a dream where the air whips around you and there's never a floor or end to graciously splat across. An eternity of flailing limbs and rushing air, eyes so dried from the wind they begin to crack like egg shells.

Help me, he thought. Helllp meeeeee!

All the king's horses and all the king's men . . .

Tick, tick, tick. The clock's one-syllable laugh. Flies feasted on his skin, buzzing down the tubes of his ears, using ropes and pick axes to ascend through his nostrils until they reached the command center where, much like the movie *Being John Malkovich*, they were able to see through his eyes, only now his eyes saw through theirs in strange gridded fashion where every image was distorted through a hundred segmented views.

Humpty Dumpty murdered his wife, Humpty Dumpty took his son's life.

A plague of shadows transformed into scuttling demons, their centipede claws clicking and clacking against the hardwood floor and marble counters. Each time they came forward, they became a little bolder, like seagulls at a beach picnic, darting closer, inch by inch, until the bravest one would eventually reach its talons out, snatching a chunk of flesh off Blake's exposed arms or legs.

Jing Jong, Jing Jong.

Who issss iiiitttttt?

In the maddening silence, Blake came to what might amount to the greatest epiphany of his life—Humpty Dumpty hadn't fallen. He had jumped.

Jing—

Jong.

The doorbell continued to chime.

Chapter 10

Day Six Continued

1

"There's no need to worry."

Adam looked down at his fingers, nails bitten to the point he was now chewing skin. He set his palms down on his legs and watched the other people in the restaurant. An older couple, both massively overweight, mopping up their plates; a young girl, maybe two or three, climbing over the back of a cushioned booth, her mother lifting her back over and setting her down without breaking from her conversation; a young black waitress moving toward them then into the kitchen, pretty face, her gold dangling earrings bouncing with every step.

Even prettier legs.

It felt strange to be surrounded by people who were just living their lives, eating meals on their way to the next item on their things-to-do list. People who weren't wondering if they would be alive tomorrow.

"She's going to be fine. Drew will take care of her," Joje said.

Adam sipped his Mountain Dew, avoiding Joje's gaze. It was almost surprising how easily he could understand Joje now, despite his speech impediment. Adam suspected that with time, even the most grotesque of horrors could become commonplace.

"What's wrong? You can tell me anything, and it stays right here, between you and me."

"This isn't . . . fun anymore," Adam said. "What you're doing? You've taken it too far. It needs to stop." He twirled the straw in his drink.

"So why don't you stop me?" Joje asked.

The little girl squealed as her mother once again lifted her over the booth.

"We're in a public place, people all around, why don't you shout out that you've been kidnapped or have someone call the police? If things have gone too far, you should ask why you've allowed it."

"I can't stop you, I'm just a kid."

Joje laughed, his face lighting up with amusement. "Don't try your games on me. I know you better than you know yourself, better than your own father knows you."

Adam glanced out the window to their left. Dusk was settling into night like a blanket, its folds draping lower to the ground. The beat-up station wagon they had taken down the mountain was parked next to a white minivan that had backed into the space, a stick-figure family of four plus a stick dog all waving on the back of their filthy window.

"Is she going to die? Jenna?" Adam asked.

"Would that bother you?"

The question bothered him, had for some time, mainly because Adam didn't know. He had always thought he wouldn't care if something happened to her, now he wasn't so certain. He felt her hand gripping his even now and had to shake it off.

"Drew will make sure she gets the care she needs," Joje said.

"And what if he doesn't take her to a hospital? What if he just tells us he took her there and instead leaves her in a ditch or, or kills her?"

Joje shifted in the booth, sitting forward and resting his arms on the table. "Drew's not like you or me. He's an idiot, just does what he's told, so yeah he'll take her there. But would your life be that different without her in it? Would you be any different? Or would you maybe stop hiding from who you really are, start becoming your true self?"

The black waitress returned, setting their plates of food in front of them. Her name was Shayna, tag hanging from the open V-neck shirt, bringing it down and to the right just enough to see a little of the cleavage beneath. Like the first tear in the wrapping of a birthday gift, letting you see just enough to make you want to see more.

As soon as she left, Joje asked, "You like her?"

Adam dropped his head, dipping a fat steak fry in the saucer of ketchup.

"You don't have to pretend around me, Adam. Be yourself. Do your parents know?"

"Know what?"

"I didn't think so."

"What, that I like girls?" Adam was surprised by the anger in his voice, more so by Joje's ability to draw it out of him. This was the first they had spent time alone together.

Joje's bottom lip twitched, drawing his left eye down; it looked like he was repeatedly winking at Adam. Creepy. He cleared his throat, glancing at his plate of untouched food, then was back, the movement on his face gone. "How old were you when you made your first kill?"

Adam stopped chewing and swallowed his fry in large chunks that hurt going down.

"You can always tell by the eyes. That special glint. It doesn't come cheap. Was it just one? Or have there been others?"

"Just one," Adam said. He felt like he was both vomiting out his soul and having a stalled car lifted from his chest at the same time.

"There'll be others," Joje said, picking up his Philly cheesesteak sandwich and taking a large bite. Clumps of greasy beef and melted cheese dropped onto the plate. "I knew we would share a bond—I knew it!"

"How . . . how many have you killed?" Adam felt an exhilaration rising within him. Here was someone who could actually understand him, maybe even accept him for who he was.

Joje shook his head, motioning to the waitress approaching. She refilled both of their glasses, asking if everything was okay. They both watched her walk away this time.

"Got a girlfriend?" Joje asked.

Adam recognized the change in subject but was okay with the deflection. They could move back to warmer climates when they were no longer in public. "No, I mean—I had a few back home, but not here."

"Isn't this your home?"

"It's a house, not a home," Adam said flatly.

Joje nodded as if he completely understood. "You prefer blond or brunette? Or ginger?"

"Brunette," Adam said.

"So Jenna's out," Joje said with a laugh. Adam couldn't help but join in. "Dwew told me about your tapes—classic. But you don't want a girl like that. There are much better rides with a lot less maintenance per mile. In fact"—he snapped, pointing his finger at Adam—"I know the perfect one! Unless you wanna wait till Sha-Nay-Nay gets off work?" He nodded toward the kitchen, where the waitress had disappeared.

Adam knew he was supposed to speak but found himself unable. He felt spellbound, as if he were being hypnotized. Was this what Adam did with his friends back home? That same effect—them hanging on his every word, wanting to please him—he now felt for Joje. He didn't understand. He was supposed to be immune to this.

Despite everything, he felt himself relax. He was in the hands of a master.

"I didn't pick your house at random you know?" Joje said.

"I know."

"You do? Of course you do. But you don't know why I chose you."

As Joje told him the reason, Adam found himself relaxing even more, understanding—real understanding—settling in, making itself at home. His life was no longer just a house, four walls with furniture and a family of stick figures, present yet empty of reason, of meaning. He was coming home for the first time in a long time, and his life would never be the same again.

2

Blake blinked.

He swallowed, though there wasn't enough spit to wet his throat.

The house had been immersed in darkness, a thick, unforgiving black capping every surface like oily snow. At least in the only corner he could see.

The corners of his mind were equally dark.

The digital display of an oven clock provided a recessed glow, and whatever moon floated over the waves outside teased a shadow here, beam there.

Such a tease.

They aren't coming back for me.

3

The truck idled at the curb of the street in front of a one-story bronze building that had metastasized into a hospital, wings sprouting from every side. Stu refused to drive into the parking lot, said they had cameras in there.

The stale air pushing through the plastic vents smelled like a squirrel had climbed in to the truck's engine and died there.

Jenna was cradled in Drew's arms, lying across the bench, her feet lifeless in Stu's lap. From her toes to her calves, she looked like some swamp creature out of a horror movie, the kind his old boss used to make, with more shots of boobs than monsters. Flakes of dead skin as thick as twigs were gathering on Stu's pants. Drew had almost forgotten he had been the one to do that to her.

"You could always say she died before we got here," Stu said. "I'm surprised she didn't."

But that wasn't the problem. The problem was Joje wanted him to kill her. At least it was the first problem.

On the drive back down the mountain, Drew had had plenty of time to think, discovering three overreaching problems that, unresolved, would get him caught, killed, or worse.

The fourth problem, he had realized, was that he had never been good at solving problems.

"Joje would know. If I was lying to him," Drew said.

Stu nodded. They all knew Joje's uncanny ability to sense a lie, however minute.

"What if she wakes up?" Stu asked. "You know that's why he's not walking in there. Might as well slap cuffs on yourself if you take her in."

He was right. It was the second of his problems, one he had yet to work out. Because if she woke, she would talk, and if she talked, there would be no shortage of security and police officers to bring Drew down.

But he was *so close*.

If he thought Jenna might live without a doctor, he'd disappear right now, but to go out alone . . . what would the point of this past week have been?

"Look, uh, I've got more I need to do, so let's either dump her or I tip my hat 'cause you're a braver soul than I," Stu said.

"I'm going," Drew said. He leaned forward, lifting his hands from beneath Jenna's head as if going for the door but bending lower, reaching down to the floor. "Help me with her."

"I'm not steppin' outside," Stu said, not realizing what Drew was reaching for.

When he came back up, it required only a movement of a few inches. The hilt that fit so succinctly in Drew's grip pressed forward, the attached blade sliding into Stu's chest just below his sternum. Drew twisted the blade, pinning him to the driver's door. Blood burst from Stu's mouth, spilling over his chin and into his beard, his eyes wide as if he had one more question for Drew.

He probably did.

Drew waited until Stu's eyes glazed over, his head lolling forward. One of his arms plopped onto Jenna's leg, and she stirred beneath him. His third problem hadn't been that difficult after all. With a little luck he'd find a way to manage the others.

He wiped at the sword's handle with a scrunched-up napkin he found in the seat. He wouldn't be taking it with him. The thought was disheartening; that sword had been a part of his transformation, like Adam picking up the Sword of Grayskull and discovering he was He-Man the whole time.

I have the power, Drew thought, and no one—not even George—can take it away!

He looked down at the creature stirring in his arms, more beautiful than any of the buxom blonds Welchsetzer had used. And used. Drew had always gotten his turn, but only when it was time to take out the trash, leaving him empty and craving more. But with Jenna it would be different. A dumpster may still be at the end of their union, but not after their first time. Not after their hundredth.

With the napkin in hand, he opened the door, taking care to

wipe at any edge he may have touched. He lifted Jenna into his arms like a sleeping child and descended the two metal steps down to the sidewalk. A lit-up stone sign read, "USC Verdugo Hills Hospital," but might as well have read, "This Way to a New Future."

Drew took a step forward, then another, his future now within grasp. In his arms Jenna moaned despite being unconscious.

He could get used to that moan.

One problem at a time.

4

Between the sloppy notes of a Jimi Hendrix guitar solo sped up at four times its normal speed, the prattle of his current mental state discussed on an overhead projector in a classroom the size of Tokyo, and the insane screaming in his head, Blake heard a thump at the back door. Then another.

No wonder Jimi's solo was getting increasingly messy. He passed it off as just another piece of sanity dissolving, but the thumping continued.

Coming, he thought, the laugh in his belly never rising to his chest.

Someone was trying to break in.

"Dad! Dad?"

Adam was back for another haunting jaunt. This time would he repeat, "'It's all *your* fault, all *your* fault?'"

The door broke open with a crash, the chill of the night air sweeping in uninvited. Blake felt suddenly naked, serenely so. He was lying on a beach, a sprinkling of stars overhead. Water too warm to be the ocean broke just before his body, retreated, coming back to prod again. His clothes were wet, and he was cold—deathly cold—yet not shivering. Shivering required energy his body simply couldn't expend.

"Dad?"

Adam stood over him. He was no longer lying on a beach; he was at the bottom of a grave, earth opening beneath him as he sank , his son growing more distant above.

"We're back, we're safe."

Warm water lapped up against Blake's face and side. "You're not real," he said.

"Dad, it's me, come on!"

The moonlight split through the shutters over Adam's face, erasing his eyes, leaving only his hair and smile, a wide swath of darkness between.

"Come on—you've got to try!"

His neck rotated back as if in a cinch, each fraction of an inch clicking into place another notch. He cried out in pain—Tick, tick, tick went the square clock.

The door to the cage was open, and yet Blake still couldn't move. Countless times he had imagined his rescue, his body spilling out like beads from a broken vase, pouring onto the floor as soon as the latch was thrown open. But like a sandcastle that doesn't fall apart when the plastic mold is lifted, his body had formed to the cage, the crate.

His new home.

At least it's warm here, he thought, a cloud of heat dispersing from the water around him.

"We're home, you're okay, Dad. We're okay."

Water slopped up over his face and into his mouth. He breathed it in, choked, coughing, his lungs and chest heaving, the movement like a thousand hot needles spreading through the muscles in his back and shoulders and side.

Every exhalation brought an exclamation, suffering beyond imagining. He was going to rip in half, a baby was forcing itself out, a camel going through the eye of a needle, only he was the eye. Hands rubbed his body, his shoulders, his arm that felt it had detached from the rest of him, his hand, its flesh undercooked. He brought it up and over the outer lip of the crate, his fingertips poking through a gridded square.

From the outside.

He was kicking, thrashing against the waves, but they were too strong, the currents slapping him away like a doll. He'd never reach his son—Adam would die, drown, and Blake would hear his cries and see his splashing and hear him scream his father's name

"Dad! Calm down!"

And these four torrential waves would box him in on every side, a cubed vortex, pinging him back with every attempt to escape, reminding him he had come so close, so close,

"Say something!"

So close.

Metal prongs clung to the top of his skull, raking into his flesh, ripping out hair as he slid his head backward, backward until he was

Drowning, water in his ears, crawling down his nostrils, a thin film above his eyes over which everything wavered—Adam, shifting back and forth without moving, face a blur.

He lay on the marble kitchen floor, the coolness of the stones like the caress of a corpse.

He lay an inch beneath the water in his pool, if he slipped from this step, he would drown, he couldn't remember how to swim.

He lay, Adam holding his head in his hands, looking into his eyes as if he no longer recognized his own father, shouting, shouting,

His words unclear beneath the surface of water,

Shouting his name, shouting

"Dad,"

We're home.

5

The fire crackled in the middle of the pool, a cinder spitting out into the sky before dissipating midflight. Wherever it had intended to go, it never made it.

Blake sat at the lip of the pool, legs dangling in the water. Every few seconds he would gasp, muscles tensing, his body taut. And then he would remember where he was.

Adam stood nearby, Joje leaning back in a patio chair by the table, granting them space. A colorless moth flew overhead in tired loops.

Adam told him about the men who had kidnapped him and his escape, how if Joje hadn't shown up, he would be dead.

Thank God for Joje.

Jenna had been hurt and taken to a hospital. He asked which one. Neither of them knew.

"Did anyone come by the house? Anyone hear you?" Joje asked.

Blake didn't know.

"Well, there's an unmarked van across the street. I don't think they know you're here. Probably don't have a warrant or they'd already be inside, but you can bet they'd like to bring you in for questioning," Joje said.

The flames crested and dipped so similar to the waves of the ocean. Blake was mesmerized by them.

"We had to park out on the main road," Joje continued.

"The PCH," Adam said.

"Right. We came around through the back."

Blake couldn't believe how many shades of orange and yellow hid within each flame.

"We got a dog," Joje said. "You should see her, a real beauty."

Weal booty.

"What kind?" Blake asked, the fire reminding him of Conrad.

"Wrong question," Joje said. "Care to try again?"

Blake didn't. Eventually Adam helped him to his feet as he took his first tenuous steps, leaning on his son for support. He felt like a mannequin, knees and joints refusing to bend, his jerky movements so uncoordinated.

"Did the water help?" Adam asked.

It hadn't. Or maybe it had, just not enough.

"No lights," Joje said, following them inside. "I want them thinking we're not here."

The dog crate was directly in front of the broken door, the lock's latch busted, pieces hanging. Adam led him around the table pretending not to notice Blake hyperventilating at the sight of the cage. They stopped at the fridge, pulling out a bottle of Vitamin Water. Nothing had ever tasted so good.

"There's something you need to see," Joje said. "In your office, where they won't notice the lights."

Blake grabbed a second bottle as well as a bag of baby carrots.

"What kind of dog?" he asked as they crossed the family room. The shattered TV still leaned up against the wall, the newer shinier version hanging above it.

"Just a bitch, nothing special," Joje said. "We shouldn't stay long, she'll be getting lonely back at the car."

"You're not staying?" Blake asked. "Don't make me go back in the cage! Please, I'll do anything!"

"I know you will," Joje said.

Blake had forgotten about the fallen chandelier, thought maybe by now police chalk would line where its corpse had lain on their entrance floor. The aftereffects of his and Joje's fight were apparent in the living room: overturned lamp and piano bench, blood smeared on the white carpet like oil stains on a driveway. His office was only another reminder of his defeat.

"I got a text earlier," Joje said, "on my phone. My *personal* phone. From your friend?"

Now Blake understood why Joje sounded so upset. Rory Shepherd had paid him a little digital visit.

"How can he do that? My number's not listed anywhere."

"Child's play," Blake answered.

"Well, this text, it was an e-mail address and password. I didn't even know what it meant, but Adam figured it out—he's brilliant, your son, you know. So we logged in to the e-mail, and there's one message. A video."

Joje flipped open the cover to Blake's tablet, powering it on. He had forgotten about it, back in his briefcase. Had Joje found it in his car? Joje handed it to Adam. "Here, you work it."

The black screen came aglow, casting light against the far wall. Adam toggled to the web browser then went to hotmail.com. For e-mail, he typed in *blakes-effed*. Blake couldn't tell exactly what the password was; he decided he didn't want to know.

A single e-mail was available, as Joje had said, marked read. Adam opened it—no subject line, no text, there was only an ASF file as an attachment. Blake would have ordinarily refused to open such a file—especially from Rory—but right now things like that didn't seem to matter.

Adam double clicked the attachment, a small window popped up, and he clicked full screen. He looked at Blake almost apologetically.

It was a grainy black-and-white feed, but what it showed was unmistakable. Jenna's SUV pulling up to the back dock of the warehouse. It spliced forward, showing Blake walking alone up the stairs toward the building, holding a small tank. Another splice. Blake walking down the hall inside the building, alone, tank in hand. Cut to Blake holding the tank above his head as he ran past a camera. Another angle. Blake pouring the liquid gas onto explosives wrapped around a pillar. Another cut. Blake slamming into the young janitor, then leaving the screen. The janitor stayed down on the floor—he lifted his hands as if to ward off an attack. Then the feed went to static.

Blake looked from the screen to his son. It would have been better had I just died, he thought. At least then Adam wouldn't think of me as a killer.

He felt an intense need to explain himself, that he hadn't known the kid was in there, hadn't wanted to destroy that building, that Joje was the one who had done it, made him do it, that somehow he had known this would happen, had even planned this moment to make Adam think his father was less of a person; a murderer, someone he could no longer look up to or long to be like.

"There's more," Joje said.

The static gave way to a black screen, a hand appeared holding a white piece of paper with words on it written in black marker.

"Tomorrow. Midnight."

The hand let the paper drop, another one behind it.

"Payment Due"

Papers continued to drop, as the message unfolded.

"Saint Helena's"

"Stitch"

"Nice"

"Doing"

"Business"

The video ended, reverting back to a frozen frame of the SUV pulling into the loading dock. Blake squinted—could you see there were two people in the car? The reflection off the windshield made it almost impossible to tell. Not that it would matter.

Rory had him. If Blake couldn't find a way to get JT's coin by tomorrow night, that video would leak all over the Internet. Between Rory and Joje, Blake's sentencing was guaranteed.

"Wanna watch it again?" Joje asked

"I didn't know," Blake said to Adam. "I was just trying to—"

"It's all right, Dad. I know Joje made you do it."

"No. This is important—I didn't do it for him," Blake said. "I did it for you."

"You killed that kid for me?"

"No!"

"We'll help you, Bwake, to get that coin," Joje said. "We're in this together. Just our little family."

"No, I don't want Adam involved in this."

"I'm already involved," Adam said.

"No," Blake said, the word coming out more forcibly than he had intended.

"What's this Saint Helena's and stitch thing?" Joje asked.

"Location maybe? A church? I don't know, wherever he wants us to deliver his payment," Blake said.

"And stitch?" Joje asked.

"No clue."

"Why don't we go get the dog, bring her back to the house, and then we can all brainstorm for tomorrow's activities?" Joje said.

"I want to talk to Jenna first," Blake said. "Make sure she's okay."

"Of course you do," Joje said. "All in good time."

6

Drew felt like a bug beneath a microscope, under the scrutiny of every passing doctor and nurse in the vicinity. They had taken Jenna almost as soon as he had stepped through the ER doors, and now, as the seconds and minutes ticked by, he was no longer sure if he had made the right call.

A magazine was on the hard plastic chair to his right, "10 Secrets to Please Your Man" slapped on its cover. The gaunt, pale face of the model with her hair pulled back wasn't enough to get Drew to pick up its pages. Instead he waited, his thumbs circling the inner tips of his index fingers without even knowing it.

A plump nurse, with an ass so large it looked like someone had done a boob job on her behind, strolled from the double doors toward him. She moved like a walrus, shuffling one side forward, then the other. Most of the other nurses deferred to her, Drew had noticed. Must be some kind of pecking order based on who had to lug around the most weight on their butts.

He stood, wanting to be ready. Bad news could take many forms, and running might be the only option he had.

She stopped in front of him, her weight settling in like Jell-O that's just been passed. "You're the husband?"

"I am."

7

Blake lowered himself halfway down the wall before leaping to the hard cement below. His feet slapped against the patio of whatever celebrity or investment broker's house this was but once again failed him, his body rolling to the ground.

Each time he fell it was getting harder to stand back up.

He paused, listening to see if anyone had been alerted. The pool in this backyard was straight and narrow, crossing beneath an exterior wall and continuing lengthwise inside the home. Its liquid dark and quiet, as enticing as the night. Quite the contrast from the waves crashing to Blake's right, or the light spilling from inside the home.

The back walls of the mansion were glass, giving the occupants a clear view of the ocean. Apparently, wall jumpers hadn't been a consideration.

Blake flattened himself against the wall, keeping a juvenile palm between him and the house. The kitchen looked empty, its white lights casting a glow upon what could have been a laboratory it looked so clean. The room next to it must have been a dining area, small bulbs of light flickering softly. No, candles. A light was on in one of the rooms upstairs but provided little beyond silhouettes that Blake's mind turned into people staring and pointing.

He heard a scrape above and looked up. Adam, tipping one leg over the side of the wall without even a huff of exertion. Joje would be right behind. He had been keeping his distance from Blake since they had set out for the car, probably a good thing. Adam cleared the landing with ease, motioned toward the house.

"They were having sex," Adam said. "In the bedroom, when we came through earlier." Blake followed his gaze to the hovering light upstairs. "Joje thought it was two guys. I couldn't tell. Next one should be the last, another motion sensor but no dog."

Adam ducked low, creeping between the bushes and cliff's edge almost in a crawl. Blake followed, the boom of another swell breaking against rocks, causing his heart to flutter. That sound no longer provided the reassurance its digital soundtrack had only a week ago. He'd never sleep to waves again.

They cleared the other yard without incident, pausing the two times rear spotlights sprang from sensors. Beyond the last wall they were greeted with sparse weeds atop volcanic rock and boulders, sand wedged into every crevice, blowing softly with the breeze. The occasional car roared past twenty yards away on the Pacific Coast Highway.

"How big is it," Blake asked as they scrambled down a ravine, thick brush camouflaging how much farther they needed to go. "The dog? Are we gonna be able to carry it back?"

"You're asking the wrong question," Joje said.

They followed the highway down a quarter mile to a grouping of dilapidated houses that were probably condemned. Each shack looked as if it would blow over at the next gust of wind, yet year after year, storm after storm, they stood, defying nature's laws. Only in Malibu could you find a two-bedroom, six-hundred-square-foot home built in the 1920s and never renovated since that would still appraise for over a million dollars.

These homes had the same stubbornness Blake had seen in many CEOs, the ones who had built their companies from the ground up. Hardened older men, often in their late seventies or early eighties, who should have retired years ago yet continued, opposing their age, competition, innovation, and often younger children and grandchildren trying to replace them any way possible.

A sparkling white Mercedes SUV with dealer plates was parked in front of a one car garage to one of the small homes. The garage appeared to be the only thing keeping the house from collapsing in on itself. Joje and Adam both walked toward the car.

"Did you steal that?" Blake asked.

"Bought it," Joje said. "Jenna's car took a dump."

"This one had good reviews," Adam said.

"You bought a car together?"

"Sales guy even let Adam drive," Joje said with a smile.

A car whizzed past on the curved road doing at least sixty just a few feet from where they stood, its tail lights disappearing around the next bend. Where was the formidable duo, Randall and McClellan, when you needed them?

Blake ran his hands up to the windows, peering inside. It was empty.

"In the house, Bwake. We were concerned she might make too much noise. Dogs do bark after all," Joje said.

The porch was stooped, shingles sliding down the left side of the roof like children sledding in snow. The door was so sun faded it looked to be completely colorless. No damage to the doorjamb; Blake wondered how they had broken in.

Inside was a narrow hall that led to an open bathroom and closed bedroom door on the right, kitchen on the left. Lines in the carpet like wheel tracks of a stroller led toward the bedroom. Blake followed the sound of footsteps and continued into the kitchen. A stand-alone stove, yellowed countertops, and pine cabinets that looked to have fed generations of termites. The table in the center of the small room was nothing more than a piece of plywood resting on two small refrigerators the size Blake typically saw in executives' office suites. A stained glass lamp with decorated floral insignia hung like the last branch of a dying tree from the ceiling.

A million might have been generous.

"In here, Bwakey," Joje shouted from the adjacent room separated by a sliding glass door. Blake was glad architecture had improved in the past nine decades.

Before continuing into what had to be the living room, his eyes fell on a wooden block next to a microwave with a wind-up dial, the kind that cooked your food while pumping radiation into your organs. The block had six knife blades stuck into it.

Blake slid one out, examining it. A butcher knife, some cheap made-in-China brand he didn't recognize, its flimsy blade less than ideal. He placed it back in—way too bulky—and settled for a smaller boning knife, its curved steel hopefully giving him some advantage over its dulled edge.

"Bwake?"

"Coming," he said, his heart palpitations rising. His throat seemed to be shrinking—he could barely breathe as he lowered the knife to his side.

It was too obvious. Joje would see it. The humidity in the room had doubled. Blake held the knife, trying to determine where to store it. After wiping the sweat from his face, he plugged it back into the hole in the block.

He couldn't do it. It would go wrong, backfire, and send him back to the crate.

With the knife back in the block, he felt his breathing ease. It did nothing for the dull throb behind his eyes.

Passing through the glass partition, he stepped down onto the mahogany carpet that clashed so well with the rust-colored wallpaper. A small box TV sprouting antennas rested atop a beveled table, a patterned beige couch against the far wall.

Stacks of old magazines littered the edges of the room, some almost as high as the ceiling. Most had tumbled long ago, their journey down still evident by the scattered heaps they had formed. Blake detected an odd odor to the room, like mildewed rags breathing fresh air for the first time in a long time.

"Where's the dog?" Blake asked.

"Back patio," Joje said. "Unless she threw herself over, in which case she's probably dead twenty feet below. Now if she is still there, she's gonna need some . . . convincing."

Adam looked uncomfortable, glancing around the walls of the room.

"Did you bring a leash?" Blake asked.

Joje smiled. "We couldn't get it on her. She's a fighter, this one."

"I must be missing something," Blake said.

"I told you you were asking the wong questions," Joje said. "You never asked her name."

"The dog?"

"The bitch," Joje said.

A cold cord wrapped itself around Blake's intestines, squeezing, tightening. "Is Jenna out there? Is she hurt?"

"Now you're getting warm, but Adam wanted her to be a little younger. Takes after his old man."

"Who is it? Who's out there!"

"Wucy." As Joje's smile expanded, a trickle of blood leaked from one swollen nostril. "And we wuv Wucy."

Chapter 11

Day Six Continued

1

The small, wiry man standing behind the desk had more bags under his eyes than seemed possible. The bags had bags. His gaunt face and tired eyes suggested he fought a battle every day much more taxing than his job. A battle he was losing. Drew wondered how long it had been since the little guy's last whiff of the stuff that made your teeth shiny.

"Please, have a seat." The doctor gestured to the two chairs in front of his desk.

Drew remained standing.

The office was small and sterile, hanging plaques from ambiguous universities, token frame with wife and two kids, all smiles. The man obviously didn't spend much time here.

As he realized Drew wasn't going to sit, the doctor's beady eyes darted around the room. "Your, uh, wife, yes?"

"Yes."

"Well we have some positive news, her head injury was superficial, lot of blood and tissue, which is typical, a lot more blood vessels in the head than anywhere else on the body, but no cerebral damage. Her skull's intact and readings look, uh, normal. So that's, yes, like I said, very positive."

"Can I see her?"

"No, no, not yet. Her, uh, condition. Well, let me ask you, her legs? How long ago did she sustain those injuries?"

Here it comes, Drew thought, glancing at the door. Security or police were probably on their way. No wonder the man was nervous.

"The, uh, severity of the burns, well, it's sent her body into a hypermetabolic response, her circulation levels of catabolic hormones increasing dramatically, catecholamines, cortisol . . . in essence, her body's requiring an immense increase of energy just to meet basic functions, cannibalizing the proteins found in the muscles in her legs. How did she sustain her injuries?"

"A fire," Drew said.

The doctor slowly nodded as he realized Drew was done explaining. "Ah, I see. Um, is there a reason she wasn't brought in for care sooner? She had to be in incredible pain."

Drew found himself wishing Joje were here, he was always better at thinking on his feet. Drew had always used his fists to do most of his convincing.

"Is she going to be okay?" he asked.

"Yes. And, uh, and no." The doctor took a seat, his chair tilting back farther than he had intended, almost sending him sprawling. He recovered without much grace. "The degree of her burns are, as I said, uh, very severe. I'm not good at delivering bad news, but . . . we think we can save her left leg."

"And her right?"

"Yes, we, uh, refer to it as tissue death. The blood vessels, nerve tissue"—he began shaking his head—"it's irrecoverable. I'm sorry. Had she, um, been brought in earlier, there, well, we might have had some options."

"Okay," Drew said.

"Right, we'll be needing your authorization, of course." He brought out a piece of paper from a drawer in his desk. "The nurses already took your insurance information?"

"It won't be a problem," Drew said, finally sitting, turning the paper around. He signed Blake's name once, twice, three different times, initialing in another half dozen places. It didn't matter that it would never match. "How long will it take?"

"The surgery?"

"Recovery."

"A lifetime?" The doctor sat forward in his chair pinching his bottom lip with one hand, unaware. "Losing one's limb, both physically and mentally can require—"

"How long till I can take her home? Move her?"

"We'll want her here at least a week, maybe longer. As I said, depression can be—"

"Just do it already," Drew said, the doctor's babbling getting on his nerves.

When he left the cramped office, there wasn't a security guard or police officer in sight. He really didn't need Joje after all.

2

Blake closed the door to the balcony behind him, a sense of vertigo driving him to the thin metal rail overlooking the drop below. He spotted brush and rocks, a child's blue Windbreaker caught on some branches, and more trash than Blake would have guessed. What he didn't find was Lucy's bent and broken body, cast from the balcony that felt about as stable as the rest of the house.

He found her at the opposite end, cowering beneath a patio table, its chairs and table top covered with enough dust to cast it in a moldy shade of brown. She was bound, legs and hands, with plastic ties looped close to her skin. A thick cloth wrapped between her teeth.

She had been stripped to her underwear, black lace panties, matching bra, a tattoo of Japanese letters running down the side of her left arm. Blake recognized one of them. *Bravery.* Her head was bent forward, hair falling over her eyes like a waterfall caught in a picture, standing still when meant to be moving, flowing. In another setting it would have been seductive; with the bruises already forming on her arms and shoulder, it was anything but.

"What have they done?" he asked before realizing he had lumped Adam in with Joje. Had his son played a role in her kidnapping? How far had Joje made him go?

Not nearly as far as he's driven me, he thought.

He walked toward her slowly, his hands held out in front of him. Considering the state of his own body, he wasn't sure it was a

246 | B e h r g

calming gesture. "I'm sorry you've been . . . dragged into this."

His eyes moved to her pale flesh, rippled with goose bumps. She had to be freezing. Her hands instinctively rose to cover her breasts. Blake looked away, not wanting her to get the wrong idea. Then again he had been staring.

He lowered himself to the deck, sitting with his legs crossed beneath him. With effort he was able to keep his eyes on her face. "They came six days ago. Kidnapping my family and me . . . we've been living in a hell ever since. If you fight it, them, it only makes it worse."

Lucy's large eyes peered out at him behind a trail of dark hair.

"I won't hurt you."

He leaned in to remove the cloth wrapped tightly in her mouth. As he reached behind her, Lucy swung her two hands clasped into fists, catching him on the side of the head completely unprepared.

He fell back, off balance, into the leg of the table, dragging it with him a few inches. His vision blotted, and he closed his eyes, leaning his head against the plastic matting of a chair.

He really didn't have any fight left. Lucy, on the other hand, had been preparing herself for this attack for the past hour or more.

Her legs bucked forward, hammering into the cavity just below his sternum—a strangled sound burst from his mouth, and the chair that his head was resting upon slid back, his head falling straight to the deck floor.

When he could open his eyes again, Lucy was crouched on top of him; her arms, still tied together, were bent over him, one twisting his head in a choke hold, the other pressing something sharp and ridged against the side of his throat. He felt the weight of her chest shift against his back, her bare skin cool to the touch. Her gag was no longer in place as she said, "You're gonna get me out of here."

"You've got the wrong guy."

"I learned a long time ago. They're all wrong guys."

Blake thought of how ironic it would be if after all their struggles, she would be the one to end his life. "You can't fight it," he said. Partly to Lucy, mostly to himself.

"When the others come out? We make a trade. Your life for mine."

They didn't have to wait long. Unfortunately, Joje wasn't interested in a trade.

"This could make for a good joke," Joje said after following Adam out. "What does a girl whose arms and legs are bound hold you hostage with? A screw! Get it?" His smile lit up his face. "No seriously, Bwake, were you so busy staring at her boobs you didn't see her coming? Or did you just think she was faking it?" He laughed out loud, grabbing hold of the rail at the deck's edge.

"This isn't a joke—I'll do it!" Lucy said for probably the fourth or fifth time. Even with her intensity, Blake recognized the diminishing power of her words with each go.

"So do it, by all means," Joje said. "Rake that screw across his throat and let the warm blood seep over your arms and legs. Bathe in it. And when you're done, whether you kill him or not, you're coming with us. But the better you behave, the easier this will be, I promise." Her head fell against Blake's shoulder, hair tickling his face, as she began to weep. A brown rusty screw dropped from her hand, tinkling to the deck floor. Blake felt her sobs in her entire body, pressed flush to his. Despite the pain he felt, despite the contempt for what was happening, his body reacted as is often the case when an almost-naked woman clings to you. He was so aware of it, so repulsed by his reaction, that it only made the urge stronger.

At Joje's command, Adam came to help Blake up, lifting Lucy's arms over Blake's neck and pulling him to his feet. His slacks bent around the tent sticking out from between his legs. Embarrassed, he pressed his fists against it, closing his eyes. Had Joje known? Ordering Adam at that very moment? Either way, his son was painfully aware, stepping back from Blake as if he didn't know him.

"Believe me now?" Joje said to Adam. He rested a hand on Blake's shoulder. "You're a little early, Bwakey, but don't worry, we're getting there."

3

It was Adam's idea that enabled them to return to the house by car. He dialed nine-one-one from Lucy's cell, giving the dispatch operator a story about his drunk friends darting in front of cars, playing chicken on the PCH. She asked him where they were, and he told her a couple miles north of the Chart House, a seafood restaurant south of their estate. His performance was flawless, breaking into tears, whispering into the phone, telling her his friends couldn't find out he called or they'd kill him. Even his disconnect was timed, with Joje yelling at him across the driveway.

His plan, while not brilliant, did the trick. At that hour, it was easier to send the parked van outside their home to check on the disturbance versus dispatching another vehicle. When the van pulled out, the Mercedes pulled in.

A staunch odor met them in the garage; the body in Blake's trunk was growing accustomed to its new state of decomposition. Joje had pulled the unfamiliar SUV into the spot where Jenna's Escalade should have been. *So many should-have-beens*, Blake thought. And then a foreign thought, a voice that wasn't his own broke through the swirling cloud of noise in his head.

Don't let this be another one.

It was Jenna's voice, Jenna's thought coming to him when he needed her most, like a radio signal squawking through the middle of a storm in a momentary lapse of clouds.

I need you, Blake thought. Need your strength, your will!

Need or not, she was gone. Radio silence.

The house felt unfamiliar, like he was visiting for the first time. As Blake looked around the family room and down the hall to the stairs, he finally realized what it was: every mark in the home that proved people lived here had been created by Joje or Drew. The groove in the hardwood floor, the still-present aroma of bleach and ammonia flitting in from the bathroom, the broken latch to the back door, pots and unwashed dishes, dried and crusted food on the counters, trash spilling over from behind the kitchen island, the new TV, the one replaced still leaning against the wall beneath it, Conrad's crate, one handcuff still latched to its door, the other dangling.

And if they continued farther into the house?

Blake's destroyed office, blood on the white carpet in the living room, furniture overturned, white piano slathered with red, chandelier down in the foyer like a helicopter struck midflight. Blake had seen glimpses of what Drew had done with the sword upstairs when he had passed through the hall this morning, frames and vases torn from walls, pillows cut into shreds, fluff and glass littering the hall.

And in the backyard?

Two fresh graves so far. How many more might be added tonight?

The house is theirs, he thought. It always was. We were the intruders, we the ones not meant to be here.

"Home, sweet home," Joje said, as if in echo of Blake's thoughts. "We're going to retire to bed early tonight. There was a performance I was promised, and we're quite frankly running out of time. Now I don't know if we're going to be under surveillance tonight. That van might come back? It might not. But I'm low on patience, so the only screaming better be in the throes of ecstasy."

Suddenly Joje had Blake's full attention. "What?"

Lucy sat quietly on the couch. If she had understood Joje like Blake had, she wasn't making it known. Yet.

"This shouldn't come as a surprise, Bwake. In fact it should look familiar. A wife in the hospital and you home with another woman in your bed."

"What the hell are you talking about?"

"While your son sleeps, unaware of you adulterating in the next room," Joje said.

Blake felt his jaw clamp tight.

"Only this time he'll be fully aware. Won't he."

"Adam, I need your help," Blake said.

"Do you love your son, Bwake?"

Blake continued, "We have him outnumbered, and without Drew, we can take him."

"Bwake, do you love your son?" Joje asked again.

Adam still hung back by Lucy on the far side of the couch.

"But we have to work together. Adam?" Blake said.

Joje shrugged his arms into the air, looking at Adam. "Maybe you were right."

"Of course I love my son!"

"Are you honest with him?"

"Always." The distance between him and Joje was five feet. In Blake's current state he was more apt to keel over than drive into him like he had before. Joje was playing those odds.

"So if he asked a question, you would give him an honest answer. Tell him the truth, no matter what?" Joje asked.

Blake swallowed, sensing where Joje was leading him but not knowing how to change that course. "I would," he said. "I'll always tell you the truth, Adam. Always."

Adam looked so much older, as if this week had aged him not in days but years. His hair still unkempt, his face with that boyish youthfulness, but his eyes had a hardness that hadn't been there a week ago. Or maybe it had, like a rash beneath the skin, waiting to be scratched at in order to spread. Blake may have lost Adam the same day he lost his daughter, he just hadn't known it until now.

"Go ahead, Adam. Ask him," Joje said.

"Did you . . . did you kill Rachel? My real mom?"

"What?"

"Did you kill her?" Adam asked again.

Blake's eyes lost their focus, memories sweeping over the current landscape like a rolling fog erasing a city street and the shops on either side. But these memories had been rehearsed, lines rewritten, relearned until their delivery felt more honest than the truth. Actors playing roles, a forced tear at the side of a hospital bed, music crescendoing to that point where an audience wept not from emotion but from the idea of emotion—an intuitive knowledge that here was where they were supposed to feel . . . something. The fabrication of emotion, such an elaborate lie that it could feel better than the truth. And sometimes, if you allowed yourself to believe the lie, it became easier the next time, those tears so quick to roll, those scenes so much crisper and neater and fuller than the real thing. But as the layers peeled away to the raw scene beneath, Blake recognized the truth he had never allowed himself to believe. The truth he had purposely kept not just from his son, but from himself.

"Yes," he said. "I did. I killed her."

4

The emotions stirring beneath the surface were so unfamiliar Adam wasn't sure what he felt. Vindication? Betrayal? A concoction of contempt and disdain mixed with a strange empathy, just another lost soul.

"What'd I tell you?" Joje said. "The glint."

"I signed the papers, to take her off the machines that were keeping her alive," Blake said.

"So you could be with Jenna," Adam said.

"No!" Blake looked horrified at the thought. "I didn't do it for Jenna. It was for her. Your mom. She asked me—begged me—every single day! In the end, I . . . I could barely visit. It was all she said, all she thought. Adam, you have to understand she was in so much pain, even the drugs couldn't touch it. There comes a point when you can't watch the ones you love suffer anymore. It was . . . it was the only thing left I had to give her. So I gave in, signed the papers, put a stop to prolonging her death. If that makes me a murderer, so be it, but knowing what she had to go through, I would do it again. Because I loved her."

"That's the truth?" Adam asked.

"I swear. I never wanted her to die."

Adam nodded. "Thank you. For being honest."

"He hasn't," Joje said. "Two months after Rachel's death, Dr. Jasper Rominko introduced a new palliative surgery using stent placements to bypass blocked ducts and lymph nodes. It would have saved her. She would still be here today if you had loved her enough to *not* let her have her way. Instead, six months later she was in the ground and you were on a honeymoon in the Philippines with wife number two. "

"How the hell do you know all this?" Blake asked. He was shaking, whether from anger or exhaustion, Adam couldn't tell. "No one has access to that information."

"I've had an interest in you, Bwake, my whole life—stay sitting!" Joje yelled. Lucy cowered back onto the couch.

Adam watched his father turn from Joje's face to Adam's, back to Joje, then back to Adam. Was he finally figuring it out?

Blake's eyes widened. "Oh, God, you're her son."

5

Blake couldn't keep his eyes from flitting between Adam and Joje, for the first time really seeing the resemblance. Remove the red hair and freckles, and you could see it in their faces—the slight nose, strong chin, the dimple that only appeared on the left when smiling.

Just like Rachel's.

"So this is, what, some sick idea of revenge? You must know Rachel gave you up long before I was in the picture!"

"And you gave up on her, didn't you?" Joje said. "But this isn't about revenge. This is a reunion."

Blake was instantly reminded of the first moment he met Joje on the porch, his face lighting up at seeing Adam, wriggling his fingers in a ridiculous wave.

"I told you from the beginning this wasn't about your money, but that's all you think about," Joje said. "'For where your treasure is, there your heart will be also.' An old pirate saying."

"I think it was Jesus who said that actually," Blake said.

"Same difference.".

Blake felt naked beneath their gazes—even Lucy looked at him with doubtful eyes. He held his hands out to his sides, spreading his arms. "You've got me. Do what you want. Blame me for your shitty life, who you've become, 'cause I'm right here and I'm not going anywhere! But Adam? I loved your mother. If you really believe that I intentionally did anything to hurt her?" A tear fell from one eye, dropping quickly down Blake's cheek. "Then maybe you're better off with him."

"So cheating on her with Jenna while she was dying? That didn't hurt Mom?" Adam asked, his face flushed. "Did she know?"

Another tear ran down the other side of Blake's face.

"You act like you're so innocent, but this may be the best thing to have happened to us! Force us to stop living these lies," Adam said.

"So you would, what, go live with *him*? In some rundown ghetto, pulling scams to scrape by, constantly running from police—is that what you want? That's what you consider honest living? Grow up, Adam! The biggest lie is this load of crap Joje is selling you."

Adam looked as if he had been physically slapped.

Joje pulled Adam in protectively. "You still don't get it, do you, Bwake? I'm worth more than you could ever be. I wouldn't shit on what you call a life. The only scam here is you convincing yourself I'm something I'm not."

Blake shook his head, so unused to admitting defeat. But from any angle he looked, this was a checkmate. The family he had tried so hard to protect had been torn out from under him, turned against him. He had nothing left to fight for.

"We're going to give you a choice here, Bwakey, a final one, to help you keep our first rule. Remember that one? Nothing changes from your routine. And we're back to a routine now, aren't we? With the wifey in the hospital, the way I see it, you've got two options. Sleep with Wucy here, committing adultery as you've proven to do in the past, or choose the other thing you do so well—make the call to kill your wife. Drew's with her right now, and he can make sure she doesn't wake up. But as always the choice is yours."

Blake shrunk toward the wall as Joje reached behind him to pull out his gun, but it wasn't a gun he held out, it was a cellphone. The first ring sounded like a gunshot.

"What?" Drew's voice said over the phone's speaker.

"Dwew, what's the status on our leading lady?"

"Just got out of surgery.".

Surgery? Blake thought.

"Is she awake?" Joje asked.

"Not yet. I'm in her room, waiting."

"Good. Bwake's deciding her fate right now." Joje looked at Blake expectantly.

The pain behind his eyes went from an ache to a fierce stabbing sensation. It was like some ravenous creature had awoken in his head and was slowly gnawing its way out through the back of his eyes.

"Bwake? What's it gonna be?"

6

The running water in the sink was a backdrop to the liquid thoughts cascading through his mind. Blake stood in his boxer briefs, shirtless, both hands resting against the counter in their master bath as he stared at the ghost of the man presented before him. He could only look into those eyes for a fleeting second before he had to turn away, focus on the scars, the bruises, cuts, or burns. At least there were plenty of options.

"You're gonna be fine," Joje had told him. "It's old hat, this is who you are, what you do. Just be honest with yourself."

Be honest with myself. Had he ever been?

Had he been honest with Adam about Rachel? About those

awful last months? Where days had blurred into a never-ending scroll, balancing the demands of a job that required three of him, a son who asked a thousand questions about Mommy—not a one Blake knew how to answer—and then his time with her, every day going in the morning, back in the evening, the long walk from the field that had been turned into a temporary parking lot because the real one was under construction. He had had to repolish his shoes twice a day to keep from looking like a field worker. The nurses knew him by name, though he could never remember theirs. The elevator up, only two floors, but that thing had moved so slow, and when the doors finally yawned open, Blake only wished there had been farther to go, because at the end of the wide hall, sixteen steps past the painting of a young girl in an orange dress picking flowers in a field, past the nurses' station that was almost always empty (no time for solitaire in this ward), and then the door, a gray plastic sign mounted next to it, room forty-two, with a handle that had required almost no effort to push down, and yet the door had felt so heavy, wanting to remain closed. He would count to ten and then always wait one second longer; if he ever made it past eleven, he knew he would turn around, never to walk those halls again. He would slap a smile onto his face like a sticker as he walked in only to be accosted by his wife begging him to let her die.

Yes, he had been truthful. He had loved her and she him. In some way her verbal abuse during those last months was her way of helping him move on. She chose to leave him hating her rather than missing her or dwelling on what might have been. It was her last act of love.

And so he had resolved to do the same. With a signature attached to a form he had vowed never to sign. But how could anyone understand what they had given each other? Sacrifices that from the outside appeared self-serving had required a love deeper than passion, than reason—a love of respect.

Truth was often uglier than lies, heavier on the heart and brimming with the remorse that only comes from making tough decisions. And just because the right choice was made sure as hell didn't keep the anchors of guilt from pulling, constantly pulling.

It was how Blake had learned the truth—that sometimes it was better to just lie.

"Leave Jenna alone. If anyone has to pay for my mistakes . . . let it be me."

His words still rubbed against the abrasion dividing truth from lie. Because Blake had also learned that choices could be endings in disguise.

Through the steam now rising in front of the mirror, Joje's face came into view.

"Will you let me talk to her? When this is through?" Blake asked.

"Do all the talking you want," Joje said. "When this is through."

Blake was grateful for the steam. It hid the reflection of Joje's smile. "I'm going to need a few things. I'm what you might call a traditionalist when it comes to this sort of thing."

"So none of the kinky stuff?" Joje asked. "What do you need?"

"Two glasses, bottle of wine—there's a vintage port from Italy, it's the larger bottle with dark purple glass. Adam would know where to look. Cologne by the bed, to mask her smell. For after . . . unless you want to get caught. There's a rubbing oil I use, if I can find it. A cigar, lighter, and a . . . condom."

Joje turned from Blake's reflection to look at him. Did he sense something was off or would he dismiss it for submission? "That's a tall order."

It took all of Blake's reserves to be able to look him in the eye. No feigning of fear; it was as genuine as Blake's hatred for him. "We don't have to go through with it."

"Aw, Bwake, but we do. You'll see—just like Adam. When you stop holding yourself back from the real you, there's a freedom that explodes outward. A release." *A wahwease.* "No more lies. It's a thing of beauty."

How anyone could describe watching a coerced and enslaved man rape an unwilling hostage as a thing of beauty was beyond Blake.

"I'll have Adam get the wine," Joje said.

"Will you have him—I'm going to need something a little stronger. There's a bottle of absinthe in there, and maybe a shot glass."

Joje looked at him for a long moment. "Anything else?"

"No, that's all."

"And you can find the rest?"

"I can manage."

As he opened the cupboard drawer beneath the sink, filtering through tubes of creams and lotions in all sizes, hair dryers, curlers and straighteners, plastic bags of Q-tips, cotton balls, and U-shaped dental floss, one thought floated to the top above all his others. The most dangerous man is the one who has nothing left to live for. But more dangerous than him is the one who's found a cause to die for.

7

The hum and bleating of machines was the first sound to break through Jenna's unconsciousness followed by the low drone of a male's voice. She became aware of her breathing, of the uncomfortable couch or bed she was propped up in. Slowly her eyes fluttered open. She was in a hospital bed surrounded by medical equipment, lights and dots and staggering peaks and valleys registering her vitals with utter efficiency.

Sterile sheets were drawn up to her lap, a light-blue hospital gown completing her dressing. Past the IVs taped to her arm was a plastic wristband with her name on it. In case she forgot.

Jenna Crotchet. Through good times and bad, through sickness or health, till death do us part. Maybe she did need the reminder.

As she looked around the empty room, she suddenly realized it was over. She was in a hospital. *They had won!*

A seed of hope began to take root, though her fear rose like a scorching sun, ready to destroy its germinating bed.

She closed her eyes, breathing in and letting her breath out. Whatever drugs they had her on, they were the good ones. She knew she would only be awake a short while before that enticing undertow sucked her back beneath.

She was so thirsty. With effort she opened her eyes again. A call button should be hanging from one of the armrests. A flush of a toilet came from a connecting bathroom.

"Blake?" she said, her voice so thin. "Is that you?"

The door opened outward, Drew's massive form standing with the light shining behind him. "It's really me," he said.

The drugs, she realized with dismay, were not nearly strong enough.

Drew approached, pushing back a poorly upholstered chair. "How do you feel?"

"Thirsty.".

"Here." He wheeled closer a rolling plastic tray that extended over the bed. "You've got apple juice and water."

Prison food, she thought.

"I'm happy to see you're awake so soon," Drew said.

"Are my husband and son alive?" she asked.

"I'm your husband. You banged your head. It'll take time to remember."

"No one could bang my head that hard."

Drew's face tightened, darkening. "Don't count on it," he said through clenched teeth. "We're going to leave. Quietly. Anyone you call out to for help I will put a bullet through their head. Their death will be on your hands, not mine."

He held up a revolver with a wooden handle and six-chamber wheel, like a gun from the Old West.

"Can I have a drink before we leave?" she asked.

"Go ahead."

"I can't—can you bring it to my mouth?"

"I'm not that stupid."

"Then I need you to call a nurse."

"Why?"

Her body started to shake, her breaths coming in wheezes. She wasn't sure if she was laughing or crying. "Because I can't move my arms or legs."

After a minute or two, she knew. It was crying.

8

Lucy sat on the bed, hiding behind a long decorative pillow. Her legs were tucked beneath her, still bound with the plastic ties. Blake wished he could explain himself to her, tell her not to worry—at least about his intentions—but he knew he wouldn't have a chance. He was going to have to sell this performance. Considering how last-minute his preparations were, there was a good chance they wouldn't go according to plan.

Nothing ever did in this house.

"Please don't do this," Lucy said. "Please?"

Blake unscrewed the lid to his bottle of cologne, standing at the opposite side of the bed. "I have to protect my family," he said.

He dabbed a dot of the cologne onto one finger, then, walking to the end of the bed, tipped the bottle against the side of the wooden bedpost, letting an ample amount of the liquid run down. Moving to the bedpost nearer Lucy, he did the same. He capped the bottle and set it on the half wall separating the loft from the rest of the room. Joje watched without a word.

Rather than explain himself, Blake continued operating in silence. A small panel of dials was against the wall by his nightstand. He lowered one, lights dimming. Lucy was hyperventilating on the bed.

From the top drawer of his nightstand, he tore a condom from the pack and tossed it toward her. She recoiled as if it were a snake.

Smoke and mirrors, Blake thought, hoping her reaction had caught Joje's attention as he pulled out the last item from the drawer.

"It's . . . been a long time for me," he said. "I'm not sure what you're expecting but . . . you're likely to be disappointed."

"Then it won't be any different from the rest of our time together," Joje said.

Adam returned to the room, vintage port in hand, the absinthe tucked under one arm. "I couldn't find the box of cigars."

"Guess we'll do without them," Blake said.

Uncertainty gripped him. He was moving pieces on the board without considering his opponent's play, a dangerous position to be in. And his own strategy—if he could call it that—was more reminiscent of a game of shadows, the projected pieces appearing larger than they actually were.

Smoke and mirrors.

Adam brought him the bottles, transferring them to him with care.

"He's not who you think he is," Blake said.

"None of us are." Adam held out the upturned wine glasses held between his fingers by their thin stems.

Blake set them atop his nightstand. Time for the show to begin.

"Corkscrew?" Blake asked.

"Couldn't find it," Adam said. Of course he couldn't; the corkscrew meant for Drew's or Joje's throat was buried in the sand beneath an ocean. Why had Blake ever taken it from Jenna? "I think there's one on my Scout army knife," Adam added.

"Go on," Joje said from the lower landing. "While you're there, bring back the video recorder?"

As Adam left, Joje continued, "Just think how this will all be over soon, Bwakey. We'll be gone, and you'll move right back into the regular swing of things—consulting with clients, ignoring your wife, forgetting about your son. You know, all the things you've missed since we arrived. I wowee you won't remember us for long. The way you move on so quickly, with Rachel and . . . Evaline. How long before you forget we were even here?"

"I'll never forget you were here."

"No, I imagine you won't. Now turn around. Look at that gorgeous thing just waiting for you to seduce her. To take her. All in the name of protecting your family. Such a noble cause."

Lucy stared back at Blake with utter dread, her radiant face marred by swollen eyes and her calloused expression. It was as if she were still questioning her own sanity, because this couldn't be real, couldn't be happening. Only Blake saw the spark in her eyes, possibly as she recognized the horror in his own. It was real. And God help them, it was happening.

"If this performance isn't everything I hoped it would be, we make another call to Dwew," Joje said.

"I understand," Blake said.

Adam returned and, at Joje's suggestion, uncorked both bottles. For some reason Joje wasn't willing to trust Blake with the knife. Blake wafted his hand over the top of the port, taking in the smell of the wine. It had a sweet scent to it, almost overbearing. It had always been Jenna's favorite, not his. Blake knew, however, when it came to wines, port had the highest alcohol content—this one even higher than most. The absinthe was just in case the port failed.

Blake tipped a small amount of the absinthe into a wine glass. He knocked it back, gagging as the heat poured down his throat. He had forgotten how strong that was. And how awful.

"Start from the side of the bed on the right," Joje said, instructing Adam with the camera.

"You want me to go up there?" Adam asked.

"We need close angles. I want you weaving in and out, hovering just above them."

Adam moved back to the upper landing, coming around to the

opposite side of his father, Lucy and the bed between them.

Blake turned his back to Joje as he filled one wine glass from the bottle of port. The other he filled with absinthe. The fumes of almost pure alcohol carried up, clearing his sinuses as if he had swallowed a chunk of wasabi.

"Lucy," he said, proffering the port. She did not reach for it. He sat on the bed, scooting himself toward her. She lashed out, tossing the pillow at him and causing the glass to dump.

"Don't touch me!" she spat, distancing herself from the slosh of red liquid bleeding into the bedspread.

Thank you, Lucy, Blake thought.

"You're going to let her do that to you, Bwake? This is how you conquer?" Joje shouted.

Blake looked directly into the digital camcorder his son had pointed at him. "My name is Blake Crochet. I live at Sixteen Vanilla Banks, Malibu, California. My family has been kidnapped by two madmen who have forced us to commit acts against our will and better judgment. To any whom I've hurt, I'm so sorry. To my family," he paused, looking up at Adam. "Sorry isn't enough. It shouldn't have taken this for me to realize my life is nothing without you. In this life or the next, I hope you can forgive me. And to my kidnappers—I hope you rot in hell!"

The object Blake had pulled from his drawer had been kept low, hidden from Joje's view. Blake's thumb felt raw, too close to the blue flame spitting from the end of the lighter at his side. The pillow Lucy had thrown at him was just beginning to catch, yellow flames replicating along its tethered fringes.

Please let this work, he thought as blackened fringe curled up, flames sinking into the pillow and not rising again. There was no burst, no fireball, and though he had been tussling with the burner since the start of his speech to the camera, the bedspread as well had yet to take to the flame.

"Point the camera away from your father," Joje said, voice already drawing nearer. "It seems he's looking for a final lesson."

Come on, come on, come on!

The first pillow he had lit had already gone out. A second's fabric shriveled beneath the flame but failed to expand.

Lucy's hands suddenly cupped his own, her large brown eyes boring into his. "I've got this. Stop him."

Without a word Blake transferred the lighter to her, its blue flame continuing at a steady pulse. He tried running the numbers in his head; maybe he had dumped too much of the wine out, the soaking of the sheets and bedspread preventing the flame from spreading. He could go for the absinthe but not without it blowing in Lucy's face—he had heard of a man who tried to drink what the Czechs called a flaming pistol, a burning sugar cube dropped into a glass of absinthe that set the alcohol on fire, only this man's lips had burned away, the inside of his cheeks hollowed out to the point you could see through his skin it was so transparent. If he threw that second glass at the lighter, Lucy would go up with it.

He turned to face his adversary, realizing once again he had miscalculated, hadn't fully considered the course his actions would run. As desperately as he needed a miracle, he was in no position to petition divine intervention. He may not be the murderer Joje was making him out to be, but how many skeletons, skin and gristle still clinging to bone, resided in his closet? The countless people he had stepped on, livelihoods he had destroyed, businesses he had crushed in the wake of his own ascent. Was success even possible without climbing on the shoulders of those around you? With cleated hooves stepping on faces and bodies, forcing them into the mud so your shoes would stay sharp and shined and you could stand another inch taller?

A day in a box, a week with a monster, and Blake was no longer the man he once had been. His own blue flame had been set against his body, his soul, setting ablaze the cardboard beliefs he had thought were golden. His only option at this point was to hope that the flame inside would leap farther and faster than the one behind him.

9

Drew showed no more emotion than a Cabbage Patch doll, retreating from Jenna after her declaration of paralysis. He pulled aside a hanging curtain meant to surround her bed. Leaning against the wall was a fold-up wheelchair.

"You're not going to scream. You're not going to cry for help. Because if you do, I will plunge this into the back of your neck."

He held up a small scalpel, its quarter-inch triangular blade as deadly as the sword he had kept with him earlier. "Then you really will be paralyzed."

Jenna swallowed hard. She wished she could have had that water.

Drew unfolded the chair, wheeling it toward her.

"What did they do to me while I was out?"

"Surgery," Drew said.

"They used anesthesia, didn't they?"

"How should I know?"

"*You*. You told them to do it, didn't you," Jenna said. "I have a reaction with anesthesia. My nervous system shuts down. I couldn't even get an epidural when I was delivering!"

Drew tilted his head at an angle, watching her. *Observing* her. "How long does it last?"

"I don't know, I haven't had it since I was a kid. They put me under for a root canal. I ended up in the hospital for two weeks."

"You don't know why you had surgery, do you?"

"I don't even know where I am," she said.

Drew grabbed ahold of the blankets at the end of the bed, drawing them back in one full swoop. Jenna's nightgown, the blue hospital dress her ass would be hanging out from, stopped halfway down her thighs. Below, her left leg extended, skin still a horrific sight, but it was her right that caused her breath to catch, her heart to skip a beat.

Her foot and calf were no longer there.

Bile rose in her throat, searing her esophagus both on its way up and going back down. Her knee, swollen to the size of Drew's thigh, was wrapped protectively, a cone funneling down to the part of the bed with no indentation from where her foot or leg should have been. A clear thick tube slunk out of the wrapping, brown and red chunks visible every few inches along its curve.

Her eyes were welling to the point she couldn't see. "You had them do this to me? This!"

"I saved your life," Drew answered.

"You've taken everything from me! Everything I ever cared about. I don't even know who I am anymore." Her breaths came in ragged spurts. "Why . . . why couldn't you have just killed us?"

"George has his reasons. You were mine."

"I swear to God I'll kill you," she said. "I will rip your throat out with my teeth if I have to, but I am going to kill you!"

"Plan B it is. Strangle you till your unconscious and then wheel you out."

At least if Drew took her now, there was a good chance she would die. Infection, dehydration, without the proper care at this stage, it wouldn't take long.

Though a few days will be like an eternity with him, she thought.

"I have to make sure," he said.

"Of what?"

He didn't answer. Instead he plunged the scalpel into her left thigh. Though the blade was short, there was no doubt with the force of his impact he had severed more than skin and arteries—this had gone straight through muscle to the bone.

His eyes never left hers, watching for the smallest sign of pain, the slightest tremble. He pushed the handle of the blade left and right, digging in farther. She stared back unflinching, refusing to give him the satisfaction.

"Imagine that. You were telling the truth," Drew said.

He let go of the handle, leaving the blade sticking from her leg like a junkie in the throes of a soaring high, unaware of the still-protruding needle. A trickle of blood rolled down her thigh, spreading on the white sheets of the bed.

"We're gonna change," he said. "Less questions that way."

He came around behind her, tearing at the gown and dragging it over her body. Her arms slumped back to the bed, lifeless, the gown snagging on her hair until finally breaking free. She now sat on the bed naked from the waist up, the panties they had dressed her in as thick and attractive as an adult diaper. One arm lay in her lap turned upward, the other resting at her side.

"I could get used to that view," Drew said. He glanced at the door leading out of the room, probably wondering how much time he could get away with before someone came barging in.

"I'm cold," she said.

"I thought you couldn't feel anything."

"My head, it feels like . . . glaciers colliding."

Drew came around, staring down at her chest with a twisted smile. "I'll have to find a way to get more anesthesia if it keeps you from fighting back."

Her shirt was on the seat of the wheelchair next to him. He grabbed it, leaning over her from the side and lifting one arm, his bare flesh pressing against hers. He tilted her head forward to bring it through the outstretched shirt.

Now, she thought.

Her left hand reached down, clasping at the handle protruding from her leg. She ripped it out with one quick pull, reminding herself she loved pain. Turning the blade, she thrust it into Drew's stomach. He lurched backward, one arm slapping her across the face so hard she was almost stunned. Unfortunately for him, his arm was entangled in Jenna's shirt. She tried scratching at his face with her other hand, but his arm slipped free of the shirt just in time. Instead she pulled the blade back out and swung it upward, putting everything she had into her lunge.

The blade slid deftly between soft tissue, warm blood bursting and covering her hand and arm, splashing onto her leg. It felt like an egg breaking, its yoke dripping out in a continual flow. Drew staggered, turning slightly toward her. In her horror she let go of the handle, yet the blade remained wedged into the flesh just below his chin, sticking straight down.

Blood trickled from the corners of his mouth. He tried to speak, but only a gurgle came out, thick with froth. He wore an incomprehensible expression on his face as if he couldn't understand why she would do what she had done.

"You were wrong. This whole time? You were *mine*," she said.

He dropped, legs giving out, his head connecting with the rail of her bed, and with it Jenna heard the scalpel drive through his skull, rail becoming hammer, scalpel the nail.

His face, completely motionless, rested atop that rail, his body propped against the bed as if he were kneeling in prayer. His unseeing eyes somehow still conveyed a sense of surprise.

Jenna broke down and cried like she had never cried before, huge gasps of grief, relief, revulsion, rejoicing. When she thought she had regained herself, she pressed a finger against Drew's forehead and pushed. His body slumped to the floor, hitting the wheelchair on its way down.

When the nurse finally came in to check on her, she found Jenna laughing hysterically lying on the tile floor in a pool of smeared blood. Her "husband" was in a similar state with one major distinction: he was not laughing.

Next to Jenna's hand, partly immersed in a pool of red, was an old flip phone.

10

Joje's phone began to ring to the unmistakable tune of the Rolling Stones' "Sympathy for the Devil."

Woo-hoo, Blake thought.

Joje stopped at the foot of the landing, pulling the phone from his back pocket and holding it out. "Do it now!" he yelled into the speaker. "I want him to hear her die! Kill her now!"

Silence from the phone.

"Dwew!"

"It's not 'Dwew.'"

That voice, that angelic voice, broke through every dark cloud swirling over Blake's head. "Honey? Jenna!"

"Here," she answered. "And I'm not going anywhere. Drew's dead. In case you were wondering."

Blake couldn't keep the smile from his face. "I love you," he shouted. The words were unfamiliar. He hadn't planned on saying them, but they were words he didn't regret.

"Love you too dar—"

Jenna's voice cut off midsentence, but her message had been received. Loud and clear.

The phone dropped from Joje's hand, bouncing off the first step to the carpeted floor below. He was trembling. "Where's Adam?"

Blake looked back—both Adam and Lucy were gone. They had used the call as the distraction they needed to get clear of Joje. A smoldering pillow atop the bed was the only evidence of their attempted diversion. That and the strong aroma of sweetened alcohol.

Joje was bent over, a fist held to his mouth. It was so odd to see human emotion on that face. Blake half expected Joje to break character at any moment, laughing or shouting.

Or smiling.

His grief for Drew looked heartfelt. "This is all wrong!" he shouted. "All of it! It wasn't supposed to go this way."

"Cops are on their way. You must know that," Blake said. "Probably seconds from our door. Go. Leave. We can still both walk away."

"Adam," Joje said, squaring his shoulders. "Are you coming with me?"

"I—I don't know," Adam said without raising his head from behind the side of the bed.

Joje exhaled a long breath. "It's not the journey, it's the destination that matters."

"Dad—get down!" Adam yelled, jumping up and over the corner of the bed to pull Blake back.

The roar of the gun echoed in the room. Blake felt the vibration of a bullet skim just past his face, a loud thunk following as the projectile meant for his skull sunk into the bed's headboard. He had time to see Lucy standing by his nightstand, clear liquid flinging from the glass in her hand, then he hit the bed, and the room exploded.

The initial blast of heat went up with a whoosh that seemed to suck the air right out of Blake's throat. Adam was propelled off the bed. Blake slammed into the corner bedpost. The post suddenly burst into flames, fire consuming the cologne Blake had poured down its side.

Blake rolled from the bed, falling forward and dragging himself down the three steps to the lower level of the room. Above him orange and yellow flames billowed out across the ceiling like clouds set to fast-forward. Joje was on the ground, hands covering his face, the gun nowhere to be seen.

As quickly as the burst began, it ceased, a vacuum drawing the flames back. And then a second wave rushed forward. Like the tide of the ocean. The bed was ablaze, front bedposts now flaming pillars, the ceiling above turning a cancerous black.

"Adam!" Blake shouted, but before he could move, Joje was on his feet, rushing toward him. He didn't have the strength to fight back, not anymore. The crisp smell of rising smoke, the crackling of flames.

Joje stepped over Blake, rushing up the steps onto the landing that had become a roaring furnace. Jenna's dresser and the silk curtains along the window had caught fire, oppressive heat now pushing against Blake like a physical presence.

Joje was down, crawling beneath the bed. Blake climbed back to the upper landing, another roar sending him to his knees as flames licked the air above his head. Joje slowly backed out, dragging with him his fourteen-year-old brother. Thick swaths of gray smoke followed in their wake.

Blake pulled his son up, wrapping one arm around his shoulder to keep him standing. Adam was unresponsive, his feet bent back on the floor, arms dangling at his side. Joje stood, wrapping his arm around the other side. A silent agreement seemed to pass between them as Blake looked at Joje, and then together they walked Adam carefully down the steps.

Joje bumped into Jenna's armoire, a drawer crashing out, bracelets of gold and silver and dark exotic stone spilling onto the floor.

A body slammed into Joje on his right side. He lost his hold on Adam, Blake falling against the doorframe as his son's full weight rested upon him.

Lucy stood from the ground, her shoulders and arms covered in black streaks. She steadied herself against the wall, staring at Joje, who was still on the ground.

She brought her leg back and kicked him in the stomach, then groaned, clutching at her bare foot. Joje rolled to his other side, facing away from her. Blake could see in her face the intense desire to kill the man who had taken her.

"Wait," he said. "I need him . . . help carry my son."

The look she turned on him was so reproachful Blake almost cowered back.

And then Joje's hand shot out. He grabbed her by the ankle, pulling her to the floor. She screamed, falling atop him. Joje rolled over to pin her beneath.

"Let me go!" Her hands flailed. She must have connected, because the next moment she scrambled out from beneath him.

Joje lunged forward, his fist coming down like a hammer. It barreled into Lucy's right ankle and foot, catching her just as she was bringing the foot up and forward. The scream that followed was louder than the crackling flames behind them.

Blake hefted Adam back up, placing both his arms beneath his son's armpits. Adam lay limp, his head lolling back and forth. A blast of hot air surged forward, and Blake didn't have to look back to know the fire was spreading, and fast.

With the tiniest of steps, he shuffled forward, his back groaning with every movement. Lucy was up, hopping on one foot while leaning against the wall as she made her way down the hall. Joje was just getting to his feet but wouldn't be long behind her.

An earsplitting alarm shrieked just overhead, the sudden noise causing Blake to almost drop his son. "George! I need your help!" he called, words lost in the pitch of the alarm. "*Joje!*"

He either heard or sensed Blake's cry for help. In that momentary glance back, Lucy left the safety of the wall, limping toward the banister and staircase.

"Help me!" Blake shouted again as Adam sagged lower to the floor.

Joje wobbled. He took a step toward Blake, turning to look behind him, then froze. Blake saw the tension in his body as his muscles prepared to launch. He shot back toward Lucy in a full sprint. The look on her face as she saw him tearing toward her was a look Blake would never forget. It was also her last.

She took the first step down, still staring back, that look of terror distorting her normal beauty. Blake wasn't sure if in her speed she miscalculated the spacing of the stairs or if perhaps Joje gave her just enough of a shove to send her off balance, but he watched her pitch forward at an unrecoverable angle and then disappear below his line of sight.

Her disappearance did nothing to mute the sounds of her quick descent.

Like a strand of fireworks all tied together, the chain of repetitive thunks as Lucy's body bounced from mahogany rail to ebony stair seemed like it would never end. The staircase must have elongated, adding steps between steps, the shrill shriek of the Whistling Pete stopping almost as abruptly as it began. But that scream was no firework. Each collision caused Blake to shudder and crawl a little further back into his mind. Bones crunching, limbs breaking, Blake saw it all without being close enough to witness. Hearing was seeing.

A final plomp as Lucy's body came to a state of rest followed by an even louder silence. Joje stood at the top of the staircase looking down.

"Help," Blake croaked, unable to drag his son forward another step. He could feel Adam slipping. He tried to reposition himself but ended up on one knee instead. Smoke clung to the ceiling above, descending in wisps like dangling spiders. Blake's vision was narrowing, turning black on all sides, becoming a slowly shrinking tunnel.

Adam was being pulled from Blake's grasp, slipping, slipping. Blake's eyes shot open and he stood, careening into a wall. The heat pressing at his back prompted a forward movement. After a few gangly steps, he felt solidity return to his body, enough to continue moving at least.

Joje was still at the top of the staircase, though now Adam was flung over his shoulder in a fireman's carry, his head and arms hanging limply down Joje's back.

"It really is a beautiful home," Joje said.

"Wait, I'm coming!"

"Beautiful home, beautiful life. Thank you for letting me be a part of it."

"No, wait!" Blake stepped forward, tipping to the right. Bracing himself on the wall, he continued. Joje had already begun walking down the stairs. Blake made it across the hall, clinging to the banister.

At the top of the stairs, he took a moment to survey what had become of his house. The smoke swept into the foyer and high ceilinged antechamber like a waterfall in reverse, fire spreading to the outer walls of the hall. At the bottom of the staircase, Lucy's body lay, her head twisted at an angle Blake had only seen achieved on Barbie dolls in the clutches of tormenting brothers. The artwork and decor on the walls all had gouges and tears through them, lines that could be traced with a missing sword. The remnants of the chandelier lay in a heap like the carcass of some wild and forgotten beast.

Blake took the steps down, careful not to pitch forward and follow Lucy's lead. *Just one more name to add to the list of deaths I'm responsible for*, he thought.

Halfway down he had to stop, the cough leaping from his throat doubling him over. Blake heard the front door wrench open and watched as Joje stepped through, exiting with his son.

"Wait!" He clambered down the remaining steps, pausing only a moment before stepping over Lucy's body. There was no rise or fall from her unmoving chest.

"Joje! Wait!"

Blake stepped outside, tromping down the path from their door leading to the driveway, slapping away palm fronds.

"George!"

He rounded the corner, the trickle of water from the fountain in the corner anything but soothing. The Mercedes was already backing out of the driveway.

"*Wait!*" Blake yelled, running to catch the vehicle that was transitioning from reverse to drive. "I'll do what you say! I'll do whatever you say!"

As he hit the sidewalk, he saw the window on the passenger side roll down. Adam looked out at Blake, his eyes foggy, unclear. Joje leaned across him, one arm wrapped around Adam's head in a brotherly gesture.

"Remember, Bwakey, it's not the journey, it's the destination."

The car accelerated, speeding up the curved road toward the gated entrance at the end of their street. Sirens were circling nearby, squawking like angry seagulls. Blake stood alone in the middle of the road, surrounded by darkness and the plush shadowed landscaping of empty homes. A flare of pain shot upward and into his head, a viper snaking its way through his nostrils and into his brain. And then biting. He screamed his son's name until his voice produced only threads of whispered air.

And then he screamed some more.

Chapter 12

Day Seven

1

The hard metal chair had gone from uncomfortable to unbearable. There were only so many positions you could rotate through when forced to sit for eight hours straight.

The hard plastic table in front of Blake had three words etched into it, a feat that should have been impossible, considering anyone in this chair would only have their fingernails to work with. But like the weathering of rocks over time, the thousands of occupants seated in that unendurably hard and rust-stained seat had each etched their part, tracing those lines until plastic spec by plastic spec they were as engrained as if they had been chiseled.

Blake ran his fingertip along each letter.

"DIE PIG DIE"

There was no mirror on the wall, with people hovering behind, sipping coffee, and telling jokes about each other's ex-wives. This room was bare. Four brick walls, one door—locked—the table, the chair, and a small camera mounted above the door and pointed directly at the seat Blake was in. When the detectives had been in the room, they stood, a simple gesture that not only made Blake feel powerless, but let him know they weren't here to be his friend. No good cop, bad cop routine. This was pissed-off cop and his even more outraged partner. They had left two hours ago, by Blake's count. With no clock in the room, it was hard to tell.

Today marked the seventh day of Joje's pwoject. If God created Earth in seven days, Joje had learned to destroy it in six.

Joje.

Blake shuddered. He didn't even have a last name—if George was his name in the first place. All he had was a ghost, an apparition that had torn his family apart from the inside out.

Yes, officers, I know there's a body of a half-naked girl at the bottom of my stairs, my neighbor's decomposing corpse in the trunk of my car, and the doctor you were so kind to refer buried in my backyard, but a psychotic killer with a lisp, who conveniently disappeared right as you arrived, is the one who really did it!

Maybe if Blake had told them the killer only had one arm, they might have taken him more seriously.

Blake was reminded of Tom Jones's slogan as if he were whispering from his grave: "Because the only crime is letting them put you away."

"DIE PIG DIE"

But he hadn't come to them without some evidence. His son was missing, and Jenna, she had supplied Drew. According to the little he had gleaned from his interrogation cleverly disguised as a conversation, he understood a separate investigation was ongoing as to the murder committed by his wife. He had a feeling the police were looking for his son about as hard as they were trying to expedite his acquittal.

At least they had found the decency to take the handcuffs off. His fingers absently traced the words on the table for what must have been the hundredth time. Only this time he imagined the words slightly altered:

"DIE JOJE DIE"

The fire department had converged on the scene much later than the police, not having the benefit of an anonymous tip from a woman in a hospital. By the time the hoses were shut off, the right side of the house had collapsed, master bedroom and loft meeting family room and kitchen. The front of the house was tarred in black, that oily-looking substance leaking down the walls and garage.

Blake had glanced toward the house only once, when the upper section fell into the lower, the thunderous crashing causing all eyes to gravitate toward it. Other than that he had kept his eyes fixed on the stars, seated on the curb, his arms cuffed behind his back. It had reminded him why they had chosen that house. A little piece of paradise.

A loud clack caused Blake to almost fall from his seat. The bolt slid free in the heavy door. He looked up, hopeful, anxious, then remembered what side of the table he was on.

The door swung open with a shriek that a little WD-40 could have mended. Deputy McClellan entered with a smug look on his long face. A woman officer closed the door behind him, brown hair in a ponytail, stout, and even less sympathetic looking than McClellan. Blake hadn't met her before.

"Where's Randall?"

"He went home," McClellan said flatly.

"He was bringing me breakfast," Blake said. He couldn't believe how pathetic he sounded, even to himself.

"Yeah, well, there's a funny story to that, 'cause when we got to McDonald's to order, they weren't serving breakfast anymore. And since we hadn't asked what you wanted for lunch, I figured we'd come back and ask."

Blake brought his hands to his head. "I'm trying to cooperate."

"Kirkpatty, you mind getting the camera for me?" McClellan said.

The stout woman came around the side of the desk. "Put your hands on the table facing down, thumbs touching."

Blake wondered what made this woman smile. He did as he was told, and she slid a pair of handcuffs back in place at his wrists, wrangling them tighter than they had been previously. "Please stand. Do not move your hands from the table," the female cop said.

"Don't make Kirkpatty repeat herself," McClellan said. "Word to the wise."

Blake stood, his knees knocking against the table as the woman McClellan called Kirkpatty snatched the chair and carried it back toward the door. She climbed on top, pulling out a wire from the back of the camera and letting it dangle down. If Blake's legs hadn't been tingling in pain from the sudden rush of blood, he would have laughed.

"Is this where you threaten me? Rough me up? Because you couldn't come close to what I've been through this week."

McClellan stared back, eyes unflinching.

Blake's composure began to break. "Do you have any news of my son? Or wife?"

"They're still holding her downtown," McClellan said. "Considering the extent of her injuries and recent surgery, I don't think she'll be going anywhere for some time. But don't you worry, 'cause when she does, it'll be in a cell across from yours. The only difference I see between you and her is that she's admitted to the murder she committed."

"That was self-defense and you know it.".

McClellan's hands shot up as if Blake were holding a gun on him. "I ain't no lawyer. My paycheck can attest to that."

"And Adam?" Blake asked.

McClellan just shook his head. "Come on, we need to book you. I'm assuming you'll want that call now?"

"Can I talk to my wife?"

"I think we can have that arranged," McClellan said.

Kirkpatty led Blake down a narrow hall, winding around a desk with no legs stacked vertically against a wall.

"Hold here," McClellan said as the corridor intersected with another outlet. A desk—this one with legs—was unoccupied, tape dispensers and staplers strategically placed to keep the stacks of manila folders from tumbling down. "Where's Boyd?"

"He was right here," Kirkpatty said.

"We'll wait till he gets back," McClellan said. "Can't have either of us alone with him." As if Blake posed some serious threat.

McClellan leaned against the edge of the desk, his backside pushing against the folders, which slid back, toppling to the floor in a cascade. "Aw, damnit!"

Kirkpatty went around to help on the other side of the desk.

"No, I've got it. Just, go find Boyd so we can book this asshole," McClellan said.

As soon as she was gone, McClellan came back around the desk, grabbing Blake by the arm. "This way," he said.

"What?"

"Shut up."

McClellan brought him back into the hall they had come from, leading him farther down, then to the left. His grip on Blake's arm was anything but friendly. McClellan glanced around before opening a door and pushing Blake through.

"Take the second door on your right, follow the stairs out." He remained at the door.

"I don't understand."

"You want a chance to save your son?"

Blake glanced around the room he had entered. A few computer terminals sectioned off by cheap cubicles, whiteboard against the back wall so full of scribbles it looked like a prop for a scientist's lab. He turned back to McClellan just as the door clicked shut.

His hands were still cuffed, he realized. Was McClellan setting him up?

You want a chance to save your son?

Shoving all rationale aside, Blake ran toward the second door. He pulled at the handle—locked. It was a setup. He looked to see if McClellan was about to burst back in, gun in hand. They'd probably give him an award for killing the wanted suspect attempting to flee, no questions asked.

The handle in Blake's hand gave, the door pushing inward. He laughed silently, remembering *The Far Side* school for the gifted comic. Seems he had joined their numbers.

The room opened into a stairwell. A thousand voices screamed in the back of his head, telling him to turn around—this was the police he was dealing with, not some juvenile delinquent. As the mental debate continued, he heard the bone-crunching impact of a body falling down the stairs, flung into walls, railing, steps, and landing. He winced with every thud. That there was no body falling made no difference.

He descended, clinging to the metal rail, mindful not to join Lucy in the downward tumble through his mind. At the bottom landing was a door with a push bar, its circuitry leading above to an alarm box. It read "Emergency Exit Only—Alarm Will Sound."

"Die, pig, die!" Blake shouted, slamming against the bar, the door jerking open with a stutter. The alarm immediately sounded.

A short slab of sidewalk quickly gave way to grass. Blake was grateful for the softer landing as his legs gave out. He hit, rolling like a child down a hill, only without the laughter. His teeth were chattering though he wasn't cold.

Stumbling to his feet, he continued, no regard for where he was going. Any moment a bullet would slam into his back, severing his escape. And maybe his spine.

A dog barked nearby, and Blake forced himself not to waste the precious seconds determining from where. The building ended in a neat corner, all hope slipping from Blake's grasp—of course the property would be gated. A security station was at the gate's exit, or entrance, thirty yards from him, a line of empty police cars parked between.

"Blake! Blake!"

It took a moment to register his name being shouted. They were coming for him.

"Malibu Blake!"

He followed the direction of the voice. Joje sat in a brown coupe, waving him over.

What the hell?

Blake took two steps toward the sedan, eyes clearing as he moved. It wasn't Joje; it was the Asian cop, Officer Randall.

"Hurry!"

Blake moved quicker, glancing back at the exit he had come from. A man and woman were coming out and pointing toward him. He stepped off the curb and into the parking lot, opening the passenger door and jumping inside. Before he had closed it, the car began to reverse.

"Get down like you're giving me head," Randall said. "Lower if you can."

Blake didn't understand what was going on, but he did as he was told, dropping flat against the seat, his head resting next to the driver.

"You got some friends in high places," Randall said. "Or low ones. Keep down."

They were at the guard gate. Blake watched as Randall gave a half wave out the window, barely slowing, then the station was fading farther and farther behind them. Eventually Blake sat up.

They rode in silence until Blake was able to find his voice. "Why . . . why are you helping me?"

"Who said we're helping?"

They were coming down Overland off of Santa Monica, the angel atop the big Mormon temple playing them a silent tune.

"What does he have on you?" Blake asked. Randall continued looking straight ahead. "Come on, you wouldn't be risking all this for my innocence. Rory Shepherd—what does he have on you?"

Randall shook his head. "Look, McClellan and I, I mean, we're good cops, you know, we don't tithe our busts, we try to do our civic duty, I guess, but who doesn't have some dirt on them? I don't know this Shepherd guy you mentioned or what kind of shit you're involved in, and to tell you the truth, I don't want to. But this guy, he knew everything about us, and I mean everything. From the hell storm raging around you? My guess is you're his bitch too."

They drove in silence, Randall turning onto the 10 freeway heading east. To Blake's lack of surprise, there was plenty of traffic.

"He didn't give you a choice, did he?" Blake asked.

"He give you one?"

Rory Shepherd's network of coercion had reached its tentacles out to officers of the law this time, ensuring Blake had the chance to pay back his debt. Now that he knew, Blake wasn't surprised. It was exactly how Rory would work.

As Randall fought his way through the bottleneck of cars, Blake settled in to the decision he was being forced to make, reacting exactly as Rory would have hoped. No predictive intelligence software or AI needed. Sometimes there are no choices, just reactions and the consequences that follow.

2

"I've got an officer here from Santa Monica precinct, needs to speak to the wife. Looks like the husband skipped out."

"You shittin' me?"

"Nah, feel bad for the SOB who let him slip the coop. I'm okay to put her on the line?"

"There's no tap on the phones. It's more difficult than bangin' a one-legged hooker from behind to get that set up in a hospital."

"Eh, he said they've got it taken care of on their end. You sure she can't hear you out here? I mean, you might want to watch the analogies."

"Hey, I'm not sayin' she's a hooker, but she sure as hell could be. Shame."

"Yeah, a shame your mother never taught you how to treat a lady."

"Oh, I treat 'em all right. In and out. With the phone call, I mean, not the ladies."

Jenna's eyes were closed when the laughter stopped and the door to her new room opened. Despite the drugs and her exhaustion, sleep evaded her, but if she kept her eyes shut, they might leave her alone.

She wasn't sure if they believed her; her injuries had done a much better job of convincing them than her story ever could, but she was still handcuffed to the bed rail.

At least they had believed her enough to send a squad of cars to their home last night. She hadn't been told much but had picked up on pieces of conversation, content with the knowledge that Blake and Adam were alive. But now a new question begged answering: Why would Blake run?

As much as she wanted to avoid thinking, avoid speaking, she needed answers as much as they did. She opened her eyes.

A uniformed officer stood at the end of her bed. He had a baby face, hair gelled and crusted with a part down the side. "Sorry to disturb you, ma'am," he said. He had kind eyes, or maybe Jenna would think everyone's eyes were kind compared to the glares of the two psychopaths she had spent the week with. "You've got a call. It seems your, uh, husband has—"

"I heard," she said.

The blush that brazened his face made him look younger than twenty. He carried a phone over from a small chest of drawers that had probably remained empty since the day they had been purchased.

"Who's calling?" she asked. "What do they want?"

"Detective De Hare, ma'am. And you'll have to ask him yourself." The officer picked up the receiver, having the operator transfer the line. He handed her the phone.

"Look, I know you have questions for me," Jenna said into the handset, "but I need some answers too. Now what the hell is happening with my husband?"

The voice that responded brought a chill through her entire body.

"It's me, baby—don't say my name. Make it seem like you're talking to the police."

Jenna closed her eyes, hoping the officer at her bedside would take the tear sliding down her face as fear or frustration, not joy.

"You saved us, sweetheart. Your call—it gave me the time to

make my own move."

"But why would my husband run away? I don't understand," she said.

"He's got Adam," Blake said, and Jenna could hear the tears in his voice. "The game's over. He got what he wanted, and it wasn't you or me or our money—it was our son!"

"No! The police will find him, right? Keep him safe?"

"They won't be able to, but I know someone who can, someone who orchestrated my escape. But there's something I need to do for him first."

"This doesn't make any sense," she said, sniffling into the phone and not caring. "I just—I want this to be over."

"It will be soon. I just, I wanted to call to tell you how much I love you and that no matter what happens, no matter what you hear about me, just know I'm doing everything I can to get our son back. To right a few wrongs."

Jenna was moving into the boundaries of hysterics. This time she wasn't sure she could pull herself back.

"You're the strongest woman I've ever known. Your will, your belief, it's what's kept me going. It's what I'm holding on to still. Now say 'I'll cooperate any way I can,' and I'll take it to mean you love me."

Jenna wet her lips, tasting the salt from her tears. "I'll cooperate any way I can," she said. "Any way I can."

She heard Blake exhale a short breath into the phone. "I love you too, baby. Love you too." And with that he was gone, the sudden silence of the line worse than any gunshot in her ear.

3

Randall kept the engine running, Blake's first clue his reluctant escort was terminating their relationship. They were parked outside a tall building on Alameda in downtown LA. Strangers passed by just outside Blake's window, high-powered men and women in high-priced suits, their crisp haircuts and purposeful walks in contrast to the homeless men and women shuffling in their midst.

"That's the Metrolink in there. There's an envelope in the glove box with two hundred dollars. Buy yourself a ticket someplace and then go from that someplace to another place 'cause the next time we meet, it won't be under friendly circumstances."

"Two hundred bucks? How am I supposed to get my son back with that?" Blake asked.

"Not my problem," Randall said.

"It is your problem. A family in the city you swore to protect was tortured and almost killed under your watch! We were set up for those murders and you know it. Now you tell me how that is not your problem."

Randall turned to meet Blake's glare. He no longer looked like the cop that wanted to be buddy-buddy. "I think we've gotten off to a misunderstanding. You are not my friend, you are not my problem. You are the lead suspect in a criminal investigation that involves the murder of three individuals so far. The only problem I face is finding you and bringing you to justice, and the only reason we're sitting here in this car and I'm letting you walk out that door is because I had no choice. Now I'll give you thirty minutes before I bring the manhunt here as a courtesy, but don't for one minute mistake me as your friend."

Blake punched Randall square in the jaw with a left hook, the unexpected blow landing with more force than he had anticipated. He kicked off the passenger door, launching himself into Randall to keep him from reaching for his gun. A finger jabbed into one of his eyes, another into his face, but Randall's flails were all defensive, trying to allay the furious onslaught of Blake's fists. He felt murderous, blood surging in his head, his chest, his limbs.

Randall lifted the handle of the door, angling to position himself out of Blake's reach. Blake used his momentum to throw Randall out—he tumbled onto the street, rolling twice to shrieking brakes and blaring horns.

Blake slammed the car door closed, reaching for the gear shift when the front driver's side mirror shattered, tiny shards of glass blown inward.

Randall's feet were planted, his pistol drawn and aimed at Blake's head. He had recovered quickly. "LAPD! Out of the car!"

"And here I thought we were friends," Blake said.

"I'm taking you in right now," Randall said. "Now put your hands on your head, slowly."

"You're not gonna shoot me."

"I said—"

"I'm in your personal vehicle. How are you going to explain what I was doing in your car? Considering the amount of time I've been gone, they'll know it was you who picked me up and got me out of there."

"That won't matter."

"It does and you know it."

Randall seemed to tally the same results in his head. "Fine. Now get in the Metro before another squad car drives by wondering what the hell is going on."

Blake shook his head. "I'm not taking the Metro. Report this car stolen, and I'll make sure you go down with me."

Randall shifted his feet, gun arm going slack.

"Thanks for the help." Blake hit the gas, pulling out into the lane and merging with traffic. The puzzled cop standing in the street, gun in hand, might have been flipping him off as he drove away. But Blake chose to believe Randall was wishing him luck, pointing him onward in the direction Blake was flying, a direct course to where every little choice he had taken in life was now about to collide.

Come and find me, he thought, not knowing if he meant it for Joje, Rory, or the police, who had no doubt sent his name and face to every substation in all of Southern California. The wind whipped at him from the broken window, and for the first time in a long time, Blake felt he was back on top. When he later abandoned the car, the glove box was one envelope lighter and in the trunk a metal attaché case was popped open, the foam cutout empty where a gun should have been.

4

No stars could compete with the glowing billboards and spray of city lights below the hills of Hollywood. Blake stood in the shadows of a eucalyptus tree on Briar Knoll Drive, the road and landscape at such a steep pitch his left foot was almost two feet lower than his right. His breathing was as light as the evening breeze, a calm detachment having overtaken him.

He watched the last of the houseguests depart. They ambled toward a Porsche utility vehicle parked in front of the house. Husband and wife, or more likely executive and escort. They followed in similar footsteps as the previous guests who had left—drunken staggering with wild hoots and occasional pawing. They eventually found their way in, the Porsche's engine singing as the couple coasted down the hill.

JT's party was over, or so he thought. The real party, however, was just about to begin.

Blake drew back the top of the pistol he had taken from Officer Randall's car, checking for the fiftieth time that a bullet was chambered. The gun was just a prop, something to show JT how serious he was, how desperately he needed his help. Blake allowed himself to believe that.

He stepped from behind the brush and tree where he had been stationed for the past several hours. It felt good to move. He hadn't dared sit, knowing he wouldn't have been able to stave off the sleep his body so desired.

Crossing the paved road, he stood in front of JT's yard. The terrain was expansive, driveway circling around a large lighted pond. The front porch of the house extended out in an awning supported by large, elaborately carved marble pillars with almost the look of an entrance to a hotel where one might park their car when checking in. A high-end luxury hotel. Squared bushes were lined in front of the columns, retaining walls supporting the illusion that the yard and home were built on level ground. The large front entrance was an attempt to make up for the lack of a back yard, as JT's home was one of those daring houses in Hollywood Hills clinging to life by mere timbers and creative engineering.

A light mounted on the corner of the house sprang to life, replacing shadows as Blake made his was across the driveway. He took care of it with an upward thrust of the gun, glass tinkling onto the stamped pavement. He thought about going around the side of the house, looking for a rear entrance or garage door, but dismissed the idea when the front door opened.

JT swung out, dressed in a tuxedo shirt, one side's shirt tails untucked. "What'd jou forget?" he said, then blinked repeatedly. But Blake wasn't disappearing.

Blake knew what he must look like—haggard, tired, bruised and broken, a gun held tightly in his hand. JT would come to the only conclusion that made any sense, that Blake was here to kill him.

Before Blake could shout out and tell JT his real intentions, JT beckoned him. "Damn, Bwake. Migh' as well come in."

Blake's breath quickened at the pronunciation of his name before he remembered how tossed JT was. Still, as he stepped inside his former boss's house, he couldn't shake the mounting feeling of dread.

JT pressed the palm of one hand into his forehead, massaging it as he walked Blake down a narrow hall. The interior of JT's home was all new age: sleek and uncomfortable furniture, odd wall hangings, and abstract sculptures. Yet another testament to the idea of artists being tortured souls.

Blake followed JT into a long but awkwardly narrow living room that connected with the open kitchen in back. Empty champagne bottles were scattered on the table and counters, glasses and dirty dishes piled high.

JT said, "Tabby, dim the lights, set the fire to four, and lock exterior doors." The lights dimmed and fire came aglow as if a ghost had responded to his requests. "Excuse the mess. We were celebrating."

The word seemed so foreign to Blake, the idea of not having to worry every second of every day, whether you and your family would live or die.

"Mind setting the gun down?" JT asked. "'Less you really are here to kill me."

Blake hesitated. "I'd rather keep it."

JT picked up a wineglass from the array of dishes on the counter. Its coppery liquid gleamed as he put the glass to his lips. Blake noticed a smudge of lipstick on the other side of the glass; if it hadn't been JT's before, he didn't seem to mind.

"Shouldn't you be incarcerarated right now?" JT asked, struggling on the word. "Holding me hostage won't win any favors with a jury."

"You invited me in."

"So I did."

JT crossed in front of Blake, with no acknowledgement of the gun gripped tightly in Blake's hands. He fell into a black leather chair, his head leaning against one armrest, legs hanging over the other side.

"Help yourself to a drink. If you can find any liquor left."

"This isn't a social visit," Blake said. "I need your help."

"The great Blake Crochet, consulting practitioner for the common business cold needs my help? You know what everyone calls you, don't you? In the fortune community?" JT pantomimed quotation marks around the word *fortune*. "Crotch consulting. Where you're better off paying for a blowjob. Though both come with hot air, only one leaves you with a happy ending."

Blake gritted his teeth, ignoring JT's smile. How had he ever put up with this nasty little man? "I'm not asking for my job back. My son's been kidnapped, and I need your help with the ransom. I'm also not asking."

"Aw, come on, Blake. Didn't your mother teach you how to ask nicely?"

"Where's your Liberty nickel?"

JT righted himself in the chair. He seemed to be looking at Blake differently.

"One way or another I'm leaving with it," Blake said. "And don't you dare tell me it's not here. I know you keep it close."

"Do you know what dollar value is ascribed to the average American teen? Their net worth?" JT asked.

"He's not an average teen. He's my son."

"Doesn't matter. It's a *negative* number. So with all your consulting expertise, would you suggest a client steal an investment worth upward of five million, valued at potentially ten times that, in exchange for an asset with a negative net worth?"

Blake cocked back the hammer. "If you value your life, you'll take me to where you store that nickel. Now."

JT stood, teetering only slightly. "Well, come on."

5

Back out in the hall, JT opened a door to a cast iron spiral staircase leading down. "Watch your head," he said as he began his descent. Blake followed. JT spoke to Tabatha, and the room came aglow from the canned lights in the ceiling above.

Blake's arm wrapped around a spoke of the staircase as he stared down at the drop below him. The room had no floor—just a staircase extending down to a forty-foot drop to the tumbling mountainside, another fifty feet at least before the hillside was lost to the tops of trees and brush. Then Blake noticed the pool table levitating in the air.

JT stepped from the ladder to a see-through floor—whether glass or some other composite material, Blake didn't know.

"It's quite safe," JT said, meandering over to a wet bar against the far wall and uncorking a bottle of bourbon. "Low-iron glass, seven and a half feet thick. Same engineering firm that did that Skywalk in the Grand Canyon."

He poured two glasses, then, almost as an afterthought, picked up a third. "Did you want one?"

"No. Thank you."

Blake stepped tentatively onto the floor. Trusses and steel beams barely visible extended out of the darkness below, reaching toward him like claws.

"Tabatha, set temp to seventy-four. Always gets a little cold in here," JT said. "Didju know we took the company public?"

"What?"

JT slammed the first glass of bourbon back without even a hint of a grimace. "You should drink. You were integral to the launch."

"It would take months to plan, execute . . ." Blake's words trailed off, thoughts spinning recklessly forward.

"A business is as fragile as a house built over a hill. At first, at least. But erect enough support, you no longer need the foundation. You outgrow it. You're suddenly just . . . hovering."

He refilled the empty glass.

"Ever seen a floating building, Blake? You'd know if you had. The whole world would know, because you can't see a building float without telling the world about it. Google was the first floating building I ever saw. And that's when I knew. I had to have one."

"The coin, JT."

JT grabbed the second glass and walked across the floor only staggering once. His other hand brushed against the pool table in the center of the room as he passed it. "The thing about floating buildings—the real ones, not those held up with strings—is they appear overnight. One day they don't exist, the next they're everywhere, on every tongue, filling a vacuum no one knew existed.

Lightning in a bottle—you can't replicate it."

At the far wall, he pushed something on the wooden rack holding pool cues. The rack pulled away, revealing an electronic display screen embedded in a metal panel. A safe?

"What people forget is that even floating buildings began attached to some hill," JT continued.

Blake raised the gun, leveling it on JT's chest, the pool table between them. "I'm not here for a drink and I'm not here for your philosophy. I need that nickel or I won't see my son again, so you are either going to help me or I will make you help me."

"You dumb little shit—have you not heard a word I've said?"

"I need that coin, JT!"

"Tabatha, display my . . . floating building."

A panel in the ceiling unlatched with a mechanical drawl, descending slowly, black metal arms extending from the ceiling as it lowered. It stopped just above the pool table like some futuristic device displaying a luminescent cube that looked almost otherworldly. In the center of the transparent block was a single nickel, a fossil caught in amber.

"Not quite as thick as the floor you're standing on, but it still weighs a quarter of a ton. You're welcome to it," JT said.

Blake's eyes moved from the impregnable coin to the man who had doused what little kindling of hope he had remaining. He felt an electricity in the air—the gun in his hands wanted to be fired.

"Put it away. You're not going to shoot me," JT said.

"You have no idea what I'm capable of," Blake said.

"Actually you're wrong. You've had Betti what, a month now? Before the whole kidnapping thing? The amount of information collected from you in one month of monitoring could fill the Library of Congress three times. Just one month. Symbio is not some small jettison, and while we're starting with predictive marketing, that's not the endgame. It's about control—a true new media—understanding how someone thinks so that you know exactly how to bend them to whatever you need them to believe. It's what we did with you."

A sudden bout of vertigo hit Blake, whether from the drop visible beneath them or JT's words, he couldn't be sure. He steadied himself by gripping the side of the pool table, though it didn't stop the room from swaying.

Bourbon sloshed from the glass in JT's hand. "Sure you don't want that drink?"

The timing of it all suddenly brought random numbers into order, x's, y's, and z's finding their place in an equation that meant billions for JT and his company at the low cost of one family's sanity. "This whole thing—the kidnapping, the warehouse, the former employee seeking revenge—it was all to put the spotlight on Symbio?"

"Well, it's tough to run a traditional marketing campaign for a company touting the future of marketing. We had to just . . . *be*, overnight becoming the collective consciousness of predictive software and AI. We're actually calling it symbiotic intelligence rather than artificial intelligence. Tests much better in focus groups and really turns our brand into the market. Like tissue and Kleenex."

"Tissue and Kleenex? You had them set my wife on fire! My son is missing, and at least three people are dead!"

"Floating buildings aren't without their costs."

Blake pointed the gun down and pulled the trigger.

JT jumped—the bullet sinking into the glass floor in front of him. A web of cracks cascaded out from its entry point. The glass in his hand fell to the ground, shattering, chunks skidding across the no-longer-quite-as-see-through floor.

One rotund chunk spun in place at Blake's feet.

He couldn't tell if the bullet had made it all the way through or was lodged somewhere within the layers of folded glass, either way, his message had been delivered.

Blake fired again, the kick traveling the length of his arm. The noise of the gunshot was amplified by the glass floor as if thunder were rising from the ground. He was no sharpshooter, but his second shot landed less than a foot from the first. The glass floor was beginning to look like a river of ice cracking beneath their weight.

"If I can't take the coin, I'm taking you," Blake said. "That's what Rory really wanted anyway."

JT looked at Blake like he was mad. "Rory Shepard?—Don't!" he shouted, stopping Blake from firing another round into the floor. Barely.

Both of JT's hands rose, palms out as if trying to calm a feral beast. "All right, I'll go! Let's head back up."

Blake shook his head. "I want you standing right there. Now what do you know about Rory?"

"Who do you think came up with the marketing campaign that was Blake Crochet?"

"You . . . hired Rory?"

"I told him what I needed. He brought me you," JT said.

"No, that . . . that's impossible. Why would he break me out?" Blake ran one sweaty hand through his hair. "The warehouse—they were his instructions."

"Nothing but empty servers and old machinery. Should have known, Blake. Rory only works with a person once."

Blake did know, had known, but he had wanted to believe, *needed* to believe, that someone, even someone as demented as Rory Shepherd, would be willing to help. How could anyone not extend a hand knowing what he and his family had been subjected to?

But he should have known. Rory had no empathy.

"He's not going to help me find my son, is he?"

Blake grabbed ahold of the glass cube levitating over the table. The tile holding the cube swayed back and forth, long extended arms rattling above. "He's just like this! Your floating building. Full of promises, but with nothing to stand on."

Blake shoved against the cube, trying to rip it free from the metallic arms dangling down. JT stepped forward, face full of fury, the wrinkled creases and lines on his pocked cheeks falling into a position much more natural than a smile.

"You ignorant son of a bitch!" JT grabbed at Blake's arms, and then Blake had the gun in his face, mere inches away.

"I have nothing left to live for."

"Tabatha," JT said, his cold, small eyes unwavering in their ferocity, "magnets on!"

A low humming sound like a pipe with air in it vibrated through the room. Blake felt an immediate pull on his gun, his hand wavering back and forth before ripping his arm back, the gun flying loose back toward the staircase. With a loud clang the gun settled on the railing.

"Tabatha is the home model version of Betti but with a few upgrades. Like home security." JT took a wide arc around the pool table, arriving back at the bar. This time he grabbed a bottle of brandy, dropping two ice cubes into a new glass. "Tabatha, incapacitate our guest."

Blake felt the sting in the back of his arm before he heard or registered any motion—a tiny dart half an inch in length stuck from his right triceps. He heard the twirling and clacking of ice cubes in JT's glass, and then he was falling into the waiting arms of darkness.

6

"Does it look handled to you?"

"It could be a lot worse."

"For what he's being paid . . . never have happened."

Blake's whole body twitched. It felt like ice had been injected into his veins and was coasting slowly toward his heart.

"We can turn this to our advantage . . . A second storm of media coverage . . . Closure we might not have otherwise had . . ."

Whatever drug had been administered in that dart was still riding its course, whipping Blake's consciousness around. Rushing waves toppled from above, a wicked undercurrent pulling from beneath, and somewhere between the two, Blake struggled to remain afloat.

"Can't have him capable of talking . . ."

"Plenty of ways to . . . Can doctor the video surveil . . ."

"Calling the shots . . . Reminder of who hired who . . ."

The looming voices brought Blake slowly from his drug-induced trance. As his eyelids slowly responded to his repeated requests to open, he realized he hadn't stopped falling. Shadowed mounds of dirt and brush and the tops of trees moved toward him in a silent howl. And without even the faintest rush of air.

He sucked in a staggered breath as feeling began returning to his face. He wasn't falling, he was still lying against the glass floor. JT hadn't even bothered moving him.

It was a strange sensation staring straight down into an abyss of darkness, an abyss he was more than familiar with. A tingling in his neck and shoulders turned into a searing burn as if his body were thawing from a deep freeze, one body part at a time. In some ways maybe he was—thawing from a freeze of being unable to act, the psychological barriers of his trauma slowly breaking down.

JT's agitated voice carried in the small room. "Much more serious. When this is through I want him buried beneath a concrete building."

The other man in the room had a strong British accent. He had a deep voice but not a booming one. It was more of a caress. "I can only carry out orders that are . . . feasible."

"He's a man like anyone else. I don't care what it takes, how many resources. You find this Rory and you snip him from his little network of meddlers. Or someday someone's request will be to topple our empire."

By the grunt coming from the other man, Blake surmised the argument wasn't yet over. His face was angled toward the pool table, JT's shoes moving in and out of view. He couldn't tell exactly where the other man was standing—or sitting. Or doing cartwheels for all he knew.

"This isn't a circumcision. One snip won't cover it."

JT's glass striking the paneling of the pool table caused Blake to flinch.

"I pay you to make things happen, so why are we still discussing this?"

They were talking as if Blake were already dead. In their minds he probably was.

Blake slid his body back half an inch, away from the pool table. He had to put some distance between the two men if he was to have any chance.

"Shame 'bout the floor," the Englishman said.

"I'd pay to have it redone ten times for the coverage this'll bring," JT said. "Hell, a hundred times if we leverage this right."

The sole of Blake's shoe rubbed against the glass floor, making the faintest of chirps. His silent escape was at an end. He scrambled up from the floor, and his feet immediately gave out—he tumbled backward, the momentum of his fall pushing him farther from JT and the mystery man in the corner.

"Blake. Pleased to finally make your acquaintance." The man in the corner had risen. He was tall yet his build fit him as well as the dark three-piece Armani he wore, black silk shirt beneath. His hair was the silver of refinement not age, his face hard, dark circles beneath his eyes earned. "Ty Harrington. Symbio's head of security."

Blake knew what that meant—he was a man in the know, a man who had probably had as much to do with his family's kidnapping as JT himself.

A man who had been brought over to finish the job.

"Do you know where my son is?" Blake asked.

Only one side of Ty's mouth rose in a smile that looked as pitying as it did sympathetic. "Sorry, mate. Not my department."

Blake pushed himself farther back, scooting along the floor until his back was against the railing of the stairs. "You've got it all wrong, you know. You didn't hire Rory—he hired you. You've been working for him and didn't even know it."

JT turned to look at Ty. "You see the level of competence I've been working with?"

"I know who he is," Blake said, pulling himself to his feet with the aid of the rail behind him. "I may be the only person alive who knows. Don't you see? It's why he had me released."

Blake grabbed hold of the gun still stuck to the railing, pointed at the bar. The magnetic pull was so strong. But some ties were stronger.

"Yeah, good luck with that," JT said. Ty unbuttoned his suit jacket, revealing a holster tucked beneath.

"It's why he keyed my voice as an override command," Blake said. He tightened his grip on the hilt of the gun, bracing himself against the rail to provide what leverage he could. "Tabatha. Disengage."

Blake swung the gun away from the metal railing, leveling it on JT. He hoped they didn't notice the sweat trickling down his forehead.

"How did you—"

"Shut up!" Blake shouted, cutting JT off. The gun began to waver—let them think he was nervous. He wouldn't have the strength to hold it for long. "Tabatha, alert the police there's been a shooting, download a recording of all conversation in the past hour and then power down."

"Tabatha, disregard last orders!" JT shouted.

"Fine, stay powered on Tabatha," Blake said.

"The last four orders! Tabatha disregard last four orders!"

The room went dark, lights extinguished, the hum of the vents going silent with a final loud knock as the temperature control shut off. Blake's arm fell to his side, the resistance of the magnetic pull no longer sapping the energy from every muscle in his frame.

"What the hell?" JT said.

Blake stepped onto the bottom step of the staircase and raised the gun in the dark. He fired, the spark like lightning flashing against a blackened sky. Several sparks flashed from the other side of the room, loud clangs ringing off the metal rail in front of him. A hammer struck against his hand, fingers going numb. He dropped down, lying against the staircase and shielding his head while he continued to empty the clip. At last the chamber clicked empty.

"He's out," Ty said. "Got him at least twice. He won't be going anywhere. You hit?" The question wasn't for Blake.

"No," JT answered. "Your aim's as good as your consulting, Blake! Tabatha, lights."

The room sprang to light. Blake squinted against the sudden change, feeling more sluggish with every drawing breath. He wondered if JT had ordered the room to hit him with another dart.

He held his shaking hand in front of his face. Two of his fingers had been blown off, bone and gristle sticking from their ends swathed in blood that looked black not red.

"Oh, holy shit." The words were Ty's. JT, for once, was unable to come up with a sufficient curse.

As Blake's eyes adjusted he looked out at his handiwork. Entry points in the floor arced in front of the pool table, the ground no longer revealing cracks but rather the aftereffects of a collision, splinters spawning splinters like a shattered windshield. The two men in the room were standing on glass as fragile as a spider web.

"Rory wins," Blake said. "Not you, not me. He's the only one getting what he wants."

"You're wrong. And this"—JT gestured down toward the floor—"is as replaceable as you and your family. Sorry, Blake. You lose. And Rory will never get his hands on that coin."

"It wasn't the nickel he wanted. It was my son, and what your nickel represents . . . your floating building."

Before JT could respond the floor blew outward, pool table disappearing into the dark stream beneath. Like a black hole, the darkness ripped the remaining shards and chunks of glass out. the bar, table, and chairs disappearing to the sudden angry howl of wind. Blake never saw Ty disappear—he was one moment there, the next gone—but he caught the look on JT's face before those invisible and nightmarish black talons reached in, snagging him then retracting back down. The look was an unintelligible one. Symbiotically unintelligible. A look of sheer horror.

The staircase no longer attached to a floor wobbled beneath

Blake's weight as if it wanted to join the rest of the room. A cloud of dust kicked up from the side of the hill, hiding the remnants of furniture, glass, and bodies as they floated down the slope and out of sight. When the dust settled it was as if the hill had swallowed them whole, Blake catching only faint traces of glass reflecting moonlight.

"I hope you're happy!" Blake shouted into the night. "I hope you have what you want!"

Somehow he knew Rory, or rather Joje, would be listening.

Chapter 13

Day Eight

1

"I understand you're ready to talk."

The cuffs on Blake's wrists were well used, their metal shine dulled, gouges and tiny dents more numerous than rhinestones in a woman's bracelet. He nodded surreptitiously.

"And you've denied your right to have a lawyer present. Is that correct?"

His hands were shaking. Such a strange effect to watch those finite vibrations, his body acting independent from his mind.

"Yes, that's correct."

He focused on the wrapping over the stubs of his missing fingers. He couldn't feel them, couldn't feel the pain. Pain had simply become synonymous with living, a state of being, like a blind man who wakes one day not bothering to open his eyes.

"And you have reason to believe that the supposed man who kidnapped you and your family this week was Rory Shepard, a wanted fugitive in over twenty-eight states."

"No," Blake said.

"He wasn't Rory Shepard?"

Blake closed his eyes against the intense white light bleeding down from the ceiling. "No, it wasn't 'supposedly' Rory. It was him.

2

St. Helena's Foster Care was in a part of East Los Angeles where Caucasians weren't a minority—they didn't exist. The "home" was in an urban industrial building along East Cesar Chavez, the drone of cars between the competing 5, 10, and 101 freeways, turning any conversation into a shouting match.

Blake handed the keys to JT's black Jaguar XK to the two dark-skinned men who had been sitting on the steps of an abandoned church across from the home, La Iglesia del Dios Recordado. A black trash bag blew inward, exposing an open window, broken scraps of furniture within. Blake wondered when the change in management had taken place, the Church of the Remembered God becoming instead forgotten.

A police car drove past. A heavyset woman in shorts and hideously undersized tank top screamed at a young girl with ratted hair, then snatched her by one arm, dragging her around the corner.

Five minutes to midnight.

Blake approached the doorway. The smell of urine was strong. He raised his hand to knock.

3

Blake hadn't seen Officers Randall or McClellan since stepping into the downtown Los Angeles Police Department off East First Street. Nor had he been allowed to see his wife despite his repeated requests. The men sitting in front of him weren't police officers, they were FBI. At least they had been kind enough to bring in a donut and mildly warm coffee.

"Look, I believe you believe this man was Rory. If you manage to make *us* believe, you'll be the first person on record to have ever seen him."

The handcuffs were beginning to rattle with the shaking that had now traveled from Blake's hands to his arms. "I should've seen it. He kept saying, 'I wowee, I wowee' . . ."

"I worry?"

"Not 'I worry,'" Blake said. "'I Rory.'"

"Why don't you start at the beginning for us."

4

Someone whistled, that forceful hail Blake had never been able to manage using fingers in your mouth. He turned, hand still raised at the door. A black boy, so skinny the flesh on his arms clung to the bone, stood at the corner of the street. Staring at Blake.

The kid nodded. He couldn't have been more than ten. His chin was smaller than the rest of his head, giving him the look of a drawn caricature at a carnival, or maybe it was his uncombed afro. He wore a stained nightshirt, his feet bare against the cold and litter-strewn sidewalk.

Blake walked over to join him, more aware than ever of the scraps of metal and glass, broken needles and garbage he was stepping over.

"You're Stitch?" he asked.

Now that he was closer Blake could see the long, thick scar that ran across where the boy's right eyebrow should have been. It climbed his forehead, disappearing beneath the tangles of stringy hair.

"D'you bring it?" He was chewing gum. Or tobacco.

"Is this your home?" Blake asked, gesturing toward Saint Helena's. Any plans of beating Joje's whereabouts out of whomever he was supposed to meet quickly fled.

The kid started walking away.

"Wait!" Blake cried out after him.

"Show me the coin," Stitch said.

Blake brought out a thin leather case. He had found it in JT's glove box, a way to keep his insurance and registration in one place. But it could have as easily held a valued coin.

The kid stopped, now intrigued.

"You should keep it," Blake said. "Don't give it to him. You know how much it's worth?"

"Not as much as my life."

Blake smiled. He liked the kid. "How do I get ahold of him."

Stitch shook his head.

"How do you get ahold of him?" Blake asked.

Stitch held his hand out, lips closed.

"He took my son," Blake said. "I need to find him, tell him I know who he is. And I will expose him if he doesn't send Adam back. Can you tell him that?"

The kid's bright eyes remained fixed on the case.

Blake sighed. The exasperated release of a man admitting defeat. "Is this where he grew up? Joje? Rory?"

Stitch wriggled his fingers, bidding Blake to hand him the envelope.

Blake held it out. Stitch grabbed the other end. Blake still held on to his side.

"Don't become like him," Blake said, then released it.

Stitch bolted down the street then scampered up a block wall. At the top of the wall, he opened the envelope. He spent some time looking at what was inside, a single piece of hair along with a message for Joje and the location of the Liberty nickel, just in case it was what he wanted. Stitch looked back up at Blake, his face expressionless, then disappeared on the other side of the wall.

Head down, Blake turned back, remembering he had given his car away. He had passed a police station a few blocks north. Maybe he'd be able to make it there in one piece.

5

The bars slid shut with a pervasive ring. An hour later Blake still felt the rattle in the fillings of his teeth. There was no bed in this cell, just a long metal bench like you would find on a bleacher. Blake stood until his legs gave out, then sat on the ground, the base of his neck leaning against the cold metal seat.

It hadn't been enough. When truth was more fanciful than lies, he should have known better than to stick to it. He pissed in a seatless toilet at the back of the cell. A meal was brought at some point. He ate some of it.

Blake looked up at an officer calling his name. From the unpleasant look on the guy's face, he had been calling Blake for some time.

"Stand up, spread your legs, and put your hands against the wall."

Blake did as he was told.

Through several hallways, they buzzed him in to a locked room. The officer held the door back for him. Jenna was inside.

Blake looked back at the portly officer at the door, who simply nodded back at him. Blake rushed into the room. Jenna was in a wheelchair, a blanket covering her lap and draped down around her.

"Careful," she said, but when Blake embraced her she squeezed back, her arms wrapping around him, hands gliding up and down, wet cheeks pressing against his own.

"How . . . Why?" Blake began.

"I don't know," she said. "Does it matter?"

"Have they charged you?" Blake asked.

"Shhh," she answered, bringing him back down to her and holding him.

"I'm so sorry—"

"No! None of that," Jenna said. "We're alive. It's over."

"Adam."

She ran a hand through his hair, the other caressing his bruised and mottled face. "We just have to believe."

"And you? You're okay?" he asked.

A faraway look came over her momentarily, and then she was back. She pulled the blanket up around her, exposing the metal rack at the bottom of the chair where her feet were resting. But it was only one foot. Farther the blanket rose, until her right knee came into view, covered in wrappings. Nothing emerging from the other end.

Blake couldn't dam the guilt that swept through him, but Jenna gently lifted his face to look into hers.

"Believe with me?" she said.

Through the tears, soon Blake was nodding.

6

Blake wheeled Jenna into what appeared to be a conference room, the long table in the middle of the room much nicer than any of his previous holding rooms. A thin black woman with a beige skirt and enough jewelry to prove she was not only married, but married well, greeted them at the door.

"I'm Lieutenant Whitaker. Thank you for joining us." She extended a hand to each of them, gold bracelets accentuating the movement. The gesture of kindness seemed so foreign. Before Blake could ask any questions, she continued. "There's been a . . . development."

Blake recognized the two FBI men from what they had deemed his "story time." Two other men and one woman were new faces in the room. One of the men stood, moving out a chair so Blake could push Jenna up to the table. He sat beside her.

"Did you find him?" Blake asked. "Our son?"

The lieutenant exchanged a glance with one of the new faces, a large man with a thin black goatee. In that brief glance his hope was shattered. Jenna took hold of his injured and bandaged hand beneath the table, encasing it with both of hers.

"We have reason to believe your . . . story," Whitaker said, standing across the table from Blake and Jenna. "And that the kidnapper was in fact who you say he was. At this time, unfortunately, we don't have any leads to his whereabouts or the whereabouts of your son."

Jenna's grip tightened on Blake's hand, his arm flinching back at the sudden jolt of pain.

"Sorry," she said and moved to wipe the tears from her eyes.

"I don't understand," Blake said. "These two said I should've been a writer, what with the crazy shit I came up with. What changed?"

Again that shared glance.

"Enough!" Blake shouted. "Either tell us or throw us back in a cell!"

"We're hoping for your cooperation," Whitaker said. "No one's ever been that close to Rory before. With a little luck and your help, we can use that information to determine what he's planning next."

"What he's planning? He's planning on disappearing! With our son!" Blake's head was pounding from the incompetence in the room.

The large man with the goatee spun his chair to face Blake, one leg up, crossed over the other, as if they were old friends having the most casual of conversations. "We received an e-mail," he said. "Did you want waters by the way?"

Blake stared down at the table in front of him, trying to keep himself in control. "Who'd he send it to?" Blake felt the man's eyes begin to drift to Whitaker. He slammed his fist down on the table. "Who!"

"Every damn one of us," Whitaker said. "And keep your voice down. You're still under custody."

"Every agent and police officer even remotely involved in your two cases received an e-mail at approximately eleven forty-two this morning," the other man said. "Sent to our departmental e-mail and, as far as we can surmise, every officer and agent's personal accounts as well. The district attorney was also copied, as was the mayor."

"So what . . . ?" Jenna said.

"As far as our sources have been able to ascertain, it appears the message was sent from the president of the United States' own e-mail account."

"It's him," Blake said.

"What's it say? What's he asking for?" Jenna asked.

But Blake already knew. There were no demands. There never had been.

Whitaker took over, motioning toward one of the men at the end of the table. He rose, turning on the small flat-screen TV mounted on the wall. "We felt it appropriate you see for yourselves," she said. "Dim the lights?"

The man who had turned on the TV typed into a wireless keyboard, opening an e-mail account on the TV screen. Blake felt his body tense as he read the subject line before it was even clicked on.

Subject: Farewell

The e-mail contained a single link that had been opened before. The officer or agent or whoever was typing at the table clicked on it. A video screen opened up.

On the screen Joje smiled into the camera. The same smile Blake saw every time he closed his eyes. After a quick buffer, the video began to play.

"I'm sending this to help a good friend of mine. Blake Crochet."

Blake felt a shudder that wouldn't come out, as if every internal part of him was contracting and trembling, unable to accept the reality this video presented.

Joje was speaking without a speech impediment.

He continued, without the slightest hint of a lisp. "I accept full responsibility for the unfortunate loss of lives over the past few days surrounding the Crochet family. Everything Blake has told you is true, with one exception. I did not kidnap his son. Adam Crochet, now Adam Shepard as of nine a.m. eastern standard time, willingly chose to come with me."

Blake felt like his ears had been filled with hot wax—the pressure in his head unable to escape.

Adam Shepard.

Joje continued speaking, though to Blake his words were just the monotonous buzz of an angry swarm of bees. Until Adam came on screen.

He looked older. His ears were pierced, both lobes a bright reddish pink, but it was his eyes Blake focused on. Unaware, he wiped at his dripping nose.

"Jenna, Blake," Adam said, not even giving them the comfort of calling them Mom or Dad, "I want you to know I'm okay. I want to be here with . . . Rory. My brother. I'm happy."

His eyes, Blake thought. *He's scared, not happy.* Jenna's breaths next to him came in quiet sobs.

Blake found his mind wandering, reliving each decision of the past week. *So many mistakes.* The screen in front of him multiplied into a dozen more, each playing out differently as he consciously made new decisions. Joje played his message for help at the restaurant in English, and this time Blake shouted at the manager to call the cops. After slamming the crystal globe into Joje's head in his office, he quickly locked the doors, preventing Drew from finding him unprepared. Out on the cliffs while looking for Adam, Blake barreled into Joje, driving him over the edge.

The screens split into a dozen more, each new decision taking him to unforeseen consequences. A massacre at the restaurant, Blake stepping over the body of the manager and server, blood still pumping from their torsos like water from a garden hose. Blake clobbered from behind as he turns from locking the doors, Joje cracking the butt of his gun repeatedly against Blake's skull until the pounding at the doors grow as distant and soft as the beating of his heart. Joje snagging at Blake as he tumbles off, pulling Blake with him, and in the few seconds before they hit, Blake spots his son clinging to a rock where he will soon drown.

The room became a multiplex of screens, every word, every exchange, playing to an infinite array of possibilities. Blake followed them all, his fractured mind capable of viewing each screen independently, tracking each toward their inevitable and tragic conclusion until they all coalesced into one panoramic screen revealing Blake, sometimes sitting next to Jenna, sometimes alone, in this conference room, watching Joje—Rory—look down from above with a smile on his face.

Distantly he heard people calling his name, tugging against a shoulder or arm, but they were only static, one tiny screen as far away from him as his son. On every screen he heard himself make a promise—an oath—one that breathed new purpose into a life that would otherwise be vacant.

"It's not the journey," he muttered, a million screens aligning for a single moment. "It's the destination."

And his family had yet to arrive.

Epilogue

"Post-Pwoject"
Two Years Later

1

Blake's fingers came to a halt, thoughts fizzling at the slam of the front door. He lowered the screen to his Vaio laptop, peering toward the door from his desk, which occasionally functioned as the small kitchen table it actually was. His work files were spread out like giant-sized crumbs in need of a good sweep.

"Honey? That you?"

The light bleeps of the house alarm went unanswered. If it had been Jenna, she would have disarmed it by now.

Thick arms wrapped around Blake from behind, squeezing his chest and stomach until he had to gasp for air. Six months of psychiatric rehabilitation after his short stint in jail and over a year on meds, and his anxiety still had a better hold on him than he'd ever admit.

He stood, chair squeaking against the linoleum floor. He undid the clasp at his belt, gripping the handle of the sharp hunting knife that never left his side. He even required it for sleep, the hard knot beneath his pillow from the blade's case better than any sleeping pill.

"Who's there."

His voice fell flat, without the confidence he had hoped to project. Another twenty seconds and their security company, Alliance, would be notified of the illicit entry. Five minutes and twenty seconds and three security professionals would surround the home, AK-47s at the ready.

But a lot could happen in five minutes.

The door to the kitchen swung inward. It began to swing back but was blocked by someone's hand. Blake was practically chewing on his heart, it had risen so high.

A man's head peeked out from the doorway, gaunt cheeks hidden by long, bushy sideburns, shaggy hair spilling from the ball cap on his head. "Dad?"

Blake exhaled, letting go of the breath he had been holding for two years. "Adam?"

Adam stepped into the room. He looked like a bum off the street, his clothes worn and tattered, his shuffle the walk of a man who's been lost so long he's unsure if there's even anywhere to go.

He was so much taller. At sixteen he looked like he could be in his midtwenties. His eyes revealed a man who had seen more than any sixteen-year-old boy should.

Blake glanced past him at the door swinging closed.

"It's just me," Adam said.

Blake nodded, his eyes welling. "Welcome home."

He didn't walk, he ran, wrapping his arms around Adam and lifting him off the ground, damn his lower back and all.

"I've dreamed of this day for so long!"

"Me too," Adam said, his voice choking with emotion. "I didn't know if . . . if you and Mom would, would want me back."

Blake accidentally knocked the cap from Adam's head. His hands ran through his son's tangled hair. "You're all we've thought of! We spent everything we had trying to find you! Why . . . How? How'd you get away?"

Adam took a step back, pulling himself from his father's grip. Blake kept his hands on Adam's shoulders, not ready to let go of his son. "Rory . . . he passed," Adam said.

Blake saw the grief in his son's eyes. Like any father, he wanted to console him but couldn't force an "I'm sorry" from his lips. Not for *Joje*.

"It wasn't what I thought," Adam continued.

Blake brought him back in, wondering if somehow this was all a dream. "Let's get you cleaned up. Before your mom gets home."

2

By the time Jenna got back from her run, Adam had showered and dressed, Blake's clothes still a few sizes too large despite Adam's physique. They were sitting in the living room across from each other, Adam picking at the sandwich and apple slices Blake had prepared while Adam had been dressing.

In his excitement he had forgotten about the alarm and had to send the three ex-military men away. Still the three-hundred-dollar charge was worth the assurance that no albino delinquent or stuttering psychopath lurked around the premises.

Jenna came in, immediately turning to the side wall and keying in the code for the alarm. She still held the leash for Truce, their Labrador. The dog looked more beat than Jenna, lying against the cool tile floor rather than attempting to greet the new person in the room.

Blake felt Adam's eyes move to Jenna's legs as his had at first. The sleek curved carbon fiber attachment to her right leg was something he had now grown used to. He loved the fact that she still ran. She was a fighter until the very end. And there wasn't a single run in which she wouldn't take the dog.

She turned around, the leash dropping from her hand to the ground. It retracted, sliding along the tile until reaching Truce. Blake smiled up at her, letting her know it was okay. She quickly wiped at both eyes and carefully stepped down to the carpeted living room. Steps were still a little awkward for her.

Adam stood from the love seat, his eyes moving from Jenna's face not to the curved blade that was her prosthesis, but the curved belly beneath her running shirt. She was almost eight months, though to look at her she could have been only four or five.

"Come here," she said, not bothering this time to wipe the tears from her eyes.

Blake laughed as Adam rushed toward her, the two embracing as mother and son.

"Are you really back?" she asked.

Adam nodded, his head nestled against her shoulder. "I had no idea you were pregnant!"

Had either Blake or Jenna seen the smile crawling over Adam's face, they would have picked up the phone, immediately calling the security team back. They would have been alerted to the fact that something was very, very wrong.

About the Author

The Behrg is the author of literary works ranging from screenplays to "to-do" lists. Housebroken, his debut novel, was a first-round Kindle Scout selection. A child actor, The Behrg starred in such shows at Dynasty, Highway to Heaven, and an episode of The Twilight Zone. Sometimes he wonders if he ever really escaped that episode.

Stalk him at thebehrg.com.

www.ingramcontent.com/pod-product-compliance
Lightning Source LLC
Chambersburg PA
CBHW031249170626
46807CB00001B/56